S'

Anna Cato lives in Somerset with her husband Thomas, and two badgers, Bessie and Boris. As Sally Stewart she has written several historical novels including *The Land of the Nightingales*, *A Rose for Every Month*, *Women of Providence* and *The Bird of Happiness*.

STILL LIVES

Anna Cato

ARROW

Published by Arrow Books in 1997

1 3 5 7 9 10 8 6 4 2

Copyright © Anna Cato 1997

First published in 1997 in the United Kingdom by Century Books

Arrow Books Limited
Random House UK Limited
20 Vauxhall Bridge Road, London SW1V 2SA

Random House Australia (Pty) Limited
20 Alfred Street, Milsons Point, Sydney, New South Wales 2061, Australia

Random House New Zealand Limited
18 Poland Road, Glenfield, Auckland 10, New Zealand

Random House South Africa (Pty) Limited
Endulini, 5a Jubilee Road, Parktown 2193, South Africa

Random House UK Limited Reg. No. 954009

A CIP catalogue record for this book is available from the British Library

Papers used by Random House UK Limited
are natural, recyclable products made from wood grown in
sustainable forests. The manufacturing processes conform to
the environmental regulations of the country of origin

ISBN 0 09 922612 X

Typeset by Deltatype Ltd, Birkenhead, Merseyside
Printed and bound in Great Britain by
Cox & Wyman Ltd, Reading, Berkshire

CHAPTER ONE

It had been the beginning of the Long Vac when they left Oxford. Now the summer, like the holidays, was almost over, and already the Virginia creeper on the College walls was beginning to change colour. She could see it as they drove home. Beside her, Geoffrey was thanking God they'd missed the tourists for another year – even the tide of Japanese along the High was on the ebb. But made perverse by the complacent note in his voice, she said what would irritate him.

'The ebbing tide is made up for by people like us – returning academics and their wives, flowing back into the nooks and crannies of North Oxford.'

He wasn't amused, but then she'd known he wouldn't be. 'Scarcely comparable, my dear Louise; *we* belong here. The package-touring hordes merely come to have their likeness taken in Radcliffe Square.'

It was largely true, of course. The visitors seemed compelled to smile endlessly into each other's expensive cameras. She doubted if some of them saw Oxford at all. She glanced at her husband and knew that his spurt of annoyance with her had faded. He was even smiling now, though not at her. The taxi driver, instructed to take a roundabout route, was turning into Holywell Lane. Already she could see the grey gate-tower of St Barnabas rising above a huddle of Tudor houses. Charlie Jukes, a college porter even more cantankerous than most, had the 'Gardens *closed*' sign out as usual. He shared his Senior Tutor's opinion of tourists and only let them in on rainy days when most of them were too discouraged to come anyway.

Louise Carmichael heard her husband's little sigh of pleasure but resisted the temptation to provoke him again. It wasn't very likely that after nearly five hundred years of watching over the neighbourhood the tower would have collapsed during the three months they'd been away in France. But she'd been married to Geoffrey long enough to know that St Barnabas was sacred ground – its very stones and lawns were precious, no more to be laughed at than its extraordinary rules and rituals.

She half-expected to be asked to wait while he got out, but he was courteous to women, even to his wife. In any case Ruth would be on the watch at home by now, anxious to see him back from the dangers of a summer in Provence. He could wait until tomorrow to walk into the front quad and feel the ancient place wrap itself about him again.

Five minutes later they stopped outside their house in Norham Grove – her home since Geoffrey had brought her to Oxford almost twenty years ago. There'd been time enough to get used to it, but Victorian Gothic gables, and stripes of mauve and yellow brick were a far cry from the silvery, eighteenth-century elegance of Aix-en-Provence. Their Thames Valley climate was a trial, but at least its all-pervading dampness had wonderfully encouraged greenery. The myrtle, jasmine and honeysuckle that she'd planted, against her sister-in-law's advice, now veiled quite a lot of the startling brickwork. Behind the house she'd been busier still, and from the wilderness there had created the garden that was her joy and her salvation. Three months might be an unregarded moment of time to the stone tower of St Barnabas, but it was long to have left growing things in the care of a woman who didn't understand them. Ruth refused to believe that plants needed talking to, a contrariness Louise had never ceased to marvel at in someone who could usually be relied upon to talk a great deal.

She was waiting for them now with the porch door held open – a tall, ungainly figure in a Laura Ashley dress that had been designed for a daintier woman. Louise thought again how unjust it was that their mother's exceptional good looks should all have gone to Geoffrey. Ruth had inherited Dr Edward Carmichael's large frame and springy, reddish hair that she made the mistake of trying to subdue with girlish velvet bandeaux instead of getting it properly cut. Except for an unexpectedly beautiful speaking voice, she was short of feminine appeal and entirely lacking in feminine tact.

'My dear, how very *brown* you are,' she announced after

kissing her sister-in-law on both cheeks. 'Never mind . . . I dare say it will fade soon enough here.' Her brother, hugged with warmth, did better altogether. 'Dearest, *you* look splendid – a long break was exactly what you needed. Now you're not to fuss about food this evening – I've got a little supper waiting for you upstairs. It might even be a trifle *over*-ready, because I half-expected you on the earlier train. No matter – it won't have come to any harm; my special moussaka doesn't mind being kept waiting!'

Geoffrey managed to sound grateful. 'Ruth dear . . . how kind and thoughtful. Allow us five more minutes to wash our hands and collect a bottle of wine. Then we'll follow you up.'

Inside their own front door that led off the shared hall his smile faded into a frown at his wife. 'What was I to do – say that we don't want warm sherry and a dried-up mess of aubergine and lentils? She *means* so well, bless her.'

'I know,' Louise agreed. 'We must remember that at all times, whatever else we forget – Ruth means well.'

It nearly sounded right, but he knew that even when it did the words his wife said were often not the words she meant. Irony was an Oxford disease, and she'd caught it very thoroughly since coming to live there.

'Don't say it like a child repeating her catechism – believe it,' he suddenly insisted.

Her thin brown face broke into a smile, charming while it lasted, but she didn't answer him directly. 'Time we went upstairs, I think – forgiving as it is, we shouldn't try the moussaka too far.'

He didn't smile back, and she thought she knew why. Awkward, overbearing Ruth was like St Barnabas itself, not to be laughed at. Stretched on the rack he might have confessed that her affection sometimes seemed a yoke around his neck. Short of that, he would do or say nothing that would hurt her. She'd been the elder sister who had kept a schoolboy's world from falling apart when their mother finally abandoned them. Geoffrey had been twelve at the time, old enough to feel bitterly rejected, but Ruth had been there to take her place instead.

The wine that he took upstairs helped; even so it was a struggle to dispose of what she heaped on their plates.

'I feel so thankful,' she said again although they'd heard it before, 'knowing that I'm out of the cruelty chain.' Her gaze lingered on the small pile of lentils that Louise had tried to hide under her fork. '*You* don't agree with me, I'm afraid – it's having French blood, I expect, and a different attitude towards animals.'

She saw a flash of anger in the dark eyes that suddenly met her own, but her sister-in-law spoke quietly.

'If you mean that I'm not sentimental about animals, I'll agree with you. But you mustn't imply that because I'm half-French I don't care how inhumanely they're slaughtered.'

A silence fell until Louise herself found another topic that might safely bear their weight. She pointed to the dormer windows, where a soft September dusk already pressed against the uncurtained glass. Their daylight view across the Parks, always beautiful, became dramatic as well in winter when the Cherwell flooded and turned the water meadows from green to silver.

'What a pity it's too dark to see out,' she murmured. 'I used to love the bird's-eye view up here.'

'I thought you *wanted* to move downstairs when Father died.' Ruth looked round the room. In truth, nothing would have prised her from it. 'I'm sure I don't mind *where* I live.'

Louise shook her head. 'Dear Ruth, I wasn't asking you to move!' But her sister-in-law, still flushed, had been reminded of another favourite axe to grind.

'It's only lovely still because a few of us are constantly vigilant to keep it so. Left to do as they like, the barbarians in the Science Faculties would have every open space plastered with hideous new laboratories by now.'

Louise glanced at her husband but he seemed intent on considering the colour of the wine in his glass. Loyalty to fellow-dons was part of the code that academics lived by when they were under attack; so why expect him to admit how Oxford's worst defacements had come about? The Faculties of the University hadn't ever owned anything; it was College governing bodies who had been too indolent or too greedy to care what became of the land they sold.

Geoffrey roused himself at last, but only to steer the conversation into an easier channel. 'Ruth dear, how is the book going? I know you somehow always manage to finish on time, but we left you a lot to see to here this summer.'

She was soothed because he'd asked the question so gravely – the high-romantic sagas that she wrote, he seemed to say, were no less important than his own scholarly analyses of modern history. Louise had read the first of Ruth's published stories and dutifully skimmed through all the rest. Geoffrey had done neither as far as she knew, but it was all the encouragement Ruth needed to have him enquire courteously after the fate of her heroines – spirited creatures one and all, bound to get the better in the end of tyrannical Victorian ironmasters and mill owners. She was surprisingly modest about her success, and in case it should embarrass a brother who was a professional historian even wrote under another name. The sales of her outpourings hugely exceeded his but this was something she never boasted about.

She smiled at him now, content because he was home with her again. 'I enjoyed looking after things for you – though Louise's precious plants *were* a bit of a responsibility. By burning a little midnight oil I managed to stay bang on schedule. A promise is a promise, I always say, even to a grasping publisher!'

He was able to murmur something suitably admiring, but Louise got suddenly to her feet. The evening was like a hundred others shared with Ruth, but this time she couldn't bear another minute of it – the unreal conversation, the messy remains of food not cleared away, the ethnic muddle of bamboo furniture, camel rugs, and tinkling wind-bells that her sister-in-law had recently surrounded herself with.

'Forgive me if I say good night,' she said in a low voice. 'It seems to have been a very long day's travelling. Thank you for looking after the garden, Ruth, and for feeding us this evening.' She offered them both an apologetic smile, though her sister-in-law, she knew, would be only too glad to see her go. Geoffrey was looking displeased, so perhaps she'd sounded like the child saying its catechism again, polite but insincere.

'Not *quite* herself, dearest,' Ruth suggested a moment or two after Louise had left the room, '. . . unsettled, in fact. I wonder if you stayed a little too long at Aix?'

For once she was met by sharpness. 'Nonsense, my dear. This is the only *settled* home Louise has known, and she's lived here as long as she ever lived in France. The journey back was tiring, that's all.'

Ruth folded her lips together, determined not to retaliate with the truth. In any case he knew it as well as she did. Their own lives had been shadowed by a feckless, selfish mother, but they had had each other and had always known, thank God, that they were English through and through. Poor Louise could scarcely know *what* she was, and her childhood had been spent being dragged around Europe by an artist father and his equally irresponsible wife. But it was a thousand pities that Fate had led Geoffrey into a Parisian art gallery nearly twenty years ago, when there'd been girls enough in Oxford that he might have fallen in love with. His expression now looked so remote that she felt certain he thought so too, but she'd learned not to try to get him to confide in her about his marriage. Better to pour some whisky for them both and ask about the summer in Aix. That way he'd relax and stay with her for a while. If it weren't already dark his wife would be inspecting her garden by now – that was where *her* affections lay.

But Louise was indoors, walking through rooms that seemed almost too bare after the clutter she'd just left. When the house finally became Geoffrey's she'd chosen to decorate it very simply, to offset the riot of ornament outside. After a long absence, though, the rooms had become unfamiliar, unwelcoming even. This was her home but, as Ruth often managed to imply, she didn't quite seem to belong in it. Sad as this had been, because she'd wanted so desperately to belong somewhere, there had been other, more serious, failures in her life with Geoffrey Carmichael.

It needn't have been this particular city, ugly past redemption in places and achingly beautiful in others, that had lured her from France. But Oxford had already been a vision in her mind before she came. Slowly dying in a more sun-parched landscape, her father had suddenly begun to talk about it. After all the years of moving on, through France and Italy, the English wanderer had remembered a different place – rejected long ago but still vividly recollected. While he talked she had seen what he was seeing . . . green gardens under rain, and old grey buildings touched to gold by occasional shafts of sunlight.

Her father had died, but it seemed almost inevitable a few months later that the man who walked into her grandfather's Parisian gallery should have come from the very city John Standish had described. It had been nearly twenty years ago, when she was just nineteen.

That summer had been hotter than usual, and the other inhabitants of the *quartier* were complaining of the heat, already counting the days until they could clang down their shutters and escape from Paris for the August holidays. The Galeries Benoît would not be closing. André Benoît reckoned it stupid of his neighbours to leave just when visitors from abroad were ready to arrive. For a month his would be the only premises open in the Rue Jacob, with the striped awnings out and the door invitingly set wide. During the heat of the long, slow afternoons André could always escape upstairs to sleep off the drowsiness inspired by midsummer heat and Marthe's ample *déjeuner*; Louise was a capable child, knowledgeable and careful enough to be left in charge until he woke up feeling brisk again.

For an hour or more that July afternoon no passers-by had walked along the street. She might have been the only human being left alive except for Henri Rivaux, her grandfather's partner next door. Henri was probably there, poring over some antiquarian book or polishing one of the old brass instruments in his collection. He loved them for their place in the history of science, but Louise relished them for their beauty, the flowing Arabic calligraphy engraved on metal as precisely as if the scribe had been working with ink and parchment. An open archway led from Henri's Aladdin's cave into the picture gallery, and customers who bought in one place usually wandered into the other as well.

This afternoon, though, when a visitor finally appeared it was their own windows that seemed to interest him. She saw him stop outside and stare at what was displayed — two of the last pictures her father had painted. One was a still life, of sunlight reflected on a glass flagon beside a blue plate heaped with grapes. The other, her own favourite, was simpler still: a red-painted rowing boat lying on its side on the sand; nothing but the empty sea behind it and the high Mediterranean sky above. Looking at it, she'd often wondered what it would be like to climb into the little boat and row out into all that emptiness.

'Good afternoon.' The man, not quite as young as his bright hair had made him seem outside, was standing in front of her now. 'I noticed the paintings in your window . . . signed by John Standish.'

His smile was pleasant and his French too careful not to give his nationality away, but she answered in the same language; it would have seemed unkind not to after the courteous effort he was making.

'The small one, Monsieur, is not for sale . . . the other certainly.' The unblushing lie spoke itself even as she knew what André Benoît would make of it. Her grandfather wouldn't understand that she wasn't ready yet to part with the little scarlet rowing boat.

The stranger looked faintly embarrassed. 'It's really the artist I'm interested in — you see, a colleague of mine at home is called William Standish. He once talked about a brother who had left Oxford to live in France and paint. I should like to take him back some news of John Standish . . . that is, if it's the right man.'

The girl in front of him was silent for so long that he began to feel irritated by her lack of response. It hadn't been an unreasonable request, and there was no need for her to stare at him with quite such a remote, unwelcoming expression. Apart from that he would have liked what he saw — a slender figure dressed with the simple flair that seemed to be the birthright of Parisian women; dark bobbed hair that fell across her forehead

8

in an unstudied fringe; beneath it heavily lashed brown eyes under straight black brows. Not pretty, but interesting if a man's glance were given encouragement to linger. But even when she finally spoke the information she volunteered was minimal.

'There is no news for you to take except that John Standish is no longer alive – he died two months ago. You spoke of Oxford . . . is that where you come from?'

'Yes, William Standish and I belong to the same College there. His subject is English Literature; I teach Modern History.'

Her eyes still considered him as if deciding whether or not to release another bare fragment of fact. But he was suddenly aware of having misjudged her. She wasn't hostile after all – only lacking the habit of communicating with other people. He knew this about her simply because he was just as little given to communicating freely about himself.

'My father talked about Oxford just before he died – he'd never seemed to want to before.' Her mouth sketched a proud, sad little smile. 'That's who my father was, you see . . . your friend's brother.'

'William didn't mention a wife and child here . . . only that he and John never got on very well, and quarrelled bitterly just before the war started. I don't think they were ever in touch again, so William probably doesn't know that he has a niece. May I tell him your name? I'm Geoffrey Carmichael, by the way.'

She put out a thin brown hand automatically, forgetting her father's assertion that the English avoided touching strangers if they could – shipwrecked on a desert island they would manage to smile distantly and say good morning.

'Louise Victoire Standish,' she introduced herself. 'The Victoire's awful, isn't it, but it happened to be the anniversary of Liberation Day when I was born, and my mother liked the idea.'

She had switched to English, perhaps without noticing it, was even beginning to talk freely now that she'd got started. He thought she would go on now if he didn't ask a question that sent her back inside her shell.

'Are you always here, working in the gallery?'

'Only in the afternoons. *Grandpère* prefers to be in charge himself every morning, when we're busier.'

'I saw a name on the door – André Benoît. Is that your grandfather?'

She nodded, almost smiling at what she was going to say next. 'John Standish married his daughter, Nadia. It wasn't what my grandfather had wanted, I think . . . he doesn't like the English very much.'

'Well, that's fair – we're not always very keen on the French!'

Her smile broadened, then quickly faded again. 'In the end I wasn't sure *what* my father felt – pro- or anti-French. But the quarrel with his brother was because he refused to go back to England to fight in the war. He said it was stupid, bound to peter out into a stalemate. Then suddenly it was too late to change his mind because the Germans were in Paris. He and my mother spent the next five years hiding in unoccupied France; that's where I was born – in the south.'

'Afterwards I suppose you all came back to Paris?'

She shook her head at the question, looking back into a past that seemed full of unhappy memories. 'No, we kept travelling, because my father could never settle down. He'd seem happy, painting for a while, but always we'd move on again. At last I was sent back here, to live with Grandfather Benoît and get some schooling.' A wry grin suddenly lit her face. 'I know quite a lot about pictures, and cheap lodging houses, but very little about anything else!'

As an outline of her life it was brief but peculiarly vivid; he could see the little trio of man, woman and child wandering from place to place as the spirit moved John Standish. Not a happy life for a child, but even so perhaps she'd resented being excluded from it and sent back to Paris. Before he could frame his next question two interruptions occurred together: a couple dressed in the strange way of American tourists wandered in from the street to look around; and at the same moment a thickset, white-haired man pushed aside the beaded curtain at the back of the gallery and stood watching them. Benoît himself, alert again after an afternoon nap, had arrived in case his grand-daughter failed to clinch a sale.

Geoffrey smiled at her, ignoring the man. 'You'll be relieved to know I've made up my mind at last. It's the still life in the window that I should like to buy. But I must ask you to hold it for me until tomorrow – my travellers' cheques are at the hotel.'

'The still life, Monsieur . . . you're sure it's not the *other* little one you prefer?' Her eyes were on his face, telling him that, with her grandfather still standing there, he was not to seem surprised that the rowing boat painting *was* suddenly for sale after all.

'No, I'm quite sure,' he said definitely. 'Until tomorrow then.' This time his courteous nod acknowledged Benoît as well before he walked out of the gallery.

She was aware mostly of astonishment that she should have confided in the unknown Englishman, but there were also questions that she would ask him tomorrow.

For once she ignored her grandfather and he suddenly growled at her in French, certain that the hovering Americans wouldn't understand.

'I hope you don't expect to see *him* again. You may keep the painting until this time tomorrow, Louise – not a moment longer. Meanwhile perhaps you'll be good enough to pay attention to these other customers.'

She stared at him blank-faced for a moment, sadly accepting that he was bound to be right about the stranger – he always knew when a buyer was genuine or not. The man had admitted coming in not to buy at all, and it had been all the more kind of him to pretend just now. She listened politely to the Americans but let her mind wander back to what they had interrupted. She would probably never learn now about a man called William Standish, who might or might not like to have known that he had a niece in Paris.

CHAPTER TWO

She couldn't help looking for Geoffrey Carmichael the following afternoon, hoping against hope that her grandfather had
been wrong. But the long, hot hours passed and he didn't come.
Instead, André Benoît descended the stairs earlier than usual, so
that precisely when four o'clock struck he could remove the
'sold' sticker she'd placed on the painting. Ten minutes later a
provincial dealer known to them walked in, and the price was
automatically raised so that it could be haggled over and finally
adjusted to suit both sides.

'I should have asked more,' André said, when the dealer had
walked out with the still life. 'It was obvious he already had a
buyer for it.'

'You had no right to sell it at all,' Louise said coolly. 'It was
promised to someone else.'

She didn't often contradict him; he was accustomed to her
being obedient and untroublesome. But when she spoke
deliberately in English, as now, he knew it was to remind him
that she was her father's daughter; she was alien, and would
choose to remain so. John Standish had been stupid enough to
fall sick and die just when he was becoming a remarkable artist,
but at least he'd had the sense to know that France was the
country to live in, instead of his own benighted island. It seemed
entirely unfair that this girl, who had never clapped eyes on it at
all, should insist every so often that she belonged intractably to
her father's awkward race.

To make his sense of ill-usage worse, the brightness of the
open doorway was suddenly darkened by a figure stepping in
from the street. The Englishman of the previous afternoon stood
there, out of breath as if he had been hurrying. In the gloom of
the gallery after the sunlight outside he made out first the bulky
figure of the owner.

'I'm sorry . . . I meant to get here earlier but a luncheon

appointment prolonged itself.' He was pleased to have got the French reflexive verb so neatly in place, but it met with a cold smile that held no approval.

'I too am sorry, Monsieur,' said André Benoît, 'but we had given you up, I fear, when another buyer arrived who was most insistent . . .' His thick white hands sketched a gesture suggesting that life was full of such disappointments. 'However, the other Standish painting is still on offer – smaller, of course, but consequently requiring a lower price.' He leaned over the brass rod that held half-curtains of dark green velvet in place and lifted out the little picture of the rowing boat, '. . . a worthwhile substitute, is it not?'

He saw the Englishman's eyes scan the room. They found the girl who stood watching them, and asked a question of her.

'Buy it, Monsieur,' she said flatly. 'Take it back to Oxford and show it to William Standish.' Then, as if the fate of the painting held no further interest for her, she walked through an open archway into the shop next door.

Saddled with something that he hadn't wanted and could scarcely afford, Geoffrey Carmichael walked back along the Rue Jacob feeling aggrieved. He could almost believe that the snare had been rehearsed from the start between a shrewd merchant and his well-taught assistant. Far from wanting to talk to her again, he would simply remember the episode as an expensive warning against credulity in future.

But back in his hotel room he unwrapped the painting and stared at it, realising that its quality could scarcely be mistaken. He had probably been cleverer than he knew, but even if it never increased in value there would be the pleasure of owning it and the interest of its history. Then he found himself recalling the sad face of Louise Standish. She *hadn't* wanted him to have the painting, and he knew why. No plot had been hatched – she had abandoned him to her grandfather only to avoid seeing the last small link with her father leave the gallery.

The following morning, remembering that Benoît spent his mornings downstairs, he chose the second of two numbers listed in the telephone directory. A high-pitched female voice answered first, followed by a different one he recognised.

'It's Geoffrey Carmichael speaking, Miss Standish. I wonder if you'd have coffee with me this morning, somewhere nearby – say, at the Deux Magots, about eleven o'clock?'

He waited, expecting her to refuse, even half-hoping that she would. His present behaviour would astonish his colleagues at home and alarm his sister; even to him it seemed dangerously out of character.

At last Louise Standish answered unenthusiastically. 'I *can* pass that way. It's en route home from the market.' Then the line went dead, leaving him not quite sure whether the invitation had been accepted or not. But soon after he'd got to the café himself an hour later and found a pavement table, she was coming towards him – in the sort of simple, sleeveless cotton dress that every other girl seemed to be wearing, but its warm terracotta colour suited her. She looked different from the young women he met at home – *was* different altogether, he felt sure.

A hovering waiter appeared, stared at her laden shopping basket and rearranged his expression, for here was someone belonging to the *quartier*, not another unwelcome tourist to be served as insolently as possible.

'You keep house for your grandfather, I see,' Geoffrey remarked, afraid that if he didn't find something to say she might just drink her coffee, get up, and walk away.

'I shop and look after things for him . . . for the moment, at least,' she agreed. 'My mother is still in the south at Collioure; when she returns to Paris I shall be free to leave.'

'To go where?' he asked.

Her thin shoulders lifted in a shrug. 'I don't know . . . London perhaps, if I could find a job as an au pair. I wanted always to study music, but I began too late. Madame Levine next door still gives me lessons, but she doesn't avoid the truth: I play the piano rather well – for an amateur.' Her dark eyes were fixed on the coffee cup the waiter had put in front of her. She was lost in her own thoughts, unconcerned that he was there. He knew it wasn't a bid to get his attention – being alone was simply what she was used to. But she suddenly pushed the untidy fringe away from her eyes and smiled at him.

'You teach at the same place as my unknown uncle – is that what *you* always wanted to do?'

'Yes, once I'd outgrown the usual dreams of childhood. At five, of course, I was going to become an engine driver; at ten, when the war was still raging and looked like doing so for ever, I was going to drive a submarine instead! But all I really did was go away to school and, once my stint of National Service was over, return to Oxford to become an undergraduate. I'm back at my old College now – St Barnabas. It's not the biggest or the most famous; in fact it's rather small, and not much given to shouting about its achievements, but precious, and very beautiful.'

She heard the conviction in his voice, and adjusted her impression of him. Cool and self-controlled, yes, but not without the spark of passion that, according to her father, too often got snuffed out by an English upbringing.

'A peaceful, tranquil life, it sounds,' she remarked, 'despite the "raging war".'

'Even that didn't offer *us* much excitement, I'm afraid. Hitler had earmarked Oxford as his English capital and so it was never bombed.' He hesitated for a moment but then went on in the same quiet voice. 'Life *wasn't* entirely tranquil, though. My mother stuck the domestic round in North Oxford until my father came back from being a wartime Army doctor. Then she abandoned us, for London and the stage career we thought she'd given up. I was twelve at the time, and even now I still remember how all the brightness and laughter of our lives seemed to go with her.'

He'd never put that aching sense of loss into words before, and regretted a confession that was bound to call forth some pitying, useless comment from the girl sitting opposite him. But she seemed so little inclined to speak at all that he knew what else *he* wanted to say.

'I'm sorry about your father's painting but there seemed no way of not buying it yesterday. If you'd accept it as a present I'd like to give it back to you.'

Still she said nothing – for so long that he went hot with embarrassment. God knew what she was imagining now – a bribe to sleep with him perhaps, in lieu of the money the English were known to be chronically short of abroad?

But when she looked up at him and smiled his panic dropped away.

'No, I won't accept it, although it was a very kind offer. I meant what I said yesterday. If the painting goes to Oxford William Standish can see it – then perhaps he'll understand why my father didn't go back to England and do what conventional people thought he ought to do.' She glanced at the watch on her wrist, then stood up, holding out her hand to say goodbye. '*Grandpère* expects luncheon punctually at twelve-thirty, so I must go.'

'It doesn't occur to you to let him wait occasionally?'

Amusement lit her face again, giving it warmth and life. 'It occurs to me quite often, but hunger makes him irritable. Our life together is more peaceful if I keep to the rules.'

'Would an occasional postcard or letter from me cause more trouble with the rules? I'm leaving Paris this afternoon to spend a month in Lyons, and it would be nice to have someone here to write to.' He was unaware of still holding her hand until she withdrew it, flushing a little.

'Write if you like – my grandfather isn't a prison warder even though he may seem rather severe. It was better when his wife was alive, but she died before the end of the war. My mother, who insists on dramatising things, said *Gran'mère* died of a broken heart, but it was really neglected pneumonia, I think. She was a White Russian émigrée brought to Paris after the Revolution, and no doubt it *was* cruelly hard to see the Germans here when they were ravaging her own country as well.' Caught up for a moment in the recollection of so much sadness, Louise looked tragic until a clock chimed nearby, reminding her again that she was late.

'*Au revoir, Monsieur . . . bon voyage et bonne chance!*'

Then she was gone, so quickly that almost at once he lost sight of her among the passers-by. He sat down again, and found himself almost felled by the wave of loneliness that took him by surprise. Like Louise Standish, he was used to being alone, but he was suddenly aware of being in a place to which he didn't belong. Another four weeks, twenty-eight interminable days, must be got through before he could shake the dust of this beautiful but disturbing country off his feet and find equilibrium again in dear, familiar Oxford.

He made up his mind *not* to write after all to a girl who'd intruded by mere chance into his pleasantly unemotional life. He'd show William the painting when he got home and that would be that – the end of an episode that had been unsettling but too brief to matter.

A week later, sitting at a Lyons café table and making a glass of beer last long enough to allow him to stay there, he stared at the sheet under his hand – instead of the list of research queries he should have been compiling it had turned out to be the letter that he'd decided he wasn't going to write. It didn't ask for a reply, and, once sent, he told himself quite often that there wouldn't be one. But when an envelope with a Paris postmark arrived he carried it about in his pocket for a day before he opened it, like a young man at the beginning of his first love affair. After that there could be no question of not writing again – courtesy insisted on it, and courtesy was a quality for which Oxford men were renowned.

It seemed natural that a regular correspondence should establish itself. It was a pleasure to look forward to, but it had another result that struck him as still more remarkable – instead of feeling lonely, gagged and blinded by his own sense of isolation, he found himself talking to strangers and smiling at people he would normally have ignored. Life was suddenly full of rich incident that had to be shared with Louise, and in return he received from her a vividly entertaining commentary on the people who frequented the Benoît gallery. It never included cameos of her own family, but that was deliberate, he thought. Anything that was painful she was accustomed not to share.

At the end of a month it was time to go back to Oxford. He went happily, of course, but something had changed. The good research work he'd just completed, the history of Vichy France that was going to establish his reputation, even the knowledge that he was no longer the newest Fellow in Senior Common

Room at the start of Michaelmas term – these things were exciting, but they seemed as time went by not to be quite exciting enough.

He didn't confess this to Ruth, but when he strolled out into the garden late one night he was glad to find that his father had joined him instead of going to bed. A moon more gold than silver climbed the sky, attended by a single star, and the night was too beautiful not to be shared with some other human being. He knew that he would have liked to share it with Louise Standish, but his calm, phlegmatic father would have to do instead. Then suddenly he found himself talking about Louise's family.

'Before I left for Paris William told me about an artist brother he'd lost touch with there after a quarrel at the beginning of the war. By one of those chances so remote that you can't help thinking they're meant, I walked past a gallery on the Left Bank and found myself staring at two paintings – the signature "John Standish" was scrawled at the bottom of them.'

'You went inside, of course, and asked about the artist,' Edward suggested, when his son seemed to need prompting to go on.

'Yes, I went inside . . . I even bought one of the paintings. There won't be any more of them because Standish had died a short while before I arrived. I met his daughter instead . . . a girl called Louise whom William hadn't even known about.'

'Is *that* the end of the story?' his father asked, to break another silence that had fallen.

'I don't know . . . probably, although I hope not. She's not beautiful – in fact she's rather an odd mixture of a girl; but I'm afraid it's due to her that I keep looking at the women here and thinking how dull and ordinary they now seem.'

'Would this unordinary mixture enjoy North Oxford, do you suppose?'

'I have no idea,' Geoffrey said, aware that what concerned him most had now been touched on. 'All I do know is that she hasn't had much to enjoy so far – dragged at the heels of Bohemian parents selfishly absorbed in each other, and then dumped on a grandfather who could have strayed out of a novel by Stendhal.'

'Dear me!' Edward Carmichael feared it was an inadequate response, but a glance at the moonlit face beside him suggested that his son hadn't even heard it. 'You could always,' he said more loudly, 'invite Miss Standish here to stay. Ruth would enjoy looking after her while you were in College.'

It was, Geoffrey realised long afterwards, only the second error of judgement he had known his father to make. But for the moment he let out a long sigh of relief. 'Yes, that's what I'll do . . . ask Louise to come on a visit. She sounds desperate where she is – you see, her mother has returned home.'

Edward managed not to say that he didn't see at all.

In the end, the plan came to nothing. There was no reply to Geoffrey's letter of invitation and he didn't know why until he eventually received a note from Louise with a London address on it. She was already working there, in the home of a diplomat at the French Embassy, as companion-cum-help-cum-house-keeper to the diplomat's wife.

In Oxford the first term of the academic year was always hard, with lecture and tutorial timetables to be worked into a smooth routine, an intake of bemused new undergraduates to be shepherded along, and third-year students already beginning to get neurotically intense about their chances in Final Schools. Wrapped up in the urgent demands of College life, Geoffrey put off from week to week the thought of finding the time to go to London. Louise's letters had become short and scarce – deliberately offhand, it seemed, as if she regretted the intimacy they'd rushed into. He didn't mention her name again at home beyond saying that she seemed to be settled in a job in London.

Christmas was almost upon them when he was buttonholed by William Standish in the Fellows' Quad late one afternoon.

'Come to my study, Geoffrey. I want to talk to you in peace, and you're a terrible chap for going everywhere at a run. Let the little perishers wait, say I. They've got more time ahead of them than we have.'

There was nothing to be done but follow the shambling figure up the staircase that led to his room. He had been its occupant for twenty years at least, to Geoffrey's knowledge, and during all that time little or nothing had ever been thrown away. Books flowed out of every shelf onto the floor, and any occasional chair that surfaced above the flood was piled with pamphlets or odd items of clothing that William had put on and removed again.

'Place is too small,' he muttered, 'but at least I know roughly where everything is.' He cleared a chair by removing from it a professorial gown green with age, a pullover and a disreputable pair of shoes, and invited his guest to sit. 'Term going well?'

'Strenuously but well,' Geoffrey agreed with a smile. 'Thank God we shall soon be able to draw breath for a week or two.'

His glance fastened for a moment on the picture above the fireplace. Under the strangely compelling impression that it was what Louise Standish would have wanted, he'd given it to William with the news that his brother had married and begat a daughter in France. There'd been times since then when he'd regretted the gesture. Lost in a scholar's world of Shakespearian texts and Jacobean commentaries, William hadn't seemed very grateful for it, or more than mildly interested in the story of his brother's life in France. There was also the fact that the damned painting grew on one: Geoffrey realised that he would have liked it hanging over *his* fireplace, even at the cost of reminding him painfully of Louise.

William poured Madeira into glasses that were beautiful but rather smeared, and examined his guest's expression. As usual it gave very little away. Carmichael was still young, but seen as a coming man, in the College and in his own Faculty. It was a pity, William thought, that he was also so hard to know.

After a slow sip or two of wine Professor Standish delivered his news. 'Went to London yesterday . . . been thinking of it for weeks and putting it off as a matter of fact; but ever since you told me John's daughter was there I knew I'd have to go.'

He was still looking at his visitor, and Geoffrey stared back, one fair eyebrow faintly raised. Not for anything would he have put into words the thought that hammered in his brain – *he* should have been the one to go and see Louise, not this well-meaning but ineffectual man who had been too long out of the real world.

'Was the visit arranged, or did you just go and thump on the diplomat's door?' he asked almost insolently.

William looked over half-moon glasses, curious to know why his self-controlled guest should suddenly be angry.

'I wrote to my niece and invited her to lunch with me. Jukes, who knows everything, recommended Simpson's-in-the-Strand as a nice, respectable place to take her to . . . and so it was.'

Geoffrey looked down at his glass, afraid of giving away the extraordinary feelings that seemed to be sweeping over him. He found himself thinking inconsequentially that he couldn't imagine how Louise Standish would have looked – he'd only seen her in the summer heat of Paris, in a cotton dress, with her slender brown arms and legs bare.

'I hope you both enjoyed the meeting,' he said at last, struggling to sound as if he meant it.

A charming smile made William look almost youthful. 'Speaking only for myself, I fell in love! It's a long time since that happened and I'd forgotten how very pleasant the sensation is.' He gave a little sigh that suggested other pleasures also mislaid over the years, and then returned to his story. 'Louise was wary to begin with, wanting to make it clear that she would have taken her father's part in our quarrel. But I was cunning, Geoffrey . . . I talked about Oxford instead, and I haven't been blessed with such an audience for years! Then *she* told me about John, and one way and another there seemed so much to say that we could have "tired the sun with talking and sent him down the sky".'

'Why did she leave Paris so suddenly? She seemed chained to her grandfather's house and gallery when I was there.'

'Her mother returned. Louise didn't say so, but my impression is that Nadia Standish sees her as a threat – understandable in a certain neurotic kind of woman, I suppose, when her daughter grows up beautiful.' William pointed to the painting above the fireplace. 'I told Louise where that had finished up, thanks to you. She seems to think you're kind, and very generous . . . but a poor correspondent now!'

He was surprised by the flush of colour under Geoffrey Carmichael's fair skin, and by the suddenness with which he got to his feet.

'It's time I went, William – thanks for the drink.' His hand was on the latch of the door when he turned to ask the only question that mattered. 'How did Louise seem – happy?'

The answer he waited for came slowly. 'She did her best, but I'm quite good at hearing what people *don't* say, and she looked much too thin. The truth is, I think, that she's lonely, tired, and seriously overworked. Once her employers discovered how well she could cook the polite fiction that she was an equal member of the household was over. Madame entertains lavishly while her "companion" slaves in the kitchen.' William ruffled his hair worriedly. 'I begged Louise to come here – I've got a little money put by – but she said that wouldn't do. She'd find another job when she couldn't bear the beastly de Vercors woman any longer – though I'm not sure how that's to be done when she has so little time free.'

Geoffrey heard him out, but merely nodded in response.

Two days later he took the train to London himself and called, without arrangement, at the house in Holland Park. A teenage girl opened the door, and when he asked to see Mademoiselle Standish admitted sullenly that she was there but '*très occupée*'. He insisted as pleasantly as possible that his visit was urgent, and then was abandoned on the doorstep while the girl went away. A moment later Madame de Vercors herself appeared, hard-faced, elegant, and not at all disposed to have her helper distracted from preparing an imminent luncheon party. Perhaps Monsieur would have the goodness to call some other time?

By now murderously angry but aware that he had no right to barge into the house uninvited, Monsieur replied in her own language that he would return at half-past two. On his next visit he ignored the front door and chose instead the area steps that led to the kitchen entrance. He supposed it was still rage that made his heart thud at twice its normal rate, but when Louise stood there in front of him all he was conscious of was the long weeks of missing her, and the overpowering longing to be allowed to take her away.

'I was made to feel out of place upstairs,' he said unevenly, 'so I thought I'd come to the servants' entrance instead.'

Her pale mouth tried to smile, and she managed to speak above the lump in her throat. 'Well, I suppose that's where I belong! Madame de Vercors only announced that she'd had to send an inconvenient caller away. Her daughter went so far as to describe you – tall and fair . . . *très Anglais*, in fact! I'm sorry they didn't recognise a grand academic gentleman from Oxford.' She was afraid she was talking too much and too flippantly, but it was the only defence she had against bursting into tears. Never in her lonely life had she felt quite so alone as in these past months in London, and now the de Vercors family would seem *more* unbearable still when Geoffrey Carmichael went away.

'I should have come sooner . . . meant to, Louise; but there always seemed to be a thousand other things to do. Then William told me about the life you lead here.'

Her thin shoulders lifted in a shrug. 'It doesn't matter. I'll find another job soon – cooks are quite sought after in London.'

He stepped close and took hold of her hands – still remembered as being beautiful, but a burn-mark on one of them stressed her status in this unpleasant household, and he was sharply aware of wanting to remove her from it.

Louise could feel the warmth of Geoffrey's hands against the coldness of her own skin. Less palpable but just as intense was her awareness of some rising tide of anger in him. She wasn't sure where it was directed – at her employer, or herself for the mistake she'd made in rushing over to London. But she was certain of one thing: he was concerned for *her*, and that knowledge was unfamiliar and suddenly sweet.

'William said he'd asked you to come to Oxford and you'd refused. Would you still refuse, Louise, if I asked you?'

Her eyes searched his face, looking for a meaning she might not have understood. 'To . . . to come for a visit?'

'No, for good – as my wife.' He could scarcely believe that he'd said the words that were still echoing in his brain. They hadn't been in his mind at all during the journey to London.

But they were the *right* words — that was perfectly clear to him now. They were the truth he'd been evading ever since he'd asked if he might write to her from Lyons. 'We don't know each other very well yet,' he said awkwardly, 'so marriage could wait . . . you'd have to be sure first that you liked me and Oxford enough.'

The effort at lightness was brave, she thought, when she could feel his hands trembling.

'You're sorry for me,' she muttered. 'There's no need — I'm used to managing on my own.'

'So am I, but I find that I don't want to any longer.' He let go of her hands, but only to grip her shoulders and be shocked by the fragility of them under his fingers. It suddenly seemed impossible that she shouldn't marry him, when he knew so certainly what was best for her.

'My dear, if I promise not to rush you into making up your mind, will you leave this awful household and give *us* a try instead? William is longing for you to come, and my father would love you at first sight. There's a piano at home — you could practise all day if you wanted to.'

It was absurd to try to bribe her with a piano and her smile said as much, but he couldn't yet bring himself to say that he didn't want to go away and leave her there alone. She sensed his reluctance and understood it because it was the same as her own; emotions were dangerous, unfamiliar things best kept well in hand. They both knew this; it was the most painful lesson life had so far taught them. But there might be different lessons they could learn together if they felt brave enough to try.

'I'm inclined to think I should like Oxford,' she said at last, 'but it doesn't seem fair just to take it on trial. If you were serious . . . about marrying . . . perhaps that is what we should do.'

His taut face relaxed into a smile that she found full of unexpected amusement and tenderness. He should have expected such French matter-of-factness from her, and probably it was their best way of dealing with an unusual situation. Astonished with himself for feeling so little embarrassment, he was becoming more and more convinced that giving instinct its head was something he should have tried before.

'Come and try to love Oxford,' he begged with sudden urgency, still unable to ask her to love him as well. 'It's bound to seem miserable just now – cold and damp and full of winter flu – but promise me you'll give it the benefit of the doubt until spring comes.'

Torn between laughter and a sudden desire to weep at his kindness, she agreed that she would, but refused to be persuaded into abandoning Madame de Vercors on the eve of Christmas.

'Well, let me at least break our news to her,' Geoffrey suggested. 'I should like to, in a manner as wonderfully *anglais* as I can contrive!'

Her chuckle at this suddenly reminded him of William Standish, but she shook her head. 'Leave it to me, please. Having hurled my thunderbolt, I can let her down lightly by saying that I'll stay until her Christmas parties are over.'

Geoffrey finally agreed, remembering that he would have some explaining of his own to do. The house in Norham Grove was easily big enough for them to share with his father and Ruth, but now it would need splitting into separate apartments. For the moment there seemed nothing more to say, and they stared at one another, uncertain what should come next in a relationship for which neither of them was quite prepared. Then Geoffrey leaned forward to kiss her cheek and of its own volition his mouth travelled on to cover hers, though only very briefly. Perhaps that was very *anglais* too, she reflected, and smiled at the thought. But when he wanted to know what amused her, she answered gravely.

'I was thinking we have a lot to learn about each other.'

'So we do, but that's what Oxford is – a fine place for learning!' he said, touching her cheek in a shy gesture that pleased her.

A moment later he was climbing the area steps to the street, and she was left alone to consider what she had agreed to. It was too soon to think about her marriage to a man she scarcely knew – she'd have to come to that idea by slow degrees. Better to consider the place called Oxford, that had lodged itself in her father's memory, and where she was to learn all the things she didn't yet know.

But her thoughts were interrupted by the ringing of a bell upstairs, where afternoon tea was now required. She remembered the woman who waited there and suddenly felt sorry for her. The poor creature had chosen for a husband the sleek and viperish Raoul de Vercors. She should have looked instead for a quiet-voiced man with gentle hands, and kindness in his smile.

CHAPTER THREE

A month later her first glimpse of the city she was now committed to came as something of a shock; her imagined vision of it required adjustment in the face of reality. Lovingly eloquent about a place still 'whispering the last enchantments of the Middle Ages', her uncle had forgotten to mention its depressing ugly suburbs and railway station, and its dowdy-looking shops. On a bleak morning in January Oxford seemed steeped in cold provincial gloom rather than romance. But she had promised Geoffrey not to be cast down. Spring would come, and so would delight eventually.

Astonishment came first, when he stopped the car outside the strangest house she'd ever seen. Violently coloured bricks had been contorted into so many gables, turrets and curlicues that she closed her eyes, hoping to find she'd imagined them when she looked again. But they were still there.

'Victorian Gothic, it's called,' Geoffrey was explaining beside her, half-rueful and half-proud. 'North Oxford is rather famous for it — you'll get used to it in time.'

She doubted whether he could be right; it seemed more likely that it was something one had to be born to. But her attention was diverted by the opening of the front door. A tall man and a scarcely smaller woman were waiting for them there — Geoffrey's father and his sister, Ruth. They were going to share this ugly house together — he'd made that clear — but she realised that she hadn't thought about them at all. Now it was a great deal too late to do so. She wondered how she must appear. Being half-foreign might excuse a certain amount of oddity, but there was no blinking the fact that in rushing into this marriage she was behaving very oddly indeed. For a moment panic spiralled almost out of control, and she opened her mouth to implore him to return her to the railway station. But he spoke first himself and it was too late to say anything at all.

'Come and meet my father. You'll like him, I think.'

She tried to smile at Edward Carmichael, and saw such kindness in his face that the knot of fear inside her loosened to a point where she could breathe and listen to the simple words with which he made her welcome. Ruth kissed her on both cheeks and said more emotionally that she had always longed for a sister. Perhaps it was going to be easy after all, even though they'd knitted themselves together so closely after being abandoned by Sybil Carmichael. Louise felt optimism return and, when Geoffrey smiled at her, gladness as well. She was going to belong somewhere at last; with time she would discover what was expected of her, and even learn to feel secure.

Ruth, talking all the time, at once took her on a tour of the rambling house.

'My grandfather was born here,' she explained proudly, 'soon after the house was built in 1877 – high noon of great Victoria's reign! Perhaps it seems old-fashioned to you, coming from a sophisticated place like Paris. But we haven't ever wanted anything changed. Continuity is so terribly important, don't you agree?'

Louise stared at dark flock wallpapers, fringed brocade curtains, and overstuffed furniture, unwilling to believe that Geoffrey enjoyed living in this dusty Victorian high noon. But Ruth's eyes were upon her, and it was too soon to say that continuity of ugliness seemed no virtue at all.

'There's nothing sophisticated about my grandfather's rooms in Paris,' she said instead. 'He would agree with you that things should be solid and well used.'

It wasn't quite the eager response that Ruth had hoped for, but allowances had obviously to be made, and she had forbidden herself to be anything but delighted with Geoffrey's fiancée.

They had reached the top floor and now it was easy to exclaim with genuine pleasure. Louise stared down at what was spread before them – green spaces traceried with the outlines of bare winter trees, and further off the silver gleam of water.

'How lovely . . . and how unexpected, to find fields in the middle of Oxford.'

'They're called the Parks,' Ruth corrected her, 'and of course they belong to the University – everything does that counts, you'll find.'

'I have a lot to discover,' Louise admitted, trying not to feel depressed again. 'Between them Geoffrey and my uncle William must keep me from making too many mistakes.'

Ruth's large hands suddenly clutched her arm. 'You must let *me* help you. An uncle you don't know can't be of much help, and my darling boy scarcely has a moment's peace as it is. The first thing you must learn, Louise, is that College dons are not like ordinary men, and Geoffrey especially takes his duties very seriously.'

It was a relief to hear Edward Carmichael calling up to them that sherry was waiting to be drunk in the drawing room.

'In honour of the bride-to-be,' said Ruth, still determined to instruct. 'We usually keep wine for high days and holidays.'

'We shan't any more – we shall drink it every day.' Had she actually shouted the words that echoed in her head? Presumably not, because Ruth was bouncing down the stairs in front of her, still talking gaily about the joy of having a wedding in the family. She meant well, Louise told herself. That would be the important thing to remember in future about her sister-in-law.

Downstairs Geoffrey was busy pouring wine, but his father's eyes inspected her, as a matter of professional habit perhaps. 'You look pale, my dear – not at the thought of living here, I hope! If there are things about the house you don't like, you must change them; we shan't mind.'

She was careful not to look at Ruth, but sipped her sherry instead, and managed to listen calmly to Geoffrey explaining the arrangements for their wedding.

Ten days later, just before the beginning of something that everyone called Hilary term, they were married in the lovely, simple chapel of St Barnabas. It hadn't, muttered William Standish in the course of giving her away, been mucked about with, thank God, by the Victorian restorers. She was deeply grateful to have his arm to hold. It was warm and real when nothing else about the occasion seemed to have any reality at all

– not the girl who was herself, dressed in a hat and fitted coat of cream moiré silk with violets pinned to its lapel; not the serious, fair-haired man waiting for her at the chancel steps; and least of all the small congregation invited to come and watch their lives being joined together, all of them Geoffrey's family and friends, except for William. For a moment loneliness pierced the haze of unreality with an arrow-thrust at her heart, and she failed to hear what the clergyman was saying. The news that she was marrying an Englishman, as Nadia Benoît had done, predictably hadn't been well received in Paris. Only her old piano teacher, Hortense Levine, had bothered to regret not being present to see her married. The future lay here, among these people who were strange to her. Even the man now standing tall and straight beside her was unfamiliar in his formal clothes. But he was promising to love and cherish her and she had no doubt that he would – Geoffrey Carmichael would fulfil his promises. He took her hand and smiled at her, and she decided that she wasn't afraid. They would learn happiness together.

She didn't falter again until they were on their way out of the chapel. Geoffrey felt her stumble and looked down to see that her pale face was suddenly flushed with colour.

'My mother is here,' she murmured, 'with Henri Rivaux – Grandfather's partner! It's just like her to suddenly decide to come, I'm afraid.'

Geoffrey thought of the Master's wife being asked to fit two more places round her luncheon table, but bravely said it didn't matter. 'I'm very glad for you, my dear – it's very right and proper that she should be here.'

The phrase 'right and proper' was a strange one to apply to her mother, but she hoped that if the visit were brief he might not need to discover the fact. It was true that when Nadia Standish emerged to kiss her daughter and be introduced, her new son-in-law looked a little surprised. A wedding guest swathed in black from head to foot *was* surely unusual, even if her husband had died within the last year? But he bowed over her gloved fingers, and was examined by huge, kohl-rimmed eyes in a face that was haggard but still beautiful. A black velvet beret was tilted rakishly over her red hair, and elaborate jet and enamel earrings dangled almost to the collar of her cape.

'You are *not* what I expected,' she announced. '*Enfin*, more . . .' the right phrase failed her, but her hands sketched a gesture instead, suggesting some kind of surprised approval.

Geoffrey, faintly blushing, embarked on a hasty round of introductions, while Louise performed the same duty on behalf of Henri Rivaux. Dr Wharton, with an anguished glance at his wife, pressed the visitors to join them in the Lodging for luncheon, and they straggled across the quadrangle, with Nadia clinging to his arm and supposing from the wording of the invitation that what awaited them was some dingy boarding-house parlour.

Walking with Henri, Louise was told how they came to be there.

'I was going to visit Oxford soon in any case, to consult the curators of the museum here about a rare instrument. Nadia heard me talking to André, and suddenly decided that I could escort her to your wedding at the same time.' A faint smile touched his mouth, hinting at more humour than she'd discovered in him before. 'Your mother is not the easiest travelling companion, my dear, but the occasional problem en route is a small price to pay for this!'

His glance travelled appreciatively round what Geoffrey would have told him was Oxford at its most perfect: grey stone buildings, mullion-windowed and creeper-hung, framing velvet green lawns, and an ancient tower from which the blue and gold College flag was flying – Charlie Jukes' personal contribution to the day's festivities.

'It's beautiful *now*,' Louise said, 'but Geoffrey insists that it will take my breath away in the spring!'

She was rather breathtaking herself, Henri noticed, in her charming jonquil-coloured coat and hat. Through all the years he'd known her in Paris she'd been simply André's small grand-daughter, a solitary child made wary by the knowledge that she was only there because no one had known what else to do with her. England seemed to be suiting her very well – a fact that would surely have made John Standish smile wryly if he'd known.

The splendour of the rooms they were shown into came as another surprise, sufficient to silence Nadia while the first glasses of champagne were being served. She'd been parted from her matador's cape, but the skin-tight black dress beneath was not such as Oxford wives normally wore to College luncheon parties. Afterwards, sitting at table on the Master's left, she was slightly intimidated at first by his formal, exquisite courtesy. By the time choice burgundy followed champagne and Pouilly-Fuissé she was seeing her host quite differently and was able to explain to him what a great artist her husband had been.

'Not appreciated *here*, of course,' she said with sorrow. 'In England everyone must be the same, *n'est-ce-pas?* Genius is frowned upon.'

'I'm afraid prophets are often without honour in their own country, Madame Standish,' Dr Wharton suggested tactfully. 'It's their penalty, perhaps, for being so far ahead of the rest of us!'

She was about to agree that this might be so, when a remark of Geoffrey's floated across the table in the course of a different conversation. His eyes had rested on her critically from time to time, she thought, and she was sure already that he was cold – this a woman like herself could tell immediately. Poor Louise, to have married a man with no passion in his soul. But sorry as she was for her daughter, she couldn't allow him to speak lies about France. She waved long, white hands in the air, demanding everyone else's attention around the table as well.

'No, *mon cher*, you are quite wrong. Me, I can tell you how it was because I was there; not you. In Vichy France the war years were *entirely* terrible, not easy at all.'

He was nettled by her contradiction, especially since the rest of them had heard it, but he remained polite. 'Not *easy* anywhere, I suppose – certainly not here.'

'Some bombs you had *par ci, par là* . . .' Nadia conceded, '*not* enjoyable. But the agony of seeing invaders trample over your country . . . this you English didn't know. Because I am half-

Slav, for me it happened twice – France, and then Russia. For you it happened not at all.'

Geoffrey allowed her a courteous smile. 'All that happened was that this country spent its wealth and greatness on the salvation of the rest of Europe.'

She turned huge, imploring eyes on her host. 'I speak of the suffering of the heart and my son-in-law speaks of wealth.'

'My dear lady, you are both right,' Humphrey Wharton said, looking desperately in the direction of his wife. But relief came in the form of William Standish getting to his feet to offer Nadia a courtly bow.

'I'm going to ask Mrs Wharton and the Master to excuse us, my dear. This is Louise and Geoffrey's day, but when I am meeting my sister-in-law for the first time I too have something to celebrate! Will you honour me with a visit to my study? We must talk about John before you have to rush away.'

Watching anxiously, Louise saw her mother begin to smile again. Nadia needed admiration as flowers needed sunlight, and William, bent over her hand, exuded all the charming warmth that her son-in-law so deplorably lacked. He escorted her almost tenderly to the door, and as it closed behind them Louise thought she heard the faintest sigh of relief.

She didn't need to be told what the rest of them were thinking – an excitable Frenchwoman might have been strain enough; but half-Slav Nadia Standish, with her outré clothes and intense theatricality, was altogether too much. Even Geoffrey thought so; she could see him exchanging a faint grimace with Ruth, sitting further down the table. For the first time in her life Louise felt a rush of affection towards her mother and a twinge of anxiety on her own account. These Oxford people she had come among expected everyone to be the same as them. That was bad enough; but it would be even worse if they believed that no one else *could* be quite the same as them.

Despite his wife's raised eyebrow, Dr Wharton was signalling to the steward to serve more wine to save a luncheon party that had gone sadly flat. Toasts were drunk, and the conversation recovered cheerfulness and even gaiety again when Geoffrey described the difficulty William must be having to find his guest anywhere to sit down. But it was a relief when the Chaplain volunteered to escort Henri Rivaux to his appointment at the museum, and the rest of them could offer their thanks to Mrs Wharton and leave.

There was still William to be rescued, but first Geoffrey took his wife up a warren of staircases to his own rooms. Within the ancient stone walls there was pleasant modern comfort here, and no disorder. The huge number of books were neatly shelved and, she guessed, alphabetically arranged.

'Of course,' Geoffrey agreed when she said so. 'I hate muddle, and having to waste time looking for things.'

Louise braced herself against the edge of his desk and took a deep breath. 'You had to put up with a muddle today, I'm afraid – my mother confused things by coming, didn't she?'

She wasn't sure whether she wanted him to be honest or tactful, then gratefully heard him manage to be both.

'Never mind, my dear – it was an interesting confusion! And our disagreement about France was my fault. I shouldn't have mentioned the war at all.'

'I know she hovers on the edge of being absurd,' Louise admitted, 'in fact with a child's brutality I used to think she *was* absurd. But now I understand her better. It isn't all make-believe; she really does feel everything intensely. That's why I was such a nuisance to her – she wanted to love, and be loved by, my father completely. She's lost without him . . . almost afraid she doesn't exist any more.'

Geoffrey came towards her, with more tenderness in his face than she had looked for in a reticent man. 'We'll agree that she's anything you like as long as she doesn't want to stay with us *too* often! My dear girl, this isn't the merriest of wedding days for you, I'm afraid, going straight back to Norham Grove, as if we'd been staidly married for years. As soon as term's over, I promise we'll find somewhere exciting to visit.'

With his arms around her and this new sweetness in his smile it was easy to believe that she didn't mind at all. 'Getting married is enough excitement to be going on with,' she pointed out. 'I think I'd *rather* begin in our own home, as a matter of fact.' Her expression changed suddenly, reminding him of Nadia Standish in its swift alterations. 'This will be the first real home I've had – being parked on my grandparents to be got out of the way wasn't the same thing at all.'

Beneath the charming wedding hat her face seemed to have become mysteriously beautiful; he was aware of it with a growing sense of delight. In fact, more emotions altogether than he could manage were crowding in on him, but he struggled to remember that he'd promised to make haste slowly. They had first to get to know one another; trust would grow with time and patience, and with trust love would come as well.

'Your mother and mine would have made a good pair,' he said as lightly as he could, '. . . monsters both in their way! Now, shall we go and rescue the gallant professor?'

She smilingly agreed, and he kissed her mouth because it wasn't to be resisted and a man could surely be allowed to kiss his wife, even in the monastic calm of a don's study. Then, hands clasped, they walked down and up the staircases that led to William's door.

He was brewing tea for Nadia beside an open fire. The room should have looked the same as Geoffrey's but in fact, Louise decided, didn't resemble it at all. Here, untidiness had been brought to a fine art, and it smelled different too. Coal soot was mingled with the scent of old leather and tobacco; and now, trying to make an impression on these entrenched aromas was his guest's exotic perfume.

William saw Louise sniff appreciatively and grinned over the teapot he was holding. 'I'm hoping the Chanel No. 5 will last until the young gentlemen come up tomorrow – my reputation as a ladies' man should soar!'

They drank strong tea in the warm, friendly room where it was easier to talk than round Mrs Wharton's elegant luncheon table. Nadia looked happy, and Geoffrey more completely relaxed than Louise had ever seen him – perhaps because he was in his true element in this scholar's paradise, just as William was. She smiled at the uncle she would never have known but for Geoffrey, remembering that William was one of the Oxford people, hiding great erudition under grace and kindness. There was no reason to fear them after all.

The time came at last to deliver Nadia to the station, where Henri was to meet her for the journey to London. They arrived early and she stood shivering in the cold, damp air of early dusk. Gaiety had drained out of her face, leaving it tragic again.

'*C'est triste, cette ville,*' she murmured, looking around the bleak platform.

'It's still the middle of winter,' Geoffrey pointed out firmly. 'Things get better soon.'

Nadia's faint shrug agreed that it might be so. 'Well, never mind, but I hope you have chosen somewhere more . . . more *séduisant* for your honeymoon, at least.'

'Not immediately,' he said rather stiffly. 'A new term starts tomorrow. We shall have to wait until the Easter vacation.'

She stared up at him, trying to remember that her passionate-hearted husband had been an Englishman like this one.

'So where do you go now, if not away together?' she wanted to know.

It was Louise who answered. 'We go home, of course, *Maman*. The house is more than big enough to share with Geoffrey's father and sister – you met them at lunch today.'

Nadia closed her eyes, recalling a woman in a distressing shade of blue who had stared at her as if watching a specimen in a zoo. Women did not all have to look the same, *évidemment*; Nadia was prepared to concede that she herself might not be appreciated by everyone else, but even so . . . She clutched her daughter's arm urgently.

'*Écoute, ma chère – il faut changer tout ça. La soeur . . . c'est une femme complètement affreuse . . . impossible!*'

Louise thought the situation could only have been saved by laughing about it, but her husband's set face told her that laughter was beyond him. Instead, still trying to treat it lightly, she said, 'Geoffrey understands French as well as we do, so if you have any more unkind things to say you might as well say them in English.'

About to do so, Nadia was interrupted by Henri, breathless from his gallop along the platform and still caught up in the pleasure of what he'd been allowed to handle at the museum. He was too excited to notice anything wrong and eager to explain that it would be necessary to come back again and again to Oxford.

'Me, I don't think so,' Nadia had got as far as saying flatly when, by the grace of God as Geoffrey saw it, their train came trundling in. A flurry of goodbyes, banging doors, and blowing whistles made the moment seem more or less normal; then, apart from a solitary porter, the platform was empty except for themselves. Louise looked at Geoffrey hoping that now, at least, he might smile. But with an effort that was almost visible he made no comment on his mother-in-law and something else was jerked out of him instead.

'I hate this railway station — always have ever since I first started going away to school. I was never quite sure that I'd find my mother still here when I came back.'

Louise thought again of what he'd said earlier about Sybil Carmichael and about Nadia — monsters both. In a way she could see that it was true, but there was pathos as well in Nadia that he ignored; and surely it was possible that his own mother had grown desperate to escape from a life in Norham Grove? She shivered suddenly at the thought, and at once Geoffrey's rigid expression melted into concern.

'My poor girl, you must be frozen in your thin clothes. Let's . . . let's get out of this perishing wind, shall we?'

She thought he'd changed his mind, and would have said 'let's go home' if her mother's horrified amazement hadn't still echoed in his ears. It had seemed a perfectly natural thing to do until a few moments ago, to share a too-large family house. But now he was unsure. Like herself, in fact, he was unsure about a lot of things. She turned to face him, so that he had to stand still and look at her.

'I *am* very cold,' she agreed, 'and I want to go home . . . *home*, Geoffrey. It's where we begin, you and I. I prayed hard in the chapel this morning for us to make each other happy. That's all that matters — not what my mother and your sister think of each other; not what my grandfather thinks of Englishmen; nor what the Master of St Barnabas thinks of me!'

37

Amusement tugged at Geoffrey's mouth at last, bringing his face to life.

'I'm afraid Humphrey was terrified of Nadia, but clearly very taken with you. Louise, my love, it *is* going to be wonderfully all right. I should have shouted that aloud before your mother and Henri left.'

Her smile agreed with him. Together two people who knew loneliness and rejection at first-hand would make it all right. She didn't see how they could fail.

Nearly twenty years later her husband's wedding-day boast was something she could still vividly remember. He never referred to it now himself, and she supposed that it had got lost among the more important matters that occupied his heart and mind. There were always University Committees to be joined, tutorials to hold, dinners at High Table to attend, articles to be written, or – better still – politely scathing reviews of what other academics had been unwise enough to publish. Ruth had been right that first day of her arrival at Oxford – College dons were not as other men. But the long years since had proved that about some other things Nadia had been right as well.

The clock in the hall chimed ten – still much too early to expect to sleep, even though she had used tiredness as an excuse upstairs. She could read or listen to some music, but if her light was out when Geoffrey finally came to bed, he would sleep in his dressing room. He always did when he came back late from College; her acquaintances among the North Oxford wives would think him a very considerate husband. She always knew how they regarded *her* – half-French of course, but also rather odd in other ways. She had done better than she deserved, they reckoned, and Louise supposed that in some ways she had.

CHAPTER FOUR

At eight o'clock the next morning Geoffrey walked into the kitchen, punctual to the minute as usual. It had taken him years to get used to the idea of breakfasting here instead of in the dining room, and even now it seemed an informal, slapdash sort of thing to do. But the table was attractively laid, with pride of place given to a bowl of orange and bronze dahlias that Louise must already have been out in the garden to pick. He remembered once pointing out that the flowers she filled the rooms with were dying from the instant she cut them. She'd smiled and said it didn't matter – they'd been appreciated, so dying wouldn't hurt them. The remark was typical, a reminder that after twenty years of married life they still saw things differently – like Ruth's supper last night, endured by his wife, but not for long enough. It was a habit with her now to escape from them, in mind if not in body. He wanted to say so, shout that it was wrong of her, but self-discipline was too strong, and all he said instead was, 'You've been out in the garden early, I see.'

'Yes . . . it must have been a cool, wet summer here. A lot of things need cutting back before they strangle each other to death.'

'Excellent, my dear.'

He hadn't listened – she thought he never did when she spoke about the garden; but in any case his whole attention was probably on St Barnabas again by now. He'd enjoyed the summer at Aix but he was deeply content as well that it was over. There was the start of new term to think about; better still, the start of a new academic year. It was the best thing she knew about him – a great many of his colleagues had lost the joy of teaching, but Geoffrey never had.

She watched him tip cornflakes out of the packet and for once he didn't even notice that she'd put the willow-pattern bowl down the wrong way round. Normally he'd correct it carefully so that the three little men forever crossing a china bridge weren't walking on their heads.

'Don't worry about lunch for me,' he said politely. 'I'll eat in College.'

Another silence fell which she suddenly broke with a casual comment of her own. 'If you're wondering what *I'm* going to do today, I think I shall try to seduce the Vice Chancellor.'

She waited for him to murmur 'Excellent!' again, but he'd heard her this time. His eyebrows drew together in a faint frown, but instead of disapproving of her bad taste he apologised instead; it was the weapon that he always chose to fight with – unfailing courtesy.

'I'm sorry, my dear . . . I'm afraid my mind *was* elsewhere. But I expect you're quite glad not to have your gardening interrupted by a husband needing to be fed at lunch-time!'

'Very glad,' she agreed cheerfully. 'Three months of French middays meals have been much too much for me.'

'Without having any discernible effect,' he observed. 'Ruth thought last night that you'd *lost* weight, if anything; in fact she was concerned about you.'

It was so intolerable to be discussed by Ruth that she couldn't keep the edge out of her voice. 'I hope you explained that I'm reaching the dangerous age when a woman easily gets irritable, and grows either rather thin or extremely fat.' For good measure she added something else that he wouldn't like. 'I shall go and visit Anna this morning, as well as work outside.'

'Just as you please, of course.'

His voice was expressionless but she knew how much he longed to ask her to ignore their nearest neighbour. Instead of a dozen pleasant women who might have become her friends she'd chosen the exotically strange Hungarian creature next door. Geoffrey acknowledged to himself what irked him most about Anna Ouspenska: she reminded him too vividly of his mother-in-law. With time and a late, unexpected remarriage – to Henri Rivaux – Nadia had calmed down a little; but nothing had made Madame Ouspenska more acceptable to North Oxford. It was unfortunate that she and Louise should share not only a harmless passion for music but also a sense of not being quite as their other neighbours were.

He stood up and walked round the table to kiss his wife's cheek. Her face *was* too thin – he could see the shadows beneath her cheekbones – but it had always been like that. The passing years had made so little outward change in her that he was sometimes misled into thinking that she was still the girl he'd fallen in love with in Paris.

'I *like* the brown face,' he said gently, and it wasn't until he'd walked out of the room that she remembered Ruth's unfortunate greeting of the night before. His parting kindness left her feeling ashamed of her own edginess. With no real hardship to complain of, perhaps she *was* turning into an irritable woman made tense by the prospect of becoming middle-aged.

Out in the garden tranquillity as always returned. Absorbed in the task of restraining a rampant clematis that wanted to entwine with anything it met, she finally registered the sound of a lawn mower starting up next door. It would be Anna, of course, reluctantly embarking on a task she hated, and happy to be interrupted.

Louise walked round to the garden next door, passing an unfamiliar car parked in the drive, but there was no sign of a small figure dressed in the clashing shades favoured by her friend. They were an antidote, she said, to the colours that William Morris had inspired too many North Oxford ladies to wear – a depressing mixture of sludge green, ochre and peacock blue. But today, instead of Anna's pink shirt and magenta trousers, there was only a soberly dressed man in view, steering her antiquated mower. He cut the engine when he caught sight of the visitor, but made no attempt to walk towards her.

'Good morning,' Louise said, with a pleasant smile. 'I expected to find Anna here. Burglars don't normally lend a hand with the lawn, so I suppose that's not what you are.'

His expression didn't relax but he briefly explained himself. 'My landlady went away yesterday, to play something she called baroque music at a festival in Bath. I'm here alone at the moment.'

Louise could place him now. Anna's two upper floors were rented out in self-contained apartments to visiting academics.

'Of course, I'd forgotten the festival,' she confessed. 'My husband and I live next door, but we've only just come back from a summer in France.'

She saw no pretence of interest in his face – nothing, in fact, except a scarcely concealed impatience for her to leave; but he'd said that he was alone, and she couldn't help noticing the blood-stained handkerchief he'd tied roughly round one hand.

'If you can bear to stop cutting grass for ten minutes I'll find a plaster for your hand, and make some coffee,' she suggested.

He considered his makeshift bandage. 'The mower's revenge – it disliked having the rust of years scraped off it so that it could be made to work efficiently.'

She registered what she'd missed before – an accent that labelled him, even though it was less obtrusive than most. 'You insist on things working efficiently, of course.'

'In my funny old American way, yes, I do,' he agreed, and then took her by surprise. 'Coffee would be welcome if the offer was serious.'

They walked in silence towards her own house. If he preferred it that way she didn't mind, but it was unusual in an American. The transatlantic visitors Geoffrey brought home erred on the side of chattiness as a rule.

She left him in the kitchen, holding his hand under the cold tap, while she fetched the first-aid box. Cleaned, the wound looked sore but not serious, and once she'd strapped it up he seemed to think no more about it. When the coffee was made she suggested taking it outside. The morning was beautiful, with the golden, benign warmth of September; but her reason for bringing him outside, she realised, was not to enjoy the sunshine. The truth was that he seemed overpoweringly large indoors. Out here the scale was better, and the charm of the garden might even beguile him a little.

He stared at the lovely greenness all round them, but not with any noticeable enjoyment. 'There isn't a lot of scope for this sort of thing where I come from.'

'New York?' she hazarded.

'Most weekends, when I can get there to see my wife and children. Otherwise I'm at Ann Arbor – the University of Michigan, in other words.'

Hazily aware that New York was a long way from Michigan, Louise supposed that he'd chosen the arrangement. Even foreign academics seemed reluctant to indulge in domestic life.

'You may get to like gardens if you stay here long enough,' she suggested after a slight pause. 'Though not necessarily! Anna has lived in Oxford for fifteen years without catching the infection. She fondly imagines that what she has next door is a garden, instead of a patch of weed-filled turf.'

The man beside her gestured at what Louise had created around them. 'Whereas this, I take it, is the real thing . . . your life's work perhaps?'

The edge to his voice made clear what he thought of it, and again she was struck by how untypical he was. Visiting Americans were usually so urbane that she'd imagined them hand-picked for Oxford. For a moment she toyed with the idea of claiming the garden as a hobby, indulged in when she wasn't leading students through the mysteries of Elementary Particle Physics or Electron Spectroscopy; but life being the confounding business it was, he would probably turn out to be a scientist himself.

'Yes, I think I'll claim this is *my* work,' she finally agreed, 'even though I detect a certain reluctance in you to take gardens seriously. I'll make large claims for my painting, if you prefer, or for playing the piano rather well.' She smiled at his expression. 'Perhaps not . . . I can see you share the Oxford view . . . they're considered accomplishments here, not serious works at all.' Then she withdrew her attention from a conversation that neither of them seemed to enjoy; it would be more interesting to decide whether a little weeping purple beech tree would or would not look right at the far end of the lawn.

Aware of her lack of interest, he found himself resenting it. 'Perhaps we should introduce ourselves,' he suggested, and got to his feet to offer a mock bow.

'Dr Daniel Goodman, on sabbatical from Michigan – second-generation self-made American, as no doubt you guessed. My grandfather was Fritz Gutemann when he arrived in New York from the Ruhr sixty years ago, as an immigrant steel worker.'

Her dark eyes were suddenly on his face and there was no doubt that he had all her attention now.

'Why not, of course, be proud of your grandfather, and your German ancestry,' she said politely, 'but it might be tactful not to make too much of it in front of your landlady. No blame to the Gutemanns, of course, if they weren't even in Nazi Germany; but as a child Anna survived incarceration in Dachau. Her Hungarian-Jewish parents did not.'

A silence fell that she saw no reason to break. She hoped instead that this large, uncongenial man looming over her would go away. But he sat down again, and she could see his undamaged hand clenched now round one knee.

'Are there any more booby traps I need to avoid?' he asked after a moment or two. 'Or do you just dislike German-Americans on principle? You shouldn't, God damn it; we come from the same Anglo-Saxon stock.'

'Diluted in my case,' Louise answered with real pleasure. 'My mother is half-French, half-Russian. I'm bound to say that she isn't *entirely* pro-German either, having spent the war years in hiding with her English husband in France.' Turning to look at her companion, she surprised an expression on his face that she couldn't read, and feared that she'd scored off him cheaply. 'I dare say it all seems suicidally silly to you, across the Atlantic,' she muttered '. . . old wounds not forgotten, nothing learned after two grievous wars. I'm afraid my husband's view of history is that we *never* learn from past mistakes.'

Daniel Goodman stared at her, free to do so now that she was picking dead blooms from the plant cascading from an urn beside her. Her slenderness, sunburned skin, and short dark hair had misled him to begin with. In the bright sunlight at close range he could see the faint lines at the corners of eyes and mouth, and her lips didn't smile with the readiness of youth. But her hands, touching the flowers gently, were beautiful.

'Perhaps I was wrong to expect a quiet, uneventful stay in Oxford,' he said eventually. 'Is my fellow-tenant next door – I

44

gather there is one on the floor below me — someone else I should handle with care?'

'She may not even notice you're there,' Louise said truthfully. 'Professor Gertrud Halvorsen is deeply immersed in Nordic studies. She wears woolly hats and socks, plays the music of Sibelius rather loudly, and avoids men below the age of seventy who, apart from frightening her, tend not to take her work seriously.'

'Dear God!' burst from his lips before he saw Louise shake her head.

'Gertrud is charming as well as exceedingly erudite,' she pointed out. 'This is Oxford, Dr Goodman; we *like* eccentrics here, always provided they don't make a nuisance of themselves. Now I'm afraid I've kept you too long from Anna's lawn.'

The cool dismissal nettled him into sarcasm. 'You mean that, apart from talking to the flowers out here, you have serious things to do as well — a husband to feed, children to see to?'

'Geoffrey often eats in College, and I have no children, so you see I'm allowed to play undisturbed.'

She gave him a brief, unamused smile and he walked away, conscious of escaping from an encounter he hadn't enjoyed. Not a successful ladies' man even on his own ground, he could see that total failure lay ahead with the women he was going to meet in Oxford. His colleague at Ann Arbor had probably been right. Go to Cologne or Tokyo, he'd recommended — go anywhere other than an old, ironic place where the people speak in pleasant, low-pitched voices, but like to confuse foreigners by only saying what they don't mean.

At lunch-time Louise examined the empty larder and fridge and resolved not to put off any longer the responsibilities of a conscientious housewife. Before Geoffrey came home she must go out for food, must dust and air rooms that looked neglected, and unpack the luggage brought back from France. Aware yet again of not putting first things first — it was a fault he'd been known to accuse her of — she began with the books they'd taken away, some of them only out of an optimism that was certain to be misplaced. Who could hope to settle down with *Hard Times* and the fog-shrouded miseries of Victorian England when a summer-time Provençal landscape beckoned outside? The still unread Dickens and Flaubert had to go back onto their appropriate shelves because Geoffrey hated a jumbled library. Thinking of him, she wondered what he would make of their arrogant new neighbour next door – dislike him, probably. It was too much to hope that Dr Goodman would fly home to New York from Oxford every weekend; but at least their lack of sympathy this morning had been mutual. They could exchange chilly nods in future if they passed each other in the street.

She shopped and dusted, made pissaladière and salad for supper, put white wine to chill, and finally tackled the mail that Ruth had left waiting for her. She kept until last an envelope with a Paris postmark – her mother, almost certainly, writing to complain because they hadn't broken their return journey from Aix as well as the outward one. The summer in Paris was bound to have been too hot or perhaps not hot enough, the visitors too numerous or so scarce that ruin stared the Galeries Benoît in the face. Nadia had been an unhappy widow, and the habit of sounding plaintive remained, even though she'd been comfortably married for the past ten years to Henri Rivaux, the nephew of André's original partner. She occasionally saw fit to remind them that English John had been her 'grand amour', but with what Louise reckoned to be exceptional sweetness of character Henri merely agreed and went on taking care of her. Far from failing, the galleries were doing very well under his direction, and André Benoît, now approaching ninety, still congratulated himself on a marriage for his daughter that he'd foreseen as the right one all along. John Standish had been a temporary obstacle. Only in one way was it a pity that he hadn't lived longer – his posthumous reputation was soaring. André still occasionally sounded Louise out about the little painting William Standish had insisted on giving back to her as a wedding present. She always smiled at her grandfather and told him that it wasn't for sale.

The contents of her mother's letter weren't quite as expected after all, and she was frowning over it when Geoffrey walked in.

She handed it to him to read, knowing that although he enjoyed being hospitable, he preferred to choose their guests himself.

'Do we mind Nadia's suggestion?' he enquired eventually. 'And even if we do, can we refuse? It would seem churlish when she's asking on behalf of her stepson.'

Louise nodded, aware that although he was right she didn't want Pierre Rivaux wished on them for the three months her mother had airily suggested. He was the son of Henri's first marriage to the daughter of a rich Parisian collector, but Marie Rivaux had died when Pierre was still an adolescent. Against expectation, he and Nadia had got on very well together. She wasn't in the least jealous of him, and Louise supposed it was because she had affection for his father but no 'grand amour'.

'Yes, I'm afraid we shall have to make Pierre welcome,' she agreed at last, but so unenthusiastically that Geoffrey smiled.

'Admit it – you took against him because he was rather precious as a very young man and wore extravagant clothes. We haven't seen much of him for several years – he might have improved by now.'

She still looked doubtful. 'His taste in dress can't have got worse, it's true, and if he's coming to learn Arabic as well as study instruments at the Old Ashmolean, he may not even need much entertaining.'

'There's a committee meeting of the museum coming up soon – I can always ask the Curator to be sure to keep our guest's nose to the grindstone!' Geoffrey suggested solemnly.

It ended the conversation about Pierre Rivaux, but she was aware that her reluctance to receive him had little or nothing to do with brocade waistcoats and long hair. He was highly intelligent, which might normally be thought a virtue, but his quick brain had made him arrogant as well, and there was an excess of masculine confidence about him that suddenly reminded her of the stranger she'd clashed with earlier in the day.

'Anna is away in Bath,' she said abruptly, 'but her latest tenant has already moved in. I met him working outside. He's an American on sabbatical from Ann Arbor.'

'Then I think I know about him. Is he a Dr Goodman, or

didn't you get as far as exchanging names?' He saw Louise nod, and went on. 'He's an historian. Apart from his own research work for a book, he's here to give a series of lectures. The reputation that's preceded him is that he's a brilliant, controversial speaker hugely in demand on American campuses. It remains to be seen, of course, what Oxford makes of him.'

'Or he of Oxford,' she observed. 'Americans can usually be relied upon to smile and talk a great deal. He did neither, and gave me the impression that he couldn't really think why he'd bothered to come at all.'

'Well, he's been given dining rights in College so we shan't be able to ignore him altogether. We'll ask him in for drinks with Ruth — she's very good with Americans, bless her.'

Louise thought of the two of them together and smiled with real amusement at last. 'By all means invite them both,' she agreed cordially.

They were sitting down to supper when Geoffrey made his own quiet announcement.

'It isn't common knowledge yet, even among the governing body, but Humphrey told me this morning. He's been ordered to take things very easily from now on, and he's got to retire at the end of next Trinity term.'

Louise stared at her husband, knowing what the news must mean. Humphrey Wharton had been his friend and exemplar for more than twenty years, and if he could be said to love another man, he had certainly loved the Master of St Barnabas.

'Is he ill, poor Humphrey, or just very tired and overburdened?' she asked slowly.

'Not in danger of dying suddenly, but his heart is sending out warning signals, apparently. It's time to hand over the reins.'

'If he leaves at the end of summer term he'll miss next year's great celebrations . . . oh, Geoffrey, how cruel!'

'Yes, it's cruel,' he conceded, 'but Humphrey himself would be the first to insist that it doesn't matter. He's kept St Barnabas out in front for a quarter of a century, but five hundred years of College existence are what count; one man's contribution, great though it may be, is a mere fragment of the story.'

Louise put down her glass. 'When I go to see William I mustn't mention it, I suppose.'

'He knows already. Humphrey has no secrets from William. They were here together – as undergraduate and very young tutor. They've been friends ever since.'

She didn't ask what was likely to happen in the next part of the St Barnabas story. It was too soon, and they must first grow used to the idea of so sad a separation. She knew that there were unlamented College heads, and some whose names didn't die, for one reason or another. Humphrey Wharton wouldn't be remembered for exceptional academic brilliance, or for the self-publicising eccentricities that some dons nowadays went in for. He was just a clever, kind, upright man, who had met St Paul's requirement of a good steward and been 'found faithful'. Thinking about him, she failed to notice that Geoffrey had relapsed into silence. Only afterwards did it seem that she'd been strangely blind. Concerned about Humphrey and Edwina Wharton, she'd entirely ignored what ought to concern her most – the effect of Geoffrey's news on their own lives.

CHAPTER FIVE

In the event it needed no invitation from her brother for Ruth to make the acquaintance of the newcomer next door. She achieved it over the handlebars of her bicycle as they came to rest against the paintwork of his rented car. It was the merest scratch, nothing to make a fuss about, and, by her reckoning, a great deal more his fault than hers. But the enraged man who leaped out and stalked round to inspect the damage didn't seem to think so.

'I'm so sorry,' she said before he could speak, 'but I really couldn't be expected to guess that you intended swerving into the driveway before my own.'

'No guesswork was required,' he said between gritted teeth. 'My left indicator was blinking well before I passed you. Should I have guessed that you'd ignore it? I haven't been here long enough to learn the strange habits of the neighbourhood.'

'That explains it,' she informed him with a smile. 'No one else in Norham Grove would *dream* of overtaking me ten yards in front of my own entrance. No matter . . . no great harm has been done, and you'll soon get used to our ways, Mr . . . ?'

'*Dr* Goodman is the name. Now, if you'll be kind enough to ride on or back, I can put away what is left of my car.'

She didn't immediately follow either suggestion, but stared at him consideringly.

'You don't look like one of Madame Ouspenska's language students, so I suppose you're visiting us from some university overseas. Dear Dr Goodman, may I give you a little piece of advice? Put your car away by all means, but then forget about it. Motorcars are the curse of Oxford – indeed, they're the bane of our present-day civilisation. Let me recommend that you learn to ride a bicycle instead; it isn't a difficult accomplishment. Failing that, you may always walk, and benefit from the exercise!'

The beautiful, clear voice so at variance with her plain features and unbecoming frizz of hair stopped at last. She hoisted herself onto the saddle, waved goodbye, and pedalled on, leaving him still standing there.

A New York childhood had taught him words to shout at her, but even a week or two in Oxford were having their effect. It had been a gross error of judgement to come to the damn place at all, but he was committed to it now and must live with his mistake for a whole academic year. It had been his choice to come away – a deliberate, desperate move in the game he played of proving to Karen that she still needed him. She'd agreed that it was the best idea 'they'd' had, this temporary separation . . . giving themselves a little space, she'd called it, in the received wisdom of the moment.

But now, leaning against the scratched door of a curse he was supposed to give up – in favour of a bicycle, for God's sake – he knew with aching clearness that it hadn't been a good idea at all. Already he was heartsick for the familiar world he knew, for people he could at least understand even when he didn't like them. Here, there were no recognisable landmarks at all, and if he wasn't very careful he might even begin to share Oxford's confident belief that it was the rest of the world that was out of step.

He got into the car at last, drove it into the safety of the driveway, and climbed the stairs to the apartment on the top floor. The telephone was ringing as he walked in, and when he answered it a man's voice offered him a name he didn't immediately recognise.

'Dr Goodman, it's Geoffrey Carmichael speaking. I've been meaning to get hold of you, but my sister tells me that she's just managed to scrape an introduction herself, if you'll pardon the phrase! Why not walk across the garden and have a drink with us if you're free?'

He heard himself agree, and regretted it as soon as he put the telephone down. The name meant something to him now – Carmichael figured on the list he'd been given of the Fellows of St Barnabas. The man was an historian, almost certainly of the traditional kind, and if he lived next door the chances were that he was also the husband of a woman who seemed to prefer plants to most other things. Throw in the trick-cyclist he'd just met and it added up to a household he'd do better to avoid.

He changed into a clean shirt – American habits died hard even in Oxford – grimaced at himself in the mirror, and walked next door, to where a fair-haired man was waiting for him outside.

'You haven't called on us in College yet,' Geoffrey remarked. 'Full term begins next week but there's no need to wait until then. There must be some formalities we can help you with – a reader's card for the Bodleian, for example; or have the Faculty already seen to that?'

'They've been very kind,' Daniel replied. 'But first off I've been busy finding my way around; I don't like not knowing where I am.'

He was led into a large, cool room where book-lined shelves almost covered the walls. The hangings and chair covers were in soft colours – turquoise and jade – that enhanced the burnished glow of an old rosewood grand piano. He remembered the woman he'd met in the garden saying that she played; there was even music stacked up on the instrument to prove it.

The only other person in the room, though, was his host's sister, probably primed already with her next piece of unsolicited advice.

'If you're hesitating over whether or not to ask, I walked here,' he said when the introductions had been made.

She stared at him, then gave a loud laugh, and clapped her hands like a child. 'Geoffrey, this naughty man is teasing me!' Now that she saw him again in a more sociable frame of mind, she thought that perhaps there was no need to disapprove of Dr Goodman after all. He was definitely not Ivy League, of course – he even held himself in the wary stance of a man fighting his way through life – but his features were not insensitive, despite a nose that had been broken at some point. His brown hair and beard were closely trimmed and his eyes were striking – a bright, pale blue. All in all, Ruth decided, not hero material that she could see, but not insignificant either.

'I expect my sister advised you to give up the motorcar,'

Geoffrey commented with a smile. 'When she knows you a little better she'll recommend a vegetarian diet, as well, and the therapeutic effects of yoga – the lotus position practised twice a day is especially beneficial!'

Delighted by Daniel Goodman's unexpected laugh that seemed to prove they were now getting on well together, Ruth regretted the arrival of her sister-in-law. She couldn't help noticing that their visitor's glance, having strayed to Louise, stayed there. But amusement had died out of his face and he was looking watchful again.

'You've already met my wife, I believe,' Geoffrey said pleasantly. 'Louise, my dear, Dr Goodman and Ruth met rather too literally outside, but I'm glad to say no serious damage was done.'

She wasn't wearing jeans now; a cream pleated skirt accentuated her slenderness, and she had tucked a coral scarf into the open collar of her shirt. Daniel was offering a smiling nod but she didn't come forward to shake hands. Instead, she perched herself on the piano stool away from them. Force of habit might have led her there, but he was reminded of the remoteness that he'd noticed when they'd drunk coffee in the garden.

'Madame Ouspenska telephoned to say that she'll be home tomorrow,' Louise informed him politely. 'But perhaps you knew that already.'

She accepted the wine Geoffrey brought her and allowed Ruth to hand round bowls of nuts and crisps. Daniel couldn't decide whether she abandoned the role of hostess because it didn't interest her, or because she knew her sister-in-law enjoyed bustling round them. He shelved the problem to focus on what Carmichael was saying.

'We look forward to your lectures, Dr Goodman, having been told something of your reputation in America.'

Daniel sipped the white wine in his glass and tried not to screw up his mouth at its dryness. 'Well, what I've been told is that Oxford gives its lecturers a hard time. Perhaps that was the unhappy view of a failure who didn't make the grade over here and found himself talking to rows of empty chairs?'

'I hope we aren't accused of being uncivil to visitors,' Geoffrey said a trifle stiffly. 'It's true that not all our own academics necessarily make good lecturers, and of course students soon learn to distinguish good from bad.'

Ruth saw the gleam of derision in Daniel's face and hurried to her brother's rescue. 'We have a different system, Dr Goodman. Here it's the weekly tutorial that counts, master and pupil meeting face to face. That has always been the Oxford way. Lectures count for very little.'

Geoffrey was looking shaken by his sister's lack of tact, but it seemed to Louise that their guest wasn't offended because he didn't take any of them seriously enough — they were quaint, fossilised creatures stranded on the shores of time, not part of late-twentieth-century life at all.

'Lectures, and therefore lecturers, count for very little — I must remember that as another piece of excellent advice!' Daniel commented. 'But even the "Oxford way" can't persuade me that a failed lecturer is touched by the magic wand of inspiration once he walks back inside his study. The chances are that he only makes a god-awful tutor too.'

While Ruth rallied from this unexpected attack and Geoffrey made his guest suffer by pouring him more sharp wine, Louise thought it was time to enter the conversation. 'Ruth dear, we shan't convince Dr Goodman. Remember that he hails from the University of Michigan — so much bigger, so much more up-to-date than we are! We shall muddle on in our old, unprogressive way, but with a real lecturer in our midst we shall at least know what we are missing.'

Daniel stood up before the silence had lasted too long. She had no idea whether she'd managed to make him angry now because his face and voice were expressionless. 'I hope that means one empty chair the less, Mrs Carmichael,' he said, looking at her. 'I shall do my best not to disappoint you.' Then he walked to the door, having none of the indecision that afflicted visitors who saw that it was time to leave, but couldn't bring themselves to go. Geoffrey followed him out, and Ruth saw that she too was not going to be encouraged to stay.

'Much nicer than I thought when we had our little

contretemps outside,' she offered as a parting opinion. 'Americans can sometimes be a little humourless, but there was a definite twinkle in Dr Goodman's eye once or twice, didn't you think?'

'Why shouldn't there be? I'm sure he finds us all worth laughing at already, and Oxford's richer oddities haven't dawned on him yet.'

As always with her sister-in-law, it wasn't quite the agreement Ruth had hoped for. She'd so wanted them to be what she thought of as 'really close', both devoted to the precious task of looking after Geoffrey. Closeness hadn't come, even after twenty years of living in the same house, but she was at least certain of one thing – she had done her best; it was Louise who hadn't cooperated, just as she'd refused to this evening. Her behaviour to Dr Goodman had been unnecessarily sharp. Geoffrey, loyal, kind saint, could make what excuse he liked – his wife had returned from France in a state of mind that neither of them could understand.

For once Louise would have agreed with her; she'd certainly been rude to Daniel Goodman. But then Geoffrey came back into the room and made the mistake of sounding patient and forbearing. 'My dear, you don't have to like our new neighbour, but you were a trifle severe with him. Or did you imagine that he would take your little speech at its face value?'

'Oh, I don't dislike him to the extent of underestimating his intelligence,' she replied. 'I shall even go and listen to him perform – a performance *is* what it will be, shouldn't you think? I prefer my academics to be like William – full of sweetness and humility.' She gave no indication of the sort of academic she found her husband to be, and Geoffrey couldn't bring himself to ask, but he was provoked into something less than sweetness about a man he liked very well.

'Academics should also only do the work that is worthy of them. An anthology of love lyrics doesn't strike me as a fitting farewell to scholarship for someone in William's class.'

Louise's smile reappeared. 'Come now, Geoffrey! The anthology is William's charming way of saying thank you for what he's loved most in English literature. He's going to dedicate it to all the ladies who have given him pleasure – in one way or another!'

This ended the conversation more happily because even Geoffrey had to enjoy the thought of that.

The next morning, however, typing the fresh batch of manuscript William had sent her, Louise recalled her husband's opinion with regret. What he found wanting in the new anthology was seriousness. Love, even in all the fascinating permutations William was presenting, couldn't be reckoned an important enough subject to justify a scholar spending precious time on it.

She was still at the typewriter, deciphering her uncle's minuscule handwriting, when someone tapped on the window beside her. Anna stood there grinning at her, arms full of Michaelmas daisies that shaded from palest mauve to imperial purple.

'Darling, look – aren't they beautiful? When I made the taxi driver stop while I got them for you, he said they grow like weeds in his garden, but that's the sort of disagreeable thing taxi drivers like to say.' She disappeared from sight, and Louise got up to meet her at the kitchen door.

Kissed and warmly hugged, she was examined by Anna's bright eyes from under a mop of hair currently tinted an improbable shade of gold. Her monkey face contained no single feature that was beautiful, but even now Louise could see why men still found her irresistible. Intelligence and warmth and a heart merry even after much grief made up the secret of her allure.

'You seemed to be away ages in France, my friend, but I hope that's not how it seemed to you,' she suggested.

'Aix was beautiful,' Louise said, choosing the easiest way of answering something that wasn't quite a question. 'But in the end Geoffrey was glad to get home, and so was I . . . only I'd forgotten that you would be away, so when I called round I met your new tenant instead. It was clever of you to get him to mow the grass – I understand that he doesn't normally get his hands dirty in gardens.'

'You don't like him,' Anna observed calmly. 'Nor do I yet, but I'm hoping we shall warm to each other in time.'

She watched while Louise arranged the daisies in a tall copper vase, her thin hands persuading them to stay where she placed them.

'Flowers don't do that for me – they flop instead and turn their heads the wrong way,' Anna complained. Then, as usual, she suddenly changed conversational gear. 'You *look* brown and well, so why should I feel worried about you? Tell me that, please.'

'I have no idea,' Louise answered, faintly smiling, 'but even Geoffrey seemed to find it necessary to apologise this morning for neglecting me to attend to College affairs. Perhaps it's my day for being worried about!'

Anna's intense stare still considered her friend. 'I think you should neglect Geoffrey for a change. Not too many affairs of your own – that would be tiresome – but just one kind, exciting lover, Louise darling . . . wouldn't that make a nice change?'

'You speak, I suppose, out of your own accumulated experience on the subject,' her friend suggested solemnly.

'My experience isn't quite as wide as your sister-in-law and the other ladies of North Oxford like to believe. Nevertheless, I do know this – provided no hurt is done, a little loving here and there is entirely beneficial. It is especially true of the English, who seem to believe that physical desire should be known only to the young.'

Trying to keep her mouth from twitching, Louise enquired whether a possible candidate sprang to mind.

'Not yet,' Anna admitted. 'The large Dr Goodman might have done, but Americans usually make boring lovers, and in any case there's a wife he is inconveniently attached to in New York.'

'We have also already established that I don't like him,' Louise pointed out gravely.

'That too!' Anna still pondered the problem while her friend, now making coffee, thought it time to offer a change of topic.

'It's not an immediate worry – I shall be much too busy for lovers for at least the next three months. My mother's stepson is to lodge with us while he studies in Oxford. Being a Frenchman, he will require frequent delicious meals, endless philosophical arguments, and a reasonable supply of attractive young women whom he can try to seduce. Geoffrey must help with the arguments, but I'm afraid the rest will be up to me to provide.'

Anna put the interesting problem aside for a moment, to offer news of her own.

'My dear, there is more than an interesting Frenchman to keep you busy. At Bath I got talked into providing something myself – a chamber music concert here in two weeks' time. I shall need you for the Schubert Trout Quintet, and Beethoven's Opus Sixteen.'

'No, definitely not, Anna – I'm an amateur who tinkles away for her own amusement. Not even for you will I perform in someone else's drawing room in front of a lot of carping academic wives.'

'You know very well that you play better than most of the professionals they hear. In any case it's for Hospice funds so *they* won't carp and *you* can't refuse.' Anna's twisted grin appeared. 'No one's drawing room, by the way, and not just wives present. We shall appear in the Holywell Music Room, before the cream of Oxford society.'

'It gets worse and worse,' Louise muttered. 'I'm to make my public debut, at the advanced age of thirty-nine, in Europe's oldest surviving concert hall. I suppose you know that the first local music critic even railed against Handel for playing there with his "lousy crew of foreign fiddlers"!'

Anna waved the critic aside. 'He's long dead, one would suppose, and we shall look *much* more beautiful than the fiddlers. I think I can make the Sheriff and the Lord Mayor come, but I rely on Geoffrey to bring the Vice Chancellor.' She put down her coffee cup and suddenly stared at Louise with eyes from which the gleam of amusement had fled. Her monkey face now held only the most profound despair.

'I've kept the worst piece of news until last,' she murmured. 'You aren't the only one to be offered a visitor.'

Louise was accustomed to her friend's sudden swings of

mood, but even for Anna this plunge from high to low was more than usually extreme. 'Someone you dislike very much? You can always say no.'

'Someone I don't even know – my own daughter. Think of that . . . imagine it if you can. The infant girl I had to hand over to the Torrance family twenty years ago wants to come *here*. God help me to turn her away, Louise, for that is what I must do.'

'Why? *Why*, my dear friend?' Louise asked gently. 'If she's only just learned about you, how can you blame her for not coming sooner?'

'I don't, but I've prayed that she would never come at all.' Anna flung out her hands in a gesture of desperate appeal. 'Look at me – am I anything to be proud of, with my wrinkled face and dyed hair, and my doubtful reputation among the worthy ladies of North Oxford? No, let my daughter stay among her French relatives. She belongs with them, not me. When I answer her letter I shall tell her so.'

'You must do what seems best to you,' Louise said finally, 'but think well, Anna love, before you write. She may never ask again if you refuse to know her now, and I don't see why she shouldn't share my opinion that our worthy neighbours are fools!'

Anna's tragic face creased into a grin, but her eyes were full of tears. 'Heresy, *ma chère* – it stands to reason they must be very intelligent. They're Oxford ladies!' She wiped her wet cheeks with the palm of her hand, and stood up to leave. 'We shall do our best for them, though, in the Music Room. Leave William's little poems alone, Louise. From now on you and I must concentrate on Schubert and Beethoven.'

She kissed her friend and went away without reverting to the subject of her daughter. Louise cleared away their coffee cups and then went to sit at Sybil Carmichael's piano. But instead of raising her hands to play, she sat motionless, thinking about an unknown girl who waited in France for an invitation that Anna wasn't going to send.

CHAPTER SIX

That Oxford should fly so completely in the face of Nature every October seemed to Louise only in keeping with the place. When trees and plants and some animals more sensible than most were putting themselves to bed for the approach of winter, Oxford was waking up. Even the weather usually entered into the spirit of this transformation and for a little while there might be a rare, frosty sparkle about the High, before the damp vapours of November began to drift among its towers and pinnacles.

A new term had begun. The pavements outside College walls were clogged with parked bicycles again, and freshers up for the first time wandered around trying to look like unconcerned old hands embarking on their second or third year. Louise normally enjoyed this throb of life through the time-hardened arteries of the city. She liked to see the new undergraduates filing into the Sheldonian to be claimed by their respective colleges and formally made scholars of Universitas Oxoniensis. This year, though, as Geoffrey set off with hood and gown for the matriculation ceremony she had the strange feeling that for once she would have preferred no Michaelmas reawakening. Fresh beginnings had become dangerous, liable to lead them she knew not where.

Geoffrey said nothing more about Humphrey Wharton beyond admitting briefly that the news of his retirement was common knowledge now, having been announced at the first governing body meeting of term. It seemed safe to assume that the next Master would be Edward Castleton, the most senior of the College Fellows, but she left the subject alone since it was so unmistakably what her husband seemed to prefer. Anna remained equally silent on the subject of her daughter, and altogether there seemed to be too many topics now that the people around Louise wished not to discuss.

Her only disagreeable certainty was that Nadia's stepson would arrive in Oxford the day before their concert in the Holywell Music Room. She hoped fervently that he would dislike chamber music enough not to attend. In between their frequent rehearsals Anna grappled competently with publicity, programmes, and all the other details of a public performance, while her reluctant pianist rose early to keep the autumn work of the garden from getting too far behind. Then, with each day's stint of pruning and planting achieved, she would go indoors to practise.

One afternoon, afraid of becoming over-familiar with what she now knew by heart, Louise allowed fermenting nerves to drive her into a barn-storming account of some quite different music. At the end of it, tired but appeased for the moment by its exhilaration, she remained sitting at the piano. Then a shadow moving on the open window distracted her and she looked up to see Daniel Goodman watching her from the garden.

'Have you been there long?' she asked coolly across the space between them.

'I wasn't meaning to intrude.' For once he sounded diffident, as if there were uncertainties of his own that he was contending with. 'I came to deliver a paper I thought your husband might like to read, but an avalanche of chords crashed down on me. Do you often play like that, as if all the hounds of hell were chasing you?'

' "Like that" is how Liszt mostly has to be played. But if you mean is that the sort of music I prefer, then the answer is no.'

'We can continue this discussion by shouting at each other, or I can go away. Which would you prefer?'

It was absurd to think of loneliness in connection with so self-sufficient a man, but something in his voice conveyed the impression that for the moment he didn't want to be sent away. She thought of the distance separating him from his wife in New York, and changed what she'd been about to say.

'The storm is over, but I'll play something quieter if you would like to come in and listen. The door's unlocked.' Daniel moved away without answering, and a moment later walked into the room.

'You mustn't expect me to know one piece from another,' he warned her. 'My journey from New York slum to comparative success had to be single-minded; there are a lot of things I didn't have time to stop and discover, and music is one of them.'

'Then I'll explain that what comes next was written by a young Frenchman called Claude Debussy. No passion or argument here; it just paints a lovely picture. Think of the sea on a still night – a full moon rises and pulls a ribbon of silver across the dark water.'

She began to play and he closed his eyes, reluctantly aware that this was the only way to listen and see the picture she had drawn for him. When the last quiet note had died into stillness he got up and walked over to the piano. At close range she was obliged to register again his sheer bulk and barely reined-in vitality. It was *this*, she thought, that made her feel uncomfortable with him, when she was accustomed to men who made no parade of their masculinity.

'I have an uncomfortable impression that the first time we met I was fool enough to jeer at you,' he said unexpectedly.

'Why not?' Louise asked with a faint smile. 'It was probably my fault for sounding like a Victorian governess with a few small accomplishments.'

'Well, let's say the fault wasn't entirely mine, because I think that's how you meant to sound. I'd suggest it's the way the English always like to confuse foreigners, except that you owned to being partly something else. If it amuses you, though, I'll admit to being very confused – I have been since the first day I arrived here.'

She was aware that it had cost him something to make the confession. He wasn't a man who enjoyed admitting to being at a loss in any situation.

'My father was a painter called John Standish,' she explained slowly. 'His brother William still lives in Oxford although he's retired now from being a Fellow of St Barnabas. If anyone can explain Oxford to you, he can. I'll take you to have tea with him one day.'

Daniel Goodman's quick grin was becoming familiar now – she didn't know whether its derisive edge was something

Oxford's peculiarities inspired or whether he always found the world a place to laugh at. ' "Going out to tea" doesn't happen where I come from,' he observed. 'It sounds such an unlikely thing for me to do that my children won't believe me when I tell them; their theory is that they always know how their parents will behave.' Louise's expression had become remote again, and he was provoked into dragging her attention back to him. 'I was forgetting, though – the difficulties that parents and children have with each other aren't of any interest to you.'

Louise lifted her head to stare at him, and he saw the brightness of anger in her eyes, although her voice was very quiet.

'There was no time for difficulties with our children. One of the twins – David, we named him – was stillborn. His brother, Dominic, clung so hard to life that we thought he might survive, but on the second day he died too. I was ill afterwards, and we couldn't have any more children.'

It was, Daniel thought, heartbreak almost beyond bearing expressed in the fewest possible words. He felt sick with regret for having needled her so cruelly, and angry as well for a mistake that she could have let him avoid making. 'Why couldn't you have adopted children?' he said roughly.

'We chose not to for reasons that won't interest you very much.' She sketched a gesture that said the subject was closed. 'I expect you miss your own children.'

He wondered what she would say if he offered her the truth – that his family's New York life barely seemed to include him now. 'Hal's twelve, Kate is fifteen,' he explained instead, '. . . my wife's choice of names; she was heavily into Shakespeare then, being more cultured all round than I am. She's also a very successful public relations expert, which is why she lives in Manhattan while I work at Ann Arbor.'

Louise acknowledged to herself that she had been unfair. Here was no academic who didn't need closeness with his family. Their separation from him was a wound that hurt enough to make him seem harsh and intolerant, but he wouldn't thank her for knowing that about him.

'I ought to be practising Beethoven,' she said instead, 'and you must have a lecture to prepare. Are you going to sneak up on our historians here and disarm them with guile, or sail into battle with all guns blazing?'

He didn't smile, and spoke with a return to the brusqueness she remembered from their first meeting. 'Guile is something else I haven't had time or the inclination to acquire. The quick knockout is my usual style, but I doubt if it will go down well with the die-hards ranged against me here. I assume that they are likely to include your husband.'

She couldn't tell whether it was the remembrance of his unsatisfactory private life or of other professional antagonisms that made him hostile, but she resented a slur that Oxford had so far done nothing to deserve. 'I don't think you should make any assumptions about us at all,' she said coolly. 'Logic sometimes gets stood on its head here − or was *Alice in Wonderland* another unnecessary piece of luggage that you didn't have time to stop for?'

He smiled again, with the same lack of amusement as before. 'I guess it's *all* too rarefied for me here, Mrs Carmichael . . . wine so dry that it takes the roof off your mouth, baroque music − whatever in God's name that may be − and College dinner customs that were probably invented just to embarrass visiting barbarians like me! I'll say good-day now . . . the paper I brought your husband is on the table in the hall.'

He left with the suddenness she was becoming used to and she was free to return to her interrupted practice. But her thoughts still lingered on the past half-hour. Never in all the years since her babies had died had she spoken of them to anyone but Anna; to have done so to this hostile stranger simply because he'd made her angry now seemed shameful. She remembered, too, a moment when she'd thought him vulnerable and had rashly offered him the pleasure of a visit to William. Presumably that had been seen as a mistaken attempt to smooth down a self-made American's rough corners; this American would rather die remaining the way he was. She speculated for a moment about whether or not to warn Geoffrey of the lecture battle-lines being drawn and decided against it. He was already on edge − probably convinced, although he didn't say so, that she was about to make a public exhibition of herself in the dubious company of her friend next door. The concert should have been a low-key affair, he thought, if it had to take place at all; not the three-ring circus it had inevitably become with Anna Ouspenska as its moving spirit.

Between Geoffrey's efforts not to discuss any of the issues that occupied his mind and her own determination to stay calm at all costs, Louise thought their meal-time conversations were becoming so unreal that she even began to look forward to the arrival of Pierre Rivaux. Whatever virtues he lacked, the ability to keep talking was not one of them.

When his taxi finally drew up at the gate she walked outside prepared with a welcome that was almost sincere. Only it wasn't his dapper figure and seal-smooth dark head that she saw first, but a woman clad in folds of purple velvet that made up some sort of travelling outfit. Nadia emerged, holding out both hands to her daughter.

'Darling! I suddenly realised *quite* at the last minute that of course I must come with Pierre. How, I asked Henri, could you be left to perform in public without your own mother present? He agreed that it was impossible, so here I am, to lead the applause and sit with Geoffrey in the place of honour.'

Kissed on both cheeks and examined by a pair of eyes that were still as dramatically emphasised with make-up as they'd been twenty years before, Louise did her best to sound delighted. Geoffrey would be delighted too, she said, and so would the Vice Chancellor with whom they would probably have to share the place of honour.

'Delight all round, in fact,' murmured Pierre, who was now kissing Louise himself. '*Chérie*, I knew you would be pleased!' His eyes gleamed with so much malicious enjoyment of the situation that she responded by smiling wholeheartedly.

'I am very pleased to see *Maman*, and provided you have come prepared to behave yourself, dear Pierre, I am even quite pleased to see you.'

His grin showed very white teeth in an olive-skinned face,

and she could see why he would have no difficulty in attracting women. He looked lithe and fit, and intelligence gave interest to a face that wasn't conventionally handsome. His command of English was excellent, but concealed under an accent that he used to great effect. Now, he busied himself paying off the taxi while Nadia shielded her eyes from the house. She had visited it too often over the years not to have grown used to it, but it pleased her to pretend that it was gifted with organic life that enabled it to grow steadily more extraordinary each time she came.

'I suppose Ruth is still here?' she asked, in the tones of one who hoped against hope to be contradicted.

'Of course she is,' Louise answered with firmness. 'It's her home. What's more, she's dining with us this evening, to meet Pierre.'

'Of course,' Nadia repeated. 'The poor boy must accustom himself, *n'est-ce-pas*, to all that is truly remarkable about England.' Then, pleased with herself for producing an unanswerable remark, she swept towards the house while Louise helped Pierre with a pile of luggage and enquired under her breath, 'How long for?'

'A few days only, *ma chère*. My father is coming to London for a sale. Then they'll travel home together.' He grinned as she stared at the enormous valise he was struggling with. 'It's not the average woman's wardrobe for a month – only Nadia's toilette for the seat of honour! She will refuse to be outshone by Madame Vice Chancellor.'

With her guests left to refresh themselves after the journey, which in Nadia's case meant relaxing in an hour-long bath, Louise rearranged the dinner table, put the finishing touches to the menu, and waited for Geoffrey. He looked tired when he came in, and she wished she did not have to give him her unwelcome news.

'I hope Pierre arrived in good order,' he said with his usual courtesy.

'Yes . . . but I'm afraid he brought Nadia with him. She says she's come as a good mother should, to see us through an ordeal.'

'Oh, God,' he said faintly.

His wife's mouth twitched, began to smile, and suddenly they were both helpless with shared laughter. Nor was that the end of the surprise because he leaned forward to kiss her laughing mouth, and then they stared at one another. But the strangeness of the moment was interrupted by Pierre, coming into the room to shake hands with Geoffrey.

The evening went well, with Geoffrey unexpectedly careful to pay his mother-in-law the little compliments and attentions that were all she needed to make her happy. Nadia contented was enjoyable company, and with the encouragement of Pierre's bright eyes on top of her brother's good Burgundy even Ruth showed signs of sparkle.

The following day Geoffrey took charge of Pierre's most urgent introductions, to his Arabic expert and the staff of the museum in Broad Street, and to the Maison Française in Norham Road where he could find comfort if he should feel homesick. Louise left Nadia to wander through the few Oxford shops she didn't despise, and after an hour's hard practice took herself off for a calming walk through Christ Church Meadows. She ended up in the Cathedral, not with the conscious intention of praying about the evening ahead, but in order to emerge with some sense of proportion, and panic under control. An hour before the concert was due to begin she set off with Anna, leaving Geoffrey to follow with the rest of the family.

Squashed into the only seat still available, high at the back of the hall, Daniel saw them come in, escorting the other privileged members of the audience. He recognised Carmichael, of course, and Ruth, but not the couple with them – an elegantly dinner-jacketed man, and a woman who would have been conspicuous even without her tendency to wave graciously at the hoi polloi crammed in uncomfortably all around.

Daniel had been asking himself for some time why he was there at all, squeezed into this small, crowded place, which looked as if it should have been the music room of some classical, eighteenth-century country house. It was the kind of Oxford occasion calculated to make an outsider feel still *more* out than in, and the programme notes in his hand might have

been written in Chinese for all that they conveyed to him –
what, in the name of heaven, was tempo rubato or a leading
seventh supposed to mean? He was glared at by an intense-
looking lady on his right who suspected that he might fidget,
and ignored by the young woman sitting on his other side, who
emerged from a curtain of black hair long enough to stare when
he said good evening, and then retired behind it again.

Cowed by his neighbours and angry with himself for having
been fool enough to come, he watched the performers taking
their places – two men and three women in evening dress. He
recognised only two of them. His landlady, holding her fiddle in
one hand and bow in the other, was an unexpectedly dignified
figure in bronze-coloured silk. Beside her, acknowledging the
welcoming applause, was Louise Carmichael. Then she sat
down at the piano and, from his high perch, he could only see
the coral silk of her skirt spread around her, dark head, and
slender bare arms poised over the keys, waiting for Anna's nod.

They began to play – Schubert, his programme said – and he
resigned himself to sitting still, at least until he could escape at
the end of the first item. Then something happened that he
hadn't bargained for: he could hear and actually follow what was
going on. *This* was chamber music, this intricate, closely woven
argument between the instruments. The high, sweet song
invented by Anna's violin was seized by darker-sounding strings,
and disputed for by the still deeper rumble of the cello. A final
glorious free-for-all was tamed and brought to harmonious
peace by the insistent silver voice of the piano.

Daniel found himself smiling at the stern-faced lady on his
right, who had melted into a state of rapt contentment.

'*Such* a pity it ever has to end,' she confided, and he realised
with a sense of shock how close he was to agreeing with her. He
thought no more of leaving, forgot that he was uncomfortably
cramped, and heard the final roar of approbation with almost as
much regret as his new friend beside him. It was an uninhibited
response for Oxford – he'd expected languid applause. But then
he remembered that one of the heroines of tonight's performance had expressly warned him that it would be foolish to make
assumptions.

The audience filed out slowly but he got to the doorway at last just as Geoffrey Carmichael approached it from a different gangway. There was a white-haired man beside him whom he politely introduced and Daniel identified.

'Your niece assured me once that you'd be able to explain Oxford to me better than anyone else,' he said to William Standish.

'Do you feel in need of explanations, Dr Goodman?' William asked cheerfully.

'Yes, but I dare say I can manage without if you have more important things to do.'

A charming smile lit the face he was watching. 'I doubt if I could claim that – I'm now one of the ancient of days! Why don't you join us for a glass of wine? I live only just across the street.'

It seemed a friendly invitation impossible to refuse, but he found that there was nothing impromptu about the entertainment after all. The small house he was led to seemed to be already overflowing with guests, and waiters whom Daniel recognised as College servants were circulating wine and food. As all Oxford occasions seemed to be, this was a family affair, but a family to which he didn't belong. Feeling out of place again, and still bemused by what he had just been listening to, he wished that he'd refused William's invitation. Geoffrey Carmichael was busy being attentive to important guests, Anna was at the centre of a crowd, and Louise Carmichael, looking tired now, seemed content to be sheltered by the elegant stranger who had escorted Ruth to the concert.

Daniel sipped wine he didn't want and was on the point of edging his way out when William Standish reappeared beside him with the exotic-looking woman who had sat with the Carmichaels. Nadia, introduced, responded inevitably to the challenge. With huge, lambent eyes fixed on the man in front of her, she smiled confidingly.

'My daughter, Dr Goodman, was she not entirely wonderful this evening? I can say this, you understand, because so little of the credit is *mine* – she resembles her English father.'

Daniel bowed, recalling the little that Louise had said about her parents. 'Even so, Madame Rivaux, she was quick to tell me the first time we met that she wasn't wholly English.'

Nadia's face glowed as if he'd offered her some rare tribute that she knew was due. 'I am very happy to hear that, *mon cher docteur*. If Louise is a little different from all these women here, if she has some music in her soul, *that* comes from me!'

A conversation on this level Daniel knew that it was beyond him to sustain but William, thank God, was arriving with reinforcements in the considerable shape of the Lord Mayor. He bowed and moved away just as a small gap appeared in the crowd clustered round Anna. She grinned as he reached her, and he was aware of a certain resemblance to the woman he had just left. They had the same habit of buttonholing anyone they met; the difference was that Nadia Rivaux wanted to talk about herself, while Anna wanted to listen.

'I didn't expect you tonight,' she said frankly. 'How nice to find that I was wrong!'

'And how much nicer to find a woman who'll admit it,' he pointed out with a rare smile. 'Huge success isn't going to your head, I'm glad to see.'

'It *is* quite huge, I think,' she agreed with a surprised look round the room. 'I've sometimes thought my dear Walther was wrong to advise me to settle in Oxford, but I should have had more faith in him.' Her bright eyes examined Daniel's face for a moment. 'You, I think, are still wishing you hadn't come, but perhaps *that* will change also.'

Someone else claiming her attention saved him from having to answer. Now he'd surely lingered long enough for politeness' sake and could make his way to the door. But suddenly between it and him was the slender figure of Louise Carmichael, for the moment unattended by her devoted escort. He saw the astonishment in her face and anticipated what she might have wanted to say.

'I'm not gate-crashing – your uncle invited me in.'

'My surprise wasn't at seeing you here, only that you should have bothered to come to the concert. Even people who pretend to like music go out of their way to avoid the chamber repertoire you've listened to tonight.'

'But I'm not "people", Mrs Carmichael; I'm an awkward ugly customer who can never keep to the rules.'

Only her faint smile allowed that this was probably true; unlike her mother, he thought, she preferred to detach herself from discussion of personalities.

'Well, I'm afraid you won't have enjoyed the programme, so it was all the more kind of you to come.'

'I came intending to leave early, but the Schubert-lover next to me would probably have murdered me, and then I found I didn't want to.'

A real smile transformed her face and he saw her for the first time – a woman who was sometimes beautiful and might easily be desirable. Even with the thought came other awarenesses – he found he could smell the fragrance she used, wanted by touching it to prove the softness of her skin. Thrown sharply off balance, he rushed in with a comment that sounded even to him stupidly inane.

'All Oxford seems to be here enjoying itself.'

'Oxford is doing what it enjoys most,' she agreed, 'exchanging barbed compliments and morsels of gossip.' Her glance wandered round the noisy, crowded room and he knew as certainly as he knew anything at all that she wanted *not* to be there. He might have blurted out something else – suggested taking her away even – but the next moment it was too late, and she was introducing Nadia Rivaux's stepson, who had returned to hover close to her. The Frenchman bowed and waited, and made his meaning clear; Daniel understood that he was now expected to withdraw.

A steely smile, a bow of his own that came nowhere near Pierre Rivaux's elegant performance, and he was free to go at last. Outside, the night air was cold but welcome. It would cool his heat and his anger, even if it did nothing for the confusion left by an evening that had been full of unsettling surprises. Tramping morosely back to Norham Grove he told himself that there was one thing he was still certain of. He hadn't told Anna Ouspenska so but there was no chance of a change of mind for him; it had been a mistake to come to Oxford. That was a hard admission to make for a man impatient of errors, but at least it explained why he now walked along feeling so thoroughly at odds with himself. And perhaps it also explained why he hadn't told Louise Carmichael that Schubert's music was still singing in his head.

CHAPTER SEVEN

The afternoon following the concert coincided with Louise's usual weekly visit to her uncle. When William opened his door to her he had the grin of a guilty cherub on his face and a toasting fork in one hand.

'Tell it not in Gath, or even in Oxford,' he whispered, 'but we're spoiling ourselves with buttered toast for tea. My clever young doctor says it's bad for ageing arteries, but I'm afraid mine are going to have to lump a bit of butter now and then, and it certainly can't do yours any harm.'

Louise cheerfully agreed, but he heard the little sigh of relief with which she collapsed on the rug in front of the fire. The weather had turned cold and uncharitable, but he doubted if that was the reason for her look of whiteness.

'Tired, my dear? Usually there's nothing more exhausting than failure, but I dare say a great success needs recovering from as well.' He handed her a slice of toasted bread to butter while he brewed tea. 'I expected Nadia to come with you today, if you felt energetic enough to come at all.'

'She's back in London by now. Henri telephoned to say that he'd arrived a day early, and he needed her at dinner with an important client tonight. It was like watching a drooping plant reviving under a shower of rain – she was already bored with Oxford, and with me.'

William bit into the toast Louise offered him and wiped butter off his chin. 'Not bored, but perhaps a little jealous. She's only confident and happy when her thunder isn't being stolen by someone else.'

'I know,' Louise agreed slowly. 'It's why there was so little room for me when my father was alive. *She* needed all his love and attention. Uncle Will, have you had the happiness of knowing that you mattered most, came first, with another

73

human being? It's something we all need to happen to us once at least, I think.'

He stared at her downbent face, saw its sadness, and feared that even her marriage hadn't brought her the necessary reassurance she'd just described. They never discussed her life with Geoffrey, and publicly she managed to give the impression of being a completely contented wife. But William thought it wasn't true – she simply made do with what she had, in the manner of women the world over. *Their* adroitness made workable a system still mainly arranged by men.

'No, I don't think I've known that special kind of happiness,' he admitted in answer to her question, 'but it's probably because I didn't deserve to.' He fitted another slice of bread onto his fork before asking a question of his own. 'You're not merry today, my dear girl – reaction after too much hard work and excitement, or something else?'

She looked up to find him watching her, and his wise, kind eyes made a lie impossible. 'Something that I shan't tell Geoffrey about. I was in the supermarket at North Parade this morning and bumped into Robert Morgan's wife. Normally we just exchange insincere smiles. Today she walked along beside me, to congratulate the Carmichaels on what she called a successful piece of publicity. For a moment I didn't know what she was talking about, but she soon made herself clear. I had managed to draw a lot of attention to myself last night, and Geoffrey had no doubt made good use of it with the Vice Chancellor. As a tactic in the College battle it was seen to be unfair. Until then I didn't even know there was a College battle, but I could see that she didn't believe me.'

'I've no doubt Gwyneth Morgan is a devoted wife, and an excellent breeder of small, future scrum-halves,' William said with careful moderation, 'but she is also a fierce Welsh harpy, Louise, and you should know better than to pay the smallest regard to what she says.'

'I agree with you – it doesn't much matter what she says to *me*. But what do you suppose she's saying to everyone else she meets – just that she enjoyed a pleasant evening at the Music Room? I doubt it.'

'So do I, and she will find cronies glad to add their pennyworth of malice as well. Still I insist that you must disregard them – *they* are not the people whose good opinion you should value.'

'I don't, and perhaps I've made it too obvious in the past. But Geoffrey hasn't said what's going on, and *I've* been altogether blind, it seems. I just assumed, as the longest serving Fellow, Edward Castleton was bound to follow the Whartons into the Master's Lodging.'

'That could happen,' her uncle agreed cautiously, 'but it doesn't necessarily follow as night follows day. The governing body may find itself divided, in which case the lobbying begins.'

'Gwyneth Morgan at least pretends to know a good deal more than I do. She implied that Geoffrey was being put forward as a candidate, but I'm sure she's wrong, Uncle Will. If he covets another job at all, it would be the Regius Professorship. He loves teaching too much to give it up for anything else.' She stared at her uncle's face and added desperately, 'Don't you agree?'

'Ten years ago I would have agreed, my dear; now I'm less sure, because the College is his life. If the traditionalists who want changes to come slowly rally behind him, then I'm afraid he'll feel obliged to become their man.'

'And against him will be the scientists led by Robert Morgan, I suppose – looking for an influential outsider, with research grants in his pocket and money he can tap for the College.'

'It's their view of the way it should go. Don't blame them too much,' William suggested gently.

Louise lifted her hands in a little gesture of despair. 'We seem to be damned either way. It would break Geoffrey's heart to see the long humanist tradition of St Barnabas lost; but he would hate just as much to be at the centre of a bitter Common Room struggle.'

William took one of her hands in his and gave it a little pat. 'What about you, my dear – what would *you* hate?'

'Moving into the Lodging, I'm afraid,' she confessed sadly. 'I don't have very much of Geoffrey as it is. There'd be nothing left for me at all if he became the next Master. But I should hate even more to see him defeated by the sort of tactics Gwyneth Morgan and her friends will use . . . "damn with faint praise, assent with civil leer, and without sneering, teach the rest to sneer" — isn't that how Oxford operates?'

William nodded regretfully. 'Yes, as do academic societies the world over, though I hope Oxford may bring a little more elegance to the process than elsewhere.'

She nodded, but after a moment veered away suddenly to another subject. 'You met our new neighbour last night — an American called Daniel Goodman. My impression is that *he* doesn't like Oxford ways very much, either.' She frowned over the crumbs she was flicking off her lap into the fire. 'He's due to present his first lecture next week, and that's another worry. We're given to believe that he's a controversial speaker at the best of times, but since he doesn't seem to enjoy being here I can imagine him fairly letting rip for the pleasure of fluttering a few Oxford dovecots.'

'Dear me,' said William mildly, 'but perhaps we should be grateful for a little excitement!' She didn't smile, and he spoke again in a different tone of voice. 'You're anxious about Geoffrey, but you needn't be. Any historian worth his salt enjoys the cut and thrust of controversy — it stops him getting in a rut. Of course, we must expect that if he *should* get into an uproarious public debate with Goodman, Gwyneth Morgan would see *that* as an unfair tactic too!'

Louise produced a reluctant grin at the thought of her husband doing anything uproariously. 'You're a great comfort to me, Uncle Will. For two pins I'd forsake North Oxford and ask if I could move in here with you!'

She didn't mean to be taken seriously, but beneath the surface lightness lay some distress of spirit that Geoffrey Carmichael *ought* to sense, if he would only disengage his mind for long enough from the concerns of St Barnabas. Feeling unable to say so, William asked a different question.

'What about your other problem, by the way? He seemed to be behaving very nicely last night.'

It might have been a trick of the firelight, but he thought he saw colour rise under her skin.

'Oh, Pierre's turning out not to be a problem at all. Either *he's* improved a great deal or *I've* grown less intolerant. He even seems to have become kind, which I certainly didn't expect.'

William didn't query the word, even though he thought he'd have chosen 'proprietary' to describe Pierre's attitude the night before.

'I take it he's here to acquire the expertise in scientific instruments that his father has. That will equip him to run half the Benoît galleries eventually. What, I wonder, will happen to the rest?'

She gave a faint shrug. 'We shan't know until my grandfather dies. He isn't likely to break the habit of a lifetime now by informing us of his intentions in advance.' The sound of the St Barnabas gate-tower clock striking five made her scramble to her feet. 'Time I went, Uncle Will. Thank you for the tea . . . and other comfort!'

A smile and a kiss on his cheek and she was gone, pedalling homewards. But the traffic lights at the junction of Broad Street changed to red as she approached them, and while she waited the unmistakable figure of Daniel Goodman loped out of the Clarendon archway and crossed the road. There was time to watch him turn into the King's Arms before she had to move on. He'd probably been ferreting in the Bodleian for yet more ammunition to hurl at his opponents next week, but even so she disliked the thought of his sitting lonely over a cup of coffee. He seemed to have deliberately discarded the sociable habits she'd thought were the birthright of all good Americans, but surely it would have been more pleasant to share the end of the working day with a companion than to plot all alone the rout of his fellow-historians?

Her vision of him was inaccurate today. With only one chair vacant, he was obliged to murmur, 'May I?' to the girl sitting alone at a small table. She shook back her hair and nodded, and the gesture and her pale face were familiar from the night before – the same sullen expression, air of foreignness, and isolation in the middle of a crowd. The only difference was that her hands were gripped round an untouched cup of coffee in a way that seemed to suggest despair.

Daniel thought of his own daughter – not so very much younger than this girl, with just that same 'damn your eyes and leave me to suffer alone' expression on her face, and the same inability to ask for help when she needed it.

'English coffee *is* barely drinkable,' he suggested quietly. 'May I get you something else?'

'No, nothing . . . thank you.'

Her accent he placed none too certainly, but the Oxford guidebook written in French that protruded from her bag confirmed his guess.

'I hope you enjoyed the music last night,' he tried again. She looked so blankly at him that he spoke with a tinge of irritation in his voice. 'You *were* at the concert, surely? I sat next to you.'

The next pause lasted so long that he thought she wasn't going to bother to answer at all.

'Yes, I was there,' she agreed finally. 'I hated the music.'

He had the impression that he was now being examined through her veil of hair. It had been a mistake to recognise her, perhaps – she might have misunderstood his intention. About to make an excuse to leave, he was stopped dead by her next remark.

'Do you look for a girl to buy? My mother was a *famous* prostitute . . . I am not bad myself.' As if to prove it she pulled back her hair in a gesture that was openly provocative and smiled at him.

'Thank you,' he managed to mutter, '. . . but I have a wife and . . . and children just about as old as you.' Certain now that he must make a rapid exit, he got up to go, but her hand shot out and caught his in a desperate clutch.

'I don't even know my mother . . . I've never met her. That is terrible, *n'est-ce-pas, Monsieur*?'

He was tempted for a moment to think that, if she wasn't unhinged, she was playing some ridiculous game with him. But the grip of her hand was real, and so were the tears that had begun to stream down her white face. He was aware that the people at the next table had abandoned their dull conversation the better to listen to this one, and that the girl beside him was balanced on some knife-edge of emotion that could tip her over into full-blown hysteria if she wasn't handled with care.

'You are a stranger here,' he said gently. 'Shouldn't you go home? Are there some friends I can take you to?'

'I don't know *where* to go. I came to see my mother but it is impossible to go to *her* now. Oh, I am not able to explain in English . . . she was the violin last night.'

'If Anna Ouspenska, last night's violinist, is your mother, I know her. She is surely the lady to take care of you.'

'No, I won't go,' the distraught girl shouted, 'it was *stupid* to come.'

Torn between pity and acute embarrassment, Daniel kept hold of the only fact he had. 'Stay here a moment. I must make a telephone call; then I'll be right back.' He wasn't sure that she even listened to what he said, but she made no attempt to move, and it seemed safe to leave her. He found the number he wanted, and prayed that there would be an answer. Only the ringing tone jeered in his ear, insisting that no one listened to it, but just as he was on the very point of giving up Louise Carmichael breathlessly spoke her name.

'It's Daniel Goodman here, Mrs Carmichael, needing a little help. Do you know if my landlady has a daughter she's expecting to see?'

'There *is* a daughter, and I believe a visit was mentioned, but shouldn't you be asking Anna herself? I've only now come in, so I'm afraid I can't tell you whether she's at home or not.'

Louise's cool voice made him hurry on. 'Don't hang up on me, please . . . just listen. I'm at the King's Arms with a weeping French girl. I happened to sit next to her at the concert last night. Her English and my French aren't up to the whole story, but she seems to have come to see her mother and, for some reason I don't understand, changed her mind. She's in no state to be abandoned, and the only thing I could think of was to ask if I might bring her to *you*.'

'I think perhaps you'd better,' Louise agreed after a moment's pause, 'but you must make your weeping friend understand that her mother only lives next door. She might refuse to come in that case.'

'Expect us in ten minutes,' Daniel said briefly, '. . . and thank you very much.'

In slightly less than that Louise saw a taxi turn into the drive. The girl who got out no longer wept, but clasped her arms around herself as if she felt cold despite the fringed blanket that was draped, Mexican fashion, over her black ski-pants. She allowed Daniel to shepherd her into the house but seemed ready to change her mind when he announced that he would leave them to talk in French together. Clinging to his arm, she informed him with some fluttering of eyelashes that she would much rather go with him. She didn't care at all for women, *enfin*, and would definitely prefer not to be left with this one.

'You've obviously made a better impression than I have, Dr Goodman,' Louise observed pensively, watching him trying to detach himself from his protégée.

He glared at her but managed not to shout. 'I'm available as a chauffeur, nothing more. You'll have to ring if you need me.'

The door banged behind him, leaving Louise to look at her visitor. With that straight black mane of hair, white face, and those unconventional clothes, she could have strayed straight from the student quarter of Left Bank Paris. But a pale, pouting mouth and dark eyes marvellously fringed with lashes that needed no mascara to enhance them artificially suggested an uncertain mixture of femme fatale and little-girl-lost as well. Slightly doubtful how to proceed, Louise suggested the kitchen as a warm and friendly place to talk. She put wine and biscuits on the table and waited for what might come next.

'I offered to sleep with the American,' the visitor announced in French in a bored voice, but the woman sitting opposite her remained so irritatingly calm that she had to try again. 'He is a little old perhaps, but I usually prefer older men – they make better lovers, don't you agree?'

'I'm afraid my experience isn't wide,' Louise admitted after a small pause. 'May I call you Madeleine? Your mother once mentioned your name. She told me you'd written to her, but didn't say afterwards that a visit had been arranged.'

'It wasn't . . . I could tell she didn't want me to come. But I'd quarrelled with my stepmother by then, so I decided to come anyway. No one wants me . . . not even the man I *was* sleeping with in Dijon. Perhaps I should just kill myself.' Tragic dark eyes watched through the curtains of hair to see whether *this*, at least, might have had some effect. She was pathetic as well as tiresome, Louise told herself; the posturing and the childish longing to shock were for effect, but the unhappiness underneath was real.

'Drink some wine,' she suggested, 'and then tell me about the quarrel at home. Was that because of the man?'

'Of course — my stepmother is very *comme il faut*, although I didn't know then, you understand, that she was my stepmother. I was a bad example to my sisters! *Enfin*, we shouted at each other a lot . . . as always we have done, but this time was *much* worse. At last she was so angry that without meaning to she screamed the truth — a respectable upbringing in Dijon had done me no good, but how could it when I was just like my real mother after all! Imagine . . . this I did not know — a mother who was not *her*. I could scarcely believe, and yet it explained many things. Having made the gaffe, she would say nothing more, but of course when my father came home I asked *him*. He also was very angry that I knew, but at last he admitted that my mother was alive: he even knew where she was living. She'd been a prostitute, he said, and was again after I was born — so I had been taken away. My father didn't know why she had moved to England — perhaps there were more . . . more opportunities here, though from the men I've seen that scarcely seems likely to me.'

Refusing to be sidetracked by this interesting view of Oxford manhood, Louise stared at the girl's face instead. If she resembled either parent, it must be her father. She was prettier than Anna, but lacked the bright, warm spirit that made her mother memorable.

'So you wrote to ask if you could come?' she asked patiently.

'Of course! I didn't care if my real mother still offered herself to men . . . though perhaps she is too old now. I thought this lady who wasn't like the boring matrons of Dijon could teach me things. Her letter didn't sound welcoming, but that I understood – she was ashamed of living as she did; so I came anyway.'

'But, now that you're here, why have you changed your mind?'

Anna's daughter gave a little shrug. 'I was mistaken. I wouldn't have come if I'd known she's no different from all those other respectable people at the concert last night – even worse than Dijon, they seemed to me. I went because I saw her name on the posters, but everyone looked boring and safe . . . like the music they listened to. I came here to show that I didn't *mind* what she was, but she was one of *them* . . . being clapped and cheered by those stupid stuffed shirts. I don't believe she was ever a prostitute at all – she only gave me away because she couldn't be bothered to keep me. What sort of a mother is that?'

'I'll *tell* you what sort of a mother you have,' Louise said in a voice that shook with sudden anger, 'and you can believe *this* because it's the truth. As a child she spent four years in a Nazi concentration camp and saw her parents die there because although they were harmless, brilliant musicians they happened to be Hungarian Jews. She *was* a prostitute in Paris after the war because it was the only certain way she had of staying alive. That was how she met the man who became your father. But his family married him off to someone more respectable. She didn't give you away – you were *taken* from her because she had to go back to selling herself again. With you gone she tried to commit suicide, but the doctor who saved her also eventually married her and gave her the only secure life she'd known. He'd been a student here before the war and loved the memory of Oxford. When he died she came herself because she hated Paris without Walther Ouspenska.'

Louise stopped to look at her companion across the table, but the girl's eyes were fixed on the glass between her hands, and her sullen expression hadn't changed. Not even certain that she was listening, Louise went on. 'I doubt if Anna found Oxford quite the haven her husband had described; she was often lonely, and still not nearly "respectable" enough – until last night, when our worthy citizens here finally decided to accept

82

her. So now tell me again if you *dare* that she doesn't deserve the "safety" you seem to despise.'

Time dragged in the quiet room, but at last Madeleine spoke in a low, resentful mutter.

'She could have told me . . . asked me to come . . . but she doesn't want me – nobody does.'

Louise reached across the table to touch the girl's cold hands, resisting the temptation to shake her instead. 'You're wrong; Anna would be the first to tell you that she doesn't normally rub shoulders with all the respectable, high-toned dignitaries of Oxford – she was just terribly afraid that you'd be ashamed of her. If it weren't so sad, it would be comical that you don't find her shameful enough. You can make up your own mind whether to see her or go back to France, but you mustn't denigrate her in my hearing. Anna is my friend.'

'Naturally I shall see her now,' Madeleine said with dignity. 'It would be a *bêtise, n'est-ce-pas*, not to?'

'Well, I think so,' Louise agreed. 'But I must telephone first and warn her that I'm bringing a visitor.'

Five minutes later they waited on Anna's step. She opened the door and, slightly hidden behind her companion, Madeleine saw a small, bright-haired woman dressed in a magenta-coloured caftan splashed with orange flowers.

'Darling,' she grinned cheerfully at Louise, 'I'm still getting over last night, and not at all respectable, as you see, for entertaining! But where *is* your visitor?'

'Right here,' Louise explained in French, 'and she'd rather you *weren't* dressed respectably.' She stepped back and let the porch light shine on her companion's face. Anna stared at it for a moment.

'I don't . . . don't know you, I think . . . and yet I *do* . . . of course I do . . . dear Holy Mother of God, you're . . . you're Madeleine!' Tears began to trickle down her face but she went on talking feverishly, almost to herself. 'My letter was so cold . . . in case you came and then hated me, you see . . . but oh, my darling girl . . . come in . . . come *in*!'

The silent figure she spoke to seemed rooted to the spot, but when Louise gently pushed her forward she managed at last to find something to say. '*M . . . Maman . . . oui, c'est moi, Madeleine.*'

Louise pulled the door shut behind them, blinked away her own sudden tears, and went home. There she remembered the chauffeur who might still be waiting, and rang his number.

'I don't think you'll be needed again, Dr Goodman. Anna and her daughter have just begun a conversation that has twenty years to catch up on. It was kind of you to take care of her, by the way – I think I might have forgotten to say that earlier.'

'You did – or perhaps you thought that kindness wasn't what I had in mind originally.'

She paused a moment to consider this. 'I don't think so . . . I'm sure your motives were very pure. In fact, you looked more like a man desperate to escape than one who'd had seduction in view. I can't describe our arrival next door, but after last night's triumph as well, Anna's cup of happiness is full.'

'I hope it stays that way,' Daniel commented brusquely.

'Why do you say that?' she asked 'I promise you there isn't any doubt about Anna's happiness.'

'My doubts concern the girl – *Unruhestifterin*, my grand-mother would have called her. It means a maker of trouble, if you aren't familiar with German.'

Louise heard the click of the receiver at the other end – still not a man to waste words or observe the social niceties, Frau Gutemann's grandson. That had been obvious last night, too. She replaced her own telephone, wishing very much that she could think him merely irritable at having been embroiled in other people's emotional confusions. But all too easily she could see what he meant about Anna's daughter. William had said they should be grateful for anything that broke the humdrum round, but she disagreed with him. Excitements only meant agitation and loss of tranquillity. She went to the novel that lay by her armchair, but didn't even pick it up. Her mind swung maddeningly between two conversations – the one going on next door, and her own morning encounter in the supermarket with Gwyneth Morgan. Anna's life would be altered by her daughter's arrival as certainly as the Carmichaels' uneventful existence would be affected by what was happening at St

84

Barnabas. Geoffrey would be selected as a candidate for the Mastership, or he would not; but either way it was bound to be important, and sooner or later he would have to tell her so. This was cause for agitation enough, but there was something still more painful to consider – a marriage with so little confidence left in it that she had to hear from other people what was likely to change their lives.

CHAPTER EIGHT

At breakfast next morning she was greeted by her husband with the kiss that always followed a night spent separately. It had become part of the ritual — after a shared bed no kiss was needed. Last night, following dinner in College, Geoffrey had considerately slept alone.

'How was guest night?' she asked, thinking that it would have been a more interesting question to put to Pierre, who had gone as Geoffrey's guest.

'Rather enjoyable, I think. One or two eyebrows quivered at our friend's unconventional idea of evening dress. But since he looked much more dashing than the rest of us, and twice as comfortable, envy won over stuffy disapproval in the end!'

Geoffrey smiled at the thought, but then applied himself to toast and marmalade, and there was time to consider him across the table. He usually seemed younger than his age, which was just past fifty now. Unlike some fellow-dons, he ate and drank in moderation and took sufficient exercise — might, in fact, have coined himself the very maxim of the early Greeks that ruled his life: 'nothing to excess'. His finely cut features would last well, even into old age, but this morning tiredness dragged at them. She thought it might be with the effort of pretending that they had nothing important to discuss.

At last he roused himself again. 'I can guess how *you* spent the evening — mulling over the concert with Anna.'

Louise shook her head. 'No, but I certainly called on her. Something extraordinary has happened. The daughter she was separated from twenty years ago has arrived in Oxford. By chance Daniel Goodman bumped into her at the King's Arms, and she seemed so distraught that he brought her here. When she'd calmed down a little I took her next door.'

'Strange indeed,' Geoffrey commented, 'but somehow only what one expects of Anna Ouspenska.' She could see him already skimming the front page of *The Times* that lay on the table beside him. The subject of his neighbour had been of no great interest after all and could now be put aside.

A spurt of sheer anger drove her headlong to invade what really occupied his mind. 'Tell me, please, Geoffrey. Was a decision taken about Humphrey's successor at yesterday's governing body meeting?'

Geoffrey looked genuinely astonished for a moment, almost shocked.

'My dear girl, our way of doing things is never as simple as that. There won't be an election until next term. Between now and then, having nailed their colours to the mast, the rival camps will first identify the waverers and then try to convert them with some elegant horse-trading.'

'It sounds like that infamous race in Siena – the Palio,' Louise observed coldly.

Amusement warmed her husband's face, making it come alive. 'All rode crookedly, but none more crookedly than our particular *bêtes noires*! Yes, I'm afraid it *is* a bit like that.'

She thought of Gwyneth Morgan, distilling her little drops of malice at the supermarket and of reputations nibbled away at morning coffee parties. William had said it was how the world of academe always functioned, but she hoped that he was wrong. Geoffrey's eyes were on the newspaper again; this time, though, she refused to let him evade the heart of the matter.

'I suppose the horses in *your* race have at least been named now?'

There was a little silence before he answered. 'Yes, we know the runners,' he admitted at last. 'The Science dons have got Justin Harkness to agree to stand; there are one or two others who want dear old Edward, as the longest-serving College Fellow, but I'm afraid the rest of them are putting their money on me!' He saw the expression on her face and quickly looked away again. 'There's no need to start saying goodbye to your precious garden. Harkness is bound to be the odds-on favourite – he's wealthy in his own right, and knows all the other wealthy, influential people.'

'You sound content to let him win, but how *can* you be? A stranger from outside, knowing nothing about St Barnabas?'

'Not quite that – he was up thirty years ago and managed to scrape a third in Engineering Science,' Geoffrey said with heroic fairness. 'That was before Humphrey's time, unfortunately, but there's no reason to suppose that Harkness hasn't remembered what must be cherished here.' He glanced at his watch, and announced with relief that it was time to be off. 'Lucky Pierre, with a museum to go to that keeps such civilised hours!' He was almost at the door when her last quiet question reached him.

'You *are* going to fight Harkness, though, I take it?'

Geoffrey was forced to look at her. 'Well, yes . . . I must do that, of course.' He offered a faint, apologetic smile, and then made his escape.

Automatically she stacked used plates and cups together, but abandoned them a moment later and walked by force of habit into the garden outside. Precious, Geoffrey had called it, and so it was to her, though not to him. A hard frost overnight had sealed everything in a glittering carapace of white, reminding her of the samite – 'mystic and wonderful' – that had sheathed King Arthur's sword, Excalibur. For once the sky was a clear, delicate blue, and somewhere nearby a robin was celebrating the fact with a trill of winter song.

She was still listening to it when Pierre came out of the house to find her. He stood watching her for a moment, aware of being puzzled, and disconcerted, and excited, all at the same time. He'd come reluctantly to Oxford, preferring the world he knew at home. Study was not a problem, he was used to that; observing the people around him was also something he was accustomed to enjoy; but to find himself impressed had been no part of his plan. Oxford *did* impress, it seemed, and on top of that there was the woman in front of him who was disorientating him most of all. He'd known her off and on for years – a thin, self-contained creature, now nearly middle-aged. It was ridiculous that she should so occupy his mind. He had only to look at her – face devoid of make-up and pinched with cold – to know how absurd the attraction was. But suddenly she turned round and smiled at him, and attraction seemed too pale a word. Obsession would have been nearer the mark. It wasn't rare for him to want a woman – but to long to take care of her, that was something new and disturbing.

'Louise *dearest*, I suppose you realise it's freezing out here,' he managed to say. Exaggerated, teasing tenderness was the note he'd struck with her and now couldn't seem to change, but he supposed it did as well as any other.

'It's cold, but too beautiful to be indoors.' She pointed to a spider's web, perfect in its silver filigree sheath of hoarfrost. 'Look – so lovely that I even forget its purpose – to lure some unsuspecting insect into providing the spider with his breakfast!'

Pierre bent to examine it with the seriousness he might have brought to inspecting a priceless Maghribi astrolabe in the museum. His concentration on the matter in hand surprised her, but then he was surprising her in all sorts of ways. Finding herself wrong about him didn't matter, but occasionally she was disturbed to find him watching *her* with just that same care he was applying now.

'Geoffrey says your roll-necked silk shirt caused something of a stir at High Table last night,' she suggested lightly. 'I hope *you* were entertained as well, by all the strange rituals that go on.'

He looked up to stare at her and for once there was no gleam of satirical amusement in his face. 'Oh, I find everything strange and interesting here.'

'Academic gowns worn at table, but removed at dessert, I suppose you mean . . . sherry in one room before dinner, coffee in another afterwards. The College traditions must seem pointless unless you think of the continuity they represent. You should hear Ruth on *that* subject!'

'I'd rather avoid hearing her on any subject whatsoever,' Pierre said frankly, accepting that the conversation had been steered into a safer direction. 'But right now, *ma chère*, I'm more concerned to take you back indoors before you freeze to death out here.' He held out his arm, and after only the smallest of hesitations she bowed and linked her own through it. She wished his other hand hadn't covered hers at the same time, but in this ceremonious way they'd reached the door of the garden lobby before someone else came towards them round the side of the house.

Madeleine Torrance was still dressed in the skin-tight trousers of yesterday, but her blanket cape had been swopped for a colourful sweater borrowed from her mother – Louise recognised Anna's clashing purples and pinks.

'Good morning,' Madeleine said in French to both of them, but with an interested glance at Pierre. Sullenness was forgotten, and she smiled at him in a way that not only revealed excellent small white teeth, but seemed to offer an invitation that he couldn't fail to understand. A troublemaker, Daniel Goodman had said, and Louise thought again that he was probably right. This girl could no more resist making overtures to any personable male she met than she could stop breathing. The stepmother in Dijon struggling to rein her in had, almost certainly, been fighting a losing battle. The introductions over Madeleine explained why she was there.

'My mother asks you all to dine with us tonight if you are free. It is to be a little celebration for *me*, so you must please all come.'

She smiled at Louise but her glance returned to Pierre. A man so attractive and so very French among her mother's neighbours made life look interesting after all. After only a few days in England she could see that a different technique would be needed here, but with Pierre there would be no problem; they spoke the same language in more ways than one.

Louise accepted the invitation but didn't invite the caller into the house. Madeleine found that understandable and, although the contest would be unfair, looked forward to the duel ahead. She'd heard of the charm that older women had for a certain kind of man, but one who took as little care of herself as this one did could scarcely be considered a threat at all. She smiled and went away, and Pierre followed Louise back into the warm kitchen.

'I scent a story,' he said, while she brewed fresh coffee for him.

The circumstances of Madeleine's visit were briefly explained, but Louise felt obliged to add a rider. 'I know she *looks* sophisticated, and does her best to sound like a world-weary thirty-five, but she isn't really much more than an inexperienced teenager pretending to be grown up.'

'And you're afraid I might want to add to her experience,' he suggested, reading her mind correctly. 'Well, you needn't worry, *ma mie*. I find rather to my surprise that a quite different woman pleases me!'

Once again seeing no gleam of amusement in his face, she was flustered by the sudden idea that he was alluding to *her*. After years of entertaining Geoffrey's undergraduates she was acquainted with their vulnerability – could treat them with care when their hands trembled and they found conversation difficult. But Pierre wasn't an inexperienced youth, and he could take his pick of women. She was probably imagining an attraction that didn't exist – had even reached the pathetic stage of wanting a young man to fall in love with her.

'You'll be late at the museum if you don't hurry,' she pointed out, banging down the coffeepot in front of him. 'Geoffrey says it's the most beautiful seventeenth-century building Oxford possesses. It's also full of wonderful treasures that most people don't seem to know about.'

'And *you* believe that beautiful things are diminished by not being appreciated,' Pierre said, smiling at her. 'It's why you grow cold outside, staring at spiders' webs with frost and sunlight on them!'

'I was talking about the museum,' she reminded him, refusing to be dragged away from safe, impersonal ground again. 'It *should* be more known about.'

'Of course it should. The building *is* glorious, and some of its possessions are beyond price. I even find the people there fascinating as well – the place is full of wonderful clocks that never work because the man whose job it is to wind them can't bear the sound of their chimes. Then there's a puritanical janitor who keeps the poor cleaning woman standing out in the rain in the hope that it will wash away the cheap perfume she uses. Stranger still, a fierce lady-dragon at the centre of it all refuses to be seduced by my well-known charm!'

This was the light-hearted Pierre she was familiar with and

now she could smile easily at him. 'Good for the dragon-lady, though I dare say she'll capitulate in the end. Now you must hurry, and I must go and see Ruth, who will almost certainly find a reason to refuse Anna's invitation.'

The reason when it came a few minutes later was one she might have anticipated.

'Quite out of the question – didn't you remember that it's choir practice night? Never mind; I'll ring Anna. Shall I make Geoffrey's excuses as well? He hates that sort of party – such a waste of time being civil to people he doesn't like.'

'He must either go, or make his own excuses,' Louise said levelly, doing her utmost not to shout. She stared at Ruth's long, horse face for a moment, marvelling at the absurdity of a convention that said she was supposed to love her husband's kith and kin. There were times, and this was one of them, when she came close to hating Ruth Carmichael.

That shocking thought was still occupying her mind when Geoffrey came home. Told about the evening ahead, his expression seemed to say that Ruth had judged his reaction correctly.

'I should have thought a private celebration scarcely needed outsiders present,' he suggested.

'It would be more private,' Louise agreed, 'but less of a party, wouldn't you say?'

The very reasonableness of it provoked him into sounding sharp. 'Frankly I'd rather be left to eat bread and cheese here if you're not cooking, than endure one of Anna's inedible messes – all paprika and chillies and God knows what else she flings into them.'

'And more frankly still, it's unfair of me to expect you to even *think* of going. After all, you had to dine in College last night, and tomorrow, after attending Chapel, you'll probably stay on to eat there again!'

'I suppose that's meant as a reproach,' he said stiffly. 'My dear Louise, you know as well as I do that certain College duties are obligatory.'

'And so is some *modicum* of your attention spared for the rest

of us,' she flashed. 'You can't live only for St Barnabas, even if
the waverers must be convinced that it *is* all you think about.'

She could see the flush of anger under his pale skin, but he
still refused to shout at her. 'I dislike being boxed into a corner
over something that doesn't seem to me to be important. If
Anna craves party guests no doubt there are others she can ask.
But since you insist on making an issue of it, I suppose I must
go.'

'Wrong, Geoffrey – go with good grace is what I insist upon!
If you can't manage that, I'd rather you stayed here. Ruth is too
busy singing, but Pierre and I will go alone.'

She walked away before he could reply and he didn't see her
again until it was almost time to leave. The dress she'd changed
into was simple, but its jade-green colour flattered her skin and
hair, and she was made up more carefully than usual. He
thought she looked beautiful, but he was still too angry to say
so; in any case his compliment wouldn't have been offered in
front of another man. Understanding this, Pierre seized the
opportunity presented to him and raised the sherry glass he was
holding in a little gesture of approval that made her smile.
Feeling that he'd been put at a disadvantage altogether unfairly,
Geoffrey followed them glumly next door.

Already gathered there were the elderly Polish cellist who
had played at Anna's concert, and her two tenants as well.
Daniel Goodman was pouring wine, and Professor Halvorsen –
for once minus her woolly hat – smiled shyly at the new guests.
In a grey angora skirt and sweater, she put Louise in mind of a
small rabbit surprised to find itself outside the safety of its
burrow. The Carmichaels posed no unfamiliar threat, but she
was flustered when Pierre kissed her hand, and surprisingly took
refuge with her fellow-tenant. Pierre was commandeered by
Madeleine, wearing what seemed to be a slip made of black
string and very little else. It revealed most of her beautiful legs,
and altogether, Louise reckoned, allowed Anna's daughter to
offer a challenge that any red-blooded male would have to be
blind not to enjoy. Geoffrey would probably manage it, but
Pierre would be unable to resist her for very long. So much the
better *that* would be, and so much more appropriate.

She didn't know that Anna was offering a different kind of challenge to Geoffrey, whose grim determination to smile cheerfully was written on his face.

'So kind of you to come,' she said with genuine warmth, in the hope of seeing him relax. 'In fact you are *always* kind, to permit me a friendship that you don't quite approve of! There, I am brave, am I not, to say that honestly, but having Madeleine here has made me brave.'

He would have shouted if he could that her honesty was not brave but intolerable – the last straw that threatened to break his suffering back. But convention said that he must mumble something instead that Anna took for encouragement.

'Louise is very *spéciale*, you see – and that's a word that means more in French than it does in your language. At the school where we play music together the little blind children always want to stay close to her, and I notice that they smile more easily when *she* talks to them.' Anna saw Geoffrey's expression change, and quickly apologised. 'So silly of me to tell you about your wife – of course you know how lovely she is!'

He did know that about her, although he feared that there was much else he *didn't* know. On the other side of the room she was smiling at something Frédéric Grodzicki had said. As usual, the dark fringe fell untidily across her forehead, and a delicate colour touched her cheekbones. She was nearly forty now, but who would believe it when she so nearly seemed the girl he'd fallen in love with in Paris twenty years ago? Tragedy had touched their life together, but even without that could he really claim to have made her happy? The answer was that he hadn't – because her happiness came from flowers and music and the blind children who were not hers; perhaps it was now beginning to come from Pierre Rivaux as well. He emerged from this painful reflection to find Anna watching him, and went cold for a moment with the fear of what he might have blurted out. But she still seemed to be waiting, and he found himself confessing to something else instead.

'We quarrelled earlier this evening.'

Anna's monkey face creased into a grin. 'About coming here, I expect – poor company, bad food, and even worse wine! I'm sorry, Louise should have left you at home in peace.' They would have got on better without him, he thought she just managed not to say. Then, abandoning the conversation altogether, she clapped her hands and called out that it was time to eat.

The goulash, contrary to his expectations, was excellent, and the Hungarian wine exceptional. He managed to find the good grace Louise had demanded of him to tell Anna so.

'I know,' she said calmly. 'I bought all the wine merchant had – two dozen bottles. I shall share them with you, Geoffrey. My dear husband always said that wine must be shared for true enjoyment.'

'Then I'm sorry I didn't know your husband,' he said, and meant it. 'He sounds as *spéciale* as we've agreed my wife to be.' He smiled at her wholeheartedly, perhaps for the first time in their acquaintance, and Anna understood at last why her dear friend had thought it worth marrying Geoffrey Carmichael.

Across the table Louise watched them with astonishment. Hostess and guest were expected to exchange smiles in the course of an evening, but this was different – and given the frame of mind in which her husband had set out, nothing short of miraculous. She couldn't guess how Anna had achieved the understanding they seemed to have reached; but perhaps with a daughter restored to her there was nothing her indomitable friend couldn't achieve.

'Polite etiquette isn't a matter I know much about,' said a sardonic voice beside her, 'but aren't you supposed to be throwing me a word occasionally?'

She turned to look at Daniel Goodman, who was picking his way with caution through the unfamiliar ingredients of Anna's Hungarian dish.

'Just enjoy it,' she advised, 'without worrying about what you're eating. I'm sorry, I didn't mean to be neglectful – only reluctant to interrupt your success with our shy Gertrud.'

'The professor, having drunk more wine than she is accustomed to, is going quietly to sleep. I foresee that my next duty will be to convey her home soon up two flights of stairs.'

His bright, pale eyes inspected Louise's face for signs that she was enjoying his predicament, but she answered very gravely.

'Poor Dr Goodman – I'm afraid you came unprepared for the trials of an Oxford sabbatical. But you're proving so helpful and resourceful that I'm sure your grandmother would be proud of you.'

'And clever as I am, I also know when Mrs Carmichael's wit is being exercised at my expense. Do you object, by the way, to the name of Daniel? I rather like Louise.'

In the game they were playing – if that was what it was – she was aware of having been surprised by a frontal attack. She told him so, and saw his face relax into genuine amusement. It seemed to notch up another unlikely success for Anna's dinner party. At this rate they might all end up at peace with each other. Even Pierre seemed to have forgotten that Madeleine bored him, because the two of them were deep in conversation.

'I hope you've changed your mind about the "maker of trouble",' Louise said quietly. 'My own impression at the moment is that she might not be a catalyst for the *general* good, but as far as Anna is concerned she has certainly been the bringer of joy.'

Daniel stared across the table at Madeleine, whose enticing smile was now being directed at Geoffrey Carmichael. In party mood, he reckoned, with her pale face flushed with colour and her mouth laughing, she was much too attractive not to be dangerous.

'It's too soon to be sure what she's brought,' he answered deliberately. 'But this much I know already – Anna should encourage her to go back to France.'

The finality of what he said was disturbing – irritating, too, when she'd just made up her mind that things were going unexpectedly well. Still, she wouldn't allow herself to be cast down by a man who probably made a habit of underestimating the power of love to help and heal people.

'To send her daughter away is the *last* thing Anna would think of doing,' she insisted in a low voice. 'And I can't believe that God would permit her to be hurt again.'

'I'm not able to answer for what God will permit,' Daniel said brusquely. 'I only know it's time to take my slumbering friend here home before she falls off her chair.'

CHAPTER NINE

The first Goodman lecture of Michaelmas term took place without Louise there to listen to it after all. She had been summoned the evening before to Holywell Street by Mrs Maggs, the wife of an old College scout, who still ruled William with a motherly rod of iron. The doctor had diagnosed a severe bout of bronchitis, and Louise moved into her uncle's little guest room to nurse him.

By the morning of the fourth day, when he'd been promoted to an armchair in his bedroom, he announced that it was time she went home.

'I suppose you've had enough of a monstrous regiment of women telling you what to do,' she suggested, smiling at him. 'Pity . . . I rather like it here!'

William's cherubic grin reappeared. 'My dear, without you I'd have given up by now and "passed over", in Mrs Maggs' immortal phrase. She's a pearl beyond price, but her conversation tends towards the morbid. I've heard about every one of her nearest and dearest whose putting-under she's attended!' His smile faded as he looked at Louise. 'I'd love you to stay, but I can't help feeling that you're a trifle anxious about things at home.'

For once she avoided a truthful answer. 'Well, Ruth is bound to have been running downstairs with chickpea cutlets and something she calls her vegetable ragout. Even Geoffrey's brotherly love can only stand so much of that, and Pierre has probably taken to eating out.'

'But there are also one or two other worries on your mind,' William suggested.

'I feel like a nervous conductor whose players might go galloping out of control!' She could admit *that* much, but not that the conductor herself was no longer entirely reliable. Against all expectation she was enjoying Pierre's company as much as he seemed to be enjoying hers — it was a situation she found half-absurd, but also half-delightful.

'And the most troublesome player of all,' William was saying, 'is St Barnabas, I suppose. Dear girl, look on the bright side — it's very far from certain that Geoffrey will be elected.'

'I know, but that's the *worst* that could happen for him. He managed to be so casual about it that I was fooled for a while. The truth is that he believes St Barnabas needs *him*. Edward would be an inadequate Master, which in these harsh times would be almost as bad as having Justin Harkness in the Lodging. But we have to live in this agonising suspense until next term, so that those who are sitting on the fence can be pushed off it one way or the other. Geoffrey isn't a pusher, Uncle Will, but Robert Morgan is.'

Her eyes looked sadly at him out of a thin, tired face. Loving her dearly, he'd never intruded on the grief closest to her heart. Her dead babies were not a subject that a clumsy bachelor dared trample on, but he knew the struggle it had been to achieve tranquillity again. She had kept entirely to herself, though, whatever other hopes of happiness her marriage had failed to realise.

'Go home and attend to your conducting, my dear,' he said gently. 'I'm quite up to Mrs Maggs' funeral reminiscences again now!'

Louise smiled, as he meant her to, and answered cheerfully. 'And it's back to the kitchen for me. Boeuf Stroganoff tonight, I think, as a reward after Ruth's well-meant offerings!'

She was in the kitchen at Norham Grove, and weeping as usual over the onions she was peeling, when she heard the slam of the front door. Too early for Geoffrey to be home, so Pierre must have come in from his afternoon Arabic lesson. With her face still wet with tears she turned as he walked in, and found herself wrapped closely in his arms.

'Oh, my dearest girl, you're crying . . . does that mean bad news about William? What can I do to help you? Just tell me, please.'

His voice was muffled against her hair but, trying to

overcome a mad desire to laugh, she was also conscious of his nearness and warmth and longing to give comfort.

'Onions,' she managed to explain at last, '. . . *that*'s why I was weeping! William's doing very well.'

Held a little away from him, she could see the sudden change of expression on his face, and the bubbles of amusement she'd been struggling with refused to be smothered any longer. He would laugh with her for sure; it was what she'd most enjoyed discovering about this changed Pierre — that they shared the same sense of the ridiculous. But this time he wasn't laughing. Instead, she was pulled close to him again while his mouth sought and covered hers.

He was too strong to be fought against. She told herself that in some small, still-functioning corner of her mind. Useless to struggle, so why not just accept the sudden delight that he was rousing in her? She needed this warmth and excitement . . . felt in her own quickened blood and heartbeats the same desire that was leaping in him. Emotion had been banked down for so long that she'd convinced herself she no longer wanted the thrust and throb of passion. But conviction was melting now, like a winter ice floe disintegrating under the pressing warmth of spring.

'Darling . . . darling . . . let me make love to you, please,' Pierre murmured. 'We can't stop now . . . you want it as much as I do, and I shall love you so tenderly, I promise.' He lifted his head, and she could see in his face not only longing but the tenderness he was offering as well. 'It isn't just naked lust, though I'm afraid that's there too! I want to make you happy.'

When her whole body trembled it took all the resolution she could find to pull herself away from him. With her hands braced against his chest to keep him from weakening her with more kisses, she tried to speak in a voice that sounded firm.

'We *can't* go any further — should never have gone this far. You . . . you took me by surprise, that's all. Now I'm sensible again, and so must you be.'

The stammered words fell on him coldly; sensible was the last thing he had in mind to be, and he couldn't believe that he'd mistaken her own response.

'You wanted me too, a moment ago . . . *wanted* to be loved. I know you did.'

His dark, entreating eyes insisted that she must admit to what was true. Pride needed to be assured that he hadn't made so fundamental an error. But how could she do that without revealing the empty thing her marriage had become? She was still hesitating for words when Pierre's hands clamped themselves on her shoulders in a grip that hurt.

'Tell me you're just a sex-starved, neglected wife and I'm as callow as Geoffrey's students who drool over you at little sherry parties and I swear I'll beat you, Louise.'

She shook her head, afraid that her voice wouldn't function. But the distress in her face made him lift her hands and kiss them in quick apology. 'I'm sorry . . . God knows why I'm hurting you when all I want to do is take care of you.'

The gentleness that was back in his voice made her eyes prick with tears, but the moment of danger was past. She could even see now how she must answer him.

'I know about impressionable undergraduates, but an infatuation with their tutor's wife never lasts and does them no harm. You're not an inexperienced nineteen, but you're missing your friends at home and you *are* accustomed to getting a response from women. I expect I've offered a challenge you couldn't resist – married, so not readily available, and having made it too clear in the past that I found you arrogant and unlikeable!' She smiled to remove the sting from her words, but his expression was sombre.

'What happened a moment ago didn't mean anything? You were lonely and I was arrogant – is that all it was?' he wanted to know.

'By no means at all – I'm afraid you haven't stayed nearly unlikeable enough, my dear friend, and I've been thinking very kindly of you ever since you got here! What just happened was my fault as well, if I've given you the impression that I'm not happy.' Her smile wavered on the edge of tears, and he read in her sad eyes the truths that she wasn't going to admit to.

His hands cupped her face while he gently kissed her mouth, but her lips didn't open under his this time; their moment had come and gone, and he was too experienced not to know it. Without speaking again he walked out of the kitchen, leaving her trying to recall what she had been doing before he arrived. There were chopped onions lying on the board, and mushrooms, and meat – the makings of Boeuf Stroganoff. She could even remember thinking that it was something they would enjoy.

Pierre didn't reappear downstairs until Geoffrey was home and supper was ready. He was less talkative than usual, but roused himself to answer when Louise asked if Madeleine was still staying next door.

'She's likely to be for some time. Anna said she wanted a job, and for once in my life I exerted myself to be helpful.'

'What sort of job?' Louise asked in astonishment.

'I remembered that the receptionist at the Maison Française was absenting herself for the arrival of a child. A French-speaking replacement was required and I offered them Madeleine. I'll spare you a description of the clothes she intended wearing for an interview with *Madame La Directrice*. But after an unseemly wrangle in the street she yielded to force majeure and agreed to go and change them.'

Even Geoffrey smiled, but Louise thanked Pierre warmly as well. 'Dear Pierre, you were being *very* kind.' Her eyes confirmed the message, on her own account, and won a small, wry smile from him.

'I know,' he agreed, 'and the strange thing is that it's not my usual role at all. I must ask Daniel Goodman what effect Oxford is having on *him*!' Then he got up and excused himself for leaving them – there was an acquaintance he was meeting for coffee.

She doubted the acquaintance but closed her mind to the image of him walking into some bar or other in search of the pleasure she had denied him. Left alone with Geoffrey she plunged wildly into the only subject that seemed bearable.

'I was sorry to miss Dr Goodman's lecture. How did it go?'

'Very much as expected,' Geoffrey said noncommittally. 'A young, enthusiastic audience appeared to enjoy what you once rightly suggested would be a performance. It was! Goodman is a brilliant speaker.'

'But you didn't enjoy it?'

'Scarcely, when the man's views are poles apart from mine. He sees the past in purely economic terms. Germany dragged the world into war for the second time in a century because the penalties imposed on her the first time were too harsh. A megalomaniac Führer intoxicated with his own mad vision of the greatness of the Fatherland had nothing to do with it! I suppose it's the view of European history that a man of German descent might easily prefer to take, but it doesn't persuade me.'

'We might also expect him to be anti-Jewish,' Louise felt obliged to point out. 'But he's very kind to Anna.'

'Perhaps that's Oxford's civilising effect on him,' Geoffrey suggested dryly.

Then he, too, stood up, explaining that there was work he must finish. She was left alone, to clear away the remains of a meal that no one seemed to have enjoyed after all, and to sit idly at her piano until she could pretend that it was time to go to bed. It would have been a relief to find even Ruth at the door, to lessen her feeling of desperate loneliness. But no one called at all, and slowly there dawned on her instead the knowledge that a moment of truth she had been putting off for years was now unavoidably coming towards her. She'd been right to fear this year's new beginnings, because sooner or later they would present her with choices that had to be made.

Pierre remained in Norham Grove, but as a correct and rather distant guest, who worked hard and found relaxation among the new friends he'd made in Oxford. Madeleine was certainly among them, but who was now pursuer and who pursued Louise reckoned she had no right to ask. She only knew that their present situation was a strain; she longed for Christmas to come, when Pierre would go back to Paris.

Geoffrey declined to attend Daniel's second and last lecture of the term, and she therefore felt obliged to stay away as well. They were like swimmers treading water, she thought – not going anywhere; just making a huge effort merely to stop themselves being washed away. But with the Oxford logic that she had told Daniel Goodman about, the more effort that was required, the greater seemed to be their need to go on with the charade of looking calmly normal.

She didn't, as she might once have done, confide in her friend next door. Anna, happy as never before, must be left in peace; and even William – deep in the final selection of his anthology – was busy enough not to notice that her smile had become frequent but unreal.

One afternoon, after lunching with Edwina Wharton, she found that she couldn't bring herself to go straight back to the strained atmosphere in Norham Grove. The traffic-ridden din of the High was intolerable, too – but even that could be forgotten in the Botanic Gardens, she decided. Within was peace, and bare trees etched black against an apricot sky, and thin winter sunshine that even gave an illusion of warmth. She walked slowly along, letting tension seep out of her tired mind, and scarcely noticed the man who came towards her. But he stopped and spoke, and she had to look at him.

'Is Carmichael dudgeon so deep that you'd rather pretend I wasn't here?'

'Dudgeon is usually high, I believe,' she pointed out after a moment. 'Umbrage is deep.'

'Umbrage let it be,' Daniel agreed. 'Who am I to bandy words with the wife of an Oxford don?'

But he still waited for an answer to his question and she thought that such unrelenting persistence was probably the trait he depended on to wear his opponents down.

'I won't pretend not to know what you mean,' she said finally, 'as long as *you* don't pretend that small-minded academic malice made Geoffrey disapprove of your lecture. He takes a different view of history, that's all – believes that the wickedness or mad aberrations of nations must be blamed on the people who lead them. To him it seems a dangerous distortion of the truth to offer undergraduates a different theory.'

Her defence of Geoffrey Carmichael was something he didn't expect. It was irritating, too – he thought she would have been more independent-minded.

'And you agree with your husband – as a good wife should?'

'As it happens, I do,' she agreed coolly. 'But if you'll stop trying to needle me about wifely obedience I won't accuse *you* of trying to whitewash Germany's evil-doing for the sake of your ancestors.'

She expected him to be offended by this frankness but he let out a sudden shout of laughter instead that disturbed a nearby blackbird into flying complainingly away. A smile tugged at her own mouth because his amusement was infectious and it was a relief to share enjoyment.

'We'll clap hands on a bargain, if you like,' he agreed, sober again. 'No hostilities of any kind.'

They walked on together, not noticing that they had done so. For the first time in their acquaintance it occurred to her that his company was something she might learn to enjoy. He wasn't boring or trivial and, though harsh, somehow *not* unkind. 'Few people bother to come here in December – they seem to think a garden dies in winter,' she observed after a moment or two. 'I suppose I wouldn't have expected you to come at all, not being horticulturally inclined.'

'The credit goes to your sister-in-law,' he explained gravely. 'I wasn't amused when she recommended me to go by shanks' pony, but it turned out to be very good advice. I've discovered a lot about Oxford on foot. This place appeals to me because I like to picture all the people who've pottered up and down these paths for centuries – old gardeners arguing with professors of botany over their Senecio Squalida or some other precious rarity!'

She smiled at the picture he drew for her – unconscious, he thought, of the picture she presented herself. As usual she was bare-headed, dark hair ruffled by the breeze, thin face framed by the velvet collar of the dark green jacket she wore. She was so different from his beautiful wife, so uncaring of the advantages Nature had given her, that until the night of the concert he hadn't seen her as a woman who would be desirable – even if it was obvious that Pierre Rivaux had. She was gifted, intelligent, and kind, though not indiscriminately so – that much he hadn't missed; but he'd been very slow to see that she was also lovely in her own distinctive way.

Aware of the silence that seemed to have lasted too long, Louise cast around for a fresh topic of conversation. 'Almost the end of term – you'll be glad to fly home to New York for Christmas with your family.'

'Vermont,' he corrected her baldly. 'That's where we spend Christmas – my wife's people have a place there.'

His lack of enthusiasm was hard to ignore but she did her best. 'It sounds lovely – snow and sleigh bells and carols sung round log fires; or are you going to be disagreeable and tell me that my vision of Vermont was dreamed up in Hollywood?'

'I'll tell you the reality. We ski a lot if the snow is thick, carouse indoors if it's not. Either way it's all frantic hilarity and noise – not quite my idea of the way to celebrate the birth of the Prince of Peace.'

He stared, as he spoke, at Magdalen's beautiful bell-tower silhouetted against the deepening sky. With his attention elsewhere, she could look at his own profile: bent nose, and aggressive chin scarcely concealed by the small, neat beard. He wasn't a man that it was easy to like – he was too abrasive and intolerant for that. But she saw clearly now a lonely integrity of spirit about him that was surely admirable. The word 'lonely' seemed apt, even though it should have been absurd applied to a man so well endowed with family and colleagues.

'Well, the carousing may not be much to your taste,' she said at last, 'but at least you'll have the happiness of being with your family again. You and they must have missed each other.'

She was right about him, of course – there'd been nights when he'd deliberately drunk too much wine to deaden the ache of his isolation. But she was probably wrong about his wife and children. He'd written asking if they could spend Christmas by themselves for once – just the two of them and Kate and Hal. Karen had eventually replied, but only to say that the children would be disappointed if they didn't go to Vermont as usual. She didn't suggest that after a long absence she would like some time with him alone.

Conscious that her last remark had been left hanging

unattended to, Louise tried again. 'I can offer a choice of Christmas pleasures before you go home. The Choral Society, which includes my sister-in-law, will be singing Handel's *Messiah* at the Town Hall.'

'A choice, you said!'

Trying not to smile, she apologised for not remembering that baroque music made no appeal. 'There's also a carol concert in the Cathedral at Christ Church. An invitation is necessary there, but the College could arrange for you to go. I know you aren't much drawn to music, but it's always a very special evening.'

'You know about me even less than you think you know.'

The sudden, sharp denial came as a shock. Feeling that her face had just been slapped, she put a little distance between them. 'Well, at least I'm sure of one thing, Dr Goodman. Even Vermont will seem very desirable after three months in Oxford. For a week or two you'll be spared all our strange ways. You can plunge back into the real world like a stranded turtle finding the sea again.'

Unsmiling, he stared back at her. 'I can't wait to rejoin the real world. Right now, though, I'm due back in College. Can you find your way home alone?'

'Easily, thank you.' Leaving him standing there, she walked away, saddened rather than annoyed. Until that abrupt change of mood they had seemed to enjoy talking to each other.

He was invisible after that for the few days that remained of term, nor did she notice him among the congregation at the carol concert. But he *was* in the Cathedral, and took away with him on the long flight home images that seemed to have etched themselves indelibly on the retina of his inward eye. He wanted to think of Karen, to reassure himself by remembering her bright, laughing beauty and the quick mind that had once travelled so easily in step with his. But he kept seeing instead a blaze of candlelight in an ancient chapel, where boys' pure, sexless voices sang as if soaring straight to Heaven. The light had shone on Geoffrey Carmichael's fair head, and on the tear-wet face of the woman beside him. It might have been the unearthly beauty of the moment and the music and the setting. But as the slow hours of his journey passed Daniel's conviction grew that Louise Carmichael had wept for more things than these.

CHAPTER TEN

Pierre, also getting ready to go home as Christmas approached, announced almost at the last minute that he wouldn't be returning after the holiday. He didn't look at Louise as he spoke and, because she said nothing, it was left to Geoffrey to answer.

'I thought you were due for a second term here, at least with your Arabic tutor, if not at the museum.' Nothing in his voice betrayed the slightest relief that he was mistaken, but Pierre understood him well enough by now. The self-disciplined man facing him across the table might be able to conceal the fact, but he was deeply relieved to be getting rid of his guest.

'I can go on studying Arabic in Paris,' Pierre pointed out, 'and I'm needed there now – my father says that André has finally begun to fail rather rapidly.'

'Nadia doesn't say so,' Louise joined in at last, 'but I suppose I wouldn't expect her to. She prefers not to face reality for as long as she can avoid it. But if Grandfather *is* finally dying, I'm afraid it's going to be a very gloomy Christmas for you. My mother will fairly wallow in the sadness of it all – Slavs can never resist death and funerals!' Geoffrey was looking shocked, but she offered him the little shrug that twenty years of living in England hadn't cured her of. 'I expect that sounds unfeeling, but there's no point in pretending – Grandfather Benoît and I have never been able to manage anything except armed neutrality.' Memory resurrected childhood unhappinesses that were vivid even now, but she dismissed them by gesturing at the reluctant daylight outside the windows.

'Oxford at its December worst – dank and raw. I'm sorry, Pierre – I should have liked you to take away a happier image.'

His brief smile said that images of a place he was anxious to leave scarcely mattered. They stared at each other nowadays, she thought, across the barrier he'd erected since the afternoon she'd come back from looking after William. His manner was now so impersonal that she sometimes wondered if she'd only dreamed a few feverish minutes when his kisses had roused in her a longing for a life that still included love. Never since then had he even seemed to be aware of her.

But friendship, at least, obliged her not to let him go to the station alone, on a morning when an unfortunate traffic diversion sent them through the city centre. To add to the constraint between them she found herself wincing at the cheap Christmas gaiety around them.

'It couldn't be worse as a farewell to Oxford,' she muttered. 'Your last impression will be the amplified roar of "Jingle Bells" and cardboard reindeer galloping overhead!'

'Don't worry – it's the farewell itself that I'm not managing very well,' he said briefly, and then lapsed into silence again.

The train was running late, the announcer warned them as they reached the London platform. 'Don't wait, please,' Pierre politely insisted. 'It's horribly cold and your nose is turning pink already.'

It was, she understood, to be a very unemotional leave-taking; whatever longings he might have had were clearly regretted, or even forgotten altogether. So much the better, she told herself, and tried to believe it as she managed to smile at him. 'An unromantic sight I must be then, perfectly in keeping with this dismal railway station!'

He didn't answer for a moment, but his hands suddenly rearranged the scarf at her throat in a gesture that touched her by seeming intimate and tender. 'You're wrong, I'm afraid. I don't know why it should, but your pink nose makes it seem even harder for me to say goodbye to you.' His voice was quiet and level – just so might he have commented on the weather; but when her eyes met his she had to look away again.

'I hope you'll be able to escape from Paris,' she said with difficulty, '. . . go skiing perhaps – isn't that what you like to do?'

'I shall if I can,' he agreed. 'I was stupid enough to mention it to Madeleine and she badgered me to take her along. I had to point out that the slopes I ski on aren't for undisciplined novices.'

'If they were would you have taken her?'

'Certainly not. She'd have a certain gamine attractiveness if she didn't overplay her hand all the time, but I finally had to explain that a boringly self-obsessed adolescent doesn't rouse me to passionate desire.' His hand touched her cheek, making her look at him again. 'But *you*, I'm afraid, do.'

The quiet statement felt like something he'd shouted from the rooftops. She even glanced round, expecting to find an audience gathering.

'I thought the . . . the ailment was very brief – recovered from almost immediately!' she stammered.

His hands, warm and familiar, suddenly cupped her cold face. 'Is it any good – will it ever be any good – asking you to leave Geoffrey? I'd love you so much . . . take such care of you, dearest Louise.'

'I can't . . . *don't* ask me,' she said unsteadily. 'A runaway wife would ruin Geoffrey's chances at St Barnabas, and he's done nothing to deserve that.'

'Except fail to make you happy.'

There wasn't time to explain that not all the failures had been Geoffrey's; she only wanted to convince herself and Pierre that propinquity – always a danger to people who were lonely – had betrayed them into behaving foolishly.

'You mustn't worry about me, and I shan't agonise about you, even though you *aren't* an impressionable undergraduate. As soon as you're back in Paris your life there will be what matters. All you'll remember of your stay in Oxford will be rainswept gardens and dreadful coffee, and Ruth's vegetarian suppers!'

It was the best she could do, all that her tear-clogged throat would permit her to utter. But with a perfect sense of timing Pierre's train finally arrived – bustling into the station with the air of an express having not a moment to lose, and a strong reluctance to wait for lingering passengers. He had time only to leave a brief, hard kiss on her mouth, and then fling his luggage and himself on board. For a moment or two longer she could still see him, and then the train had pulled out of the station. She was left staring at a litter of cigarette cartons and crumpled Coca-Cola tins lying on the track.

Later that afternoon she was in the kitchen at home, cutting angels and stars out of gold paper, when Ruth walked in.

'My dear Louise, what *are* you doing?'

It was her sister-in-law's usual approach – to ask one question but mean another. Not what, but *why*, was what she really wanted to know, when Christmas trees and decorations hadn't ever been a feature of Carmichael life in Norham Grove.

'I thought I might be too old for this pleasure by next year,' Louise explained gravely. 'It seemed to be now or never, and I decided that it ought to be now.'

She didn't look up from the winged figure she was fashioning, and missed the flicker of irritation on her visitor's face. Ruth stared at her absorbed expression, aware once again of the frustration that her brother's wife always aroused in her. Even after all these years she hadn't got a real grip on Louise Carmichael and it began to look as if she never would.

'I saw you go off with Pierre this morning,' she said, abandoning the fruitless subject of Christmas trees. 'I know you're related to him by marriage, my dear, but I can't help feeling glad he's gone. There was quite a different atmosphere in the house while he was here – I'm sure Geoffrey felt it, too.'

Louise looked up at her at last, struggling with a shocking urge to shout that in the different atmosphere she had at least felt alive. She almost thought the words had left her mouth – could picture the change in Ruth's expression. For once the horse-like, unfocused gaze that watched but always missed what it was looking for might even register her aching loneliness. The words weren't said after all, but a variation of them still managed to disconcert her sister-in-law.

'You're right – the house *was* different. It almost felt alive.'

She saw Ruth's face flush unbecomingly, and the desire to hurt her died. Had this awkward, inelegant woman ever been loved by a man? Had she long ago had to send a lover away knowing that an abandoned schoolboy needed her? Louise felt a stab of remorse, most of all because the possibility had never even occurred to her before. For once she smiled at her sister-in-law with something almost like warmth.

'Ruth, please say that *you've* always hankered after a Christmas tree too — then we can revel in it together!'

In return she was offered a brisk shake of the head. 'A rather recent German custom, I'm afraid, foisted on us by Prince Albert. Personally I hate the thought of thousands of young trees being grown merely to die a lingering death in overheated rooms.' Ruth saw the animation fade from her sister-in-law's face and felt a twinge of regret. Principles were what one must cling to, of course, but perhaps it *had* been a pity to refuse. She could see the tree in her mind's eye, gold decorations glinting in the firelight . . . Geoffrey would have enjoyed that as a little boy.

'I only came down to check,' she said abruptly, '. . . the same Christmas arrangements as usual?'

'Uncle Will and the Whartons here for dinner,' Louise agreed, 'and Andrew Jardine, of course.' There was no surprise about Andrew, Geoffrey's bachelor colleague who lived in College. Louise cut out another star before she delivered her bombshell. 'But I've invited Anna and her daughter as well.'

Red-faced again, Ruth finally managed to reply. 'Surely a mistake, my dear,' she said at last. 'I know that Geoffrey treats Anna Ouspenska with *perfect* civility — he'd allow himself nothing less; but that is very far from saying that he'll enjoy her company at a small, intimate dinner party. And what is Edwina Wharton going to make of that extraordinary young woman — her daughter?'

'Exactly what she makes of Humphrey's female undergraduates, I expect. Madeleine may even galvanise dear Andrew Jardine into sparkling life, which is more than you or I have yet been able to do.'

Accepting defeat, Ruth turned to leave, but with one parting shot left in her locker. 'Well, quite a party we shall be, but you mustn't go to any special effort for *me*. I shall bring down some delicious little concoction to enjoy while the rest of you are struggling with dry old tasteless turkey!'

Pleased at least to have had the last word, she marched away, leaving Louise with the feeling of acute tiredness that her sister-in-law's visits always inspired. The purchase of the Christmas tree had been a desperately needed diversion – something else to concentrate on instead of the picture in her mind of Pierre making the long journey home alone. He had gone sadly, but she had no doubt that he would recover from loving her much sooner than he believed. Her own loss was likely to be more permanent. She had said goodbye to what remained of youth, and her last chance of love. Now, somehow, she must make do again with what was left.

On Christmas night, though feeling slightly ashamed of herself, Louise primed William beforehand to extol the virtues of the turkey she set before them. But there was really no need; the dinner was perfection, and there was even a moment when Geoffrey nearly tempted Ruth to abandon her spinach and nut roulade for a slice or two of golden-roasted meat. If Andrew Jardine didn't sparkle, he looked extremely happy; and Edwina took Anna's daughter in her stride after the first surprised glance. A minuscule tunic of pleated white silk above white tights revealing a length of beautiful legs might not be a conventional choice for a Christmas dinner party in North Oxford; but when Louise murmured to her husband that the outfit not only stayed on the hither side of decency but also suited Madeleine perfectly, even he smiled and agreed.

As the evening progressed she was sure of something else that she hoped was escaping the notice of the rest of the party. At their first meeting Madeleine had made it clear that she preferred the company of men to women; even so, it was unusual for a guest to ignore her hostess completely. Edwina Wharton and Ruth received sufficient attention to meet the minimal demands of courtesy; William and Humphrey, male but too old to be of interest, were smiled at; Andrew Jardine, rendered inarticulate by the briefness of Madeleine's skirt, was soon identified as being a waste of time. It left Geoffrey as the only man worth concentrating on.

Louise watched the performance with astonishment. Tempering her usual gale of sexuality to suit the unworldly academic lamb, Madeleine gazed at him sweetly, hung on his words, and even by some sleight of person managed to suggest only old-fashioned gentleness and charm waiting to be discovered beneath her outward rig. It was a scene that Pierre would have enjoyed, and Louise found herself missing him with a regret that seemed like pain. Pouring coffee after dinner, she felt acutely alone without him until Andrew stationed himself beside her, ready to be useful. He was frightened as a rule by any woman young enough not to need help in crossing the road; but Louise Carmichael didn't frighten him. In fact he loved her in a silent, completely unselfish way that he thought Geoffrey guessed at but didn't mind.

He returned from delivering coffee to Geoffrey and Madeleine, with a faint smile on his face. 'Can you believe that rowing is the subject under discussion? The poor fellow is trying to explain the difference between a University Blue and a College oarsman!' Then Andrew glanced at the larger group – Edwina and Anna with their heads companionably together, Humphrey and Ruth laughing at something William had just said.

'A happy evening, my dear Louise, but sad to think that the Whartons won't be in the Lodging this time next year.'

'Who will be – Justin Harkness?' she asked bluntly.

He fidgeted with a coffee spoon lying on the tray before he looked at her. 'I'm afraid so. The general board has lumbered us with too many scientists in Senior Common Room, you see. They're bound to vote for Harkness, because they see the future of the College only in their own terms: if St Barnabas is not to lose its standing it must be able to endow more research fellowships, and attract more eminent physicists who care a great deal about their subject but very little about the College they're attached to.'

'Does Geoffrey know what the outcome is likely to be?' It seemed a strange question to have to ask of someone else, but Andrew was too old a friend to dissemble with.

'Oh yes, he knows – that's why he's being such a wonderfully entertaining host tonight.'

It was, she realised, true – and just the sort of admirable, deceptive bravery that her husband would be capable of demonstrating. Whatever grieved him most would be so well hidden that the rest of the world might doubt that he even cared about it at all. She nodded and abandoned the subject as Anna arrived for more coffee, and sent Andrew to take her seat next to Edwina. Louise smiled at her friend.

'I was afraid Madeleine might find this evening boring – not so, apparently; she even seems to be enjoying herself!'

Anna considered the comment with unexpected gravity. 'Thanks to your dear, kind husband, who is taking such care to make her feel welcome.' Her gaze lingered on them frowningly for a moment – Geoffrey's fair colouring handsomely set off tonight by a dark blue velvet smoking jacket, Madeleine impossibly demure in her skimpy dress and revealing tights.

'My darling daughter wouldn't be welcomed everywhere in Oxford,' she confessed. 'She isn't yet quite civilised enough – even I can see that, although it doesn't stop me loving her more than life itself. It's no blame to the stepmother in Dijon; I'm sure she did her best.'

Louise heard the sadness in her friend's voice but still smiled cheerfully. 'Leave her to this strange place, Anna love – it's never been known to fail. Even some of Daniel Goodman's sharp corners are being worn away – the usual result of the drip of Oxford rain on stone.'

This brought a sudden grin to Anna's face that quickly faded. 'Of course I *want* her to stay, but I can't help knowing that she won't. I'm afraid she sees life as her father did – imagines that what she wants is hers for the taking. She wanted Pierre Rivaux, of course, and having him go back to France has unsettled her.'

'I expect he thought he was being kind,' Louise felt obliged to say.

'No doubt he was, but Madeleine mistook kindness for something else. It's an error she will keep on making.'

Was she making it now? Geoffrey's wife wondered involuntarily. Almost certainly not. She'd simply fastened on him as being the most personable male available, and perhaps also because it amused her to monopolise the husband of a woman whom she'd decided not to like. Feeling unable to say either of these things, Louise asked instead when Anna's tenants would be returning.

'Gertrud in a few days. She can't bear to be separated from the Bodleian for more than two weeks at a time! Daniel Goodman I'm not sure about, but he'll want to make the most of being with his family. There's a photograph in his sitting room. I think his wife must have given it to him because he doesn't seem to me to be the sort of man to need reminding what she looks like.'

'And how *does* she look?' Louise found she couldn't help asking.

'Beautiful – such lovely, *real*, golden hair that I almost thought I'd give up dyeing mine. Then I decided I wouldn't, because Daniel probably enjoys the contrast.'

The remark was typical of Anna Ouspenska, but before Louise could say so Edwina stood up, signifying to Humphrey that it was time they went home. Leave-takings were made outside because the night was unusually fine and clear. The moon hadn't risen, but a scattering of stars sparkled with the brilliance only seen on frosty winter nights. There was some knowledgeable discussion about which was Sirius and which Andromeda, but Louise scarcely listened. She'd been reminded instead of a day when Pierre had taken her to the Ashmolean to be shown how ancient astrolabes and orreries had explained what was then known of the universe.

'Come back from whatever regions your thoughts are travelling in,' Geoffrey's quiet voice said beside her. 'It's too cold to star-gaze out here.'

She turned to look at him, realising with a sense of shock how separate were the worlds their minds now seemed to inhabit. They had become strangers who by some accident of Fate still shared a house, and even occasionally a bed. But other people still seemed to know her husband well when she did not, and it suggested that the fault was hers. Hers also, therefore, the duty to do something about it – only she didn't know where to begin, or even if she wanted to begin at all.

'Thank you for keeping Madeleine entertained,' she at last managed to say. 'Anna was very grateful.'

'It wasn't a hardship – I found her charming and intelligent. Considering the life the poor child has led until now, she's turned out remarkably well.'

Louise murmured a silent apology to the unknown stepmother in Dijon. It was unfair to *her* to leave unsaid the fact that Madeleine was nothing if not inventive, but Geoffrey must be allowed his vision of a lonely, sensitive girl who needed to be helped. Just such a vision, after all, had inspired his marriage years ago to a different girl.

Pierre was obliged to remain in Paris over Christmas, and even his intention to escape to Klosters afterwards was thwarted in the end. January was nearly through when Henry Rivaux rang Louise to break the news. André Benoît had finally died, almost on his ninetieth birthday. For fear of shocking Geoffrey again, she didn't say that it seemed entirely typical behaviour. Her grandfather would have been pleased to drag out his dying for as long as possible. No giving in gracefully for a man who hadn't ever wanted to make things easy for his family.

Henri's voice sounded frayed with tiredness and, although he didn't ask for help, Louise's strong impression was that he needed it. Nadia was not only taking the loss of her father badly, but also letting it be known that the influenza from which she happened to be suffering would soon lead her to the grave as well. Louise found herself promising to fly from Heathrow the following day, and then went to tell Geoffrey.

He managed to smile at her. 'Well then, I must come with you of course – if you'd like me to.'

She shook her head – a habit she'd never lost, he noticed, of signalling in advance what her reaction was going to be. He thought, irrelevantly, that she would have made a terrible poker player.

'It's good of you, but I shouldn't dream of asking you to come. You'd hate having to go away just at the beginning of term . . . especially *this* of all terms.' The afterthought spoke itself because Andrew Jardine's Christmas night comments still echoed in her mind.

After a moment's hesitation Geoffrey answered her. 'It would be a relief if you could manage on your own, but which term it is makes no difference now – the election is only a formality. Harkness's supporters outnumber mine and the waverers are inclining in his direction too.' He sounded merely regretful and she knew a sudden urge to shout that his tone of voice demonstrated perfectly why Robert Morgan's candidate would win. Her husband could endure for as long as there was breath in his body; but what he couldn't do was fight. Even in Oxford, where the fighting was subterranean, not overt, it was too big a handicap.

'I'm very sorry,' she said and meant it. 'You would have made a very good Master.'

A faint smile touched his mouth, then faded again. 'But you would rather stay here – so something good comes out of it!'

Almost defeated by his determination not to appear heart-broken, she made one last try. 'Will Justin Harkness spoil St Barnabas – fill it with budding chemists and nuclear physicists whose only interest is in the laboratories where they're taught?'

'That's the trend in most Colleges,' he acknowledged. 'Classics dons may become a breed as extinct as the Dodo before long, and the rest of us will eventually follow them, but we shall hang on for as long as we can.' He saw the sadness in her face but smiled again, declining sympathy. 'Go to Paris, my dear, and forget *our* problems. Nadia will require all your attention once you get there.'

He insisted on driving her to the airport the next day, and talked of nothing in particular while they waited for her flight to be called. Not until it flashed up on the screen above them did he reveal less calmly what filled his mind. 'You'll be glad to be back in Paris – you become a different person when you're there. I'm never quite sure that you'll bring yourself to leave again.' He spoke of Paris because to speak of Pierre Rivaux instead simply wasn't possible. However inconvenient it would have been, he'd have gone with her if she'd asked him to. She hadn't asked, and he must let her go alone, but she might never come back – that was the thought that hammered in his brain. Still he must smile and kiss her cheek, and smile some more until she was out of sight, but at the last moment, almost through into the departure lounge, she turned and ran back to him.

'Be sure to eat in College ... and don't be *too* kind to dear little Madeleine! Daniel Goodman thinks she's troublesome.' Then she was gone again, a dark-haired, slender figure in a camel overcoat, quickly swallowed up although he kept looking for her in the crowd of other passengers.

CHAPTER ELEVEN

An hour and a half later the flight touched down in Paris – not long enough, she thought, to have put Oxford out of her mind. It was a serious drawback to air travel in her view – no gentle departure from one place and slow, anticipatory approach to another. She disliked at any time being hurled into the sky above London and thrown down again almost immediately at Paris. But *this* sudden arrival was more difficult to cope with than most. What Geoffrey had said wasn't true – what she was feeling was anything but gladness; more like a stupidly adolescent kind of anxiety. She resisted the temptation to check the state of her hair and lipstick, telling herself that all that had brought her there was a funeral and the need to pour a little oil on her mother's troubled temperament. Even so the conviction remained that this arrival was unlike any other, and that in her own unsettled state it might turn out to be crucial.

Dismissed by officials who showed no interest in her, she looked for Pierre, realising that he would be less noticeable here among his own countrymen than he had seemed in Oxford. She saw a hand raised to attract her attention, but it was Henri Rivaux who stood waiting to collect her.

'My dear Louise, I'm so very glad to see you.' His face beneath the closely-trimmed grey hair looked as tired as his voice had sounded on the telephone. She had come to like him very much over the years of his marriage to her mother, and thought that Nadia had been lucky in her husbands – all excitement and bohemian charm in John Standish, and steady, kind affection in this man. 'It was good of you to come quickly,' Henri was saying, '. . . too quickly for Pierre to rearrange his schedule, or *he* would be here to meet you.'

'You mean he isn't in Paris?'

'He's in Geneva, keeping an appointment with an American

collector too important to be offended. The sale concerns the most rare twelfth-century Arabic instrument we have ever handled – very beautiful and very expensive.'

'I see why the mountain has to go to Mahomet,' Louise suggested, 'but not so long ago you'd have insisted on going to Geneva yourself – Pierre must have learned a lot in Oxford.'

'Oh, I'm sure he did,' Henry agreed after only the slightest pause. 'He came back not at all the man who'd left here reluctantly, confident that he didn't need teaching. But I hoped for that, of course, and felt I could rely on Oxford.'

She was grateful for the little commotion Henri made of getting her luggage and herself into the car. By the time he was sitting beside her she decided that he hadn't meant more than he'd said, and could ask him calmly about Nadia.

'Well, she was bound to be a little upset,' he explained with heroic understatement. 'André always insisted that he'd live to be a hundred and she expected him to do what he said. Apart from that she's also been very unwell. Thank God your flight was punctual – even a small delay and she would be imagining a disaster.'

'Did Grandfather tell you what was in his will? He should have done after so many years of friendship and working together.'

She thought Henri looked faintly amused at the suggestion. 'My dear, I expect it hurt him even to confide in a solicitor! We shall know his intentions after the funeral, not before. He owned the galleries, of course, and presumably they will pass to his only child – your mother.'

'Well, yes . . . but despite being married to John Standish a long time ago, she knows very little about paintings. Can you and Pierre cope with those, as well as antiquarian books and instruments?'

'No, because *we* don't know enough either. Something, of course, but not enough. André was an acknowledged expert, called in to give an opinion whenever there was doubt. We need to keep that authority if we can.'

'So what is going to happen?'

'Nadia thinks she has the solution,' he said in an expression-less voice, '. . . a Polish count, who *may* know something about art and certainly bows over her hand very beautifully.'

Louise suppressed a grin, but felt sorry for Henri. His only hope of a peaceful future seemed to lie in the business acumen of André Benoît, who would surely have tried to ensure that, while nominally the owner, Nadia could take no ruinous hand in the running of what he'd created. But it wasn't until they reached the tall house in the Rue Jacob that she fully understood the reality of her grandfather's death. All her memories of the place included his commanding figure. To a lonely, half-alien child he'd seemed omnipresent, but although his duty towards her had been done fairly, it had been done without loving kindness. Even now she felt cold when she walked into the house, despite Marthe's smile of welcome.

Nadia, propped up in bed against a mound of lace-edged pillows, looked frail and tragic.

'I've been waiting and *waiting* for you,' she said piteously, '. . . thinking there'd been a terrible accident. You should have come sooner.'

'No accident, and I promise you we came as quickly as we could – *ventre à terre* the whole way from the airport! I'm going to bathe your face and brush your hair, then you'll feel more cheerful. Geoffrey sends his love, and so does William, and the Vice Chancellor *particularly* wished me to offer you his sympathy.'

Mollified by so much love and goodwill, Nadia allowed herself to be made comfortable, and even agreed that she might be able to toy with a glass of wine and a little of Marthe's good soup for luncheon. After that she would try to sleep, because she must recover enough strength to drag herself to her dear father's funeral. *Le tout* Paris would be present, of course, and somehow she must be there too, to say her farewells to Papa.

By the evening, bored with being an invalid, she managed to descend the stairs for dinner. Listening again to her reminiscences, Louise reflected, not for the first time, that beneath her mother's air of fragility and helplessness lay a streak of steel to match André's own. It must have taken real strength of will to run off in the teeth of his opposition and marry John Standish when she was a mere nineteen. Pray God André had remembered that – otherwise the Polish count might be installed with them after all.

In the course of the evening there was a telephone call from Geneva. Pierre told his father that the sale of the instrument having been concluded, he would take the first flight home in the morning. He wanted to be assured that Louise had arrived safely.

'He sounded pleased with himself, I expect,' she commented with a smile.

'Of course,' Henri agreed. 'He likes the entrepreneurial side of being a dealer – the battle of wits, judging the moment to yield or stand firm. Unlike me, he's very good at it; I'm always reluctant to see an instrument go.'

She thought it shed revealing light on father and son: Henri loving the things he handled for their own sake; Pierre's expertise acquired to enable him to hold his own with rich collectors ready to beat him down.

'The two of you make an ideal working combination – scholar and businessman,' she suggested. 'No wonder you do so well.'

'But only if they *stay* together,' Nadia put in anxiously. 'Henri tries to frighten me by saying that Pierre will want to leave us and launch out on his own. It's true he's been quiet recently, but that's because of the dreadful sadness in the house.'

Patiently Henri corrected her. 'I only said, my love, that he came back from Oxford unsettled . . . not quite himself. It's understandable – there comes a time when young men need to consider the direction in which they want to go.'

Louise turned a deaf ear to the slight question mark in Henri's voice, implying some knowledge on her part of what had been unsettling in Oxford. She thought she might have said instead that the time for deciding on directions came even more imperatively to dissatisfied women hovering on the edge of middle age. However hard she tried to concentrate on other things her mind went on worrying at problems all her own. Now that she'd been summoned away from North Oxford, could she bear to go back? Would happiness bought at Geoffrey's expense prove to be no happiness at all? How long could Pierre imagine that he needed *her* to complete his life? She thought she knew the answers to these questions; but it might be hard to remember them tomorrow when she faced him again.

As usual, of course, nothing about their meeting went according to the vision she imagined. One moment she was alone in the gallery, examining some limited edition prints; the next Pierre was standing in front of her, at least an hour before she thought he could possibly arrive.

'I took an overnight train,' he said in answer to the question in her face. 'Heavy snow was forecast for Geneva today. I couldn't bear the thought of not getting out of there.'

She smiled then, because she'd missed him, and because his hands suddenly holding hers said that Geneva wasn't where he wanted to be when *she* was in Paris. The answers she'd struggled to find were still clear in her mind, but already she could foresee how hard it would be to persuade herself that she must cling to them.

'You should think kindly of Geneva,' she suggested, not quite steadily, '. . . remember it as a city where you had a great success.'

'I could probably have had that here. Next time I'll convince my father that the buyer must come to *us* – it's bad psychology to do it the other way round!'

Success had made him self-confident, even a little arrogant again, she thought. Perhaps the scholar and the businessman wouldn't always combine happily. But André Benoît would have said that Pierre was right – they were dealers with artifacts to sell, not the curators of a museum. His brown hands released hers to wave the subject aside impatiently.

'Where would you like to dine this evening, *chérie* – what about the Tour d'Argent?'

'Wonderful, I'm sure,' she agreed, 'but Marthe is cooking a special dinner for us here.' She smiled at the sudden frustration in his face. 'Pierre, the Tour sounds lovely, but we *couldn't* hurt Marthe's feelings.'

'I could very easily, but it seems that you can't. I'm afraid living in England has made you sentimental, my darling one! Never mind – I'm so glad you're here that I shall behave with perfect English restraint – for the moment, at least!'

It was on the tip of her tongue to say how much she hoped he would, because the eve of her grandfather's funeral didn't seem the right time to be thinking about themselves. Pierre might see hypocritical English pretence in *that*, of course – why not just admit that their own lives were what truly interested them? Looking at his expressive face, she was certain that the answer to one of her questions had been wrong: in some way that seemed strange and wonderful she *was* still needed for his happiness. It should have been a cause for joy, but life was never straightforward. Just when she wanted him to convince her that awakened longing was another name for love, it was Geoffrey who seemed to be invading her mind – because the man who stoically went towards defeat in Oxford was the same one who had walked into this very gallery on a hot, long-ago afternoon and offered her escape from loneliness.

Uncertain what to say, she was relieved when Henri interrupted them, to greet his son and be told how the Swiss transaction had gone. They must wait until after the funeral, she told herself – nothing could be decided until then. But Henri was perceptive, and Nadia inconveniently blessed with an intuitive gift for landing on what one most needed her to miss. Pierre might imagine that he was behaving with English restraint, but there was no chance of Nadia being deceived about the electric tension that now seemed to spark across any gap between them. *She* would hear the different note in Pierre's voice when he spoke to her daughter, and watch the way he smiled at her.

The funeral was as solemn, formal and expensive as André would have believed he deserved. Nadia, veiled, caped and sable-furred like Anna Karenina, looked exotically tragic, supported by Henri on one side and Pierre on the other. Feeling scarcely adequate herself in a simple black suit and velvet beret, Louise walked behind them, shamefully aware that her mind was wandering from the present obsequies. On numerous visits to the Rue Jacob over the years since her marriage she had thought only that it looked, sounded, smelled, and even tasted different from North Oxford. Now she was trying to remember what it had been like to live there. Did she want, for good this time, to be immersed in all its Frenchness again?

After the funeral rites local dignitaries, leading figures in the world of art, and artists whose careers André had promoted, crammed into the Galeries Benoît, to drink champagne and speculate among themselves about the future. Busy talking to guests, Pierre had had to surrender his place beside Nadia and she was now flanked, Louise noticed, by her Polish friend. He smiled a good deal and only occasionally allowed a proprietorial glance to wander round the paintings on display.

At last the guests went home, but Maître Clément remained, for the last act in the long drama of André's life. Gathered round the table in the dining room upstairs, they listened first to what they expected: bequests to servants, to an art charity or two, and other institutions in which André had taken a professional interest. Then came more interesting clauses. The family house in Aix, rented out for years to a painting school, was now to be endowed so that struggling students could attend it free of charge. André's extensive property in Paris, excluding the two houses in the Rue Jacob, was left entirely to Nadia. Finally came the thunderbolt delivered by the lawyer after a telling pause. The Galeries Benoît, and the premises that housed them, went to his grand-daughter, Louise Carmichael, provided that she came back to Paris to run them. This, the lawyer concluded amid a stunned silence, had been his client's dearest wish – that his grandchild should return where she belonged. If she refused then she would merely share ownership equally with Henri Rivaux, and his son, Pierre.

Louise struggled to pin down at least two coherent thoughts, aware that the turmoil in her own mind was reflected on the faces of the others. One was that the poor Polish protégé would soon be seeking another patroness; the other was that she might have expected her grandfather to play just some such outrageous game with them as this. The truth, known clearly to André

Benoît, was that she had never 'belonged' there, either as child or adolescent. It was from *not* belonging that Geoffrey had set out to rescue her. She glanced in her mother's direction and saw tears of anguish beginning to trickle down Nadia's white face.

'Why not *me*?' she asked brokenly. '*I* should have been the one to carry on the name of Benoît. Poor dear Papa must have been too ill, too *dérangé*, to understand what was being done.' She stared with deep distrust at the lawyer she had admired until a moment ago, but he was inured to innuendo and insult by long experience, Louise thought – he took no offence at all.

'I assure you, Madame Rivaux, that your father was clear, and precise, about his intentions. All I have done is to put them before you in legal terms just as precisely.'

Henri moved to place a gently restraining hand on his wife's shoulder. 'Of course, *Maître*,' he said in an unemphatic voice. 'It has been a long, sad day, you understand . . .'

'And you are all a little *dérangés*, of course,' the lawyer agreed calmly. He looked at André Benoît's grand-daughter, wishing that his client had been more forthcoming about her. In other circumstances he would have found it amusing to guess what she would decide to do: set aside her life in England, or forego a considerable inheritance in Paris? But although he could see distress in the face opposite him under its charming velvet beret, there was no gleam of pleasure or excitement to give her inclinations away.

'I shall wait to hear from you, Madame,' he said.

A transforming smile thanked him for his services, but she still didn't speak. He was shaken hands with, reluctantly in Nadia's case, and went away wondering as usual what uproar would break out as soon as the door closed behind him.

Nadia, inevitably, plunged in headlong. Staring at her daughter, and then at Pierre, she said ominously, 'Now I understand. I didn't at first, because it seemed so . . . so *extraordinaire*, but at last the picture falls into place. Oxford was unsettling, Henri said – I see now that of course it was.'

Her husband's hand held up to stem the flow had no effect, but she was forced to stop in order to draw breath. Pierre took charge himself, smiling at her with all the charm and persuasiveness that he could muster.

'Dearest Nadia, there is *still* a lot you don't know, but none of it is bad or underhand, I promise you. Of André's strange will, of course, we knew nothing, but the rest we *can* share with you.'

This time the interruption came from Louise herself, who sprang to her feet and stood facing them – a slender, elegant figure in her simple black suit, but also a lonely one, it seemed to Henri. She smiled apologetically at Pierre for what she was about to say, but sounded too definite to be ignored.

'There's *nothing* to be shared at the moment. First, I need to think – by myself. No, there's something else to do even before that – I must try not to hate my grandfather. Tomorrow will be soon enough to talk . . . and more appropriate in any case.'

Reminded that they had just attended a funeral, Nadia could only point out that, far from hating André Benoît, his granddaughter should be feeling deeply grateful to him.

'Well, I *may* come to that in time,' Louise agreed, 'although it would go very much against the grain.' She smiled again at her mother's outraged expression, glanced briefly at Pierre, and shook her head in answer to the question his face was asking. It would be difficult enough to resolve her dilemma, but she was quite certain that it had to be done alone.

After a sleepless night, tired as she felt, it was a relief to get up. Pierre would arrive soon from his own apartment in the next arrondissement, and it was clear in her mind that she wanted to postpone talking to him. The morning was too bitingly cold to linger out of doors, but a workmen's café provided her with strong, scalding coffee to put fresh heart into her. Then she crossed the river to the Ile de la Cité and took refuge in the candlelit darkness of Notre-Dame. With the surface of her mind she followed the brisk recital of the first Mass of the day, but at a deeper level the decision fumbled towards during the long night was being tested and found to bear the weight she put on it. Now she was ready to present herself at the chambers of Maître Clément.

An hour afterwards she was back in the Rue Jacob, and a taut-faced Pierre met her almost at the door.

'We must talk *now*,' he insisted in a low voice. 'It's no help to go wandering the streets of Paris alone until you're too exhausted to think clearly.'

She didn't argue or even reply, but led the way into what had been André's small office at the rear of the gallery. With the door closed, Pierre's expression relaxed into sudden tenderness.

'Now may we say good morning properly?' His arms reached out to enfold her, but she held him off with both hands pressed against the rough tweed of his jacket.

'I wasn't wandering the street,' she said gravely. 'I've been to see the lawyer.'

A flicker of irritation crossed his face and she knew why: he would have preferred her to invite him to go too. But it wasn't important; he was certain he knew what she had said to Clément. She could *feel* his confidence.

'You're the boss now, my dear one. What was it nervous employees always said? . . . I shall try to give satisfaction!'

He had no doubt that he would – she could see certainty shining in his face. Their future together was bright, and quite beyond doubt.

'I decided to refuse – *that*'s what I've told Maître Clément,' she said baldly.

He wanted to shake her, shout at her that she'd had no right to say anything at all, much less the wrong thing, without consulting him. But she was her own woman . . . now, and always would be; if he didn't manage to remember that he would lose her.

'My dearest girl, *why*, in God's name?' he asked almost quietly. 'There isn't a more respected art-house in Paris, leaving aside the reputation my father has also built up.'

'That's a part of my reason. I could gradually learn, of course, but at the moment I know *less* than Henri does about paintings, not more. My grandfather shouldn't have needed telling that.'

'He always said that you had flair – more vital to a dealer than anything else.'

'But what he probably didn't say was that I was to be bribed to come back because he couldn't bear our independence from him. My mother finally toed the line he'd marked out and took Henri; thank God she did because your father's been wonderfully kind . . . but I refuse to be manipulated by André from the other side of the grave.'

Pierre's hands held her in a grip that would have hurt, had they been aware of it, but both were intent only on the knowledge that what was said now would decide their lives.

'Your grandfather was right about Nadia,' he said calmly, '. . . why not believe that he might be right about you? Or are you going to pretend that your English life and your English husband have satisfied you?'

She tried to remember that he had reason to think her dissatisfied – she had *given* him reason. But still his confidence and his question angered her.

'They are what I chose,' she reminded him.

'When you were nineteen, and knew no better. Nadia upset you yesterday, by implying that there'd been some plot between us by which *she* stood to lose. Well, there *was* no plot, and if you stood to gain nothing from André's will I should still love and want you as I do now.' His hands suddenly cupped her face, making a prisoner of her while his mouth covered hers. When he finally lifted his head she was trembling, and he smiled at her with the joy and certainty that he had won. 'Forget the will, my love – just say that you'll stay here with me, learning what real happiness is. Nadia won't need telling. She knows there's something between us.'

She took a deep breath to steady herself and pulled his hands away.

'Dear Pierre, the "something between us" amounts to this: *your* brief attraction to a woman ten years older than yourself, and my rather shameful longing to be made to feel young and desirable again! It's intoxicating, but not enough for lasting happiness, and even if it were, I have a husband facing the second dreadful heartbreak of his life. I couldn't add to it by leaving him now. You and Henri will enjoy running the galleries together, and I shall go home.'

The finality in her voice left him feeling sick with the

sharpness of his disappointment and anger. Barely able to control himself, he walked away and stood watching her from the door. 'You might persuade Clément to give you time to change your mind, Louise, but it's more than I can do, because I understand the truth now — there will always be some fresh reason why you're unable to drag yourself away from Oxford. André was wrong — it *is* where you belong after all.'

'It's the conclusion I came to, too,' she agreed quietly.

The furious contempt in his face was so far removed from its expression a moment ago that she seemed to be staring at a different man. Then the slam of the door echoed in her mind — a door closed on an episode in their lives that they would both recover from sooner or later.

Her final conversation with Henri and Nadia took time and patience, but at last she was free to leave and adamant that Henri, who had much to see to, shouldn't waste the rest of the morning taking her to the airport.

'You'll have to keep a sharp eye on Nadia, you and Pierre,' she said as she waited in the street with him for her taxi to appear. 'But you've had long years of practice at that!'

'A sharp but loving eye,' he promised. 'Don't worry about Nadia or the galleries, my dear — but I wish I felt as confident about you and Pierre.'

She kissed him with affection, grateful that he didn't probe her wounds. 'No need to worry about *us*, either — we shall both survive our ailments.' But Henri's anxious frown remained, and it was a relief to see the taxi arriving. She didn't look back at the Rue Jacob as they drove away. There would be other visits there in days to come, but not for a long time — not until the memory of this one had faded.

At the airport she was obliged to wait; the next flight but one for London had a vacant seat. There was time to drink cups of coffee she didn't want and to try to contact Geoffrey. He didn't answer the telephone at Norham Grove and her next call was to the College. Jukes admitted that the Senior Tutor was there, but far too occupied for trivial conversations with his wife. He, Jukes, would deliver any message, and in stentorian tones that suggested he was trying to shout across the English Channel he insisted on repeating her message word for word. Eventually Louise was able to hang up, secure in the knowledge that anyone within earshot at St Barnabas now knew that Mrs Carmichael was taking a flight from Paris that would arrive at Heathrow at six o'clock. Moreover, if her husband was unable to meet her she would find her own way home.

She was scarcely aware of the long wait or the journey; only of looking at what went on around her through a lonely fog of exhaustion. The one certainty she clung to was that, in having done what seemed right for everyone else, it must eventually prove right for her as well. Her only conscious hope was that Geoffrey would sense her need from the message Jukes delivered; just this once she wanted him to put St Barnabas in second place, not her.

Back at Heathrow she waited in the Arrivals lounge, feeling more and more like a parcel that no one seemed to want. The other passengers were either claimed or had no doubt what to do next themselves, and only she remained, bleakly facing the prospect of finding an Oxford bus somewhere in the sleet-filled darkness outside. She was already at the door when a man stopped just in front of her, out of breath from some headlong dash towards the building. Melting sleet ran down his face and beard, and not for the first time in her acquaintance with him Daniel Goodman looked formidably angry. Even so, it didn't occur to her that his being there had anything to do with her until he fetched enough breath to speak.

'I thought I was going to miss you – the weather's been atrocious all the way, and the traffic worse. Sorry if I kept you hanging about.'

'You mean you've come instead of Geoffrey?' It was madness to sound sharp when she should have fallen on his neck with gratitude, but his apology, almost thrown at her, had been no apology at all. For some reason she couldn't even guess at, he'd allowed himself to be saddled with the job of meeting her, but he clearly resented the fact.

'As it happened I was in the lodge when you telephoned, but I could have been the other side of the quad and still heard

Jukes' conversation with you. I knew that Carmichael wouldn't be able to meet you, but I couldn't think of a good enough excuse not to volunteer instead.'

She might have heard the glimmer of exasperated humour in his reply but for an anxiety that suddenly presented itself.

'Why *not* Geoffrey? Is he ill . . . hurt in some way?'

'No – only locked in a College crisis with the rest of the Fellows. It seems that the front runner for the Mastership scratched from the race almost at the last minute. With a lunatic sense of fairness your husband argued for postponing the election to give the opposition time to find another candidate; but that seems unlikely to happen. I'm only an onlooker, of course, but I think I'd put money now on *you* being the next Master's wife.'

He wasn't sure how he expected her to react, but certainly not as she did – by suddenly beginning to laugh, quietly but uncontrollably. To make it even more disquieting, she seemed quite unaware that they were still standing in the rainswept darkness, getting very wet indeed. Alerted at last to some danger he didn't understand, he grabbed the valise that she was holding and put his other arm round her shoulders in a fierce grip that sobered her enough to stare at him.

'Shall we see whether we can make it back to Oxford?' he suggested with as much calmness as he could manage. 'God knows if I can even find the way, but if not, you'll have to help me.'

CHAPTER TWELVE

He managed to find where he'd left the car in the dark, cold entrails of the multi-storey car park, and felt marginally more confident that he could now cope with the rest of this strange night.

'Get out of that wet coat,' he said, shedding his own. 'You'll be better without it.'

She didn't argue – might at that moment, he thought, have obeyed whatever instruction she was given. She had slipped out of normal connection with the rest of the world, and now was only linked to it by what she heard. Inside the car she sat with her eyes closed, head resting against the seat-back as if she couldn't support its weight any longer. They need never move at all, she seemed to say; she would just go on sitting there.

Daniel silently commended them to as many saints as he could call to mind, explained that they had serious work to do, and pointed the car in what he prayed was the right direction. An hour later, safely steering into a Thames-side village, he knew the rest of the journey would be straightforward. Now that he dared take his eyes off the road he could pay attention to his passenger. She hadn't spoken since they left the airport, and although her hands were gripped tightly in her lap she could do nothing to stop the shudders that shook her body. Her condition worried him, but when he suddenly turned the car off the road she was aware of the fact.

'This isn't Norham Grove.'

'Not yet. It's a friendly pub in Wallingford, called the George. I don't know about you but I'm hungry, and sick of driving through sleet and snow. This is where we stop for a while.'

Still obedient to the authority in his voice, she got out of the car and stumbled after him. The lamplit building in front of them seemed welcoming, and she had very little reason to arrive anywhere else.

'You look terrible,' Daniel said, as they got inside the door, and he could see her clearly. The brutality of it even penetrated her exhausted daze, sending her to stare in the mirror of the ladies' room. She saw a bone-white face, shadowed eyes, and disordered hair. Terrible was the right word, and she was shocked into attending to her appearance. Neat again at least, she found Daniel waiting for her at a quiet table beyond the bar.

'Soup and steak already ordered,' he announced, getting to his feet, 'but I let the boss here choose some wine, knowing where my limitations lie.'

'I don't think you do,' she contradicted him for the first time, and he smiled suddenly with the relief of knowing that she had regained some control of herself again. 'Thank you for coming to fetch me,' she murmured next. 'I think I should probably have said that before.'

He tasted the wine, and made a mental note of its Châteauneuf-du-Pape label before he risked a question that seemed dangerous.

'Perhaps you don't remember but you started laughing at the airport – would you mind telling me why?'

She sipped wine herself while she decided how to answer him. In the end only the truth came to mind.

'I'd just been offered a different life in Paris. It even included a man who would have loved me very well – at least until I grew too old for him. I turned it down, believing that Geoffrey faced bitter disappointment here and might need me for the first time in twenty years of marriage. Doesn't that strike *you* as funny?'

Their soup arrived, creating a diversion, and when the waiter had gone again she made a little gesture abandoning a subject on which she didn't intend to say any more. With her mind working again, conventional politeness had returned as well. 'I hope your Christmas in Vermont went happily after all.'

'It went much as I expected,' Daniel said deliberately. 'My daughter sulked because she hadn't been allowed to bring her boyfriend along, my son reckoned me a pain in the neck for refusing to let him go to an all-night skiing party, and my wife declined my invitation to join me in Oxford for a visit. She is going to be much too busy persuading her sisterhood in New York that this is the "year of the new woman".'

He had gone home with such longing for them, she remembered, but had obviously been grievously disappointed. 'Don't blame your wife for taking her career seriously,' she tried to suggest. 'She might have hoped you could take your sabbatical at a time when she wasn't launching an important public-relations campaign.'

'Sabbaticals come when they come, as you very well know. Apart from that, I prefer my "woman" as she was – making a worthwhile job of being wife and mother and linchpin of what we laughingly call a civilised society.' The angry grief in his face defeated her. As a modern-day female, no doubt she ought to support Karen Goodman – women were required to stick together if they were ever to achieve parity with men; but she couldn't help feeling that some of the sillier, shriller cries of feminists had done them more harm than good.

'For God's sake don't be tactful,' he said acidly. 'Say what you think – I'm an intolerant, jumped-up male, still ingrained with the outdated prejudices of the working class I spring from, but made arrogant as well by too much education and a bit of success!'

'I doubt if I could have put it better myself,' she agreed with a straight, judicial face.

He glared long enough for her to calculate the chances of finishing her journey alone after all. But either hunger kept him there to eat his steak, or he remembered that she'd been invited to agree with him. At last even a reluctant grin tugged at his mouth.

'I was worried about you a while ago . . . I don't know why, now. Louise Carmichael seems to be herself again.'

She nodded, but answered him with a seriousness he didn't expect. 'The restorative powers of wine and food . . . and shared disappointments, I expect. Unhappiness usually brings loneliness with it as well, because stupidly one imagines that no one else is suffering. You and I aren't what could be called friends, but we have something in common. It seems to help me to know that, so perhaps it will also help you.'

He didn't confirm or deny it, but she had the sudden conviction that she'd mistaken the reason for his hostility at the airport; it had been part of a general rage with life for always disregarding what human beings needed to make them happy.

'The existence here that you were tempted to ditch – what happens to it if your husband becomes the new Master?' he asked suddenly.

'We move into the Lodging, and I'm allowed to visit my garden occasionally, I suppose. Otherwise nothing very much changes, except that while Geoffrey becomes even more immersed in St Barnabas, I find other ways to fill my days. I shall join things, I expect, do good works, and interfere in the lives of undergraduates who would probably prefer well-meaning ladies like me *not* to offer them sherry and useless advice.' She gave a little shrug that put the matter aside, and tried to smile at him. 'What about you, Dr Goodman – is the old-fashioned male chauvinist going to stay here without a visit from his wife; or haul down his colours and go home?'

'Oh, I shall stay, and give my inflammatory lectures and write my controversial book. The curse of men like me is that we can't admit we're ever in the wrong! In any case there'd be no point in going back. I'm supposed to keep clear of Ann Arbor while my locum is there, and I'm certainly not needed in New York.'

His bright, pale eyes lingered on the face opposite him – a charming face, any right-minded male would say, even in its pale, tired state. Pierre Rivaux must have done his level best to keep her in Paris. *There* was another disappointed man – the world seemed to be full of them. Only Geoffrey Carmichael looked set to get what he'd wanted, and he'd be too busy to notice that his wife had been tempted not to come back at all.

Daniel drank off the last of his wine and managed a wry smile. 'Shall we brave that damned weather outside again? I think it's time I took you home.'

The second stage of their journey was no more conversational than the first had been, but there was a difference now.

They were both acquainted with the grief of happiness lost or never found, and a shared condition altered things.

There was no sign of Geoffrey at the house, but Ruth descended the stairs immediately – to welcome her sister-in-law home, she said, but in reality to complain about Madeleine Torrance.

'Such a pity you had to go away at all, but I suppose that was unavoidable,' she conceded reluctantly. 'The girl has made a perfect nuisance of herself, calling in to make sure that Geoffrey "wasn't lonely". As if *she* could be a companion to him!'

'She might have thought she was being neighbourly,' Louise pointed out with as much conviction as she could manage. But it wasn't a great deal and she couldn't blame Ruth for looking unconvinced.

'Madeleine doesn't know the meaning of the word. She flaunts her body like an alley cat, and that's the only kind of attraction she can offer.'

'Well, it *is* a beautiful body,' Louise said fairly. 'I suppose anyone owning it would think it ought to be appreciated!' Then she smiled at Ruth's expression. 'All right, I know she's tiresome, and not very likeable to *us* at least, but it can't be easy for her to have suddenly had to come to terms with the past. She's Anna's daughter – there must be some good in her.'

'Most unlikely in my view. After all, she's of very . . . very . . .'

'Mixed blood,' Louise finished calmly, seeing that even her sister-in-law had been stopped short by the tactlessness of the remark. 'Never mind; we shall have to hope for the best. Now if you'll excuse me I must get unpacked in case Geoffrey remembers to come home.'

Aware that there was nothing more to say, even in defence of a brother who might have been expected to welcome his wife back, Ruth went reluctantly away. Louise listened to her large feet plodding up the stairs and felt a wave of sickening regret for what she'd handed back to Maître Clément. Even if it had held no other charm at all a life in Paris would have meant not sharing her home with a woman as uncongenial as this one. But justice – lunatic justice, Daniel Goodman would probably have said – insisted she remember that *she* had been brought into Ruth's home, and probably found to be just as uncongenial. Something else also struck her about the conversation they'd just had: Geoffrey hadn't yet found the time or the inclination to tell his sister what was happening at St Barnabas; otherwise Ruth would certainly have wanted to talk about that rather than Madeleine Torrance.

She was in the kitchen, making coffee for something to do, when her husband at last walked in. After an absence of only a few days she looked at him with fresh eyes, trying to see him as a young woman like Madeleine might judge him. His features hadn't been blurred in middle age with the excess flesh that came to most people. Handsomeness, even a semblance of youth, remained intact unless he looked gaunt and tired, as he did now.

'My dear, welcome home . . . you got here safely, I see.' His hands sketched a little gesture, admitting the futility of the remark, but the hesitation in wrapping his arms about her had been fatal. Now he could only recognise another opportunity to behave naturally lost, and try to smile at her. 'Forgive me for not meeting you myself. I would have sent a taxi, of course, but Goodman stepped in. I'm afraid you had a miserable drive home.'

In another moment, she thought despairingly, they would be discussing the weather.

'Never mind the journey, Geoffrey,' she insisted. 'Just tell me what has been happening *here*. Daniel Goodman mentioned a crisis, but all he knew about it was that Justin Harkness had withdrawn.'

She sat down at the kitchen table, but Geoffrey shook his head at the coffee she had poured. 'I think we need something stronger as well!' He walked out of the room and reappeared with glasses and the brandy decanter.

'What has happened is that we've been arguing all day, in little huddles, in larger groups, and finally in a full meeting of the governing body. It was finally decided that the election *must* take place as planned, but it means that my chief opponents, effectively, are left without a candidate. Some of them will vote for Edward, on the time-honoured Oxford principle of electing someone in order to keep someone else out – me, in this case! – but we shan't know how many of them will do that until the election takes place.'

'But *why* did Harkness withdraw? I thought he'd agreed to be nominated.'

Geoffrey took a sip of brandy before he answered. 'You rarely read the *Gazette*, or concern yourself with the arcane workings of the University, so you don't even know, perhaps, that a controversy has been raging about this year's Encaenia – whether or not an honorary degree should be conferred on the Prime Minister. These things aren't as a rule hotly debated in Congregation; in fact they're scarcely debated at all. But more smoke and fire have been generated over *this* issue than over anything else that has happened for years.'

'No need to explain why,' Louise said slowly. 'Even I am aware that she's seen as a dangerous threat to entrenched and sacred academic privilege. The wickedly misguided woman wants to abolish security of tenure, for one thing. No wonder the dear dons don't want her honoured!'

'Let's say that *enough* of them don't to have managed to get the proposal voted down – but the debate has become public, unfortunately, and it's a serious embarrassment to the Officers of the University looking for increased Government grants.'

'And might it not also be hurtful or humiliating to a woman who deserves better?' Louise flashed. 'If disgust at that petty revenge is Justin Harkness's reason for turning his back on Oxford, then I think the *better* of him.'

'So do I,' Geoffrey admitted unexpectedly. 'The whole business has been deplorable, and harmful to an institution that prides itself on tolerance. But Robert Morgan and his supporters seriously misjudged their candidate. His public political line may have confused them, but he's above all else a businessman, and the Prime Minister's "value for money" philosophy seems as reasonable to him as it does to her. He sees the decision to withhold the degree as an outrage.' Geoffrey rubbed a hand over tired eyes, determined even now to be scrupulously fair.

'That's only one side of the argument, of course. An ancient university isn't just a business, and can't be treated as such; but it's too late in the night to get on to *that* subject.' He stared at his wife's face and registered its pallor. 'You look even more exhausted than I feel. Perhaps we've both had enough of today.'

Exhausted she was, and fuelled now by purely nervous energy, but there was still something left to say. 'The day began for me in the offices of Maître Clément. My grandfather's will suggested that I might like to take over the running of the galleries – that they should become mine, in other words. The proviso was that I should go back to Paris.'

The silence in the room was suddenly so thick and heavy that she found it hard to breathe. At last Geoffrey put down the glass he was still holding; his hand didn't tremble, she noticed. 'And you went to inform the lawyer that you would?'

'I went to say that I would *not*. It means that ownership will now be shared by Henri, Pierre, and myself.'

Geoffrey looked up at last and stared at her. 'You might come to a different decision – if you'd known what was happening here?'

After another long pause she answered him. 'I might, but perhaps not; in any case it's irrelevant now. We shall have the Master's Lodging to look forward to instead.' A smile, self-mocking though he didn't realise that, touched her pale mouth for a moment. 'Let's hope the excitements in store won't prove too much for us!'

She was in bed but still awake when she heard him come upstairs, go into his dressing room and quietly close the door. Among all the things that it was now too late for was certainly passion, or even the gentlest kind of shared delight; but oh, dear God, how even *comfort* would have been welcome! Desolation rose and crashed down on her with the roar of an ocean wave, and she wept into her pillow like a child – for past mistakes that could never be put right, and for all that the long years in front of her seemed not to hold.

Madeleine had news to announce to her mother at breakfast next morning.

'Louise Carmichael is back. I'm not surprised, of course – I could have told her it would be a wasted journey.'

Anna's face looked merely puzzled. '*Chérie*, Louise went to attend her grandfather's funeral – what should be wasted about that?'

Madeleine went on playing with the thick plait of hair that hung over her shoulder. 'That was the *excuse*. She went to chase Pierre. The poor thing imagined because he paid her a little attention here that he'd go on wanting her. Out of sight, out of mind – I could have told her *that* would be Pierre Rivaux's philosophy.'

'Madeleine, leave your hair alone, please, and *look* at me,' Anna insisted, trying to speak quietly. 'What you imagine you know and what is real are often two different things. I wouldn't blame Pierre for loving Louise – I'd expect him to, and any man who isn't a blind fool to do the same – but she is Geoffrey Carmichael's wife. Much as I love *you*, I shall never forgive you if you repeat what you've just said to anyone else.' Then, as if to show that the subject of Pierre Rivaux was closed, she spoke in a different tone of voice. 'How do you know Louise is back?'

'Because I saw her being brought home last night – by Daniel Goodman! Geoffrey's *wife* was smiling very sweetly at *him*, but I suppose I mustn't say that either. The only man she pays no attention to at all is her husband, if you ask me.'

'I *don't* ask you,' Anna said coldly. 'No doubt Dr Goodman met Louise as a kindness, because her husband was unable to. And that can be the end of this stupid conversation.'

Madeleine smiled at her mother's flushed face. 'Very stupid,' she agreed. 'For once Daniel was being the good friend and neighbour which usually he is *not*, I think. Me, I have been that also to poor, lonely Geoffrey. You should at least be glad about *that*!' She got up from the breakfast table, stretching her arms above her head in a gesture designed to show the compact, curved perfection of her body beneath the sweater and brief, straight skirt she wore. Blowing her mother a kiss, she danced out of the room, announcing that sour-faced *Madame la Directrice* would be waiting with another lecture on unpunctuality if she didn't now run all the way to Norham Road.

Anna stayed sitting where she was in a room that seemed very empty without her daughter's presence. She was well acquainted with emptiness. That had been her whole life after the death of Walther Ouspenska. She had loved him almost as she loved Jesus Christ – knowing them both as her Saviours. Paris without him had seemed so unbearable that she'd chosen instead the place he'd told her about. The reward for trusting him had been to find her first true friend in Louise Carmichael. But at last had come the joy of being given Madeleine back again.

Now, three months later, there was still joy, but there was anxiety as well. Her daughter wasn't to blame for that. She was the child she was – a hybrid, instinctive creature begotten of the mingled blood and genes of Anna Lazlo and Luc Torrance. The woman he had married had tried without success to force her into Dijon's narrow, provincial mould.

Anna didn't mind anxiety on her own account – she almost welcomed it as something she owed the child she'd been forced to surrender. But grief to others was a different matter. What held her motionless now in the empty room was the fear growing for weeks past that the possibility of causing pain didn't occur to her daughter. The perception that what she said or did might hurt people whose lives touched hers seemed, in Madeleine, to be entirely missing.

CHAPTER THIRTEEN

The information Madeleine had given her mother was also known in the Master's Lodging.

'Louise is back, I saw her this morning,' Edwina Wharton said with a note in her voice that Humphrey recognised.

'And you're relieved about that,' he suggested, 'because you were afraid the siren song of Paris might have tempted her to stay there.'

Not for the first time he'd seen more than she expected him to, and it came, of course, of opening the College to women students – they had wonderfully enlarged his experience of the human condition. Edwina thought he would have preferred St Barnabas to remain the all-male stronghold it had been for centuries, but he was the least arrogant of men, only stubborn when it came to principles; about opinions he was ready to admit that he might be wrong. She loved him more than life itself, and found it hard to forgive Robert Morgan for the unnecessary trouble he had caused. Robert's noisy Gwyneth she now went out of her way to avoid.

'It was a tiring day for you yesterday,' she said next, meaning by it that her husband's fragile health shouldn't have been put to so much strain.

'Tiring, but satisfactory in the end. Thank God my casting vote settled the argument. The College will have had quite enough uncertainty by the time the Statutes say the election must take place; an extra postponement would have been most unwise.'

'So Geoffrey will become the next Master?'

'Probably, though I'm afraid it isn't certain even now. Morgan's more rabid supporters will see Edward as a better short-term bet. In the nature of things he wouldn't be in the post for very long, and then they could try again; whereas Geoffrey might be blocking their way for the next twenty years.

In a sense the College loses whichever way it goes. He's the best Senior Tutor St Barnabas is likely to have, and for his own true happiness that's probably what he ought to remain.'

'Shouldn't you take Louise's true happiness into account as well?'

The dry question made Humphrey smile apologetically. 'Of course we should, but don't expect us to be more modern than we can manage, my dear! We still indulge ourselves with the old-fashioned idea that wives do what helps their husbands. In any case, Louise doesn't strike me as being any more stridently feminist than *you* have been.'

Edwina's nod acknowledged that it was true about herself. If his work had taken them to live in a Zulu encampment in Swaziland she would have gone without a second thought. But they'd been more fortunate, more certain of each other than she believed the Carmichaels were. St Barnabas being still Anglican, and rather High at that, she never spoke aloud her conviction of having simply recognised Humphrey this time round. The Chaplain might have felt obliged to frown on the idea of reincarnation, as leaning too much towards the Buddhist scheme of things.

'Wifely attitudes aren't quite what they were, but Louise will manage in the Lodging if she has to,' she said, reluctant to shed more light on her friend's marriage than Humphrey had already made out for himself. 'The undergraduates are sure to love her, but Dawkins and his slaves will *not*! No more guardsmen ranks of tulips and salvias once Louise gets here.'

Edwina sounded pleased about this, and her husband knew why. Surfeited with straight rows of scarlet flowers, she had taken on the College gardener and lost, but the defeat still rankled. He smiled and then abandoned the subject of St Barnabas, afraid that she might feel her way to what troubled him most.

That afternoon, Humphrey cut short the gentle stroll he was supposed to take and called on William Standish instead. He allowed himself to be settled by the fire, and watched the poker being applied to make the coals blaze up. Aware that his friend,

146

though troubled, might not have come to unburden himself, William grinned cheerfully.

'I always think of dear old Dr Whately's dictum when I'm doing this job ... "A woman is a creature who cannot reason and pokes the fire from the top"! What would some of our present-day lady dons make of a colleague like that, I wonder?'

'Perhaps more to the point, what would an opinionated nineteenth-century divine make of *them*, or of today's unruly student body, and the tabloid reporters who sit like scavengers waiting for any tasty morsel of Oxford gossip or misjudgement that comes their way?'

'I suppose you're thinking of the honorary degree that isn't going to be conferred. Well, of course, it's been lamentably handled, and the Prime Minister could be forgiven for thinking that the huge sums of money Oxford gets from the UGC might be better spent elsewhere. But it's a two-day wonder, at the most; something else will crop up tomorrow to knock us off the front pages.'

'I know, but it has a more lasting result for the College. If Harkness had lost in a normal election his supporters would have been obliged to accept defeat gracefully – or at least, as gracefully as within them lies.'

William smiled at the dry correction, but now knew what made his visitor look so withdrawn and sad. 'Instead you're afraid that your successor is going to get a bitterly divided and unhappy inheritance because it *won't* be seen as a normal election?'

'How can it be? It's become tainted with every kind of politics – College, University, and now national as well. I wanted more than anything else, Will, to hand on to the next Master a St Barnabas in strong, sound heart, but I'm afraid that won't happen. It seems to destroy twenty-five years of work, but even that isn't important – it's the College that matters.'

William got up and busied himself with pouring sherry while he considered how to answer.

'You're wrong about the past,' he said at last. 'What happens next doesn't change or waste your contribution one iota. The College *may* – though even this isn't certain – be in for a patch of rough water, but it's met that before in half a millennium of existence, without being shipwrecked . . . so has Universitas Oxoniensis itself, if it comes to that. This is an old and wily institution, as you very well know, and there's little it hasn't discovered about survival! Geoffrey will learn when to duck and weave, and when to fight, just as you have done, I promise you.'

It was convincing as far as it went, and Humphrey chose not to point out what they both knew – that it didn't go far enough, because the dangerous middle years of the nineteen-eighties were liable to throw up problems unknown even a quarter of a century before. He drank off his sherry and aired one final worry as lightly as he could.

'It might still *not* be Geoffrey, and I doubt if dear old Edward is in a condition to do much fighting; even ducking and weaving might be beyond him!'

William stoked the fire again, looking slightly pink. 'My ex-colleagues still tend to drop in here – I expect because I'm a convenient port of call,' he mumbled. 'I wouldn't dream of interfering in College Affairs, of course, but just letting people talk seems to concentrate their minds wonderfully. I should be very surprised indeed if Geoffrey *didn't* get elected.'

Humphrey inspected his friend's guileless expression and smiled as he stood up to go. 'You're a wicked old rascal, Will. Thank God we're on the same side!'

He thought as he walked home of what Edwina would say – that in true Oxford fashion they had left undiscussed the subject of the next Master's wife – but perhaps her uncle felt equally confident about her as well.

Unaware of being the cause of so much speculation, Louise fought her own battle alone. It would have helped to share with someone else the sorry state she was in, but not even Anna – for once – would do. Her forthright friend, having recommended a lover, would say that she was mad to have turned one away, and an inheritance at the same time. The inheritance wasn't altogether gone, and Nadia's share of André's property would also one day have to be dealt with. What kept her awake at night now was the memory of Pierre, smiling at her with such tender, confident affection and waiting to hear her say that she was going to stay in Paris. He hadn't had the right to *expect* it, perhaps, but she'd given him grounds for hope. The blame was hers, however she argued it.

The daylight hours were easier to deal with. It became a test of pride to endure smilingly Ruth's interference in the running of the house, and to play to her small blind friends as usual. Unhappiness went on the attack when she was alone, but she fought back by painting with a fierce determination that produced results even Geoffrey was surprised into approving. He thought it thoroughly appropriate that John Standish's talent should have been handed on to Louise. But he was thunderstruck at hearing that she'd offered her services to the Salvation Army hostel at St Ebbes, in an effort, she explained, to do something useful.

'What could *you* possibly do for hard-core drunks and dopers except give them the price of their next fix?' he enquired more bluntly than usual. 'That's all the poor creatures want.'

'I don't think it is. They put out their hands for money, but what their eyes beg for is to have you tell them that they still belong to the human race.'

'Perhaps,' he almost shouted, 'but it doesn't have to be *you* telling them! For God's sake, my dear girl, leave them to the people who are trained to look after them. Well-meaning amateurs are the last thing they want, and I hope someone at St Ebbes had the good sense to tell you so.'

'He did. In fact he even hinted that my good intentions were suspect too; was I not perhaps some gutter-press journalist hoping to rake through ruined lives in the hope of a story?'

An abrupt gesture with her hands put the subject aside, because Geoffrey hadn't asked the only question that needed asking. The despairing wrecks who hung about Bonn Square were nothing new, so why could she not walk past now without agonising over them? If he'd been interested enough to ask her *that*, she would have answered truthfully – she'd seen in their eyes the very same emptiness that gaped, frighteningly black and cold, at the centre of her own existence. They didn't belong anywhere, and despite all the comfortable trappings of life in Norham Grove, nor did she.

Still deep in this painful train of thought, she was hauled out of it by the sound of her husband's voice – more hesitant now, perhaps even slightly on the defensive. But she didn't register that at the time, and only found afterwards that it had lodged itself in her memory.

'If you're anxious to concern yourself with people who've been treated ungenerously by Fate, why not make a start with the poor girl next door?'

Now thoroughly distracted from herself, Louise stared at him in astonishment. 'Anna's daughter . . . Madeleine? Is *that* who you're talking about?'

'There you are, you see – the immediate reaction she receives from women who might surely show her more compassion and understanding. She wears strange clothes – of course she does; she's a child of her generation – and her education includes strange gaps, as well as some painful knowledge she's too young to have. But she's trying bravely to recover from a dreadful start in life. The poor girl needs encouragement, not the sort of snobbish disapproval that she's been getting here.'

For Geoffrey, who was normally sparing with words, it was a long speech delivered with something that approached fervent heat. Louise tried to ignore the taunting echo in her mind of what Daniel had said about Anna's daughter, and hoped she sounded neither snobbish nor disapproving.

'Call her a poor girl once more, Geoffrey, and I'll scream! She's nothing of the kind. Madeleine doesn't want encouragement from me – quite the reverse, in fact. If she thought I liked the way she behaves, she'd immediately do something else. That applies to any other woman here, but most of all to *me* because . . . well, the reason doesn't matter.'

'Oh, I can guess the reason,' Geoffrey said quietly. 'She was charmed by Pierre Revaux, but instead of noticing her, he only had eyes for you.'

Assaulted both by an onrush of remembered pain, and by sheer rage as well, Louise rammed both hands against her mouth to hold back the words that would make bad worse. Her husband had almost certainly not noticed Pierre's condition himself; it had taken the 'poor girl' next door to point it out to him.

'Pierre was kind enough to . . . to imagine himself a little in love with me,' she admitted, reluctant to add to that a syllable more than she had to because it seemed disloyal as well as unpleasantly boastful. 'Madeleine is greedy where men are concerned – she wants all their attention – Pierre couldn't manage more than normal friendliness, and that wasn't enough. The gaps in her education that you mention – are *you* by any chance attending to them?' She had meant the question literally and only realised as she saw the angry colour in Geoffrey's face that she had phrased it in a way that could be misunderstood.

'Madeleine asked to be shown the College . . . have its history explained to her,' he said stiffly. 'I was glad to do that, even though I suspected that she was being kind – afraid I needed company while you were away. But she was charmingly impressed and interested, and afterwards when we came back here her way of thanking me was to cook me what she called a real French omelette. Ruth arrived as well in the middle of it – perhaps she told you?'

He would make no other explanation because none was needed. They were talking about a girl young enough to be his daughter, who had shown herself anxious to learn, and *that*, Louise knew, was what had snared him. She took a deep breath and forced herself to speak matter-of-factly.

'Ruth mentioned seeing her here. I'm sure she's intelligent, and pleasant company when she forgets her favourite role of ill-used femme fatale. It's also true that she's had the shock of discovering her real parentage, but her father and stepmother have *not* treated her unkindly. She found middle-class French provincial life too cramping, that's all.'

'As well she might have done,' Geoffrey commented unanswerably. He guessed what Louise was about to say and shook his head. 'Don't bother to repeat Daniel Goodman's opinion of her – I'm afraid it was inspired by pique. Madeleine didn't accept a rather pressing invitation to lessen *his* loneliness, and there are men who don't take kindly to being refused.'

She recognised that the argument was lost because, convinced of the rightness of a cause, her husband would cleave to it for ever. Feeling slightly sick, she made one last effort. 'Madeleine can study whatever she wants in Oxford, and her real mother is here to wrap her in love and kindness. That being so, shouldn't you leave her to Anna? She doesn't *need* help from you that could easily be misunderstood – by her, as well as by other people.'

'I'm afraid you still miss the point,' Geoffrey said coldly. 'It's my job, in fact the whole point and purpose of my life and of this place, to offer help and instruction – and indeed friendship – to young people of Madeleine's age, especially to those of them suffering from the same rootless existence as herself. Am I not to help *her*, your friend's daughter, just because a few spiteful tongues might wag that make me fearful for myself?'

Defeated by an argument that sounded not only reasonable but right, Louise allowed him to walk away, and was left remembering how the conversation had begun. To have tried to do something herself for the despairing wrecks of St Ebbes seemed a good deal less dangerous than the rescue operation Geoffrey was now determined upon.

She rode an uncomfortable seesaw of indecision for the next twenty-four hours. Perhaps Madeleine *was* the charming, innocent creature that he believed in. The girl was Anna's daughter – that had been her own reminder to Ruth. She might be thoughtless, selfish even, but how could she be evil?

Louise had almost convinced herself that it was Geoffrey who was right when at lunch-time the next day she was pursued into the driveway by her sister-in-law, red-faced and breathless.

'You've been pedalling too hard,' she surmised cheerfully, hoping for the best.

'Nothing of the kind,' Ruth gasped. 'Come indoors, please – a council of war can scarcely be held out here.'

Louise led the way into the kitchen and seeing that her visitor looked too ruffled not to be taken seriously, poured calming sherry for them both.

'Now, tell me what's wrong,' she suggested.

Ruth took a gulp from the glass she'd been given, unmindful for once that it wasn't the vegetable juice they were always supposed to believe that she preferred. 'I hope you agree with me, Louise, that *this* is a critical moment in Geoffrey's career?' She received a nod in reply, took another fortifying sip, and went on. 'Then what are you doing to prevent Madeleine Torrance ruining it for him?'

Louise stared at the flushed, indignant face opposite her, trying hard to remember that the woman it belonged to had channelled all the love she was capable of in one direction.

'Geoffrey and I have already talked about Anna's daughter,' she admitted after a small pause. 'He sees her as someone who has had a raw deal in life. Now that she's anxious to make a fresh start, he thinks she must be given encouragement.'

'And I suppose the encouragement includes drinking coffee with him in the Covered Market, where the whole of Oxford can gape at the spectacle of a senior don entertaining a girl who looks and behaves like a . . . well, I *must* say it – a strumpet!'

'The senior don is only doing what he believes he's required to do – give help where it's needed. Dear Ruth, shall we try to give Oxford broad-mindedness the benefit of the doubt and assume that drinking a cup of coffee with Madeleine in a public place – even given her odd appearance – isn't going to be the ruin of a respected academic career?'

Ruth banged down her glass and stood up – a not undignified figure, Louise admitted to herself, even in the garb of Oxfam cast-offs and strings of Indian beads. Where Geoffrey was concerned she was devoted and disinterested, and that could never be made to seem absurd.

'You won't take anything seriously unless it's a disease that threatens one of your precious plants,' she said with genuine despair. 'What *we* assume doesn't matter. It was Gwyneth Morgan's friend, Alice Watson, who "just thought she ought to mention" having seen Geoffrey with Madeleine hanging on his arm!'

Louise summoned all the resolution she possessed because it seemed important to sound as if even Alice Watson, past-mistress in the gentle art of destroying reputations, need not frighten them.

'Geoffrey's kindness to a girl who will soon grow bored with Oxford doesn't seem to be something we need get very serious about,' she insisted firmly. 'That's all it is, you know . . . just a passing kindness, but he feels bound to offer it when he thinks it's needed, *not* when it happens to suit him.'

Ruth stared at her with something that had to be recognised at last as dislike. She longed, Louise thought, to remind her sister-in-law of the inevitably pernicious effects of French blood, wherever it cropped up. But after a struggle with herself she clamped her lips together and stumped out of the kitchen instead.

Alone again, Louise heaved a sigh of relief, but her stomach rebelled at the thought of food. The image of Alice Watson's face, avid and spiteful, was vivid in her mind's eye but there was a much worse anxiety waiting to be considered – her friend Anna, whose daughter was to have been the final joy and justification of her life. Louise put away the food she couldn't eat, drank some black coffee to neutralise the effect of midday sherry, and then left the house again to seek the only source of help that came to mind.

CHAPTER FOURTEEN

For once when she knocked on William's yellow front door only Mrs Maggs was there, interrupted in a frenzy of carpet-sweeping and cushion-banging. The Professor would be away two days, she announced, and then added in a whisper in case the shame of it should be overheard by someone passing the door, 'Gone to Cambridge, Mrs C!'

There was nothing to do but pedal home again through the icy drizzle that had set in. The bleak Thames Valley weather and the sodden, grey streets she travelled through seemed to be in perfect harmony with life itself. She would have resented one of the fleeting gleams of sunlight that occasionally appeared to give the mistaken impression that Oxford in mid-winter was bearable. In such a frame of mind she didn't immediately see a gleam of hope in the large figure striding along in front of her as she turned off the Banbury Road. But courtesy demanded that she should dismount alongside him and push her bicycle the rest of the way.

'Beastly day,' she murmured, 'especially for walking. Perhaps you're taking Ruth's advice too literally.'

Daniel turned to inspect her – wet hair plastered to her head, but a beautifully shaped head, it had to be admitted; face pale and thin, but one that now seemed to give him so much pleasure that he stopped dead to deal with the knowledge flooding over him.

'Perhaps,' he agreed after a silence that seemed long, even to him, 'but I can't help it; your sister-in-law puts the fear of God into me.'

The confession made her smile despite the agitation she'd been unable to share with William. 'Ruth is now much more complimentary about you,' she reported 'despite earlier reservations.' His brief grin acknowledged the comment but he seemed to prefer to walk the rest of the way in silence. They hadn't met since he'd brought her home from the airport, and although her own recollection of the journey was hazy, she could understand it if he chose to withdraw from the Carmichael family. It wasn't encouraging for the idea just beginning to flower in her mind but desperate times, she reminded herself, called for desperate remedies.

'I could offer you tea,' she said tentatively, '. . . that is, if you're not too rushed.'

'Never too rushed for that – I'm quite getting the hang of this tea business.'

Back inside the house, she hoped that he would wait in the drawing room, but his grasp of the 'business' obviously wasn't complete. He followed her into the kitchen to watch the preparations, and she was reminded vividly of their first meeting. Now, as then, she was too aware of him at close range; but to suggest taking tea out into the garden at the beginning of February would cause him to doubt her sanity. Nervousness made her clumsy, and she upset the biscuits that she was trying to arrange, as if their presentation on a plate was crucial. It was ridiculous – what did a tasteful display of petits beurres and chocolate bourbons matter when the only purpose of the occasion was to ask another favour of this watchful, unpredictable man, who sometimes but not always appeared to be a friend?

'I wanted to talk to you,' she began suddenly. 'Well, more truthfully, I intended talking to my uncle, but for once he let me down by not being at home. He'd even gone to Cambridge, too.'

Daniel had been there long enough to realise that it made the defection worse and he knew better than to smile.

'What needed talking about?' he enquired.

'Not what – *who*! Well, the child next door, to be even more precise.'

His intelligent blue eyes held amused understanding, but she saw him shake his head. 'Not precise at all, I'm afraid. If Madeleine *were* the child you call her I doubt if there would be a problem.'

She supposed he also guessed what the problem was, thanks

to an upbringing that had been anything but sheltered. The ways of a wider world than she was familiar with were known to him and she needn't beat about the bush. '*Did* you make advances that Madeleine refused? That's what she says you did.'

His mouth wanted to twitch again at the absurd choice of word, but he answered solemnly. 'I make it a rule to direct my ... my advances *only* where they'll be welcomed.'

Oxford was dealing with his rough corners far too success-fully, she thought with a twinge of irritation — before long he'd be almost indistinguishable from any native academic. She pushed the damp, dark fringe out of her eyes with a gesture that was familiar to him now and tried again, unaware of sounding tired.

'I can't blame you for being amused — this *is* a ridiculous con-versation, but it touches on something serious.'

'Shall I guess?' Daniel suggested with a sudden change of tone. 'Having been turned down by me, and by Pierre Rivaux, Madeleine is now aiming her darts at your husband. You're afraid that gossip could hurt him at St Barnabas, but the cause of it is the daughter of your dear friend. It's Anna's bringer of joy who turns out to be a sex-mad, self-obsessed child-woman convinced that she's Helen of Troy.'

'If your description of her is right she's also a very competent actress,' Louise said slowly. 'Geoffrey is convinced that her outward appearance is nothing to go by. Underneath it she's charmingly wistful and intelligent — the kind of a girl that he would have wanted a daughter of his own to be. Perhaps *he*'s right; but nobody looking at them together — and Ruth assures me that most of Oxford is — would be charitable enough to believe it.'

'You could try telling him that he's liable to be misunder-stood.'

'I have, and merely seemed to confirm what Madeleine has already hinted at. It's her fate to be harassed by predatory males like you, and misunderstood by women like me. If we *are* being wickedly unfair then Geoffrey must come as a revelation to her — a courteous, gentle man who merely wants to show her kindness, at some probable cost to himself.'

Daniel was shaking his head again. 'Fatal – if you can't fight as Madeleine does, don't fight at all. You'll never win by tying yourself in knots, trying to be merciful.'

'And there, I suppose, speaks a man with a New York childhood behind him!' Louise commented with a faint smile. But her eyes were still shadowed with anxiety. 'I have no faith in Madeleine and I'd hate her if I could, but she reminds me too much of my mother. They can't help being bored by other women, and they *need* the ardent attentions of men.' She picked up a teaspoon and stared at it as if she hadn't seen it before. There was more difficulty than she'd anticipated in what was to come next, but she took a deep breath and struggled on. 'Madeleine prefers *older* men – she told me so the first time we met. I suppose you wouldn't ... as it were ... consider distracting her from Geoffrey?'

A silence fell in which she had time to memorise the pattern on the teaspoon handle before Daniel found something to say.

'The answer is ... as it were ... no, I'm afraid!'

She thought for a moment that he was hurt, then discovered when she looked at him that he was merely struggling hard not to laugh. Having mislaid her own enjoyment of the absurd, she was flooded with unreasoning anger instead.

'Does it amuse you to see a good, kind man laying himself open to ruin? I pretended to Ruth that there was nothing to worry about, but she knows even better than I do that there is – because she knows Oxford better. Geoffrey assumes that no one can doubt his intentions; but they need only pretend that they do. Madeleine may not be deliberately setting out to spoil his future at St Barnabas, but doing it accidentally will have just the same effect.'

Daniel now seemed intent on the novel business of picking up sugar-lumps with small silver tongs and dropping them back in the bowl again; the conversation didn't seem to interest him at all. More angry still, she said the only thing that might succeed in engaging his attention. 'I should have guessed, of course ... you'd *like* to see him discredited.'

The sudden violent slam of his hands against the table made the tea-cups rattle. 'God damn it, Louise, I ought to beat you for saying that,' he shouted. 'Because your husband and I take a different view of history, does that have to mean that I want to see him pilloried for being a fool?'

She'd regretted the words even as she said them, knowing that because they weren't true her colours would have to be hauled down – but not cravenly. The word 'fool' applied to her clever husband was hard to swallow, and she also refused to seem intimidated by a man whose hands still easily shaped themselves into the fists that had settled childhood's streets battles long ago.

'I'm sorry,' she said stiffly. 'I should have remembered that an Ann Arbor lecture star would feel confident of beating a mere Oxford don in a fair fight.'

But the blaze of anger in his eyes had died – she thought because he was amused again by something *he'd* just remembered.

'I don't know whether I'm confident or not, but there may soon be a chance to find out. The president of the Students' Union wants *me* to propose the motion at the next debate – "that wars are necessary evils" – and St Barnabas's senior history don to oppose it!'

'Oh, dear Heaven ... a public confrontation; it's *all* we need,' Louise murmured. 'I suppose you couldn't refuse?' She saw his expression and answered the question sadly herself. 'No, I thought not.'

She looked so tired and discouraged that he was suddenly tempted to say that he'd do any damn thing she wanted – seduce Anna's daughter, tell the Union to find itself another evening's entertainment, even abandon his remaining lectures and go home if that would lessen her problems. But remembering their airport meeting, he doubted whether any of these things really lay at the heart of her unhappiness. He watched her across the table, dark hair drying in a cloud about her face, brown eyes intent only on people other than himself. For all she thought about him he could have been invisible, and that seemed cruelly unreasonable when he'd become so acutely aware of *her*.

'You can't fight Geoffrey's battles for him, and nor can I,' he said more harshly than he intended, 'but at least I do him the justice to think he doesn't want us to. If he believes he's coming to the rescue of a misused, misunderstood waif, he'll go right on doing it – that's the sort of man I take him to be. But if he's only another middle-aged male being flattered into feeling young again, then he'll convince himself that the rest of the world is either blind or indifferent to what he does.'

'The result will be the same whichever it is, and that scarcely seems fair,' Louise commented. Then with an effort that he could almost feel, she stood up, signifying that the useless conversation was at an end. But she concluded it with an act of grace that he thought typical of her. She held out her hand, and for the first time he felt the cool touch of her fingers on his own.

'I'm sorry – I had no right to ask you to help. The truth is that Geoffrey and I should be able to deal with Madeleine ourselves. We ought to be able to laugh about her together. But it seems a long time since we did that.'

She withdrew her hand and his own felt empty. 'What *are* you going to do?' he asked brusquely. 'Most wives I know would let themselves go in a knock-down, drag-out fight with the troublemaker, but I can't see that being your pitch at all.'

Louise shook her head. 'I'm afraid you're right in thinking that Madeleine might fight less fair-mindedly than me. She's already told Geoffrey that she could have had Pierre if I hadn't seemed eager to be available instead! I'm thought to have the unfair wiles born of greater age and experience, so she will use whatever weapons *she* has.'

She shrugged the malice aside and tried to sound cheerful. 'My uncle insists that academic societies are much the same the world over. I hope it isn't true of yours at least.'

'Well, Michigan is certainly nothing like this – in fact I doubt if anywhere else on earth *is*,' he said with sudden emphasis.

'Never mind, you're more than half-way towards shaking its dust off your feet, and the best of it is yet to come. Oxford is truly beautiful in the spring.'

'It's beautiful at any time,' he corrected her surprisingly, 'but there's some madness about it as well. I've taken to reading

Lewis Carroll, as you suggested. He wouldn't make a lot of sense in Ann Arbor, but I'm bound to say he does here.'

Her face revealed, as always, what she was feeling – unexpected pleasure in the confession he'd just made. She had fewer wiles than any woman he'd ever met, but her candour made her more, not less, exciting. Carmichael was a self-righteous intellectual behaving like a fool, and she was too gentle at heart: in Madeleine's tough little hands they were likely to be doomed; but it was their problem, not his. He offered a small farewell salute, made for the door, and a moment later she heard it close behind him. She was alone with her problems. They urgently needed thinking about, and it seemed perverse that what filled her mind instead was the knowledge of how strange it would seem when Daniel Goodman was no longer living next door; worse than strange, in fact – it would seem very lonely.

'You forgot about the tea,' his voice said suddenly from the doorway, and she looked up to see him standing there again, with the still-falling rain darkening his neatly cropped brown hair. Then she stared at the table – teacups unsullied, and the biscuits still in the pattern she'd arranged, neatly cream and chocolate-coloured. They seemed to make a comment so mocking on her life that she was strongly inclined to burst into tears; but when she looked again at Daniel he was beginning to grin and she was suddenly swept with him into a gale of saving laughter instead. By the time he was propped against the doorpost mopping his eyes she was able to trust her voice.

'Is that what you came back for – your tea?'

'No . . . only to say that you'd better leave Madeleine to me – I'm afraid you lack the killer instinct! I'll start by calling on your uncle myself; it's time I learned all he can teach me about Oxford.'

A rare sweet smile changed his face for a moment. Then, as instantly as Carroll's Cheshire Cat, he was gone once more and she was left staring at the petits beurres and bourbons. But her mind was on her friend next door, who couldn't help but choose to love a daughter.

★

William returned from his brief stay in Cambridge much refreshed. There was nothing better for enlivening the sad mid-winter days than a scholarly dispute with an opponent who knew the rules of the game – the courteous surface exchange of compliments, and the gleam of knives beneath.

After forty-eight hours away he was greeted emotionally by Mrs Maggs – cross because he'd ventured out of Oxford at all, but too deeply relieved to see him back unscathed to scold for long. It was well known that Cambridge was a particularly unwholesome place, given only to producing unbelievers, scientists and spies.

As usual she was primed with everything that was known in every College buttery but this time, given the Professor's family ties, one piece of gossip would have to be suppressed. Mrs Maggs refused to believe it anyway, liking the Senior Tutor and his lady. It stood to reason that Mrs Carmichael, being half-foreign herself, couldn't help the disadvantage of a shoal of queer-looking relatives. *That*, she'd told Maggs frequently to mark her words, was why Mr Carmichael had been seen about with a young girl whose skirt was several inches shorter than it should have been.

She was about to embark more happily on the news of a forthcoming Royal Occasion – dear to her heart in any case, but especially so because it seemed to make up for some of the strange people who got invited to Oxford nowadays – when she remembered that there were more personal items of news to be reported.

'Mrs Carmichael called, sir. Didn't look too chipper, I thought, but then it was one of them real nasty cold days, and rain with it as well. Came on her bicycle she did, same as usual. Someone else telephoned, name of Goodman, he said – I told him when you'd be back.'

William thanked her for the information, agreed that a cup of tea would be welcome, and had just settled down to enjoy it when, on her way out, Mrs Maggs returned with the news that the very same man was at the door.

'I said I would enquire,' she said with the grand manner that unfamiliar callers sometimes inspired, '*if* it was convenient.'

William suggested gravely that it was, and a moment later he recognised the large man who walked in.

'We met at a concert across the street, Professor,' he was nevertheless reminded, 'and I rang while you were away.'

'Of course I remember . . . my niece suggested that you call. I'm so glad you've come in time for tea, Dr Goodman.'

This time it seemed that the tea would actually be poured, and he was also invited to partake of an unfamiliar delicacy. 'It's called lardy cake – murderously indigestible, but a speciality of Mrs Maggs; be a good chap and help me eat some of it,' his host suggested.

'I had a particular reason for calling,' Daniel explained briefly, once the cake had been disposed of. 'You know Anna Ouspenska, but are you acquainted with her daughter?'

'I've met her, at the home of my niece. It's a touching story, I believe – mother and child reunited after a long separation . . . it must be a miracle to Anna herself.'

'Perhaps, but it begins to seem more like a nightmare to Louise Carmichael. It's arguable whether Madeleine is setting out to discredit Carmichael, or whether she's simply ignorant of the damage she can do; whichever it is doesn't seem to matter very much.'

Daniel was aware of a change in the atmosphere. From being a pleasant host, William Standish had suddenly become alarmingly formal.

'My dear Goodman, if you're suggesting that Geoffrey is . . . is romantically entangled with a girl young enough to be his daughter, I can only assure you that you're mistaken. I hope you won't repeat such an absurdity anywhere else.'

'I'm *not* suggesting it, but there are people who are – the rumour is already in the College Senior Common Room, because that's where I heard it.'

'Then you'd better tell me anything else you know,' William suggested quietly after a moment. 'I'm sorry if I was a trifle stiff with you just now.'

Daniel's brief grin appeared. 'If that was a little stiffness, Professor, God save me from really upsetting you.' Then he grew serious again. 'Geoffrey Carmichael's sin is only spiritual pride. He must be guide, philosopher and friend to a girl who looks one thing to him and something very different to everybody else. She's a victim who needs rescuing — ergo, rescued she must be even if the consequences to himself are disastrous.'

'Quixotic,' William agreed sadly, 'but I'm afraid it sounds exactly like Geoffrey. You could say that he also rescued my niece years ago, but that showed very *good* judgement on his part.'

Aware that his host was liable to be lost in musing about the past, Daniel dragged him back to the distasteful present again. 'Tell me what the consequences are likely to be. I'd know back home how much gossip a man in Carmichael's position could survive, but I'm no judge here.'

William frowned over the question before he answered. 'A little straying from the path of righteousness isn't unknown even among the Fellows of St Barnabas. In normal times it would be tactfully ignored unless the College seemed likely to be harmed by it. At *this* moment, of course, the smallest breath of scandal will be tended by Geoffrey's opponents as devotedly as the Vestal Virgins tended the sacred flame. I do *hope* there's a special circle of Hell reserved for the gossipmongers, with their vicious little nods and winks and veiled innuendos.'

Unable to reassure him, Daniel preferred to consider their more pressing question. 'Four weeks to the election — not time enough for Madeleine to grow terminally bored with history lessons and guided tours of College architecture, and find another victim. I'm afraid my resistance to her charms will have to crumble rather suddenly!'

William stared at him with a mixture of doubt and curiosity. 'You seem to be planning a deliberate, personal assault, Dr Goodman, but the girl belongs to Anna Ouspenska — you don't feel any qualms about that?'

'None at all; why should I? Louise Carmichael has been Anna's only true friend; she would abhor the thought of her daughter doing damage.'

'In fact, you think I'm an effete old fool even to have asked the question at all when our case seems to be rather desperate?'

Daniel smiled faintly. 'No, but I reckon you may be too like your niece! You're also too polite to ask how I come to be involved in something that concerns your family.'

'Well, it's true that I didn't think you quite saw eye to eye with Geoffrey; and I doubt if the Mastership of St Barnabas can be of huge concern to you.'

'Quite right . . . and my colleagues at Ann Arbor would be quick to tell you that I'm normally too busy clawing my way up the ladder to stop and worry about what's happening to anybody else.'

'So my wonderment remains,' William pointed out gently, watching the unrevealing face in front of him.

'Let's just say I don't like watching an uneven contest – but if it isn't that then Oxford is having an effect on me that I didn't anticipate.'

It was an answer William found so reasonable that his twinge of conscience died. This large and vigorous American was exactly the man they needed, and the fact that he and Geoffrey crossed swords professionally seemed to invest the whole thing with so much of the ironic, tolerant Oxford spirit that there was no longer the slightest need to worry about having him on their side.

CHAPTER FIFTEEN

Madeleine disliked *Madame la Directrice*, but there were certain advantages about working at the Maison Française. She could be vague at home about the staggered hours she was required to be on duty at the reception desk; better still, it was an easy walk to Norham Road. There was no need for the ludicrous exertion that their neighbours next door went in for. Ruth Carmichael riding her bicycle looked like a witch on a broomstick, and Anna's dear friend Louise had lost – presumably through such strenuous exercise – what little volupté God had bestowed on her; she was as thin as a beanpole now. That, Madeleine knew, was not the sort of female body it pleased men to observe, and much less touch. She was confident about the curved perfection of her own; every morning she mentally compared it with the statue of a nude girl that welcomed visitors on the lawn outside the Maison building. The model had been pretty enough, but she knew she could have given the sculptor even better inspiration.

An incidental daily pleasure was the war she waged against the *Directrice* on several fronts, the most open of them being her choice of working wardrobe. Instructed, finally, to be more *comme il faut* if she wished to remain there, she'd retaliated by appearing in a schoolgirl's outfit – knee-socks, loose sweater, and short, swinging kilt; all so unarguably demure that their capacity to draw attention to what was underneath could almost have seemed accidental.

There were some promising male members of the Maison, amid far too many earnest female ones for ever discussing whether or not existentialism was old hat; but, seen smiling at them, Madeleine had quickly been taught one of the cardinal rules of Oxford society. Her colleague at the reception desk had been unpleasantly blunt about it.

'Wasting your time, my ducks – we're allowed to serve, assist and occasionally supply what the academics fail to provide, but *never* expect them to take us seriously.'

Madeleine hadn't believed it – the girl beside her was ill-favoured, poor thing, and being merely the daughter of a French dressmaker and a technician in one of the University laboratories, had little hope of success.

'Watch me,' she'd said confidently, '*me* they will notice.'

Monique had agreed to watch but remained unencouraging. 'Like the rest of us, you'll get propositioned by spotty undergraduates with no money to spend. Let a dishy, living, breathing professor arrive from the Sorbonne, and you can depend on it the lady dons will have him staked out before you can say Jack Robinson!'

As the weeks passed Madeleine had watched the dismal forecast come true. Whenever a visitor appeared whom she judged worth impressing, the curtain separating academics from the rest had descended, apparently making her invisible. It had been very frustrating – even painfully humiliating in the case of Pierre Rivaux, who could scarcely be counted as an academic at all. But then had come Christmas, Louise Carmichael's dinner party, and the ripening acquaintance with someone she *could* boast about. Monique had even heard of Geoffrey Carmichael, because he and his wife were friends of the *Directrice*; even so she tried not to seem envious.

'A bit old, I'd say – well, middle-aged anyway; and I don't know why he wants to mess about with you – he's got a nice wife who smiles as if she means it.'

Madeleine was able to be truthful. 'It isn't messing about. Geoffrey is taking my education in hand . . . at least, that's what he says!'

The implications were enough to impress Monique, and only to herself did Madeleine admit that progress with her handsome, middle-aged instructor was very slow. The trouble was his wife, of course, who had come back from Paris too soon. Another week or two alone and Geoffrey Carmichael would have abandoned his habitual gentle courtesy and also the pretence that he was anxious to teach her the history of Oxford.

For Monique's benefit her visits to his rooms at St Barnabas were described in terms of feverish excitement; in reality she usually didn't get further than the porter's lodge, where a real *cochon* of a man called Jukes took pleasure in announcing that Mr Carmichael was teaching and couldn't be disturbed. But one day she'd beaten Jukes by hanging about, and Geoffrey had suddenly appeared to find her looking so cold and forlorn that she'd been taken into his warm study while tea was made. It hadn't quite led to the making of love as well, but Madeleine had taken heart from that ultimate visit. She was right to claim that she possessed an instinctive awareness of men; in fact since coming to Oxford she'd understood that it was a gift inherited from her mother. In Geoffrey she sensed both loneliness and hunger, and the pleasure of seeing his self-control finally crumble would be increased by knowing that he belonged, strictly speaking, to the woman she blamed for her own failures.

Hilary Term was reckoned by academics and students alike the worst of the three — lacking the excitement of Michaelmas's fresh beginning and its beckoning gleam of Christmas, but with none of the summer pleasures that Trinity held in store. Hilary weather was dreadful too, and altogether misery was usually unconfined. But when half the term had been washed away in relentless icy rain, small signs of hope began to appear. Madeleine took no pleasure in these. She wasn't acquainted with the Botanic Gardens, where snowdrops laid a white carpet on the grass, and even the Chinese willows to be seen everywhere in Oxford were changing from black to bronze without her noticing them. She was scarcely stirred out of winter discontent by the news she took home to her mother one evening, because it seemed to have very little to do with her.

'The French Ambassador and his wife are coming to Oxford for some anniversary or other. There's been a last-minute change of plan and they're being given dinner at the Maison. Madame's beside herself, silly creature. I can just imagine her calling him "Your Excellency" every minute, and all but curtseying to his wife.'

For once Anna sounded sharp. 'You're being unfair because

you don't like her, but the rest of Oxford does. She's a charming, clever lady . . . a credit to France, I think.'

Seeing that her mother looked ruffled, Madeleine blew a disarming kiss across the supper table and agreed solemnly that upholding the honour of *la belle France* among the English natives was of all things the most important. Obliged to smile again, Anna returned to the subject of the Ambassador's visit.

'I heard about it this afternoon, *chérie*. Louise called to tell me . . . and to implore me to share the honour of entertaining the visitors! They are to be offered a recital after dinner, and the *Directrice* has suggested some of the music we played in the Holywell Room. Me, I think we should make a different programme.'

'You are to be brought in like some poor, wandering minstrel, I suppose,' Madeleine said scornfully. 'You should refuse, *Maman*.'

'I am being invited to dine there, with the Carmichaels,' Anna corrected her. 'After that Louise, Frédéric and I will play for them. Dearest, *you* will certainly be asked to the recital, and to the reception afterwards. Is that something to get cross about?'

Madeleine thought of Monique Warren, unlikely to be asked to anything at all except perhaps the supervision of the cloakroom, and agreed that she would attend, if only to be of comfort and support to her mother.

It ended the conversation amicably, but the more she thought about the evening the more important it seemed to become, especially when the next morning the *Directrice* herself unbent sufficiently to consult her about the flowers Anna would like to receive after the performance. By now everyone knew that she would be going herself as a guest. It was an added pleasure to explain to Monique that her place at the recital would undoubtedly be beside Geoffrey Carmichael, while his wife abandoned him yet again to bask in the limelight.

Closeted with Louise to decide on the French music they should play, Anna first aired another anxiety.

'I forgot to warn Madeleine – she's bound to want to shock

poor long-suffering Madame, but it won't do to be too outré in front of important guests.'

Louise smiled at her. 'They come from Paris and London, don't forget – I doubt if anything an Oxford shop can produce will seem very outrageous to them! Now, stop worrying about your daughter who will certainly contrive to look beautiful, and tell me if we can manage Fauré's *Berceuse* between us. It's horribly difficult to play well, but beautiful enough to be worth the struggle, I think.'

The few days left to them had to be filled with practice but when Anna apologised to her daughter for leaving her so much alone Madeleine smiled sweetly.

'I have my own studies, you know – Oxford's part in the English Civil War, Geoffrey says I must now understand!'

'He's the kindest of men, overworked as I'm sure he is,' Anna said with real gratitude. 'I'm ashamed to remember that I didn't always realise that. But he *is* very busy, Maddy dear, and rather important, too – you mustn't impose on him.'

Madeleine gave a little shrug. 'The lessons are *his* idea, *Maman* – *I* don't get very excited about Cromwell and a king who lost his head . . . Geoffrey does!'

Her tutor was, in fact, too busy to do more than leave books for her at the lodge, but there came with them one day a charming note of apology for not seeing her before the evening of the Ambassador's party. In fact, she was glad to be spared Oliver Cromwell, having more important things on her mind – a dress that would rivet every eye, and some new way of doing her long black hair.

When the evening came and Anna went off with Geoffrey and Louise, it was irritating to find that she must make her own entrance flanked by the disapproving spinster next door and her elderly uncle-by-marriage. But when they called to collect her she changed her mind. In his antiquated way the old gentleman was not undistinguished after all, and nothing could provide more of a contrast to white chiffon tunic and trousers than the shapeless bundle of grey lace in which Ruth Carmichael seemed to be wrapped. Tonight Geoffrey would see a Madeleine Torrance who looked not only beautiful but entirely grown-up

. . . no need to be afraid any more, as she thought he had been, that she was too young for anything but history lessons!

Their taxi had to join a queue of cars edging slowly towards Norham Road. The driver, more polite than taxi-men usually were, seemed to be looking so constantly for someone to give way to that Ruth was finally moved to bark at him – was he *determined* that they should be the last to arrive? They almost were and had to be hurried to the only remaining empty seats at the back of the crowded hall.

Sick with disappointment at not finding Geoffrey waiting for her, Madeleine looked away from the smiling face of a secretary-turned-usherette, who would certainly hurry to regale Monique with the fiasco of their arrival – no prominent seat kept for her next to Geoffrey, no public awareness that it was where she belonged; instead, she'd been hidden in a dark corner where she might as well not have come at all.

A ripple of applause accompanied the performers onto the platform – her mother wearing black taffeta that sparkled when the light caught its scattering of tiny sequins; Louise Carmichael in glimmering jade-green silk that even Madeleine acknowledged reluctantly to herself made a contrast that was beautiful. Behind them came the upright, dignified figure of her mother's Polish friend, Grodzicki.

She intended to shut her ears to the music – it wasn't what she'd come for and would mean nothing to her anyway. But William Standish turned to smile at her, as if to insist that such beauty must be shared, and she found herself beginning to listen. It wasn't the sort of music she'd heard them play before – nothing dry and boring now; this was all delicately shifting harmonies, and colours that reminded her of the landscapes the Impressionists had painted. For as long as it lasted she even forgot her own resentments and the fear of being laughed at by Monique and her friends. But the spell was finally broken, and with the surge of applause she was herself again, impatient of the silly ritual of flowers and speeches that kept her there when she wanted to find Geoffrey. He should have waited for her, of course – she'd been confident that he would; but being wise with men she would smile and pretend not to mind.

The large room next to the hall seemed full of people but she worked her way towards the roped-off end where the evening's guests of honour were clustered. Anna, surrounded by dignitaries who included the Lord Lieutenant, beckoned to her but she smiled and edged past them. She could see Geoffrey's fair head now – in a moment he was bound to see *her*; then he would leave the people he was with. Dull-looking and elderly, they seemed; he would be longing to shake them off, and wanting to claim her. But standing there alone in the crowd she felt exposed and suddenly afraid that it had been a mistake to come. She hadn't quite the courage to join them uninvited, but if he didn't notice her everyone else would see that she'd expected to be made welcome . . . God and all the saints in Heaven *make* him notice her, please.

At last, when another moment of doubt seemed more than she could bear, he murmured something to the woman beside him and came towards her. It was going to be all right after all. He was standing in front of her, even more wonderfully elegant in evening clothes than she'd expected. She'd been clever to choose *this* man, so quietly self-assured, so confident of being in his true milieu that at last she could feel confident too.

'My dear, how splendid you look!' It wasn't quite the word she hoped for, but she had no quarrel with it as long as it kept him staring at her for everyone to see. 'But why are you alone? William was to take care of you and Ruth. He had strict instructions to conduct you to Anna after the recital.'

Confidence was seeping away again, and she was beginning to fear that even now something was going very wrong. It was time to summon up every scrap of demurely provocative charm and smile at him. 'I don't mind where William is – I thought I'd much rather conduct myself to *you*! I meant to keep you company while the music was being played, poor Geoffrey, but a stupid taxi driver made us late.'

He was obliged to smile, but she couldn't pretend to herself that he looked pleased, or that he seemed to have any intention of including her in the group of people he'd just abandoned. If she hadn't fully understood Monique's message before, she was seeing it plainly now – in this company, however elegantly, beautifully grown-up she appeared, however ready she was to please, the curtain of invisibility had descended yet again. He was simply waiting for her to realise the fact and walk away.

Geoffrey looked at her desperately smiling face, aware of several things that were occurring to him forcibly but too late. His wife had been right after all – Madeleine's grip on reality *was* insecure. How else could she have so misconstrued an interest that had been entirely impersonal? He himself had been obtuse, which was painful to admit to, and people were surely beginning to wonder what kept them standing there together.

'I'm sorry we missed seeing you earlier,' he said with more regard for tact than truth, 'but now I really must return to the guests I'm neglecting, and *you*, my dear, must go and help Anna – I'm sure she's relying on you.' He inclined his head in a courteous farewell bow and then turned away, leaving her alone.

Watching the little scene, Daniel understood why she still remained there, white-faced and rigid. It was because she simply couldn't think what else to do. When someone threw a spanner into the workings of the fantasy world she inhabited, as Geoffrey Carmichael had obviously just done, she had nothing left – no alternative scheme to fall back on, nowhere to run to and hide. He grabbed a second glass of wine from the nearest tray and went up to her, not even remembering his promise to Louise. He'd have gone as unthinkingly to the rescue of any small helpless animal.

'Did you enjoy tonight's music more than the first concert we went to?'

She stared blindly at him, making no sense of the question. Heart and mind still grappled with the knowledge that she'd been rejected, while Geoffrey went back to smile at his wife. Any other woman might have seemed bearable, but not Louise Carmichael, who deserved so little of everyone's attention and seemed to be given so much.

'You're one of *them*,' she said with bitter emphasis. 'No need to waste time on me; I'm like those poor creatures that high-caste people in India spit on . . . untouchables, don't they call them?'

'Drink this,' he suggested firmly, 'you'll feel better. I'm as much outside the magic circle here as you are – more so, in fact; you've got Anna to open doors for you. I'm just an uncouth smart-ass American who'd rather drink beer than wine and can't shake off the habit of saying what he thinks – not the way to make friends and win influence in Oxford at all!'

Madeleine took the recommended sip of wine, feeling it bring a little warmth back into her cold body. She didn't know why this large and usually unfriendly man should now be smiling as if he enjoyed talking to her, but it didn't seem surprising when nothing else about the evening had gone as she expected. At least she was no longer left alone, to be pitied or laughed at. The man beside her might be as out of place as he said, but she had the strong conviction that everyone must know it would be a mistake to laugh at him.

'I was supposed to be delivered to Anna,' she told him, 'to make myself useful by smiling prettily at a bunch of self-satisfied old men and pretend that I understand a word of what they're talking about. If I'd realised that I wouldn't have bothered to come at all.'

Daniel's bright blue glance flicked over the people talking to her mother. Among them he recognised the Vice Chancellor and the Dean of Christ Church, but cheerfully consigned them to Madeleine's dustbin.

'Quite right,' he agreed, 'I often can't understand them either, or they me. Nor can I abide these elegant little snippets that we're being offered to eat – sink your teeth in them once and they're gone; no good at all to a hungry man. What do you say we go in search of some real food?'

The suspicion lingered in her mind that he'd been watching long enough to see her abandonment. She had been happy to inspire pity in Geoffrey – had even done it instinctively, knowing that so reserved a man needed to be made to feel confident in his dealings with women. This too-vigorous American was another matter altogether, and as a general rule large, self-assertive men were *not* to be encouraged to think they had the upper hand. She would have preferred to say that she was going home, but that would mean the disgrace of being seen leaving alone, and she couldn't even be sure that there would be any taxis waiting outside.

Daniel saw the hesitation in her face and offered a smile that had wryness for himself in it but no pity for her.

'I often eat alone and there isn't much pleasure in it, even for a man who enjoys food!'

'Then I shall eat with you,' she finally decided. Her pale face had come alive again; self-esteem was restored, and a gleam of malice made her eyes look very bright. 'I should like the *Directrice* especially, but *everyone* else as well, to know that we are leaving her silly, boring party to enjoy ourselves elsewhere.'

He grinned, but shook his head. 'Impractical, I'm afraid – unless I'm to leap on a table all among the canapés and make a public announcement! I think we should resign ourselves to just slinking away.'

But even with no announcement made, Anna saw her now-laughing daughter leave with Daniel, and so did Louise. The few moments when she'd feared a scene that would cause Geoffrey mortal embarrassment had been survived. She ought to be – *was* – deeply grateful for an ally who could wage war untroubled by the pangs of conscience. But, listening with apparently undivided attention to France's genial Ambassador to the Court of St James's, she considered the unexpected idea that it wasn't war Daniel was waging after all. He'd left the room with a markedly unbelligerent air – in fact with the air of a man who had nothing but the prospect of pleasure in view.

CHAPTER SIXTEEN

The longcase clock in the hall made its usual commotion over striking eight, but for once silence reigned again before Geoffrey appeared at the breakfast table. He brought with him the faint, pleasant aroma of aftershave, and the concentrated expression of a man with too many matters that needed attending to, but this morning it wasn't quite convincing. Even though he glanced as always at the newspaper headlines, Louise felt sure he wasn't really thinking about the murderous goings-on in Belfast. It was the previous evening that still occupied his mind.

'It went very well, don't you think?' he asked suddenly. 'A credit to everyone concerned, but your and Anna's contribution was especially memorable. The Ambassador refused to believe that you aren't both professionals . . . perhaps it's what you ought to have been!'

Grateful for at least one doubt she could lay to rest, Louise shook her head. 'I should have hated solo performances, even given the necessary amount of talent. But playing chamber music makes me very happy. I think it's the same for Anna, too.'

She glanced across the table at her husband, hoping to see that about this he could be convinced. The morning was fine for once, and its bright light was revealing. His fair hair was sprinkled with silver now, and the bones of his face had become more prominent. She could see how he would look in old age, gauntly distinguished and rather frail. The long-drawn out joust for the Mastership was trying him even more than she'd realised, but it wasn't only that − another discomfort troubled him as well.

'I only caught a glimpse of Madeleine last night,' she said deliberately. 'She was looking lovely − and rather more restrained than Anna feared!'

'You glimpsed her talking to me, I expect,' he suggested after a long pause. 'It was difficult – I had to abandon her rather brutally, but thank God Daniel Goodman turned up.' He looked up to find Louise watching him, and tried to smile. 'You were right, I'm afraid – from what she seemed to expect it was clear that she'd entirely misunderstood my . . . my interest in her. I feel very much to blame for that, and it's no excuse to say that she reminded me in an odd way of another unhappy girl twenty years ago.'

'That girl wasn't nearly so dangerous,' Louise managed to say, touched in spite of herself by an explanation that hadn't occurred to her. 'In fact I told Daniel it was my mother that Madeleine reminded me of!'

She had spoken without thinking, anxious only to dispel the sadness in his face. It was a mistake, but she realised it too late.

'Why discuss her with *him* at all?' he asked with sudden sharpness. The probability that his own behaviour had been discussed as well was bad enough, but such a conversation hinted at a degree of intimacy that seemed even more objectionable. 'Were you anticipating embarrassment? Was that why Goodman appeared like a genie out of a bottle – because he'd been asked to stand by?'

The questions were flung at her, stinging as hailstones against her skin, and she was reminded of something else she'd said to Daniel – but it seemed even more painfully true now. She and Geoffrey could no longer solve problems by sharing them. Their long, slow separation of heart and mind was as hard to overcome as a current setting against two tired swimmers making for the shore. She found something to say at last, but only as much of the truth as he might find bearable.

'I didn't even know Dr Goodman would be there last night – so he certainly hadn't been asked to "stand by". I talked to him about Madeleine because I wanted to convince myself that his opinion of her wasn't the right one.'

'So on the evidence of last night we can assume that he's changed *his* mind,' Geoffrey said sarcastically, 'at least for as long as an impressionable girl is prepared to put up with him.'

'Why assume anything?' she shouted. 'Perhaps he's decided to feel sorry for a child who hasn't yet grown up – perhaps he yearns to take her to bed – he may even have had it in mind to save *you* embarrassment.'

'Most unlikely,' Geoffrey dismissed this last possibility coldly. 'I'm not his friend; not even a colleague on the same side of the professional fence. I think he might be glad to see me embarrassed.'

'I suggested that,' she agreed, quiet again but throwing discretion to the winds. 'It made him as angry as you seem to be, but perhaps with more reason.' The directness of it silenced her husband, but there was no pleasure even to be got from that. 'All this interminable term needed,' she told him wearily, 'was what I gather it's now going to get – a public debate between the two of you, on some futile argument dreamed up by the Union's president. Pride won't allow *you* to refuse, any more than it does Daniel Goodman.'

'And you despair of the stupid male vanity that will make us preen and strut in front of our supporters like a couple of fighting cocks!'

She hadn't expected his own resentment to melt into wry humour; was still more unprepared for him to stretch out his hand to touch hers resting on the table.

'Don't worry about the debate, my dear. It will be conducted in the best Oxford tradition – a lot of showy flourishing, but no real damage inflicted!' He watched a smile touch her mouth, but fade too quickly. 'I'm sorry it's all been such a beastly strain ever since we heard of Humphrey's retirement. That will be over very soon, but I could have helped matters by not climbing onto my Senior Tutor's high horse about the child next door. I don't know why I did.'

'You forgot another Oxford tradition,' she pointed out, '. . . the female of the academic species is more deadly than the male! But I expect Gwyneth and Alice and the rest of the gossips will lose interest in us as soon as the election is over. The dressing they pour over me at the moment – oil of pity mixed with the vinegar of malice – will dry up then and we shall go back to ignoring one another.'

Geoffrey saw too clearly for comfort the depth of her distaste and sense of isolation, but he returned to something easier.

'Madeleine will decide in any case that we're even more boring than her acquaintances in Dijon, and our barn-storming historian next door will finish his sabbatical and make all speed back to Ann Arbor. Life will become wonderfully peaceful again.'

Either his optimism or his contemptuous dismissal of Daniel made her perverse. 'Life in the Lodging, perhaps, by the end of the summer – so not necessarily peaceful at all,' she suggested.

He didn't want to be aware of the despair he sensed in her; told himself it was surely unreasonable – after all, most of the women he knew would jump at the position that was likely to be offered to her.

'Would it really be such a hardship?' he asked levelly. 'If so, I suppose the truth is that even after all these years you still haven't acquired a born and bred Oxonian's hopeless addiction to the place.'

Beneath his mock apology she heard the trumpet note of self-congratulation ringing out bright and clear. He'd made a better job of muffling it years ago. If she wasn't an addict yet the fault must be hers. She hadn't tried hard enough, didn't understand the treasure she'd been offered, couldn't quite match Oxford's special quality. The failure of their life together, known but not admitted even now, must become *her* failure with the rich, rare place he'd brought her to. But even while it seemed deeply unfair, she could see why it must be so. Sybil Carmichael had abandoned her family long ago for just the same reason; it was what he and Ruth had convinced themselves they now believed, because that way their mother's desertion was more bearable.

As if he'd followed her own train of thought back down the anguished years, he suddenly tightened his grip on her hand and shouted at her.

'You're not really with us at all, are you? Some enticing mirage blinds you to what is *here* – you can't get over turning down Paris and Pierre Rivaux. I'm not sure what *they* offer you – resurrected youth, perhaps, but you must know that *that* won't last.'

'You've been listening to Ruth again,' she said, marvelling at her own calmness. 'My dear sister-in-law has been trying to convince you for twenty years that it was a mistake for you to bring me here. If I manage to become an Oxford addict in the end, it will be largely to prove *her* wrong.'

A little silence fell before Geoffrey asked, quietly now, as if some brief fever had overtaken and then abandoned him, 'You *don't* regret André's gift?'

'It wasn't a gift,' Louise replied. 'It was a bribe, and since I don't regret turning it down, we needn't discuss it again, whatever Ruth or Madeleine or anyone else suggests to you.'

She spoke with such finality that there seemed nothing left to say. He nodded and stood up, would have smiled if only she'd looked his way; but she was staring at a bowl of hyacinths on the table, and after another moment's hesitation he was thankful to remind himself that he'd be late for the day's first tutorial if he didn't leave now.

William had to admit to his visitor one afternoon that even for someone born to the caprices of Thames Valley weather February's behaviour had been more than usually disagreeable. Weeks of rain were not unknown, flooded water meadows a part of the late-winter scene; but when it *should* nearly have been spring, it was spiteful of the wind to change quarter, and leave wildfowl and rowing men with nothing to do but stare at frozen water.

Having made his complaint, William threw more coal on the fire and smiled at a guest who now looked very much at home in his untidy room.

'I expect our obsession with the weather seems mad to you. Are you *ever* obliged to begin a conversation at home by considering whether today is colder, wetter, warmer, or merely just the same as yesterday?'

Daniel Goodman shook his head, grinning. 'No, but Michigan's roughly at the centre of a huge land-mass, so our climate is boringly predictable. Your obsession may be mad, but I shall miss having to decide whether the wind is light, moderate, fresh, or strong, not counting a breeze at one end and a gale at the other!'

William applied his poker skilfully, and a sudden blaze of flame lit up the unrevealing face of the man sitting opposite him. It wasn't just the beard that hid his mouth; he was in the habit, William decided, of keeping himself to himself — it made an unusual trait for an American.

'Is that all you'll miss — daily fluctuations in the weather, and a lot of lovely Gothic architecture?'

The question was less innocent than it seemed, Daniel realised, like the cherubic-faced old gentleman who'd asked it. William pretended to count himself now among the ancient of days — Oxford was thick, he said, with clusters of retired academics who drowsed away the time like sleepy bees, waking up occasionally to sip a glass of sherry or deplore the manners of modern Oxford. But it was rare to visit the little house in Holywell Street without being interrupted by some other caller, and the Professor's mantelpiece before Christmas had been witness to how many dozens of former pupils still found it necessary to keep in touch with him.

His question had been left hanging in the air but Daniel finally answered it.

'I can't be sure *what* I shall miss until I turn my back on the Bodleian and the High for the last time. But missing there will surely be, and it's more than I bargained for. I shall go home and *try* to be unfair. I'll remember silly rituals, and self-indulgent dons boasting about the books they'll never get around to writing, and old draughty buildings for ever in need of money to keep them from falling down. I'll try *not* to remember the heart-easing beauty of the place, and the sheer, damn, civilised mellowness of it all!'

'Not quite as civilised as it was,' William observed sadly, 'and not quite as self-confident either, though some might think that a good thing. I can't see the present-day University having the nerve to block the coming of trains for years, and then in a last-ditch piece of stubbornness complain that the "avoidance of natural obstacles by the route was detrimental to the geological education of the passengers"!'

He grinned at Daniel's shout of laughter and then pattered

into the hall where a telephone was ringing. When he came back his face was serious again.

'I'm afraid that was Edwina Wharton asking me to go and cheer Humphrey up – my dear friend is rather poorly.'

About to get up and leave himself, Daniel waited for another ring to be attended to, this time at the front door. William reappeared with Louise, delivering the last batch of typescript for his new anthology.

'Providential timing,' he said happily. 'I was about to send Dr Goodman away without any tea, but now you can make it for him while I nip down to College.'

He kissed her warmly, smiled at Daniel, and bustled away, leaving a little silence behind him.

Louise glanced at the man who seemed to overfill the small room uncomfortably, but looked away again, disconcerted to find him watching her. It was ridiculous, adolescent in fact, for a grown woman teetering on her fortieth birthday to find herself unsure of what might come next. But her only certainty was that no normal rules would apply because Daniel Goodman didn't believe in paying attention to them. She retired strategically behind an armchair, feeling happier for something to lean against, and remembered her uncle's parting comment.

'William really does "nip"; I've seen gasping undergraduates chasing after him in an effort to keep up.'

The picture she drew was one Daniel had seen himself, but he nodded without smiling. 'Don't bother about tea – that is if you *were* thinking of getting any.'

She was vividly reminded of another occasion. They hadn't met since then, but like any North Oxford neighbour, she had been aware of what was happening next door. She felt largely to blame for the fact that Daniel Goodman and Anna's daughter had become inseparable. To anyone else she thought she could have said so without awkwardness; then realised that with *no one* else at all would she have got herself into this predicament. She and Daniel still had none of the ease of friends, but some barrier of normal convention had been leaped and they'd been pitchforked into a kind of intimacy that made ordinary friendship irrelevant.

'Anna is concerned about you,' she said abruptly.

His answering grin was unamused. 'I expect what you really mean is that she's concerned about her daughter. I'm paying Madeleine what used in bygone days to be called marked attentions! Well, thank God someone's noticed, otherwise I'm wasting my time.'

Louise stared at him gravely, able to forget her own nervousness now that they were considering the problem of someone else. 'I feel responsible for what may end badly. I shouldn't have involved you in our affairs, and certainly not in Madeleine's.'

'She won't get hurt, if that's what's bothering you. She's enjoying what I offer her, which is simply a good time conducted as publicly as possible – I'm not asking for any payment, and with me she doesn't even have to pretend to read the books your husband kept producing for her.'

A faint smile lit Louise's face, making it look less strained. 'Anna is the first to admit that her daughter isn't studious! In fact she understands her very well. It isn't Madeleine she's anxious about.'

Daniel couldn't be sure for a moment that he understood her meaning, then as it became clear his huge laugh rang out again. Disconcerted, as she so frequently was in his company, Louise clutched at the knowledge that if coolness was her only defence against his unpredictability, her only offensive weapon was a bluntness that matched his own.

'Anna thinks you're vulnerable – missing your wife, but feeling resentful as well because she doesn't put you first. I'm sure I don't know why *that* should send you into a paroxysm of mirth.'

He admitted, still trying not to grin, that Anna was right about his vulnerability. Doubting him, Louise tried another tack.

'You began by being very offhand with Madeleine, which is all the challenge she needs to bring you to your knees. But not being nearly as experienced as she likes to think, she confuses you with a man like my husband – too hemmed in by convention and good manners not to take his congé gracefully if it's offered to him.'

'I, on the other hand, being violent and half-civilised, will be quite ready to force myself on a girl half my age when she changes her mind. You read me very well, Mrs Carmichael.'

Wishing deeply that she had never embarked upon the conversation, Louise still clung to honesty as the only way out of the pit of embarrassment she had dug for herself.

'My problem is that I can't read you at all. A moment ago I amused you without knowing why; now I've probably made you angry, also without meaning to. But it's your own fault for being so different from the men I'm used to – I don't have this difficulty with anyone else.'

'Well, that's something at least,' he said unexpectedly, straying a little closer to the chair she was still taking refuge behind. He looked at her, knowing that he had difficulties of his own to overcome. How many women had he known, younger, more beautiful, and much more aware than this one of the sexual dance between male and female, without a single faster beat of his heart or the smallest leap of desire? To be so painfully aware of these symptoms now was something else he chose to blame on this unpredictable city.

'I was *told* to give Oxford a wide berth,' he said with sudden sharpness. 'Colleagues I trusted advised me to go anywhere else. Did I listen? I did not!'

There was no lurking amusement in his face, now, to reassure her; and no anger either. Instead, something that inexplicably looked like despair.

'Is it *that* bad?' Louise asked tentatively. 'I know it can be maddening – still priding itself on the legend of a long tradition of tolerance even when it's at its most spitefully small-minded. But very few people actually manage to hate it. I've tried myself and failed.'

'Does that explain why you decided not to stay in Paris?'

She was taken by surprise but struggled to answer truthfully. 'Nothing as rational as a decision was made. Instinct just said that I ought to be here. When you met me at the airport I was fearful of having made a mistake, but all that aching regret seems to have vanished now. It's like having some ailment that seems serious until you suddenly discover one day that it's entirely disappeared.'

Daniel moved again, this time outflanking her escape route to the door.

'I'm glad *you* favour instinct as well – it's what I always bet on myself.'

Believing him, she felt very insecure. He'd agreed that he was an uncivilised man and, although she knew him capable of kindness, it was equally certain that he found the rules of polite society something to be ignored.

'I don't favour *unbridled* instinct,' she said primly, aware of the strong chance that her nervousness might soon be seen to be entirely absurd. In all probability he would smile and bow and walk away; then she would be left alone, safely unsought and undesired, with nothing to do but bring a disordered imagination under control again.

She was right about the smile, but this time his eyes weren't bright with the cold, glinting amusement she was used to seeing. Daniel Goodman smiling like this was a different man, and she must strive to remember that it should have been his wife here to evoke such warm and tender amusement. It was treacherous of him to bestow it on another woman just because she happened to be there, and even though he made no effort to touch her, she thought she knew what it would feel like to be encircled by his arms.

'William asked me a little while ago what I should miss when I went home. I could have said a dozen things,' he explained slowly, '– listening to boys' voices piercing Heaven in the Cathedral, the Master's beautiful Latin grace at High Table, Duke Humfrey's Library at night with the lamps lit and all the books around me smiling like old friends – things I shan't forget, but not the thing that really matters. I couldn't tell William about the terrible pain of missing *you*.'

She thrust her hands into the pockets of her skirt so that he shouldn't see their trembling. Her throat ached with sudden tears for a sadness that, however strange, seemed all too real; but she tried with all her strength not to sound shaken to the heart by what he'd just said.

'Anna was right about you being vulnerable. Missing your wife so much, you've just . . . just settled on me for the time being, because it's better than living in a vacuum.'

'Pierre Rivaux didn't have a wife to miss . . . did he just happen to settle on you too?'

This, at least, was a question she could deal with. 'At first he wanted to prove me wrong for having disliked him; then it got a little out of hand – probably because he was lonely here, and so was I. Perhaps you are too, but you have Karen to go back to, and children to hold you together. What you think you'll miss will very soon be forgotten.'

'I shall go back and *still* be lonely,' he corrected her gently. 'It isn't all Karen's fault. I made the same mistake with her that Carmichael made with you, although his motives were probably less selfish than mine – he wanted to serve the College, I only wanted to succeed. My sabbatical here was to give us a breathing space and prove that we were still the man and woman who'd fallen in love and were necessary to each other. It hasn't worked out like that.'

'How could it?' Louise demanded. 'People are bound to change, but as long as the people you are *now* are still necessary to each other, it doesn't matter.'

'Our problem in a nutshell,' he agreed wryly. 'Karen has become a super-smart executive lady, hypnotised with the enjoyable power of telling others what to do. I find myself travelling in the opposite direction, away from the self-made campus idol I once was. And if I stay here much longer the small flame of ambition I have left will be put out altogether by Oxford's rain and *dolce far niente*.'

'I don't believe it,' she managed to insist. 'You were born competitive, and that's the way you'll die a hundred years from now. I refuse to imagine you quietly rotting away in some academic backwater.'

He smiled again and held out his hands. She put her own into them because there seemed nothing else to do, but it was a mistake – the fit was much too comfortable, the warmth too enjoyable for safety. She tried to release herself, and couldn't because his grip had tightened.

'I dare say I shall find some battle to fight. I shall even convince myself that I've been able to forget you. Then suddenly memory will trip me up and I'll remember all the time I've wanted to smooth your fringe . . . like this, dear heart . . . and the times I've longed to kiss your lovely mouth . . . like *this*!'

The words ended against her lips. She felt the soft brush of his beard against her skin, and then his mouth on hers. Such tenderness was there that her own lips couldn't help but cling. Her whole body, wakened to life by Pierre, now seemed to be asking to be allowed to melt into *this* man's. But even that urgent prompting of flesh and blood couldn't quite deafen the small, cold voice of conscience reminding her that she'd already allowed someone else to be misled. It would be shameful to make a habit of it. She dragged herself away from Daniel, wiped a hand across her mouth as if to wipe away the sweetness that lingered there, and made a desperate grab at self-control.

'Anna should be anxious about *me*, not you,' she muttered. 'I *wanted* to be kissed a moment ago, probably even invited it. You're safer with Madeleine after all.'

'Oh, I'm *much* safer with her,' Daniel agreed unsteadily. 'My only danger comes from you, but I realised that long before you did.'

She shook her head a little, trying to smile. 'I thought we'd agreed on armed neutrality from the moment we met in Anna's garden. There shouldn't have been anything dangerous about that.'

He stared at her pale face, still trying to decide why he should find it beautiful. 'I should like to kiss you again. To be strictly truthful, I should above everything else like to take you to bed, but you wouldn't come voluntarily and I've already had to pretend that I'm not a violent man. So what do I do now – walk you sedately home and try not to mind delivering you back to another man?'

'No – I came on my bicycle, and by the time I get to Norham Grove I shall be so sane and sensible that I shan't even scream at Ruth when she drops in to lecture me for feeding Geoffrey red meat again! She's between books at the moment, with nothing to do but keep an eye on me.'

Daniel touched a finger to his own mouth, then laid it gently against her lips by way of saying goodbye. A moment later she was alone in the room, and even William's small, friendly house felt cold and empty. She was still there when he walked in, bringing with him the smell of cold, frosty air. There was no more than the usual untidiness about the room, and he smilingly shook his head.

'You shouldn't have bothered to wash up, my dear. Mrs Maggs likes to know that I've had visitors – she thinks they're good for me.'

'I didn't even bother to make tea,' she confessed. 'I doubt if D ... Dr Goodman even expects that of me now.' Without explaining a statement that seemed to puzzle her uncle, she asked about Humphrey Wharton instead.

'He's recovering again, but the sooner this election business is over, the better. Uncertainty makes a bad bedfellow for a man with a tired heart, and my old friend has been sadly aware of the acrimoniousness that has crept into the contest.' William examined his niece's downbent face, noting cheek- and jaw-bones now almost too prominent for beauty. 'No need to worry, my dear girl. I've been keeping my ear cocked, but our Valiant-for-Truth Dr Goodman seems to have scotched the gossips wonderfully.' She didn't answer and he was confirmed in the impression in his mind. 'I'm afraid you don't altogether like him, in which case I'm sorry that I left you with the job of entertaining him.'

She smiled with difficulty at William's anxious face. 'It doesn't matter. We agreed more or less amicably at our first meeting, Dr Goodman and I, *not* to like one another!' Her voice didn't tremble; in fact she marvelled that it even sounded cheerful. 'Now I must go, Uncle Will; another ten minutes and the evening rush will start.'

He kissed her goodbye, and watched at the door while she unfastened her bicycle from the lamp-post it was chained to. Then he went inside to poke the fire again with unnecessary vigour while he tried to convince himself that it was the cold evening air, not unshed tears, that had made her eyes seem so very bright. The pile of typescript she'd brought was lying on a side-table. Someone had turned the pages over and stopped at Browning's 'Lost Mistress'.

> Tomorrow we meet the same then, dearest?
> May I take your hand in mine?
> Mere friends are we — well, friends the merest
> Keep much that I resign.

CHAPTER SEVENTEEN

The future of St Barnabas was finally decided a week before term ended. One cold March morning forty Fellows converged on Holywell Lane more punctually than usual. They were greeted by Jukes with the mournful solemnity he thought the occasion required, and then penned inside the College library. The two candidates – Geoffrey, and Edward Castleton – were not present, on the assumption that, being obliged to vote for each other, they would be unable to affect the result.

Watching his colleagues assembling, Humphrey Wharton knew that some of them were more his friends than others despite all his efforts to be impartial. He knew for certain how most of them would vote, but the issue would be decided by the waverers whom Robert Morgan and his fiercer supporters might not have been able to persuade. It wasn't an unheard-of gambit to vote for a man only in order to keep another man out. Even the Chancellor himself, appointed by the combined might of Convocation, had on occasion been selected not for his own doubtful virtues, but to avoid the vices suspected in someone else.

Edward's virtues weren't in doubt; but seeing, hearing and speaking no evil himself, he assumed the same of all his colleagues. In his gentle hands the College would slide peacefully downhill, while he told himself that he'd been elected to do nothing that would offend anyone.

With grief in his heart, Humphrey called the meeting to order, reminded it with brief eloquence of its only responsibility – the true good of St Barnabas – and then asked for voting to begin.

Outside in the porter's lodge Jukes and his subordinate were still locked in battle.

'Tell you what, Mr Jukes,' said young Ron, finally throwing caution to the winds, 'I'll lay you five to one – can't say fairer than that, can I? I've bin listenin' to 'em whisperin' in corners for weeks and I reckon I know what's goin' to 'appen.'

'You know less than you think you know,' Charlie Jukes said majestically, 'but being a God-fearing man I don't see my way to taking your money. Now, stop wasting my time and get that post sorted.'

Ron picked up the bundle of envelopes waiting to be pigeonholed, then threw them down again. 'There . . . told you so! First name I see's Edward Castleton, Esq., MA. I reckon it's a sign, Mr Jukes.'

'It's a sign all right – that someone's written to him, you daft ha'p'orth. Now get *on* with it.'

Jukes was bound to sound confident – no underling could be allowed to challenge his authority; but the truth was that he shared the Master's anxiety. In times past he'd have known for sure by now what the outcome was going to be, but it was a different story when the Senior Common Room was half-full of dons who weren't St Barnabas men at all. There was no telling how *they'd* behave, but he'd know as soon as they came out, of course.

Half an hour later he *did* know, and it was all right, because he could see the Master smiling.

Ruth tiptoed downstairs the following morning, certain of finding Geoffrey working in his study at home. Saturdays were not days when he felt compelled to go down to College. She tapped on the door and stood there until he looked up and smiled at her. Confident of being always welcome, she still insisted on the charade of waiting to be invited in – a pretence that irritated Louise and sometimes even tried her brother's patience.

'Dearest, am I being a nuisance? It was a long choir practice last night, so I couldn't call in then, but I *yeam* to know what happened yesterday.'

She stared at his face, expecting to be able to guess; feared from its very lack of expression that the news was bad. Well, in some way that she wasn't entirely clear about, it must be

Louise's fault – she hadn't supported him, hadn't out-fought Alice Watson, as a good wife should.

But Geoffrey was pointing at the window. 'Look out there – that should tell you how it went.' Puzzled to know what he meant, she saw her sister-in-law, muffled against the cold in trousers and anorak, working in a flower border near the house.

'Louise assures me that snowdrops, having bloomed, need lifting for their souls' good and splitting up immediately,' he explained calmly. 'It's more urgent, but also a good deal more bearable, than thinking about a move into the Lodging at the end of the summer!'

Distracted for a moment from the unsatisfactoriness of his wife, she advanced to wrap him in an affectionate hug.

'Oh, my dear – how splendid! They *did* choose you! Well, how could they not have done?'

Geoffrey smiled at her a little wryly. 'Quite a lot of them – seventeen in fact – didn't choose me at all, so I doubt if I can claim it as a huge vote of confidence.'

Ruth waved them aside. 'Science dons, I expect – barbarians, in other words, as I'm sure poor, dear Humphrey would like to agree. In any case, all that matters is that St Barnabas is *safe* now.' She thought he looked nervous at this emotional statement and hastened to reassure him. 'I shall be the soul of tact, dearest, even with Gwyneth Morgan. Provoke me as she may, I shall *not* crow, as she most certainly would have done.'

He didn't look noticeably happier, but she knew why, of course – his gaze was fixed on the kneeling figure of his wife, now replanting the snowdrops.

'Louise has never liked *this* house,' she said, making the best effort she could not to sound critical. 'One would expect her to be glad to leave it, quite apart from the honour of being the Master's wife.'

Geoffrey was tempted for a moment to agree that since Louise had never liked her sister-in-law either, it was certainly strange that she was so reluctant to move. But it would have been a cruel thing to say, and shameful to ease his own uncertainties by wantonly hurting Ruth.

'Louise doesn't set much store by what other people regard as honours,' he said quietly instead. 'Offer her a choice between attending some grand University occasion and working out there and she'd choose her garden every time. Perhaps she's right, and it's the rest of us who are chasing chimeras!'

Ruth stared at him for a moment, discovering no sign of the triumph he should have been enjoying.

'You're overtired,' she decided briskly. 'It's not to be wondered at, but you mustn't pay *too* much attention to dear Louise's strange ideas. She's remained just the teeniest bit different, you know, even after all these years!' Ruth's smile managed to forgive a woman who'd so wilfully resisted their every effort to make her over. 'After the strain of this term you need a holiday, my dear. I suppose Paris is better than nothing but it isn't ideal. Nadia Rivaux is the most tiresomely exhausting woman I know.'

'She is also Louise's mother,' Geoffrey pointed out, 'so we can't disown her completely. I must say I should have preferred to spend the Easter Vac here, quietly getting on with things. But since Nadia insists on a party to mark the sixtieth anniversary of the Galeries Benoît, Paris it has to be.'

'For our neighbour too, I gather. I bumped into him yesterday — no, not literally this time, I promise you! — and discovered he's going to be there to meet his wife. I wouldn't quite have expected it of him, but it's something all Americans seem to cherish — an absurdly romantic vision of Paris in the spring.'

'He will be one more overcharged and undervalued tourist,' Geoffrey agreed with a smile, 'but that won't stop him finding it beautiful, at least for another year or two! After that he might prefer to be ripped off somewhere else.'

'Who might?' Louise wanted to know, hearing the end of the conversation as she came into the room. 'I hope you aren't talking of Uncle Will and Florence. He likes to think of it as his spiritual home, where only good can befall him because he loves all things Italian.' She spoke cheerfully, as if no desperate need for solitude had driven her out to work in the cold garden.

'Ruth says that Daniel Goodman is spending Easter in Paris

with his wife,' Geoffrey explained. 'Perhaps it would be courteous to include them on Nadia's invitation list.'

'Why not,' Louise agreed after a moment's hesitation, 'if you see him in College and find out where they'll be staying?' She glanced at her sister-in-law's face and read its expression correctly. 'I expect you're more concerned with us in Oxford than the Goodmans in Paris, and came down to be given Geoffrey's news.'

'I was certain of it already,' Ruth insisted, happy to forget a time when she'd just as certainly predicted the ruin of his career. 'It's an honour of course, but no more than he deserves – though I don't suppose I need tell *you* that, Louise.'

'No, I don't think you do,' her sister-in-law agreed gently.

She smiled at both of them and walked out of the room, aware that her own thoughts persisted in lingering on a different city. Imagination pictured streets and squares that she knew intimately, but in the foreground now were two people who might more easily rediscover each other in spring-time Paris than almost anywhere else on earth. She wanted it to happen – insisted to herself that it must, for the sake of something her mind loosely and rather desperately labelled the general good. Clinging to that, she need never waste another moment remembering a scene in William's cluttered little room. She could forget the touch of Daniel Goodman's lips, and his quiet voice explaining what he would miss when he left Oxford for good.

There was cold rain in Paris, giving it a certain grey resemblance to the city he'd just come from. Daniel tramped morosely through the wet streets, feeling none of the lift of heart and spirits that popular song-smiths were always promising. Liars all of them, he muttered to himself; even the damned chestnut trees were nowhere in bloom. Not that he could blame them – as the only poet he was familiar with had said of the New England spring, *he* 'wouldn't encourage a thing to blossom', either.

Paris wasn't a place to enjoy alone – that was part of the trouble, but also he was angry. Karen's brief transatlantic telephone call had said the delay in her arrival was unavoidable, but he had the feeling, familiar now, of being shunted on one side while she attended to more important things. There was another problem, too. His feet kept wanting to stray in the direction of the Rue Jacob, however many times he reminded himself that the woman who was there belonged to Geoffrey Carmichael.

At the airport the following day depression lifted a little. He saw Karen smile as she located him in the waiting crowd, and he couldn't help but notice the brightness about her that always attracted the attention of other men. Even after a long air journey she had the fresh, perfectly groomed neatness that seemed to be the hallmark of a certain kind of American woman. On top of that, of course, she had the advantage of being beautiful. He told himself how glad, how grateful, he was to see her. A moment later her New York drawl fell flatly on his ear and he had to remember that it was probably how *he* sounded as well. The blame wasn't hers if he'd become accustomed to a different intonation, different idioms.

He asked about the children. Hal had gone to Easter camp; Kate and her boyfriend were staying at the home of friends.

'Then I hope they'll keep the boy from sleeping with her,' he said.

Karen gave her little shrug. 'I expect they'll do as the rest of us do – accept what they can't prevent.'

'She's fifteen, for God's sake,' Daniel pointed out too loudly, making people round them stare. 'I hope I'd find *some* way of preventing it.'

'But you're in Europe,' his wife reminded him with her usual cool logic. 'We have to cope as best we can without you.'

It was unfair, because his stay abroad had been as much her idea as his. But he refused to allow them to sink back so soon into the old morass of cross-purpose arguments. She was late but she was there, and this might be the only chance they had to find their way back to shared ease, even to shared pleasure in each other.

The rest of the day went better. Veiled in rain-showers the famous vistas still couldn't be spoiled. Paris had its magic after all. At the recommendation of the concierge, they dined on the Quai des Grands Augustins and agreed that it was the '*expérience*' he'd promised them. So, in Daniel's view, was the bill that came with it, but he reckoned they'd needed the relaxation that came from superb food and wine. Afterwards they found that even the weather had improved – the towers of Notre-Dame across the river were etched against a starlit sky.

He steered a course back to the hotel through the maze of ancient alleys that threaded the University quarter, feeling less depressed about the night ahead. Desire for the woman he was with might even come naturally, and, if so, the pretence he'd been dreading wouldn't be needed after all.

None was, because Karen made it clear as soon as they reached their room that love-making was not on her agenda. 'Forgive me, Daniel, but I'm completely bushed – too much wine, I'm afraid, on top of a long flight and a time-change as well. I may just get my teeth brushed before I fall asleep!'

Nothing, he knew, short of fire, earthquake or flood would curtail the various preparations she made before going to bed. Hair, skin and nails must be attended to so that Karen Goodman could face another day on equal or better terms than those of any other women she met. He'd thought it a rather admirable self-discipline in the past; now it and the subterfuge she was using irritated him. His bed felt more lonely for the knowledge that his wife was within reach but unobtainable, and his mind worried at problems it couldn't solve. The only certainty reached as the night crawled past was that it would be a mistake to take Karen to the Galeries Benoît.

But he'd forgotten the elegantly engraved card propped up on the dressing table. When he woke late, having finally fallen into a troubled sleep, she was reading it while she briskly ordered breakfast on the telephone.

'I didn't know you had *friends* in Paris,' she said, '. . . stuffy academic colleagues maybe, but not ladies who send out invitations like this.'

'I *don't* have friends. Nadia Rivaux is someone I met in Oxford only because she's related to my neighbours there. All we need do is call her up and make an excuse not to go.'

Wrapped in a bathrobe, Daniel was fighting his way through layers of net-curtaining in order to throw the windows further open. Karen was unable to see his face but still aware that the conversation irked him. She knew him for a man who preferred not to socialise; even so, an acquaintance had been courteous, and she prided herself on putting together again the fragments of polite behaviour that her husband was apt to scatter all around them.

'I shall enjoy meeting Madame Rivaux and her guests, even if you don't,' she said firmly. Daniel had turned to face her now and she found his frown irritating. 'It's what I'm good at – getting on terms with people. Intellectuals in their ivory towers don't have to bother – the rest of us do.'

It was the second time in twenty-four hours that she'd cut him off from 'the rest' of them. He supposed the separation was deliberate, because it was a long time since she'd learned not to speak without thinking.

'Then we'll go where you can shine,' he agreed after a moment. 'But don't expect to find Nadia Rivaux one of your new women; she's a survivor from a different breed. Never mind – the Frenchmen present will enjoy looking at you and pretend they understand what you say, and I expect some American competition will be good for the ladies.'

Karen considered this little speech, wondering why it should have been given such a sardonic edge by an invitation that seemed harmless.

'It's the Oxford neighbours,' she guessed suddenly, landing on the one aspect of the discussion that he wished she'd missed. 'I suppose they'll be there as well.'

'Nadia Rivaux's son-in-law is an Oxford don called Geoffrey Carmichael. We take different views of history, and he reckons I'm subverting his students. His wife is half-French although you'd never know it – she's got the English obsession about gardening. In fact you could say it's her life's work. Those are my neighbours, and, yes, I think they'll be at Nadia's party.'

Karen smiled, happy to be in control again of a situation that had puzzled her. 'You don't like them! That's all it is, but there'll be other people to talk to. We need only smile at the Carmichaels and walk on.'

With the social niceties clear in her mind she was ready to consider more immediate matters: as many museums and picture galleries as they could cram into the hours available.

She was intelligent, and genuinely interested in what they looked at – virtues he'd once valued in her too much to feel any resentment that about many things she knew more than he did. But now surely a streak of feminist arrogance had crept in? Except on his own subject, it was she who knew best – from the wine they must drink at lunch to the paintings they should admire. Certain about one wine at least, he countermanded her choice and ordered Châteauneuf-du-Pape instead. The waiter looked pleased, and Daniel tried to banish from his mind the occasion that the wine evoked.

When they set out again that evening Karen chose to carry war into the Parisiennes' traditional stronghold by wearing black, aware that it was also the perfect complement to shining blonde hair. She accepted Daniel's compliment calmly, knowing that it was no more than she deserved. He thought she could have looked pleased, and then remembered that her daily fare at home was probably more fulsome tributes than he'd managed to come up with. On the way to the Rue Jacob, because it seemed safer than talking about his neighbours, he told her what he knew about the Rivaux family.

'Pierre Rivaux sounds interesting,' she said with a smile. 'I hope I shall get to meet him!'

'Don't worry – he'll make sure you do,' Daniel observed sourly, and saw that this time his wife did look pleased.

Nadia had decreed that for their sixtieth anniversary the Galeries Benoît should be truly *en fête*. With flowers everywhere, and choice paintings and objets d'art beautifully lit, the rooms insisted on the pre-eminent place that André Benoît had marked out as his own.

'*Very* smart,' Karen murmured happily as they joined the throng of people inside. 'We should have been stupid not to come.'

Bowing in the approved fashion over Nadia's hand, Daniel

unexpectedly found himself agreeing with his wife. The evening ahead had danger attached to it but now it seemed unthinkable not to be there. He would never get another chance to see Louise in the milieu she'd been born into, and it seemed necessary to know whether she belonged in this glittering, fashionable world or in a quiet Oxford garden.

He waited for the moment when they must meet, knowing what Karen was expecting – a horny-handed daughter of the soil, with unkempt skin, and the sort of dress sense that the strange females who madly tended gardens always had. Instead she found herself measuring a different woman – short, dark hair framing features not remarkable in themselves but enhanced by clever make-up, slender body revealed by folds of beautiful coral-coloured silk. The *tout ensemble* – Karen was proud of knowing the phrase – was maddeningly effective.

Louise was more prepared for the encounter, having seen them arrive. She'd been expecting to find Karen Goodman exceptional, and so she was – a diamond of the first water, Uncle Will would have said, considering himself something of a connoisseur when it came to lovely women. It was easy to smile at her, more difficult to meet Daniel's gaze and look away again.

'We've been waiting for curiosity to bring you to Oxford, Mrs Goodman,' she managed to explain. 'Your husband must have told you what an odd place it is.'

Karen smiled brilliantly. 'I can remember his exact words – "it's too damned pleased with itself considering that it's at least a hundred years behind the times". That was probably what made me decide I wasn't curious enough!'

Daniel could recall making some such statement, half-snide, half-clever. Repeated against him now, it sounded merely silly, but he knew his wife had hoped that it would. She was angry with him because he'd meant her to guess wrong about Mrs Carmichael.

'I could see easily enough what I thought was peculiar about Oxford,' he admitted after a moment. 'It took longer to give in to its magic, fighting every inch of the way.'

'Handsomely said!' Louise smiled at him as she spoke, and, because it was impossible to do anything else, he smiled back.

Karen watched the little scene and felt something akin to the unpleasantness of a sudden electric shock. The Daniel she knew had been able to conceal whatever he was feeling. Now he either couldn't hide the pleasure that came from staring at Louise Carmichael, or he didn't even know how much he gave away.

It was relief to have the moment interrupted, even though Karen thought she could identify the newcomer who stationed himself beside the woman in front of them. Everything about him – dress, voice, manner, and a kind of perfected surface diffidence – proclaimed in complete and concentrated form the Oxford academic whom Daniel had begun by finding absurd.

She wouldn't, in other circumstances, have disliked Geoffrey Carmichael's appearance; elegance, understated as it was here, was something she prized. But the feeling was strong, and growing stronger, that she must assert herself in order not to be intimidated by people so different from the ones she was used to.

'You don't agree with my husband's view of history, I gather,' she said provocatively to Geoffrey once the introductions had been made. 'Well, I suppose it does show the British Empire in almost as greedy and materialistic a light as the Third Reich – always looking for new lands and markets to swallow up!'

Even though she smiled as she spoke, Louise supposed that her intention was to ruffle into perceptible life an Englishman who hadn't immediately responded to her beauty. But Geoffrey, looking bored rather than angry, dealt calmly with what seemed to be one of Daniel Goodman's sillier remarks.

'Germany was *not* modelling itself on the British Empire when it swallowed up the rest of Europe, Mrs Goodman, and I doubt if your husband would advance that as a serious theory. Perhaps you misunderstood him.'

Louise knew that it was time to intervene. Karen had brought the snub on herself but she was looking very flushed, and Daniel would feel obliged to come to her rescue. Ignoring the cross-currents around them felt like trying to push a heavy weight uphill – natural forces were too obviously against it – but Louise tried her best to sound cheerful.

'Tonight, gentlemen, the subject of history is banned – you are here to consider Art! Failing that, you can consider the cognoscenti gathered around us instead, some of them even more extraordinary than anything you can see framed on the walls.'

Daniel followed her lead, but in a way she didn't expect. He smiled at his wife, seeming to insist that *they* were allies in whatever duel was being fought.

'I'd guess that Mrs Carmichael is an old-fashioned reaction-ary. Offer her the most brilliant example of abstract Post-Modernism, something relevant to the real world we live in, and what would she ask for instead? A seventeenth-century Dutch interior or flower painting!'

Louise heard again the jeering edge to his voice that she remembered from their first clashes. It made no sense at all that he should use it again now unless this was the only way he had of defending his wife. She answered quietly, but the weight she was pushing seemed to be getting heavier all the time.

'You're quite right – I expect I'd always choose a flower painting.'

'Well, of *course*,' Karen put in gaily, '. . . Daniel says you're a garden junky! I love flowers myself – what woman doesn't – but I'm afraid I couldn't spend all my time growing them. I mean there are other things to do.'

'Yes, and I occasionally do them,' Louise agreed with a polite smile. Then, heaven-sent, relief arrived in the shape of Pierre, edging his way towards them. She could introduce him, walk away, and perhaps find among her mother's guests someone it would be a pleasure to talk to. Then, hours from now, she could think quietly about the conversation she'd just endured. Or perhaps it would be less painful never to think of it again at all.

CHAPTER EIGHTEEN

Taken in charge by Pierre Rivaux, Karen enjoyed the rest of the evening enough to forget a moment when her husband had looked at Louise Carmichael with joy in his face. Now she could feel confident again, knowing that she was admired and impressing people. But too soon, it seemed to her, Daniel insisted that it was time they left. Unable to argue publicly, she had to go, but pleasure had evaporated again and she remembered how the evening had begun.

Outside in the cool air Daniel drew a breath of relief. 'Thank God that's over. Shall we walk? It isn't far.'

'It isn't late, either,' she snapped. 'Do you have a more exciting party in view, or are we just hurrying back to a hotel bedroom? Personally, I can wait for that.'

'Good!' he said, and pulled her into the café they were passing.

It was a place of alcoved, plush seats and ornate lamps, redolent of Edwardian lovers and illicit rendezvous – inappropriate, he reckoned, but comfortable. Louise would have enjoyed it. The thought came too vividly to mind, and he barked an order at the waiter for coffee and *fines*.

When they were alone again he spoke more quietly. 'It's time for us to talk. This visit was meant to clear the air – give us a fresh start; but I don't think it's been a huge success so far. Is that my fault?'

Sobered by his gravity, she didn't answer immediately. Instead, she looked at his hands, engulfing the small coffee cup they were wrapped around – large, powerful hands that had been familiar to her a long time ago; she could remember them touching her with surprising tenderness. She'd known him as intimately as she knew herself, but now that familiarity had gone and they were travelling in diverging directions. She had come to Paris expecting to be able to explain it to him calmly – gently even, because he was the man she'd once loved. But what Christmas in Vermont had hinted at she'd now seen confirmed; *he* had travelled further than she had. Sudden anger rose in her, shattering the calmness she'd been going to maintain. She even forgot that she'd been quite certain of no longer wanting him as a lover.

Impatient because she hadn't answered, he tried again. 'You went out of your way to embarrass me this evening, and to plant a few darts in the Carmichaels as well. I'm not sure why – all they'd done was invite you to a party. Louise Carmichael is no threat; she doesn't have a fraction of your kind of beauty.'

'No, but she has *something*, doesn't she?' Karen flashed. 'Something that keeps you smiling at her like a fool who's been transfixed! That's what Oxford's "magic" amounts to, I suppose – the lady-gardener next door. I was meant to think you found her and her stuck-up husband ridiculous, but you're . . . you're ridiculously *taken* with them instead.'

In the midst of a turmoil of anger and distress, Daniel knew he must acknowledge to himself at least the truth of what she'd just said. 'My first impression *was* the one I gave you, but it changed,' he agreed slowly, 'or perhaps I changed myself. You'd understand better if you'd paid me a visit there. The place is too old and settled in its ways for *something* not to rub off on a fellow like me with no culture he can properly call his own.' It wasn't honest to give Oxford all the praise or blame, but he couldn't have her talking about Louise.

'There you are! That's what I mean. You were never anywhere near *humble* before, and I'm not sure it suits you.' Karen warmed the brandy glass between her fingers, glad to have something to do with her hands because the moment of truth was upon them. 'Daniel . . . what I came to Paris to say was that I've changed as well as you, but in a different way – I'm *more* confident now, *more* sure of what I want to do. I'm never going to be content to sit at home waiting for you to find the time to notice that I'm there.'

'Is that all?' Daniel enquired after a moment's silence. 'Or do I sense more than just a refusal to ever be an academic's wife in Ann Arbor?'

Her eyes met his for a moment, then looked away. 'I've been offered a place on the Company Board . . . they think I'm very good, and I can't help knowing that it's true. For me it's like the professorship you'll soon get in Michigan – the top of the tree. I couldn't possibly refuse it.' She thought of asking him to feel proud of her, and decided against it. His expression contained nothing she could read, but certainly not pride. Angry that he was giving her so little help, her voice sharpened. 'I expected you to say that a divorce must wait because Kate and Hal don't need a family upheaval right now, but I didn't know then about your spellbinding neighbour next door!'

Daniel's hand suddenly crashed down on the table, making her wince. 'You know nothing about her now, except that she's been Carmichael's wife for the past twenty years, and will probably remain so for the next twenty. There's no need to drag her into a discussion about us. I think a divorce *should* wait. God knows we aren't much of a family but we're better than nothing at all until the children are a little less vulnerable than they are now.'

Being no longer quite certain whether she wanted it or not, she spared him another argument. The day had been a strain, and all she needed now was to end it.

'There's no point in prolonging any of this, is there? I'll take a flight home tomorrow. I can see the lights of the Hôtel Angleterre from here, so you needn't see me back.' Her hand touched his shoulder for a moment, and it occurred to him strangely that the gesture was meant to offer pity.

'That fresh start you mentioned,' she said almost gently, 'I don't think you could have made it either, but there'll be times when I think it's a pity.'

He let her walk out alone, ordered another coffee he couldn't drink, and then roamed the streets for an hour or more. There was nothing to think about, and nothing to link him to the world around him. He couldn't visualise the faces of his children, or even call to mind the names of his colleagues. He'd become simply a weightless void floating about the night-time streets of Paris.

*

Nadia was out of spirits the morning after her party. It was always the same after a moment of high excitement and success; now only death and the grave seemed to lie in wait. Inclined to be irritable with everyone, she was especially displeased with her son-in-law, who remained unenthusiastic about the night before. It reminded her to say again that, with the exception of her dear late husband, the English had never been able to understand the Slav temperament.

'It's true,' she insisted tragically when he smiled. 'Always you've sided with our enemies – the Greeks . . . even worse, the Turks!'

'But not in the last war,' he pointed out with his usual patience. 'Didn't we fight the Germans together?'

'Of course we did,' Louise agreed firmly before her mother could claim yet again that only the Russians had known what it was to suffer. 'In any case, *Maman*, it's no good arguing history with Geoffrey – he knows much more of it than you do.'

Nadia waved history aside. 'Perhaps, but there are other things he does *not* know . . . matters of the heart, you understand.'

It was a complaint she'd been making for the past twenty years whenever he failed to show enough emotion, but Louise knew that only tact was keeping him from saying what he thought about the party. His unvarnished opinion of most of the people gulping down Nadia's champagne would have made matters much worse.

Henri Rivaux stepped bravely into the line of fire, smiling at his wife's indignant face. '*Chérie*, no quarrelling with Geoffrey this morning; you ought to be very grateful to him for letting us keep Louise for a few more days. The poor man now has to go home alone.'

'He has a sister waiting for him,' Nadia pointed out, 'or did something happen to her that you haven't told me about?' The tinge of malicious optimism in her voice was hard to ignore, but Louise managed it.

'Ruth is very well. I told you but you've forgotten – she specially asked to be remembered to you.'

If not death, the more immediate prospect of forgetful old age was suddenly chastening, and Nadia's enchanting smile asked Geoffrey to forgive her. He smiled back – to his great credit, Louise thought – enabling them to part as usual; friends of a sort, but with relief on both sides.

He'd made no compaint about what amounted to another whim of Nadia's. His mother-in-law had shirked the tedious job of clearing out a room full of André's papers herself but insisted that Benoît blood, even diluted as it was in Louise, was required for so delicate a task. It meant his leaving for the airport alone, but only at the last minute as he said goodbye did he show Louise any resentment about it.

'Don't let that monstrous mother of yours wear you out, my dear, or keep you here too long. I can't bear to have you pulled in two between us, so you must do what you feel is right. But remember that you're needed in Oxford as well.'

It was said with the pleasant smile that pride insisted on, in case she guessed how much he mistrusted Pierre Rivaux, and how deeply he feared losing her. Henri's son might now have become no more than a charming relative by marriage, but he found it hard to believe; and even ignoring the risk posed by Pierre, there was still that seductive old witch, Paris, herself, and the life his wife might have there. But these pitiable things couldn't be admitted to; he must pretend to be the most confident of men. So he smiled, and kissed her cheek, and climbed into his waiting taxi, while she supposed that already his mind was back in Oxford, considering all that would need doing there.

She was hard at work in her grandfather's little study behind the gallery, surrounded by files and papers, when Pierre walked in later in the morning.

'My poor sweet – what a work of supererogation, as my Arabic tutor at Oxford liked to say! What *does* Nadia think you're going to find – clues to a lost Monet? An unknown Cézanne that some old lady has been cherishing down in Aix for the past fifty years?'

'Nothing as dramatic as that,' Louise answered coolly, nettled by his tone. 'A lot of this is worthless, but buried among a mountain of receipted bills and trivial correspondence and sale catalogues is the story of the Paris art world for three-quarters of a century. I don't think that's entirely supererogatory, do you?'

'I stand corrected, *ma mie!*' His dark eyes, bright with amusement and something else she couldn't pin down, surveyed her with a thoroughness she found herself resenting. It was what she had expected – his little infatuation had been something that couldn't last, wouldn't have done even if she hadn't rejected him. But *amour-propre* had also been hurt and he seemed at pains now to insist that it was a game she'd been right not to take seriously. She need no longer feel the slightest twinge of guilt about him, only regret for a closeness that had seemed more real than it was.

'You've changed,' Pierre said suddenly in a different tone of voice. 'I don't know why it is, but you're not the woman who was just a *little* bit tempted to let me love her.' His smile had no malice in it now as he still looked at her. 'Or are you going to put me in my place by saying in your cool Oxford voice that I was altogether mistaken?'

She smiled herself, at ease with him again. 'I'll admit to a *small* temptation – nothing more than that, dear Pierre. But I recovered from it, and so did you, I'm sure. That's why we *both* seem to have changed.'

He left that last suggestion hanging in the air, but after a moment abruptly switched the conversation again. 'Have you had a visitor this morning – someone from England?'

'Geoffrey left, and no one has arrived. Why do you ask?'

'Only because I followed out of the Métro station a girl I would swear was Madeleine Torrance! I lost her in the crowd, and had another call to make myself, but it seemed likely that she might be coming here.'

Louise shook her head. 'Most *un*likely, I think. If she'd come to France at all it would be to visit her father in Dijon, but it's much more reasonable to suppose you saw someone else. Half the girl students at the Sorbonne must look exactly as Madeleine does – long black hair, beautiful legs and very weird clothes.'

'Perhaps, but this girl *walked* just as Madeleine does, and that takes some copying. She'd perfected the art of riveting the attention of any man whose eyes still function.'

Louise agreed, painfully reminded of Daniel Goodman. She'd tried not to think of her conversation with him and Karen the night before, but her mind's eye still saw him smiling intimately at his wife. Memory reminded her as well of his readiness to partner Madeleine – no hardship had been involved in deflecting her from Geoffrey. It was downright foolish, no, pathetic, to have imagined that the episode in William's sitting room was anything but another of the games men liked to play.

'Well, pray it *wasn't* Madeleine you saw,' she said tiredly. 'Her latest fancy is for Daniel Goodman, and what she fancies she thinks is hers. If it should have seemed an amusing idea to come and dog his footsteps in Paris she'll bump into his wife as well. I hope he can cope with the scene that is likely to result.'

Pierre was inclined to be amused himself. 'I scent goings-on in Oxford that I don't know about.'

'Rather silly they seem now,' she answered. 'Not worth talking about. In any case, I'd rather you went away; I'm here to sort papers, not to waste the entire morning talking to you.'

She'd refused to discuss Madeleine but not, he thought, for the reason she'd given – his dear Louise was a very bad liar. His defeat with her still rankled, and he wished for his own self-esteem that he could have seen in her some evidence that she regretted it; but the irritating truth was that she didn't seem to regret it at all.

He left the room and she went back to her task, trying not to resent too bitterly the fact that her grandfather, as he grew old, seemed to have lost the inclination to throw any single piece of paper away. She tore up ruthlessly, hoping that Nadia wouldn't come in to see the destruction. A Slavonic tantrum was the last thing she felt inclined for; in fact her strongest desire, which she had to keep resisting, was just to sit and stare at the lovely reproduction of a Vermeer painting which André had positioned carefully opposite his desk. It was a thing of such light and ordered serenity that even Daniel's gibe about her liking for the old Dutch artists couldn't spoil it.

As lunch-time approached the door was opened again. She looked up and smiled with the relief of seeing Henri Rivaux walk in.

'I thought you were Nadia, come to discover me throwing André's tailoring bills away! She isn't in the mood to be reasonable today, poor love.'

'No, no . . . the skies have cleared now,' Henri was able to report. 'Marthe is grumbling about an unexpected guest for lunch, but Nadia is herself again – the "charming gentleman" who telephoned to thank her for last night's party is just what she needed, apparently, to cheer her up!'

As usual when he spoke about his wife he managed to avoid either laughing at her or sounding resentful, and it seemed to Louise a feat that was remarkable.

'I'm not sure that she deserves you, but I'm so thankful you're here,' she said with true affection.

The tribute flustered him into an admission that he would normally have been embarrassed to make.

'I've always loved her, you know – since before she ran off with John Standish and I married my first wife – so how could I change now? Her little enthusiasms for other people come and go, but it's always me she needs when they disappear.'

'She's lucky,' Louise said again, then frowned at a different thought. 'I can't remember meeting any "charming gentleman" last night, can you?'

Henri looked pained. 'My dear Louise, the cream of the Paris art world here and you were not impressed! I don't know who our lunch guest is, but your mother obviously considers that he merits a change of toilette. She's upstairs attending to it now.'

Knowing that Nadia would expect to monopolise the newcomer, Louise made no effort herself beyond washing the dust off her hands and combing her untidy hair. When she walked into her mother's salon ten minutes later and discovered who was there she was perversely glad to appear plain and colourless beside Nadia's exotic entrance.

'I didn't recognise you from Henri's description,' she said coolly, becoming very English again and dispensing with the French formality of shaking hands.

'I have the feeling that it would be wiser not to ask what that was,' Daniel commented. Plain or colourless would have seemed to him absurd words for her to use about herself, but he thought she looked tired, and he couldn't miss the distance that she'd put between them. He'd brought it on himself but that didn't make it any easier to bear. She seemed disinclined to go on with the conversation and merely thanked her stepfather with a smile for the glass of wine he brought her.

Nadia liked the undivided attention of a guest, but she was obliged to disapprove of behaviour in her normally courteous daughter that seemed offhand to the point of rudeness.

'Poor Dr Goodman is without his wife,' she announced for Louise's benefit. 'To be alone in Paris is quite sad, I think, but alas Madame Goodman couldn't stay.'

'Sad for *her* if she enjoys Paris – though not everybody does, I believe,' Louise pointed out indifferently.

'Geoffrey isn't here either?' Daniel asked, refusing to be drawn on the subject of his wife.

'He went home this morning . . . *not* with any sadness, I think,' Nadia explained, since Louise seemed reluctant to. 'My son-in-law is one who doesn't enjoy being here.' She smiled confidingly at Daniel, restored to life as Henri had said by this receptive new audience. 'Americans are wonderfully *en rapport* with Paris, I find; Englishmen, no – they seem to prefer Italy if they can bring themselves to leave their own little island at all.'

The choice did them no credit, her voice implied, but just when Louise decided that she must find the energy to protest, Marthe appeared at the door to announce that *Madame* was *servie*. As *omlettes aux fines herbes* followed Marthe's matchless fish terrine, Daniel manage to extricate himself from his hostess for long enough to discover why Louise was still there.

'It sounds a tedious job,' he commented when she briefly explained.

'It is, but I must finish it now that I've started. Pierre would find the time to help, but Nadia seems to think he might offend the ever-present ghost of her father.'

As soon as lunch was over she made work an excuse to leave them and take her coffee back to the study, but she drank it not working at all; her mind lingered instead on the reason for Karen Goodman's sudden departure, and when the door opened and Daniel walked in, she was flustered into being still more offhand with him.

'You're supposed to be entertaining my mother,' she pointed out coldly, 'and I'm very busy.'

'I know . . . that's why I'm here. I get the impression that you'd rather I wasn't, but a labour shared is a labour halved, my dear granny used to say.' He shook his head at the exasperation in her face. 'Don't scowl – her fund of homespun wisdom has made me the man I am, but maybe that doesn't help me, either, at the moment.' The rare smile that changed his face came now to try her still further. 'I'm allowed to be here. Nadia has been convinced that what her father's papers deserve is a scholar's trained eye – mine – added to the devotion of his grand-daughter!'

She had the helpless feeling that comes with beating bare hands against an impregnable lump of rock. She could shout at him to go without making a particle of difference – he'd made up his mind to share the labour. She could walk out herself and he would probably throw after her another sample of Granny Gutemann's philosophy – that she was just cutting off her nose to spite her face. At last she asked the only question she could think of.

'If you're at such a loose end here without your wife that you must find something to do, why not go back to Oxford?'

'I'd rather help you,' he said simply and she knew she must believe it was the truth.

It made no sense, remembering the way he'd smiled at the golden woman by his side last night. But it wasn't important; he'd just decided that when a fool of a woman called Louise Carmichael needed his help she must be given it whether she wanted it or not. She accepted the inevitable, and waved a hand at the bulging folders that remained to be examined.

'A lot of it's worthless. Posterity won't care about my grandfather's performance as a landlord – at least, I hope not, because it seems to have been lamentable. He was a better judge of wine, but that fact doesn't need recording either. All that matters is the part he played here in the world of art. He had a true instinct for what was good, even if it was out of fashion. It's the best thing I ever knew about him.'

The reluctant praise made Daniel smile. 'Grand-daughterly devotion *not* unbounded, I see! Well, the preliminary sifting seems fairly simple. After that an art historian would have to decide.'

She nodded and went back to the pile she was working on; then, a moment later, stopped again to ask the question that surfaced in her mind.

'What do *you* know about abstract Post-Modernism, by the way?'

He knew why she asked because he turned to glance at the lovely Vermeer picture behind him, but he went back to the folder he was tackling without looking at her. 'Nothing at all. I don't even know if there *is* such a thing. Now, will you stop chattering, please, or we'll never get this job done.'

Smiling now, she resumed her inspection of the paper she'd picked up. It was strange but true that the tedium of the morning had entirely disappeared, and so had the unhappiness festering inside her since the night before. Instead, working in the quiet room was like floating on a sea of calm contentment. She thought she could have improved on Granny Gutemann's dictum, but she'd been instructed to hold her tongue, and must work with the same diligence as the large gentleman who now sat turning over papers on the other side of her grandfather's desk.

Two hours later, when real progress had been made, Daniel finished annotating with dates and subject matter the various piles in front of him and then stood up, stretching his arms.

'I have an acquaintance to meet this evening – an old Frenchman who shares your husband's view that the Germans are the only villains of European history! If you'll promise to stop working now yourself I'll be back at half-past eight each morning until we finish the job.'

She watched him gravely for a moment, no longer surprised by anything he might suggest. 'You've done a lot already,' she said. 'I'm truly grateful, Daniel, but you needn't feel obliged to go on helping.'

'I'm not proposing to do it for nothing, or all day long either. The eminent scholar's fee will be a personally conducted tour each afternoon. You know what to look for in Paris – I have no idea. But I've seen enough museums, thank you, and the crowds who flock to them like well-programmed sheep.'

'No museums, no sheep,' she agreed after a moment's hesitation. 'But if the first tour isn't up to standard, the eminent customer is at liberty to call the whole arrangement off.'

She saw the smile that almost hid itself within his beard, but he seemed to find this clause in their agreement not even worth commenting on. Instead, he simply walked out of the room, mind already focused, she thought, on the next claim on his attention – the elderly historian with whom he was going to disagree.

CHAPTER NINETEEN

The pattern of the next few days was set – silent, companionable hours spent sifting the papers that documented her grandfather's long life; afternoons of pure enjoyment, wandering through corners of Paris that most visitors never got to know. Louise didn't analyse the pleasure it gave her to share her favourite places, but knowing that it was the only gift she could offer him made each afternoon together more precious.

She never invited him to return with her to dine in the Rue Jacob and knew why she didn't – Nadia would have watched them and sensed that she was being left out. Nor did Daniel suggest they should dine together anywhere else. The omission puzzled her until she realised that it sprang from a touching concern that she wouldn't have expected. There was nothing about daylight walks to cause embarrassment or gossip, but intimate dinners might have been a different matter.

Then one afternoon, forsaking secret places, she made him climb the steep alleys and stairways of Montmartre to visit the Sacré-Coeur – more whitely gleaming Byzantine temple than Christian church. The near-darkness inside was always candlelit, but on a day of fleeting spring sunshine a kaleidoscope of colours poured down through the stained glass as well, to give its own shifting illuminations.

When they finally left the church for the late-afternoon brightness outside it seemed to Louise that ease had disappeared. For the first time in their rambles together she felt obliged to talk for the sake of breaking a silence that had become uncomfortable.

'I wanted you to come here on this sort of day. It inspired a French organist called Henri Mulet to write some music that exactly describes those patterns of colour on the flagstones. I could play it for you on the piano, but it sounds even more beautiful on its rightful instrument.'

She glanced at Daniel's face and doubted that he'd even heard what she'd just said. Something other than organ music was occupying his mind.

'Another morning's work will see André's papers finished,' he said abruptly. 'I'll waive tomorrow afternoon's fee, though. The guide can take a rest – our walks are over.'

She had the feeling of having walked into a door that had been slammed in her face. There was almost physical affront, but also something much worse than that – a bitter sense of rejection in place of the closeness that had laid enchantment on the past few days.

'The scholar can take a rest, too,' she answered after a small pause. 'I'll offer him my thanks now for much help received, and finish the papers myself.' Terrified of having made assumptions that were shrivelling as fast as the first frost blackened her dahlias at home, she went rushing on. 'We can say goodbye now. You'll be wanting to ... to go off somewhere else, I expect.'

She got no further than her first step away from him before his hands clamped themselves on her shoulders, biting through the thin tweed of her jacket. When he spoke his voice was rough with pain and sadness.

'Listen to me, Louise. If the choice were mine I'd *never* say goodbye. I'd walk with you to the world's end and count myself lucky above all men. But you have a husband; I, for the moment at least, still have a wife.'

Life was going on all around them but she was aware of none of it. All that counted now was the warmth of his hands, the anguish in his face, and her own turmoil of grief and joy. But the question she'd carefully buried in her mind insisted on being asked.

'Why did Karen go home the day after Nadia's party? You seemed a couple that night.'

'She only arrived here at all to explain that she'd been promoted, and that living in Ann Arbor looked even less of a prospect than it had before. I think a divorce was in her mind, but she didn't argue when I said our marriage, such as it is, must remain intact until Kate and Hal are through the difficult teenage years. She doesn't mind – she's leaving me for a job, not another man.'

Louise made a desperate search for something to say. 'It sounds a civilised sort of agreement, but it's still very sad.'

A faint, improbable gleam of humour lightened Daniel's face. 'I'm afraid it became a little *less* civilised because Karen had caught me looking at you! Renowned for being as inscrutable as the Sphinx, apparently I gave myself away. It made her angry and snide at Nadia's party, and silly enough to fracture even Geoffrey's Oxford courtesy. That's why I had to weigh in myself.'

'And flattened the "garden junky" in the process! I took that *very* amiss,' she said with difficulty, 'even though it's probably what I am.'

Daniel's hands cupped her face so that she had to look at him. 'I hope you've also taken it amiss that I've managed not to touch you all this week. The roughneck seems to have acquired self-control at last. In fact I've become so damned decorous that I scarcely know myself.'

She managed to smile at a word that still didn't suit him, even though tomorrow was too near, and already she could feel the grief it held in store. 'You're touching me now. Is that to say goodbye?'

'I'm afraid it's only to say that self-control is crumbling fast.' A moment later he had pulled her towards him and found her mouth with his own. The kiss was too sweet not to be repeated, a second, a third time. By then she was crushed against him; the world had slipped from gravity's clasp and was spinning out in space.

Daniel lifted his head at last and tried to find his voice. 'Will you spend this evening with me? Just once? I warn you that if you say yes I shall try to spend the night with you as well, but you'll still be able to say no.'

She knew with what vestige of common sense remained that she should drag herself away from him and leave without a backward glance. But it was more than flesh and blood and heart would allow.

'If you're feeling rich we'll get dressed up and go to Maxim's, and pretend that we aren't the people we know we are,' she agreed unsteadily. 'Just for one evening I think I could manage that.'

He smiled the rare, tender smile that seemed to have become her private possession, then took her hand and led her down the hill.

'Why did you bring us here?' Daniel asked the question as they were left alone to sip coffee and fine brandy. 'I wouldn't have suspected your tastes of running to little pink lamps and gilded mirrors and murals that are only just on the right side of decency!'

'My tastes don't as a rule,' Louise agreed, thoughtfully contemplating the luscious nude lady painted on the wall behind him. 'But we didn't come here for the slightly overblown décor, or even the superb food and wine.' She looked at him over her glass, and he saw the sadness that hid beneath the surface of the evening's gaiety. 'We came to step out of the real world for an hour or two, to live our own particular fairy tale. I keep expecting that intense-looking gentleman with the violin over there to break into the opening bars of *Der Rosenkavalier*!'

He smiled because she wanted him to, but for him the evening's enchantment had nothing to do with Maxim's *fin-de-siècle* effervescence. It wouldn't worry him if he never came again. The only thing needed for happiness was to be able to look at Louise, and it was wrong past bearing to know that *that* might never happen again when he loved her with such grief and rich delight.

'I'm not familiar with *Der Rosenkavalier*, or almost anything else you care to mention,' he admitted. 'I'm a very good historian – pace all those others who don't agree with me! – but that's *all* I am, you have to realise. You're worse than Karen for my self-esteem, knowing intimately what I've barely heard tell of, but when she jeered at me for falling into the trap of becoming humble, she got it all wrong. The truth is that I'm as proud as a peacock for having the good sense and perfect taste to fall in love with you!'

He said it lightly but she wasn't misled. The matter was

serious for them both, and desperate entreaty was in her face when she looked at him.

'We're too *old* for that, Daniel . . . aren't . . . *can't* be in love. In real life the fairy tale ends for good at midnight; there's no happy-ever-after. In three months' time you'll go back to your family, where you belong. If I belong anywhere it's in Oxford.'

His hand covered hers where it was clenched round a glass on the table. 'Please don't tell me this isn't real. It's as real as anything I shall ever know, and God knows I'll pray that nothing else is half as painful.' He gripped her hand for a moment longer and then let it go. 'Time I took you home, I think. Prince Charming is beginning to feel his age!'

Outside in the Rue Royale they had to wait for a cab. While Daniel watched out for a free one she stared at his face lit by the street-lamps above them. It was dearly familiar to her now, but not yet nearly enough explored. There was altogether too much they still didn't know about each other, and they had one chance left to find out. It seemed suddenly unthinkable to waste it.

As a taxi slowed down beside them the knowledge in her mind spoke itself in words, quite calmly.

'I should like to go back with you, Daniel – not to the Rue Jacob. Just this once.'

If he hesitated, made the mistake of asking whether or not she was sure, she knew that she would change her mind. But he simply helped her inside, and gave a direction to the driver. They might, she thought, with a twinge of misplaced amusement, have been doing this for years. But amusement was more bearable than guilt, and much more bearable than the fear that was beginning to grow inside her. There couldn't be a woman less equipped than she to become a passionately explicit, demonstrative lover. Anti-climax stood waiting to scream with laughter at her, and when it did she would know how thoroughly she had disappointed him and humiliated herself.

But the act of making love when they got to his room had no guilt in it, and not the least chance of failure. Nakedness seemed natural between them after all, and loving each other was what they had been born for. Entranced by the rapturous ease of giving and taking pleasure, she even laughed out loud, and heard Daniel's shout of delight when she tried to explain.

'I expected to be racked with shame,' she said with wonderment at herself, 'not wallowing in the happiness of being a fallen woman!' She reached up to touch his face, no longer unsure of what she did because whatever they did to each other had become instinctive and right. 'I never dreamed that *this* was how love is meant to be . . . I'm so glad I *do* know now.'

'My heart's blood, I'd love you for ever if I could . . .' but her hand moved to stifle what else he might have said; hadn't they agreed that 'for ever' didn't come into a real-life fairy tale?

He fell asleep after she did, and woke to find her dressed and ready to leave. 'Not so soon . . . please, not *yet*,' he entreated.

'I'm going now,' she said gently. 'Being a coward, I hoped I might be able to creep out without having to say goodbye. I must go and finish what I stayed to do, and then return home.'

'I'll come with you . . . Louise, *wait*, my love.'

He caught her wrist and held her imprisoned. 'You're anything but a coward – in fact you've brought self-sacrifice to a fine art, but you ought to have learned by now that graceful acceptance of the inevitable isn't my style at all.'

She smiled because he wanted her to, but her eyes were bright with tears. 'The inevitable is nevertheless what we seem to be faced with. It's time to go our separate ways, my dear love . . . in your heart you know it as well as I do. But I shan't feel guilty – that would be to spoil something that was entirely beautiful.' She pulled herself away from him and fled, and a moment later the door closed behind her.

The Rue Jacob was waking up when she turned into the street; it looked impossibly as usual – the awnings already out on the Hôtel Angleterre, the pavement in front of the florist's shop being swept and watered. Then she realised that nothing else had changed at all . . . only *she* had changed completely. It made a dangerous gap between herself and the rest of the world – something she could fall through and be lost in for ever.

But Henri, drinking his first, peaceful cup of coffee of the day, took her arrival so calmly that her moment of panic died away. She even remembered that she was much too old to have to make explanations, and that he was the last man on earth to insist on them. He poured coffee for her as if it was natural to see her return from an early-morning walk, and smiled at her with warm affection.

'I was afraid you'd been working too hard, my dear, but you look . . . well, beautifully not tired at all.'

She thought he almost certainly guessed, this quiet, kind man whose lifelong habit it had been to observe rather than participate. It would have been possible to tell him the truth, but she sensed in him no longing to be told. Instead she explained to him as calmly as she could the work that had been completed in André's study.

'There's a little more to be done; after that everything that's left will have value for an art historian. It's also, of course, the material for an account of the Galeries Benoît themselves.'

'Which perhaps *you* ought to write?' Henri suggested.

'I don't think so,' she said with a faint smile. 'For one thing I could have too hard a job being fair to my grandfather! I think it's something you should do yourself when you can leave the galleries to Pierre.'

Henri made no comment on this and asked another question instead. 'Is Dr Goodman coming to help this morning?'

Her colour rose a little but she shook her head. 'No . . . there's . . . there's no need now; I can finish it alone. Then I must go home.'

'Of course, my dear. With Geoffrey's move in the autumn you must both have a great deal to arrange.'

She merely nodded this time, feeling herself sliding with dreadful ease into the ways of iniquity and deception. Since Daniel's appearance at her mother's luncheon table she had given no single thought to Geoffrey, or to their move into the Master's Lodging. But Henri placidly sipped his coffee, and remembered something else.

'By the way, someone called here yesterday afternoon, asking for Dr Goodman, although I'm not sure why she expected to find him in the Rue Jacob. Her name was Mademoiselle Torrance.'

Louise forced herself to explain through suddenly dry lips.

'She's Anna Ouspenska's daughter, living with her in Oxford at the moment. Daniel rents rooms in Anna's house. I suppose Madeleine thought we might know where he was in Paris.'

'When I explained that you were both out she didn't seem inclined to come in and talk to Nadia.'

'She thinks talking to women is a waste of time; she's happier with men.'

'Not happy at all, was my impression of her,' said Henri definitely, '. . . in fact, rather a strange girl altogether.'

'Well, let's hope she goes home soon, otherwise Anna will worry about her.' It was another untruth, Louise realised sadly. What she really wanted was for Madeleine to stay safely in France, out of reach of their lives. But it was no kindness to Anna to hope for that. She must bury the thought in her mind, along with the unease of knowing that Pierre had been right about Madeleine being in the locality.

It was a huge effort to decide what to do next when her only inclination was to sit remembering, moment by moment, what had happened to her since yesterday's visit to the Sacré-Coeur. But she forced herself to concentrate on the obvious first steps – a shower and a change of clothes would help her regain some hold on normality. But when she walked into the study half an hour later Daniel was already there, with papers spread around him.

'You weren't supposed to come . . . I told Henri so,' she said unsteadily, made breathless by the joy of finding him.

'I explained that academics have a tiresome habit of wanting to be in at the end of a job – that way they can be sure of taking some of the credit!'

His smile, his whole face, was so full of tenderness that her racing heart steadied again. The world was safe while he was there. The gap between herself and reality was something she could step over after all.

'I keep forgetting you're an academic,' she admitted, 'you're so little like the ones I know.'

'A compliment? No, perhaps not! Now, sweetheart . . . we have to finish off this tedious work before you show me

Versailles. No historian worth his salt can admit to never having been there.'

The sudden doubt and sadness in her face made him reach out to grip her hands. 'I haven't forgotten the inevitable – you'll go back to Geoffrey, and I shall eventually fetch up in Michigan again. But today – and tonight also, I pray – is ours. Who else does it help if we *don't* enjoy the little that's within our reach?'

' "Look thy last on all things lovely every hour",' she quoted slowly. 'An English poet recommended that, and of course it's exactly what we must do.'

Afterwards she remembered very little of what they looked at that afternoon. Conscious only of his hand holding hers, and of his smile when she occasionally turned her head to look at him, they could have been anywhere on earth for all she registered of what they saw. But afterwards over dinner 'Chez les Anges' – a name earned for the restaurant, she explained, by the celestial coq au vin it always served – she remembered to ask what a celebrated historian had made of Versailles.

Daniel considered the question seriously before he answered. 'True to my theories of economic cause and effect, I reckoned up what it had cost generations of French peasants to produce the wealth needed for all that useless magnificence. How could the Revolution not have been inevitable?'

'I didn't quite believe in your theories,' she admitted with a faint smile, 'and suspected you of not believing them either! I'm sorry, Daniel.'

'And so you ought to be!' But his hand reached out to cover hers resting on the table. 'The truth is that at the moment I can scarcely remember what my theories are – I can only think about us. For the first time in my life I'm feeling helpless, and sick with rage at myself for not knowing what to do.'

She shook her head while she struggled to sound certain enough to convince him. 'Doing what we know is right doesn't make us helpless. It *has* to be right, Daniel, for you to think of your children, and for me to remember the man who tried to rescue me from being unwanted.'

'He couldn't have tried hard enough, because – unlike most women I know – you'd be so easy to make happy.'

'It wasn't his fault,' Louise had to insist. 'We hadn't been married long enough before disaster overtook us; I was still only used to dealing with pain on my own. I shut Geoffrey out, but by the time I was rational enough to know what I was doing it was too late – he'd found his own salvation at St Barnabas. But he still honours in his own way the agreement we made at the beginning to trust our happiness to each other. I've betrayed that trust, and my punishment will be never to be able to tell him.' She watched Daniel's face, thinking that she must be certain of remembering it clearly – not to be able to recall, feature by feature, how it went together, and changed when he smiled, would be more than she could bear.

'You seem to be telling me that you can't abandon a man who did you a kindness twenty years ago,' he said with deliberate bluntness. 'That's masochism carried to the point of madness, my dear one, and I wouldn't permit it if I had a chance of doing anything else. But I can't, try as I will, see you enjoying a life of sin with me at Ann Arbor; I'm not even sure that you could tolerate the place at all. It's about as different from Oxford as anywhere could be, but all places of higher learning seem to have one thing in common – they're unhealthily inward-looking.'

Louise blinked away the tears that would keep forming, and tried to smile instead. 'I *told* you we were past the age for falling in love. Twenty years ago I'd probably have taken the life of sin in my stride. But at going on forty I can't help remembering that you certainly loved Karen once, and that I intended to love no one if I didn't manage to love Geoffrey.'

Daniel's hand touched her cheek in a tender gesture that no self-styled roughneck New Yorker should ever have known. 'We're only past the age of making another mistake. You'll have to take it on trust for now, but I shall go on loving you until I die. I don't know whether I shall ever be allowed to prove it to you, but I'm bespoke now. That's a word Oxford has taught me . . . but then it's taught me a lot of things I didn't know.'

There seemed to be nothing more to say, and only one thing

left to do – to go back to Daniel's room and become as nearly one body as the two human beings could achieve, engulfed by longing for each other and the awareness that so little time was left to them. The uncertainties of the night before weren't remembered now – there was only urgent need, and leaping desire, and the tenderness left behind afterwards, like foam on the seashore after the wave breaks and goes home.

Still lying safely held by Daniel's arms she found the courage to say what must be said.

'I'm going home tomorrow . . . today, I suppose it is. I *have* to, to do the best I can without you. Will you give me a little time – stay away as long as you can?'

He tilted up her face and saw it washed silver-pale by the moonlight slanting down on them. 'I can't cancel next term's lectures, but I *could* find somewhere else to live. Shall I do that, my heart?'

She shook her head, trying not to weep. 'No, I'd always be wondering where you were . . . longing to bump into you and dreading it as well. Besides, Anna wouldn't find another tenant this late in the year. We'll meet occasionally, I expect, and manage to smile and ask each other how we are . . .' Her voice failed, but for a little while longer she could feel his arms tighten about her and be comforted.

CHAPTER TWENTY

The flight reached Heathrow late in the afternoon, and this time it was her husband's fair head she could see above the crowd in the Arrivals hall. It took a deliberate effort to walk towards him, to smile, and to have her cheek kissed – the only public display that Geoffrey would ever permit himself. It felt like being touched by a stranger; she had to remind herself that this man was entitled to kiss her and examine her closely.

'My dear, you've been working too hard.' His quiet voice at least was familiar – she remembered it from a time that seemed to be long past. 'I expected it to take you days to get through the mountain of papers André must have left behind.'

She took a deep breath and heard a calm voice that seemed to be recognisably her own. 'Nadia probably wanted to get rid of me as quickly as possible – she accepted an offer of help from Daniel Goodman.'

'And from his wife also?'

'No, she had to go back to New York, so I suppose he was . . . glad of something to do.' It was all she could manage until a different subject offered itself. She found it when they were settled in the car, nosing their way out of the airport car park.

'How's Uncle Will . . . and Ruth? Has she been looking after you?'

'Devotedly – you know Ruth! She offered to feed us both this evening – I had to accept, of course.'

'Of course!' She saw him frown a little and realised that if irony had been carefully ironed out of her voice, so had warmth as well. 'I hope term started well,' she added as a peace offering.

'Oh, well enough, I think. But Humphrey is looking very tired. I shall be thankful to ease the burden off his shoulders.'

It was true, she realised, and something to be remembered. Her husband was less interested in power for its own sake than most men – he believed that he was needed at Barnabas, and he was probably right. He also wanted to release Humphrey and Edwina, and in that he was certainly right.

Geoffrey always drove fast, and well, disliking a passenger who talked to him all the time. She could close her eyes, relax for a little while the guard she was keeping on herself. It would get easier . . . she repeated it silently like a litany she could learn to believe in. The day would come eventually when mind and body didn't ache for Daniel.

Beside her, Geoffrey glanced occasionally at her white face and tried to believe that what ailed his wife was the natural exhaustion of ten days spent under the same roof with Nadia Rivaux. He didn't speak until he turned the car into their own driveway, and then heard himself say what he'd been telling himself for miles past that he *wouldn't* say.

'You look so tired that you'd better go straight to bed – I'll make your excuses to Ruth.' She tried to smile, grateful to be let off a purgatorial visit upstairs, but it suddenly provoked an outburst that wasn't typical of him.

'I should have known better than to leave you in Paris – I *did* know it was a stupid thing to do.'

With a shock of relief she realised what he meant and was able to answer him.

'I've told you before – I don't regret giving up the galleries. Even less would I have wanted Pierre's little infatuation to last, but I can promise you that it *hasn't*.'

'Then something else is distressing you – is it still the thought of leaving here? Shall I make College history by resigning before I'm even installed?'

He didn't mean it – she wasn't intended to believe that he would contemplate such a betrayal of Humphrey Wharton and the men who had chosen him. The dissembling made her angry but she made a huge effort to speak lightly.

'Even if you *were* prepared to go that far, Ruth wouldn't let you! I shall be myself again after a night's sleep, and now you must go and enjoy your supper with her.' Then she got out of the car and went indoors, not waiting to see if he followed her.

The following morning the breakfast table was neatly laid when Geoffrey went downstairs. He could tell himself that normality had returned; his anxiety about Louise the evening before had been a figment of his imagination. She put coffee in front of him, smiled, and remembered to enquire about Andrew Jardine, whose turn of Proctorial duty was coming to an end – conversation about such things would see them safely through breakfast. Geoffrey left for College feeling happier; the Paris danger seemed to be over and he'd exaggerated in his own mind whatever distress he'd imagined in Louise.

At a later hour, one that Anna would consider reasonable for a visit, Louise raided the garden again, this time for an armful of pink and orange tulips.

'Picked with you in mind,' she said cheerfully when she arrived next door. 'No one else I know would put them in the same vase.'

Anna accepted what she considered to be a compliment, but inspected the face of her friend. 'You stayed too long with Nadia – she sucks your blood and leaves you looking pale.'

'There was some tedious work to do, sorting out my grandfather's papers,' Louise explained. 'I should probably still be doing it if your lodger hadn't kindly lent a hand.'

In such terms she could talk about him, clinging to the hope that every time she did a little pent-up longing for him would escape, like steam being allowed out of a safety valve.

'I thought Daniel was going to Paris to meet his wife,' Anna commented with surprise.

'He was . . . did, I mean. They attended Nadia's party together, but Karen left after that – some dizzying promotion called her back to New York.'

'Beautiful she is, judging by her photograph, but stupid she must be as well. I'd choose Paris and Daniel every time, wouldn't you?'

Louise bent down to deal with a shoelace that needed retying. Then, a little flushed, she raised her head again, having apparently forgotten Anna's question.

'I didn't know Madeleine intended going to Paris. She called at the galleries, but Pierre and I were out – there was only Henri for her to talk to.'

Anna's monkey face screwed itself up into an expression of

anxiety. 'She said she had friends to meet there – I suppose she meant you and Daniel. The truth is that she can't bear to be left out. If you were going to be there, that's where she would be too.' Anna brought coffee to the table, then sat down looking at Louise with sad, intelligent eyes. 'She has saved a little money since she came here, but it won't last long in Paris. Dijon she thinks of as a prison – only desperation would drive her back there. She has youth to offer and a very definite animal allure, but where can that lead, except to a life she seems to think of as well paid and glamorous? I *know* what it is, my dear friend – servitude as degrading as any slavery ever was.' Her husky voice broke on the words, but she knuckled her eyes to keep herself from weeping. 'I'm afraid I shall never see her again – she thought Oxford was *worse* than Dijon.'

Louise tried to sound both gentle and firm. 'Anna, drink your coffee and listen to me, please. Madeleine hasn't the slightest intention of becoming a prostitute, if that's the anxiety in your mind. It amuses her to talk about it, but only to *épater le bourgeois* like me! I even doubt whether the lover in Dijon was anything but fantasy. You should persuade her to burst into print – she could be Ruth brought up to date, another Françoise Sagan, with the stories she spins!'

Distracted for a moment by an idea that appealed to her, Anna sipped coffee, then banged the cup down again, shaking her head. 'It's too late, dearest – she won't came back now. All I can do is pray for her happiness, even though I *know* that happiness isn't to be had that way. It's something we make for ourselves, or not; Madeleine hasn't the gift.'

'She may learn the trick of giving, if only to receive something back. In fact, she's too intelligent *not* to learn. And if her giving is never from the heart, as it has to be for most of us, that will be an advantage she has over the rest of us!'

Anna stared again at her friend's face, noting its sadness and fragility. 'You don't like my daughter,' she said without the slightest offence. 'Sometimes neither do I; but I love her more than I can say. She's part of me – I *have* to love her whatever she does.'

'She'll do nothing very terrible,' Louise insisted definitely, 'and I'm certain that she'll come dancing back to Oxford before long – for the same reason that took her to Paris. She seems convinced that her life is bound up with ours. The story isn't finished yet; she'll stay here at least until it is.'

'You sound very sure, my dear, how can you be?' Anna asked, torn between doubt and hope.

'I consulted my crystal ball this morning,' Louise said gravely. A smile wavered round her mouth for a moment, then disappeared. 'It gave me no information about your other wanderer, but you probably aren't concerned about him!'

Then before Anna could speak again about Daniel she went back to the only haven she knew. A cherry tree that had been 'wearing white for Easter-tide' was already snowing petals in the wind and she had missed its day or two of perfection. It seemed reason enough for the tears that were trickling down her face.

Trinity term had well begun by the time Daniel got back to Oxford. He'd returned as late as he dared, but there was a lecture to be prepared and delivered. The weeks in France had let in more changes than he'd bargained for. Already College gardeners were mowing lawns again with the air of men reinitiating some sacred, post-winter rite, and blossom hung everywhere in great swags of white and pink and gold. Spring and Oxford suited each other, he'd been told; now he could see that it was true. Allowing for having been blinkered and half-deaf before, he didn't think he could altogether have missed noticing anywhere else such greenness and such birdsong. The truth was that he was *dangerously* alive now, but that had more to do with Louise Carmichael than Oxford.

Anna was kind enough to say she'd missed him when he got back to Norham Grove. Madeleine, on the way out of the house, could barely bother to fling him a greeting.

'It serves me right for going away,' he said smilingly to Anna when she looked mortified afterwards at such behaviour. 'Your daugher's probably found a more suitable escort than me, and if she has it's just as well – I was finding it hard work keeping up!'

'You were being kind, and getting very bored, I expect. In any case Madeleine went away herself. I was afraid she wouldn't come back, but my dear Louise *said* there was no need to agitate myself and she was right.' Anna looked thoughtfully at the face of the man in front of her. 'Paris wasn't a huge success all round. My daughter returned cross, Louise looked more tired than when she went, and your wife apparently didn't even stay – I'm sorry, Daniel. Never mind. One more little term here and you'll go home yourself.'

He nodded but returned to the subject of the girl who'd just swung out of the door, with a provocative flick of her skirt for his benefit.

'*Has* Madeleine got a new fish hooked on her line?'

'Someone she met when he wrote an article about the Maison Française for a local newspaper. He's a talkative Irishman called Niall Redmond who even bothers to be charming to me when he calls here!'

'And our neighbours next door – how are they?'

'As usual, I think – well, perhaps not quite. My dear friend is so often outside that I'm afraid she's saying goodbye to her flowers one by one.'

'You'll miss *her* as much as she'll miss them,' Daniel suggested, wondering why he'd thought it would be easier to talk about Louise than pretend to himself that she didn't entirely monopolise his thoughts.

Anna's hands sketched a void she couldn't express in words. 'Imagine having just Ruth instead! Even after years of being neighbours, she still looks at me down her long, thin nose as she would look at a gypsy who's pitched his caravan in Norham Grove. She thinks I'm out of place here. Perhaps I still am, and Louise a little, too; but I can't be sorry – it was the beginning of our friendship.'

He nodded again and made an excuse to climb the stairs to his own rooms. Anna's 'little term' stretched ahead of him like an athlete's gruelling marathon that he couldn't hope to win. He'd considered again the idea of finding somewhere else to live but always rejected it, as Louise had done. He wasn't an adolescent to be overcome whenever the love of his heart appeared in the garden next door. He was, for God's sake, an old hand at squaring up to Fate, who had better start now by concentrating on a lecture that was to demolish the conventional historian's analysis of the Crusades! The following morning found him out of the house too early for the Bodleian to be open, but a tramp round Christ Church Meadows was better than running the risk of coming face to face with Louise.

By the end of the day, tired of working, and assailed by the need of someone he might call a friend, he found himself knocking at the yellow door in Holywell Street.

'I was passing by . . . can keep right on passing if you're otherwise engaged,' he suggested when William Standish opened the door.

'Come *in*, my dear boy — thought you were still in France,' said William with the warmth that drew people to his little house. 'You can't have eaten yet — you've got that "lean and hungry" look of a scholar who's forgotten about food all day. I can't offer you a stalled ox, but if you'll share the pâté I was about to start on, and a bit of Stilton, then good company will make it a feast!'

It was the Professor's special grace, Daniel thought, this way of reversing roles so that taker suddenly found he was made giver instead.

'I'm not sure how good the company will be,' he admitted. 'Perhaps I should warn you of that.'

William noted the weariness in his visitor's face but didn't comment on it. 'A glass or two of Burgundy will help. You've been rootling in the past too much — it's an occupational hazard for historians!'

His sitting room had, as usual, defeated Mrs Maggs by returning to the happy disorder that prevailed around William as soon as she left the house. Daniel didn't notice it, being unable to think of anything else but the memory of kissing Louise here for the first time. Mechanically, he looked round for a chair to clear and sit down on, and found his eye caught by a name on a newspaper by-line.

'A scavenger,' said William with unusual asperity. 'A sticker of pins in the side of the Establishment to see if he can make it bleed. I dare say we're asked to forgive him because his grandfather was murdered by the Black and Tans. The more likely truth is that he finds scurrility pays.'

'Harsher speaking than usual from our gentle professor,' Daniel commented with a smile. But he could see why, when Redmond had dared to compare Universitas Oxoniensis to an ageing, narcissistic 'queen' forever preening at his image in the looking glass.

'The one-sidedness of the attack is what makes me angry,' William admitted. 'When the gutter press squirts venom over the Royal Family *they* can't descend to the same abysmal level, and nor can this ancient university. Its foibles permit irony, but not Redmond's kind of vituperation.' He inspected Daniel's thoughtful face. 'I dare say *you* find the foibles absurd. Why should an undergraduate "come *up*" for a new term even though he might hail from ultima Thule? Why should Lord Crewe's Benefaction mean strawberries and champagne for senior academics instead of a hand-out to the more indigent among them?'

'And why,' asked Daniel, entering into the game, 'should Great Tom thunder out at 9.05 each evening, not nine o'clock, just because Oxford's 1° 15' west of Greenwich!' He sipped the wine that had been poured for him and grew serious again. 'Redmond's name was mentioned to me yesterday, as it happens – by Anna Ouspenska. She seemed relieved that her daughter had found herself a suitable companion for once. If she were to read that rag over there she might be feeling less happy.'

William conjured up a picture of Madeleine in his mind's eye and gave a little sigh. 'I used to imagine that I should like to have a daughter. She'd be a small, pretty thing, and I'd teach her to love the English poets as I do myself. So much for an old man's foolish vision – I fear it would make today's young ladies laugh themselves sick!'

'My own daughter, Kate, among them,' Daniel agreed, 'but I'd take the risk of sending her here. New York and Oxford make excellent correctives for each other – our pace and brashness, your inertia and finesse!'

The Burgundy had helped, but William remembered his

guest's face at the front door, and still sensed the despair that dragged at him.

'Has it been a risk for *you*, coming here? Have you foregone something precious at home for an experience that Oxford has failed to provide?'

The quiet question took him off guard. After a moment he answered it with painful honesty, aware that nothing less would do for this good friend.

'Oxford has provided just about every damn thing it could, but the most precious of them I shan't be allowed to take away. That's a hard lesson for a smash-and-grab man like me to learn.'

William's smile was so full of kindness and understanding that Daniel suspected he'd given away his trouble.

'Oxford's most lasting lesson, perhaps: possession isn't what matters; knowledge of the thing desired *is*,' suggested the Professor, and then Daniel *knew* that he had.

The annual celebration of May Morning might reasonably have appeared on any list of local oddities. Especially given the vagaries of an English spring, it bordered on idiocy to rise before dawn to listen to a Latin anthem being sung from the top of Magdalen's bell-tower. Daniel owed prior notice of the event to Ruth Carmichael, who held forth about it when he overtook her walking home.

'Quite pagan, of course,' she said with a faint air of disapproval, 'and quite unpleasantly damp as well, more often than not — it *usually* rains, Oxford weather being what it is. For those who can afford it tomorrow morning a champagne breakfast in a punt on the river will be considered *de rigueur* afterwards; for those who can't, a cheap, noisy revel will do instead. Needless to say, my sister-in-law still persists in thinking it a pretty ceremony!'

Until that moment he'd had not the smallest intention of rising in time to trudge all the way to Magdalen Bridge. Now, short of dying in his sleep, he would be there — to gainsay this woman, and to gather a memory that would link him to Louise.

'I'm glad I met you,' he said with such unexpected vigour that Ruth almost blushed. It had been her impression until now that she and Daniel Goodman were not quite kindred spirits. Tempting as it was to think she might have been wrong, the fact remained that he wasn't Geoffrey's kind of historian. She must remember that and keep a cool, Carmichael head even though he was being so agreeable.

'There was to have been a debating joust between you and my brother at the Union, Dr Goodman,' she said archly. 'I'm told that *you* decided against appearing.'

Only the truth – that he'd wanted to do away with one of Louise's anxieties – would have wiped the smile off Ruth's face; short of that, amazing affability would have to confound her. He'd had time to learn that rudeness merely stimulated this warrior lady to battle.

'I'm a man who likes to win, Miss Carmichael – that isn't easy if your heart's not in the right place, and now my view is that wars *can't* be anything but an obscenity.'

He waited for her to take a merry swipe at his ancestors from the Ruhr, but for once she disappointed him.

'You're so right! Englishman must never fight German again. I feel that very strongly. We may never understand the French – a law unto themselves, I always think – but we do have much in common with Teutonic peoples.'

He gave her the benefit of the doubt – she hadn't deliberately sneered at her half-French sister-in-law again – but it was a relief to part company with her at the gateway to her own house, before affability wore too thin.

He set his alarm clock before going to bed, crawled out to make himself coffee in the half-light of a very unMay-like dawn, and left the house in a frame of mind that was anything but celebratory.

It had, as Ruth predicted, begun to drizzle, in the sly English way that pretended not to wet whatever it fell upon. But it was rain for all that – enough to dampen his spirits still further and confirm a strong impression that Oxford was sending him out of his mind. He wouldn't be seen dead in Ann Arbor doing anything as stupid as this, even if it existed to be done.

Five hundred yards ahead of him another madman – no, a mad woman – travelled into the mist. Making a faster pace, he would overhaul her soon, and no doubt they'd wish each other a straight-faced 'good morning', before he walked on. No, dear God, he'd do nothing of the kind, because now he knew who it was in front of him. He began to run and caught up with Louise before she could cross South Parks Road.

CHAPTER TWENTY-ONE

He saw the apprehension in her face turn to joy.

'Oh, Daniel . . . I'm so glad it's you! There aren't enough people about, and I was afraid that if I ran, whoever seemed to be chasing me would run faster.'

He wanted to wrap his arms about her, but this was Oxford, not a byway in Paris where they were unknown. All he could do was command his racing heart to slow down so that he could speak.

'Are you all right? I think about you all the time, when I'm supposed to be concentrating on some blasted, totally uninteresting Crusade! I dread seeing you, fear missing you, and altogether feel like a teenager trapped in calf-love for the first time. But it's much worse, in fact, because I know that isn't what I am.'

'I'm managing quite well,' she said with an attempt at a smile. 'I expect you are, too, really.'

He smoothed the damp, dark fringe out of her eyes, and thought it was how he would most easily remember her – with the sheen of rain on her hair and face.

'Can you be on the same crazy errand as me? Ruth didn't say that you joined in – only that you approved of pagan springtime goings-on.'

'Geoffrey had to spend last night in London, so Ruth and I endured dinner together. May morning cropped up in the conversation and, as usual with my sister-in-law, I found myself in the defending corner. Then I decided that I'd better put my feet where my mouth was.'

'I wish I'd known. I'd have provided the punt and the champagne.'

'For that you really do have to be young enough not to mind the rain!' She looked at her watch and tried to sound severe.

'We shall be late if we don't hurry – they start to sing at six o'clock.'

'And we did come out to hear the singing, after all,' Daniel agreed.

He took her hand and fitted his stride to hers, aware that the grey, misty morning seemed appropriate now – a perfectly ironic mismatch with a celebration of the coming-in of summer.

'*Is* it some sort of bacchanalian orgy we're going to?' he asked. 'Ruth's long nose, quivering with indignation, implied as much.'

'It sometimes becomes a bit riotous, but it begins magically – no traffic in the High, voices taking flight from the top of the tower, and all the girls with flowers and ribbons in their hair.'

'Mad, but pretty,' Daniel agreed.

'Merely mad some think, including Mr Khrushchev when he came here. He asked why it was done, and the President of Magdalen looked down *his* nose and explained – only because it had been done for the last five hundred years!'

She turned to enjoy Daniel's smile, but spoke seriously again. 'I haven't always been happy here, and I can see a lot of things that are wrong. But for as long as Oxford's spirit is civilising – and I think it still is – then I hope we can manage to keep it standing, and being true to itself.'

Daniel lifted her hand to his mouth and kissed it. 'Even a man from Michigan must say amen to that.'

They were no longer walking in an empty world, he suddenly noticed. In ones and twos, in dribbles that coalesced into streams, people were emerging from alleys and gateways, all moving in the same direction as themselves – like the children of Hamelin, answering the Pied Piper's call. There was no need to know the way, and no need to talk now. They were part of the crowd; they stood and listened to the choir's disembodied voices in the middle of the crowd; and still they knew that this May dawn would always seem in memory to have been spent just with each other.

'It's time to leave,' Louise said when the last note had floated away on the wind. 'Now the dancing will start and it begins to get noisy.'

'It's also time for breakfast,' Daniel insisted. 'I'm so famished that a genteel spread at the Randolph won't do. Can you stand something less fancy – George's in the Covered Market maybe?'

Barely hesitating, she nodded, and they began the walk along the High in silence. Afterwards precious time might seem to have been wasted, but they were together again, touched shoulders and hands occasionally – it was happiness enough after being alone.

'How's Madeleine?' Louise suddenly remembered to ask. 'I expect you know by now that *she* went to Paris too – in fact she called in at the galleries one afternoon, looking for you. I forgot to tell you when . . . when . . .'

'. . . we had other things to discuss,' Daniel finished for her. 'She's all right, according to Anna, but I'm off the list of people she's prepared to talk to – unfortunately she saw through me in the end. It doesn't matter now; she's found a dashing new beau – a real one this time.'

'I'm glad, I felt guilty about her. A man she can really call her own is exactly what she needs – at least, if he's a nice man.'

Reluctant to comment on Niall Redmond, Daniel was glad to arrive at the entrance to the Covered Market. He steered her through its labyrinth of alleyways into the homeliness of George's Café.

'Maxim's it isn't!' he said with a grin. 'But I can recommend something they call dripping-toast.'

His appetite, though, when the food arrived, seemed to have dwindled, like her own. They drank coffee and struggled not to watch a clock on the wall that seemed to be ticking away the most precious minutes of their lives.

'Tell me about Ann Arbor,' Louise said suddenly.

He had to search for words to describe a place he took for granted.

'I suppose I'd have to say it's vast, compared with Oxford; huge campuses, but with none of the ancient, protective spirit that the Colleges here provide. The Vietnam war stirred up a lot of unrest but things are quieter now – the spectre of unemployment seems to wonderfully concentrate the minds of students and teachers alike.'

'Your economic theory again!' Louise commented with a smile. 'Will you stay there for ever?'

'No . . . nor even for very much longer. I've had it in mind for years to find a philanthropic millionaire with enough money to burn to help me start a school somewhere for children who've been branded as no-hopers. I was one myself until an inspired teacher took me in hand. Now I'm arrogant enough to think that *I* can make the misfits want to learn.'

'I don't doubt it,' Louise said quietly, 'but can you find your millionaire?'

'I shall when the time comes.'

She smiled across the table at him, not doubting what he said. With no difficulty at all she could picture him drawing a response from even the most cussedly hostile or sadly backward child. It would become his life's work, and he would accomplish it brilliantly while she pottered through her privileged, aimless days in the Master's Lodging.

'You mustn't smile at me, my love, at least not quite so heartbreakingly,' he said. 'I've just spotted two of George's other customers – Madeleine and her new friend, sitting over by the window.'

Louise pushed her coffee cup away, made dizzy by the speed of her slide down into reality again. 'She seems determined to shadow us! But at least I'm now reminded that it's time I went home. Shall we go?'

'Yes, but not looking guilty,' he said gently.

She turned her head away for a moment, and when the need to weep had been mastered, managed to look at him again. 'Quite right – let May Morning jollity be our cry!'

It was even possible, she found, to return Madeleine's sly smile as they walked out, but jollity was nowhere in sight, and joy had surely fled for ever.

'I'll catch a bus, I think,' she said hurriedly. 'Don't bother to come with me, Daniel.'

'We're going to walk back together, my dear one, because I haven't finished what I was going to say; but first you have to forget about Anna's tiresome daughter, please. I've done very little work since I came back from Paris, but I've put in plenty of thought and I can't have it wasted by you not listening to me.'

'I'm listening,' she agreed, like an obedient child.

He smiled at her approvingly, but grew serious again. 'I told Karen that a divorce would have to wait – bad for the children, I said pompously. The truth is that I was too angry with her to think straight. Intelligent, almost adult teenagers see through sham more certainly than any other of God's creatures. What good can we possibly be doing them to pretend their parents still have a marriage that works? They probably despise us for that, and therefore discount the rest of what we should be teaching them.'

'I think you're right,' Louise said after a long pause. 'If you and Karen can separate without bitterness, and if Kate and Hal can be certain that you still love them, that *must* be the best way of limiting the damage.'

'So . . . with the Goodmans settled, more or less – what about the Carmichaels?'

She stopped suddenly and he had to turn and look at her.

'Daniel . . . if you were thinking about us as well, we *aren't* a reason for a divorce. My marriage may not be much more satisfactory than yours, but Geoffrey isn't like your wife, wanting release from it. He's still crippled as it is by his mother's abandonment of them. For me to walk away from him as well . . . I couldn't do it; happiness can't be bought at such a cost.'

He saw the sadness and the certainty in her face, and knew that nothing he could say would make the slightest difference. She was reduced to this one last handhold on what her heart said was right, and she would cleave to it for ever unless Geoffrey himself released her.

Eventually he mastered the obstruction in his throat and summoned up a response.

'Then I shall have to learn to picture you in the Master's Lodging, instead of at Norham Grove. I shall finish out another year at Ann Arbor while I lassoo my millionaire; then I'll start my school. I'll do the work I have to do, and I shall miss you to the end of my days.'

She didn't answer, and they walked the rest of the way in silence. There seemed nothing left to say.

When Geoffrey returned from London later in the day he remarked at once that she looked tired.

'A dawn start is catching up with me,' she explained after a moment's hesitation. 'I went to listen to the May Morning anthem, and so did Daniel Goodman. Ruth had predicted that it would be wet, and she was right.'

'Another memory of Oxford, then, that Goodman won't forget – singing in the rain!'

She managed to smile at the small joke, thankful for one concealment the less in having confessed to her early-morning walk. But relief didn't survive beyond the following day when her sister-in-law came downstairs to deliver a shock that set her heart racing.

'Look at this,' said Ruth, brandishing a local newspaper. 'The usual photographs of undergraduate horseplay on Magdalen Bridge yesterday. But I can't think what *you* were doing there – that *is* you, isn't it, with Daniel Goodman?'

Louise nodded, feeling slightly sick. 'We met by accident on the way, and left before the dancing started.' Her eyes skimmed the text alongside the photographs. 'Mr Redmond, whoever he may be, seems to share your killjoy view of May Morning!'

She had the rare pleasure of silencing Ruth, but was herself silenced later in the morning when Anna mentioned the photograph as well, and explained who Niall Redmond was.

Madeleine felt confident at last. There need be no pretence this time – about a gentle schoolmaster who avoided touching her and then abandoned her, or an unimpressionable American twice her age who'd declined several invitations to take her to bed. At last she'd been most definitely *taken*, and no feat of imagination was required. Virginity had technically been lost before, during a furtive and unenjoyable afternoon in Dijon, but she'd never blamed Monique for doubting that it was a *vraie affaire* – there were limits to what artistic licence could achieve.

About Niall Redmond there could be no doubt at all. She

needn't even explain what an exciting lover he was – her colleagues could see that for themselves whenever he came to collect her. He was clever and charming and experienced; but would he stay? One evening, after the love-making in his flat that followed their dinners together, anxiety drove her into talking about the future.

'Anna likes you very much, but she's getting suspicious that you're not *entirely* good for her precious daughter! She says you're too clever and ambitious to be a local journalist here for long. Are you?'

'Of course. The sky's the limit for a bright fellow like me. Now don't tell me that you didn't realise that!'

'You haven't even told me why you came here – wasn't that strange for an Irishman?'

Niall gave the lazy smile she found so exciting. 'I reckoned it might be a good place to start making a name for myself, and that's how it's turning out. There's God's plenty here to write about – as you very well know yourself.'

She knew, and she'd shared with him what she knew. For a moment she was uneasy about that – even regretted a little giving in to the temptation to paint her friendship with Geoffrey Carmichael in lurid colours when she saw that it amused and interested her lover. No actual harm would come of it, she was sure of that, even though she scarcely bothered to read what he wrote. She certainly hadn't minded pointing out to him yesterday a couple who'd been too wrapped up in each other to notice anyone else. Louise Carmichael had been her *bête noire* all along – a woman who didn't deserve her husband, much less the other men who seemed so ridiculously taken with her.

But Niall was lighting a cigarette, a sign she already recognised. Instead of making love again he'd suggest getting dressed and take her home. She'd been a fool to irritate him by mentioning Anna.

'I hope Louise Carmichael enjoyed seeing herself in your newspaper with our American lodger,' she said with relish.

Niall, blowing a smoke-ring at the ceiling, seemed unexcited. 'Embarrassing for her, and it also has its amusing side after the gossip there was about Carmichael himself – but it didn't dish his chances at St Barnabas. I hoped it would.'

Madeleine turned to stare at the man lying beside her. 'You dislike Geoffrey as much as I dislike *her* – why?'

'It's the system I'm after, but to attract readers a story needs people. One photograph doesn't amount to much – there were hundreds of other people on Magdalen Bridge, and although we can misrepresent, we're not supposed to invent!'

She didn't believe him. His target was the man, not the system. He'd only taken an interest in *her* when he discovered that she was intimate with the Carmichaels. Since then he'd enjoyed making love to her, but when he got bored he would smilingly drift away; he was that sort of man. She was stung into releasing a piece of information that did amount to something.

'No need to invent. I *saw* them – Louise and Daniel – kissing as lovers kiss outside the Sacré-Coeur in Paris, and it wouldn't have stopped there. What do you guess they went back to do at Daniel's hotel?'

'*This*, I imagine!' He was stubbing out his cigarette, restored to sparkling good humour. Taking her back to Norham Grove would wait after all, because he was no longer looking in the least bored.

As Niall had predicted, the May Morning photographs caused no particular stir. But in its next appearance his twice-weekly column returned to worry at a favourite bone: the cynical old institution that publicly wrung its hands over student morals but turned a blind eye to the private behaviour of its academics. This was followed two days later by a swingeing attack on the secure, privileged life of College dons, whose wine cellars were still full when many teaching posts were left unfilled for lack of funds.

'Predictable, tired stuff,' William Standish said dismissively when Geoffrey called on him one morning. 'I thought we'd heard the last of Belloc's poor old dons – "Compact of ancient tales, and port . . . and learning of a sort"! Redmond must find a less shopworn aphorism to beat us with.'

'This one will still do,' Geoffrey pointed out, grim-faced.

'But he *has* found something else. Here's what most of Oxford will be reading by this evening.'

Corruption was the story this time, especially as it was liable to appear in the election of Heads of Colleges. It gave no names, argued only general principles, and yet cleverly left the reader in no doubt that a crusade was being waged against a particular offender.

William read the piece through, then dropped the newspaper with a little snort of disgust. 'I suppose you think he's aiming at St Barnabas since no other College has held an election recently. Why should he? Did we once do something to ruffle Mr Redmond — throw him out, or not accept him at all?'

'I think he's aiming at *me*,' Geoffrey said quietly.

'*Why?*' William almost shouted. 'My dear man, you're tired and over-worked, reading too much into a piece of cheap invective that could apply to dozens of people.'

Geoffrey wiped a hand over his face and tried to smile. 'It was I who sent him packing out of College one day. He had the effrontery to go snooping into private rooms in the cause of "investigative journalism"! Jukes was doing his best to get rid of him but being unpleasantly baited with the freedom of the press when I appeared on the scene. I lodged a protest, of course, with this rag he writes for, but I expect the editor reckons that little confrontations are good for sales.'

'What do we do?' William asked. 'Send a dignified explanation of the procedure for appointing College heads? Preserve an even more dignified silence, which will impress no one but ourselves? Or have a couple of large rowing blues crowd Redmond into a corner and smile sweetly at him? I think they'd enjoy that.'

Geoffrey's face relaxed at last into a smile of genuine amusement. 'My dear William, you've been watching too many American thrillers on television — this is Oxford, not Chicago! I'm afraid we must wait and see what happens next. Perhaps Redmond has amused himself enough.'

But with the next issue came a more vehement restatement of the original theme. Surely it should be a matter of public concern that academics, already highly placed and climbing higher, were free to pollute the clear stream of youth. Female students were especially vulnerable. Which of them could afford to say a middle-aged, lecherous tutor nay, and have that refusal reflected in their Final Schools results? And then there were the academics' wives – understandably bored with their husbands, and the revels available to them in Oxford – who went abroad for extra-marital pleasures. The Montmartre district of Paris, for example, was known to be particularly enjoyable. In a final salvo of indignation the article pointed out that it was these same men and women who sat without a blush through sermons on the godly life in the University Church, and dutifully took their turn at rattling charity collecting boxes.

The newspaper dropped on the doormat on a Saturday morning, considerately allowing itself to be read without haste at Oxford's breakfast tables. Geoffrey skimmed through it, then handed it to Louise.

'Must I?' she asked with a little grimace of distaste. 'Why pay this man the compliment of reading what he writes?'

'I think you *should* see this,' he insisted, then pushed his plate aside, as if toast and marmalade no longer appealed to him.

She read it through, aware that her body felt suddenly cold, and a pulse had begun to hammer in her throat, but at last she found something to say.

'The May Day photograph and now this. Can Redmond really be hounding *us*?'

'Not us – *me*. I think there's no doubt about it now. I'm meant to be the academic climbing higher as a result of a rigged election.'

White-lipped, she made the obvious connection. 'In which case I'm the academic's wife, in Paris. What have we done that he should hate us so much?'

'I don't know that he does, although I've certainly had one brush with him. Redmond is in a hurry to make a name for himself; a personal crusade that he can pretend to believe in is a very effective way of doing it.'

In the middle of the distress that was making her feel sick she recognised the authentic, measured voice of the man she had married. Even now there were no shouts of anger, no furious swearings of revenge. He remained true to himself, and simply didn't care how that made him seem to anyone else — ineffectual, supine, or admirably cool and fair.

'Don't be upset by the reference to Montmartre,' he said, finally glancing at her stricken face. 'That was a bow at a venture. It's where most visitors to Paris go — why not academics and their wives?'

For a moment it was insidiously tempting to agree, but Madeleine had been at large in Paris and she was now the constant companion of Niall Redmond. Between them they *knew* what had happened when Louise Carmichael went to Montmartre, and the article was intended to tell her as much.

'Madeleine is this journalist's close friend,' she said slowly. 'She could have seen me in Paris with Daniel Goodman. After poring over papers each morning, we'd go walking in the afternoons . . . He wanted to see the places that tourists don't normally go to.'

'Like Montmartre, I suppose,' Geoffrey agreed with super-human restraint. 'In that case perhaps we should agree now to steel ourselves for whatever photographs might appear next, in the unlikely event that Madeleine had a camera with her.' He looked from his wife's downbent head to her thin hands, gripped together on the table. Then he spoke again in a different voice. 'My dear, if she *is* doing this for spite the blame is mine. I encouraged her to think of me as a friend, and then cruelly turned my back on her when I found her an embarrassment.'

The temptation to make *him* responsible was almost unbear-able now, but it wouldn't do; she knew that as almost the only certainty she could cling to.

'Perhaps the trouble began with your kindness to her, but I'm to blame for the rest of the muddle. Your chances at St Barnabas were being ruined by the gossip about her, so I asked Daniel to . . . to divert her away from you. It wasn't difficult because she was getting a little bored with history, and the incident that evening at the Maison Française also made her angry. Daniel seemed to offer more than you did and she was happy for a while. Then, because we were all going to be in Paris for Easter, she decided to go too – she hates to be left out. I'd got in her way with Pierre, probably put a spoke in her wheel with you, and now even seemed to be monopolising Daniel as well.'

'Montmartre wasn't a bow at a venture?' The quiet question barely reached her, but now came with no shock of surprise. This moment had been waiting for her all along; it was almost a relief to have it delayed no longer.

'She could have seen us there – it was . . . almost our last walk together.'

Any other man, she thought, would shout at her, demand to be told what else had happened. If he asked her she would have to tell him the truth, but Geoffrey didn't ask, and refused even to look at her. At last she understood why. What he didn't know as a fact, put into words that would become uncancellable, he could avoid accepting, or even thinking about.

The question that he asked instead was quite unexpected. 'What are Daniel Goodman's plans?'

'To finish his lectures and go home. Nothing has changed.'

Her husband's face was always schooled to conceal emotion, but even so she sensed in him release from some burden of anxiety that had been nearly intolerable.

'Perhaps Redmond will now grow bored with us; if not, it's time the university officially warned the rag he writes for that he's been allowed to dance long enough on the edge of the libel laws. I hate to trouble Humphrey, but in case there is more to come he must also be warned, because indirectly the College is involved as well.'

Louise would have given a great deal to leave the conversation there, but imprinted on her mind's eye was the image of Madeleine slyly smiling at her in George's Café.

'This article is unlikely to be the end of Redmond's campaign,' she said with difficulty. 'After the singing on May Morning Daniel and I had breakfast in the Covered Market. Madeleine came in with someone and saw us there; I now know that it was this journalist.'

A silence filled the room, weighed it down with a substance so much heavier than air that she found breathing difficult.

Geoffrey was affected in the same way, she realised, because it took him a long time to speak.

'You seem to have seen quite a lot of Goodman one way and another – I thought you didn't like him.'

'I didn't . . . to begin with.' She could say no more without saying it all but, as if he understood the peril they were in, Geoffrey made a heroic effort to smile.

'I'm afraid it's dangerous to forget how small a place Oxford is – I made that mistake with Madeleine, perhaps you've done the same with Goodman. I seem to remember saying once before what a relief it would be when both of them return to their own shores. I hope you agree with me now. Life is more peaceful without them.'

He waited for her to answer, insisted on being reassured, she thought.

'More peaceful – yes,' she agreed after a long pause, 'but not more satisfying unless we try to make it so.' Her eyes held his across the table, refusing him the smallest chance to evade the truth. 'We have to do better *together*, Geoffrey. It isn't enough – at least it isn't enough for me now – to pretend to something that isn't real so that Niall Redmond's readers may be convinced he's lying.'

She waited for an answer, knowing that if he refused her one they were facing defeat. 'It's been a difficult year, and I've been neglectful,' he said at last. Her expression didn't change and he had to go on painfully. 'You probably think I've been neglectful of you for years, but perhaps neither of us dealt with our tragedy as we should have done. You are what you've always been – my dearly loved wife – whether I'm Master of St Barnabas, or anything else. Knowing that, and knowing that you can escape to your garden here whenever you need to, will you be able to live contentedly in the Lodging?'

He kept his voice quiet but he couldn't keep it even, and his hands trembled slightly. She needn't doubt, at least, that emotion was still alive, and if she still mattered to him there was hope for them after all.

'I shall manage very well,' she said at last, and saw his face break into a blinding smile.

'My dear, I think I'll go and have a little chat with Humphrey now. He's probably been upset by these wretched articles, and that isn't good for him.'

She nodded, and accepted the kiss that Geoffrey came to say goodbye with. For a moment or two longer she remained sitting at the table, then, suddenly certain of what she must do, she got up and left the house herself.

CHAPTER TWENTY-TWO

She had to go no further than Anna's kitchen door. Madeleine was there sitting in the sunshine, relacquering scarlet toenails. Her greeting was a smile that wavered between insolence and nervousness.

'I don't know who you've come to see, but there's only dear Gertrud upstairs and me. My mother is out, giving a French lesson, and Dr Goodman is also not *chez nous*.' She applied another vermilion brush-stroke and carefully studied the effect. 'Most women, poor things, have ugly feet. I'm told that mine are beautiful.'

Louise looked away, trying not to feel envious. She saw nothing particularly wrong with her own feet, but Madeleine's — thrust out for her inspection — were beautiful.

'Lucky Anna to have so perfect a daughter.'

She couldn't know how unfortunate was the remark, but, still smarting from an interview that had taken place before her mother left the house, Madeleine shot a glance of pure dislike at her visitor.

'I'll pass the compliment on and say you called,' she snapped in the expectation of concluding the interview.

But Louise merely perched herself on a low wall. 'I came to see you,' she said calmly.

Not for the first time Madeleine was aware of being denied the upper hand. She never knew why this should be so. Compared with this woman she had all the advantages — youth, beauty, and sexual allure. But still Louise Carmichael, careless of the little God had given her, had an effect on men that must be recognised. Now, to make matters worse, there were Niall's articles. She couldn't be so stupid as not to realise where his information came from — if she wasn't embarrassed, she had at least a duty to be angry; but even that seemed doubtful. So completely lacking fire, *how* had she managed to bring to Daniel

Goodman's face the expression it had worn in the café that morning?

'I *hoped* I was right in thinking you don't go to the Maison on Saturday mornings,' Louise said pleasantly.

'I don't go at all now. The girl with the baby was fool enough to want to come back. Personally I hated that cow of a *Directrice* and the work was boring anyway.'

Unable to do anything more to her toes, Madeleine shot a glance at her visitor's face instead. The bright light was cruel, revealing a fan of tiny lines at the corners of eyes and mouth, and too little flesh to soften cheek– and jaw-bones. Altogether Louise Carmichael was showing welcome signs of age and strain.

Feeling more confident, and more anxious than usual to keep the conversation on herself, Madeleine enlarged on the future. 'I'm thinking of becoming a journalist. It seems a more interesting life than just dwindling into a bored and boring wife. Even the same lover for too long would be a real ennui . . . don't *you* agree?'

Louise considered for a moment the idea of strangling her with her own dark plaits of hair. It was a bizarre fantasy of course, but when so much of any conversation with her wandered into the realms of make-believe it was hard not to catch the infection. She was a maddening, conscienceless, pathetic mess, but still she was Anna's daughter, not to be given up for lost without a struggle.

'Marriage doesn't have to be boring,' she pointed out at last, 'but I can see that journalism might suit you better. Your friend, Mr Redmond, could probably help you to get started, but my advice would be to leave his gutter-press tabloid behind as soon as you can.'

The smile that came with this calm advice was more irritating than the advice itself. 'You know nothing about it,' Madeleine was stung into shouting. 'Niall is very clever . . . Everyone is reading what he writes. Even a London newspaper has asked for him. Soon he will be' – the English words failed her – '*comblé de succès* and . . . and . . .'

'You won't see him any more,' Louse finished, not ungently.

'Of *course* I shall. I'll go with him.' It wasn't true – Niall had made it painfully clear that he would travel faster alone; but she couldn't admit to that now. 'Why should I stay here and be treated like a child, by my *real* mother, who's supposed to love me?' She hoped she sounded bitter and defiant, and confident of what she was going to do next; but Anna's sudden transformation into an accusing stranger had shocked her, and Niall had laughed and shaken his head when she persisted in asking to go with him to London.

The tell-tale quaver in her voice gave her away. Beneath the truculence was uncertainty and fear, reminding Louise of their first conversation in the kitchen next door after Daniel had brought her to Norham Grove. Even after all that had happened it would still have been surprisingly easy to weep over a girl who was such a hopeless mixture of confidence and uncertainty, promise and despair. If middle age fell prone to failure and grief, what chance had youth of remaining unscathed?

'I'm disappointed in you,' she said, abandoning the sympathy that Madeleine would certainly reject. 'You're more intelligent than most of the young women I know, even including Geoffrey's undergraduates, but you seem to have learned nothing in the months you've been here.'

'What was I to learn?' Madeleine shouted again, holding fast to rancour. 'That Oliver Cromwell won your stupid Civil War? That if you've been to Oxford you can boast about it for the rest of your life?'

'You weren't taught *that* by my husband – he would only have said that it was something to be proud of.' Louise got down from the wall, but only to move to an empty chair beside Madeleine's.

'You ought at least to have discovered by now how much your mother loves you. Nothing in her whole life, not even her affection for the man who rescued her, counts beside that. Some parents, I believe, think that loving their children means never judging them. Anna knows that true loving requires more than that. If she guesses that you are behind some of Niall Redmond's spiteful little attacks on us, she's bound to tell you that it's a poor way to treat your friends.'

'You *aren't* my friends!' Madeleine cried. 'Geoffrey was supposed to be . . . I even *liked* him. He was unhappy and I was going to . . . to comfort him, because *you* were so stuck on Pierre. What happened? He left me to stand alone for everyone to laugh at. I wasn't sure about Daniel, but at least we had a good time together. I thought we'd do even better in Paris when his stupid wife went home, but *you* were in the way again. You always have been.' She hovered on the verge of saying that she'd trudged behind them all the way to Montmartre. To no great walker, it had been an effort only rewarded by the little scene outside the church. But Anna's anger that morning had been intense, and in a straight fight between them Madeleine couldn't be sure even now that her mother wouldn't take this woman's part.

Determined that she wasn't going to discuss Daniel with anyone, and least of all with the girl beside her, Louise returned to what else Madeleine had said.

'Geoffrey wanted to help you, and you, I now see, wanted to help *him*,' she began seriously. 'But all that Oxford could see was a scandalously unsuitable relationship between a stunning young woman and the middle-aged academic who was hoping to become the next Master of St Barnabas. Geoffrey finally accepted that on the night of the French Ambassador's party. He abandoned you because he had to, but he's felt unhappy about it ever since.'

Madeleine gave a little shrug. 'I was getting bored with history lessons, and he wasn't getting any nearer being interested in *me*. I'd be inclined to think it's what delving into history does to a man, except that I can't help feeling it hasn't made Daniel any less effective in bed.'

With an effort that Louise congratulated herself on afterwards, she managed not to blush. For an insane moment she could imagine vouching for a performance that had been very effective indeed, could even anticipate relief in confessing to the joy of being wholly alive again. Madeleine would understand *that* at least, if she understood nothing else. But the temptation was momentary, and the purpose of her visit had been to offer understanding, not receive it.

'The thing to remember about Geoffrey and Daniel is that they're both teachers,' she went on diffidently. 'In their own ways both of them wanted to help you, because they see that as their function in life. It didn't occur to them, that you might get so much more pain than profit from their lessons that you'd want to hurt them in return.'

There was a long silence, and time for Louise to calculate the chances of Madeleine taking enough offence to flounce indoors. But at last she muttered an unexpected reply.

'I suppose I shouldn't have followed you around in Paris, but I was angry. That's why I told Niall. He said he wanted to expose this *place*, but I realised after a while that only the scandalous hints about people counted for much, with him or anyone else.'

'Sadly true, I'm afraid,' Lousie agreed. 'Oxford itself is too used to being laughed at, criticised, or even raged against to take any notice of the attention it gets. It sails on through the centuries, a bit chipped and dented here and there, but still serenely confident of being indispensable!'

Madeleine's sulky mouth almost twitched into a grin, and when she spoke again hostility had been replaced by something that sounded almost like regret. 'I'm glad I came, as a matter of fact – I can't imagine now *not* knowing my mother. But I don't belong here as she seems to do. The trouble is that I don't know *where* I belong – certainly not in Dijon; but Niall doesn't want me in London either, except for an occasional night in bed. I can't make that my life's work, can I?'

'It's obvious what you must do,' Louise said firmly, trying not to smile. 'Make up your quarrel with Anna as soon as she comes home, and then tell her that you're going to become a better journalist than Niall Redmond. You could even train for it – in Paris, perhaps – if your father can afford some `fees.' Real amusement lit her eyes for the first time. 'Oxford's influence has finally rubbed off on me, you see – I now give learning its due!'

She stood up again, touched Madeleine's cheek in a shy, friendly gesture that surprised them both, and went home.

Now that the conversation was over she could see how slight had been its chance of success. But, with or without the threat of legal pressure on the newspaper, she thought the articles might now cease. Niall Redmond had achieved his purpose of getting people to notice him and could scarcely go on beating the same old drum. In any case, Louise felt certain that he would no longer be able to rely on Madeleine to spy for him. Trusted to be a friend, a friend she might become as far as she was able. It wasn't much to have salvaged, but it was something.

The June afternoon had suddenly turned to a blaze of midsummer heat. Two elderly gentlemen, rakishly panama-hatted against the sun, shared the green, peaceful garden around them. A slightly off-key piano tinkled in a distant room, and voices drifted towards them from the tennis courts, but otherwise the entire College seemed to be theirs. William looked wistful for a moment, remembering other times. His long wicker chair was comfortable for a man whose waistline was expanding; but oh for a punt on the river again, on a golden June afternoon!

'Final Schools weather, as usual,' he remarked. 'I watched the poor little devils marching like lambs to the slaughter this morning – ragamuffins suddenly neatly rigged out in black and white, all afraid that madness or amnesia might attack them before they could open the first examination paper!'

Beside him Humphrey smiled but didn't answer, and William had to speak again. 'Nearly there, old friend. Just Encaenia to get through, and a lot of farewells at the Vice Chancellor's garden party. Then you can hand the baton over to Geoffrey. Edwina must be counting the days. The pair of you have earned a bounteous retirement.'

Humphrey thoughtfully polished his spectacles and replaced them.

'Geoffrey came to see me a week or two ago, about those wretched articles. He seemed to think they were aimed at *him*; even offered to stand down if there were more of them that might damage the College. I told him not to be a bloody fool, of course, but I can see why he reckoned Redmond's smutty innuendos were intended for him and Louise – they had a venomous, personal ring to them. Edwina's nostrils were breathing fire every time a piece appeared; like you, she regards Louise almost as a daughter. But a warning shot has now been fired across the newspaper's bows, and I pray that that will be the end of a distasteful business.'

William pondered for a moment what he should say; generalities would be safest first, perhaps. 'The difficulty is that a clever journalist like Redmond always mixes fact with fiction. People don't need much persuading that we're a protected species, living too comfortably, working too little, and entirely sheltered from the harsh realities that everyone else has to contend with. It's an easy step from that to touching up the picture with hints of licentiousness and adultery and the breaking of all the rest of the Commandments. Veiled hints are damnably hard to challenge or refute, and so the smears remain.'

Humphrey considered in his turn, and grasped the nettle offered to him. 'I didn't for a moment think of asking any questions, Will, but I am not as blind as my dear Edwina seems to think. For months past both Geoffrey and Louise have had to make more of an effort *not* to seem strained than even I could miss. It's been a difficult year in every way, I know, but all along I've feared that things weren't entirely well with them. Edwina thinks that Louise is the worse sufferer – I suppose she's bound to. Being a prudent man, I don't say that my heart has ached for Geoffrey too.'

He waved a long, thin hand to say that they'd trespassed enough on private ground, and William was left to offer the best comfort he could. 'They'll manage, left to themselves. Redmond's gone, thank God, so until the next fire-raiser appears, eager to demolish this ancient institution, perhaps we can all relax.'

Humphrey still looked grave. 'There *are* abuses that the University must grapple with, we all know that; but hacking indiscriminately at a great old tree is no way to cure its ailments. We *can't* let it be brought down. What it represents in the life of this country is too precious, and Geoffrey understands that. It's why I needed him for St Barnabas. That's my faith, Will, and if I were called upon to testify to it I hope I should do so as bravely as Cranmer and Latimer and Ridley died for *theirs* in the Broad not so many centuries ago.'

'You would,' William said simply. 'There isn't a doubt about it.'

The solemn business of conferring honorary degrees was over. The Latin orations that nowadays few people understood had echoed round the crowded Sheldonian, and the academics, colourful but uncomfortably hot in gowns and hoods, had made their stately processions. Now, at the Vice Chancellor's garden party, it was the ladies' turn to see and be seen.

Daniel ambled about, stopping occasionally to speak to someone he recognised or be introduced to a wife he didn't know. He supposed he would remember it long afterwards as a quintessentially English occasion, half-enchanted, half-absurd. Being there only as an observer would have pleased him; he'd have been free to enjoy the rich variety of oddities spread out all around. But the observer's heart wasn't in the game of mockery any longer; the damn place had beaten him in the end.

He didn't look for Louise, knowing that she was certain to be there. The moment would come when he'd find her standing in front of him, and he was prepared for it. He'd even be able to find something to say. Being a man who hated to be taken unawares, he'd practised several easy phrases. And then, suddenly, when he saw her, he wasn't nearly prepared enough after all. She wore the soft coral colour that suited her so well, echoed in a velvet ribbon round the crown of a wide-brimmed hat of natural straw. He wanted to shout that among these floral frills and furbelows that English women seemed compelled to wear only *she* was beautiful . . . He wanted to take her by the hand and shout that God had surely meant her only to belong to him.

But Geoffrey stood beside her. He hadn't done that on the other public occasions Daniel could remember. Then there had been other people to attend to, but perhaps he'd learned his lesson now. They couldn't not be greeted – Daniel didn't need to be told that people, seemingly involved in other conversations, were watching them. He commanded his legs to continue moving; he managed a little bow, and even a sort of smile.

'I noticed you both in the audience for my last public performance – a courtesy beyond the call of duty, I'd say.'

Her face, shadowed by the brim of her hat, was delicately made up, only entirely familiar when she smiled. She couldn't say that pride had driven Geoffrey to the lecture, and that a longing to see the lecturer had driven her.

'I'm afraid you played a trick on us,' she murmured instead. 'We went prepared for some final, blistering attack, and were given instead a wise and gentle discourse on the necessity to learn from past mistakes.'

'A perfect apologia, in fact, for the continuing study of history,' her husband added. 'It set the seal on an outstanding series of lectures.'

'Generously said by an opponent who didn't agree with the rest of them! We're not as civilised as that in Ann Arbor.'

Geoffrey smiled faintly, and half-turned away from them to speak to someone who had come up to him.

'I read those articles,' Daniel said quietly to Louise. 'Madeleine has been in hiding in case rage got the better of me.'

'No great harm's been done. One or two ladies have avoided me this afternoon, but Geoffrey has friends in high places. We, and St Barnabas, will survive more or less unscathed. When . . . when do you go home?'

'The day after tomorrow. I'll spend the rest of the summer in Vermont, knocking into shape one *more* history book that will make no difference to the world's mistakes.'

He sounded defeated, and it seemed the one grief that she couldn't bear. Shadowed by the hat's wide brim her eyes were full of pain but they met his steadily.

'Anything you do makes a difference,' she insisted in a low voice. 'It always will.'

'Do I have to say goodbye to you like this, here?' he muttered.

She nodded, unable to trust her voice now. It was almost a relief to see Geoffrey extricate himself from the Registrar's wife and rejoin them. He glanced from his wife's white face to the expression on Daniel's, and spoke too loudly in a voice he didn't recognise.

'I *know* I'm getting old when I find myself preferring the sort of garden party that gets rained off!' He tucked Louise's hand within his arm and tried to smile at her. 'My dear, you look a little weary, too. I'm sure Dr Goodman will forgive me if I take you home.'

She wouldn't weep, couldn't disgrace him. There was nothing left in the world to do but hold out her hand, feel Daniel's fingers grip it for a second or two, and then walk away with Geoffrey. In five or ten years' time when he'd become Vice Chancellor – even now she could see *that* fate coming inexorably towards them – all these people would be *their* guests, thronging the gardens of St Barnabas. Among them, unknown to her, there might walk a lost, unhappy soul, just as she was walking now.

CHAPTER TWENTY-THREE

After the last of his students had trooped in and out, making their farewells, Geoffrey still lingered in his study. Already the College felt different, and within a day or two it would settle into the peace of the Long Vac. For the third-year men and women a whole charmed life was ending – no more weekly essays to be battled with into the small hours; no sonorous grace in Hall; no time left to dance and skylark. But he hoped they'd take with them the more precious memory of having belonged to a place that he believed to be uniquely beautiful.

There was no reason why he couldn't lock his study door on the reports still waiting to be written; they could wait a little longer. But he still sat there, too tired to make the effort to go home. A tap at the door made him frown, but he relaxed when Andrew Jardine walked into the room.

'I know the signs,' his visitor said feelingly. 'You need a stiff drink, a week's sleep, and then a good long holiday.'

'The drink we could share *now*,' Geoffrey suggested and got up to pour whisky for them both.

Over the glass that he was handed Andrew regarded his friend. 'Like me, you're sad to see the promising ones disappear, and sadder still to have wasted so much time on the rest who will have benefited from it little, if at all.'

Geoffrey shook his head. 'No . . . I was wondering what they thought of *me*! Perhaps they were envious because, unless I disgraced myself in some way, I'd got a job for life? Well, not a real job at all, I could hear some of them thinking – a piece of cake, a sinecure, if that's a word that Oxford has taught them. Or were they indulgent instead? Better let the poor sod go to a soft life in the Master's Lodging, because what use would he be in today's cold, harsh world outside? Yes, being on the whole a tolerant lot, I expect *that's* what they were thinking!'

The folds of Andrew's mournful, bloodhound face rearranged

themselves into a smile. 'End-of-term blues, and the Oxford curse of too much introspection! Let me remind you that we require our new Master to be full of confidence, about himself and about the goods we offer. As a matter of fact, you *are* confident, but you *do* need that holiday. It's been a trying term . . . well, a trying year altogether.'

Geoffrey left the adjective uncontradicted although it struck him as heroic in its understatement. Andrew knew something of the strains of the past few months; he was an old and trusted friend who could have been told the rest of them. But he treasured for Louise an affection that came close to reverence. Geoffrey saw no reason to spoil that for whatever relief *he* might get from chattering about his wife, even if it had seemed forgivable.

'Difficult times ahead too,' Andrew remarked next, suspecting that he was talking to himself. 'Robert and his cronies are bound to want to edge the new intake towards their own Faculties. With more and more dons and undergraduates spending their days in the science labs instead of doing their teaching and learning in College, how many candidates shall we have taking Greats or even Modern Greats in a few years' time?'

'Now who's sounding depressed?' Geoffrey asked gently. 'You'd better come and stay with us in Tuscany. It's Louise's idea to rent a villa, and share it with the people we can bear to share it with – you, and William, and Anna Ouspenska. Anna's daughter may have to be put up with as well but, if so, it's your turn to extend your education by looking after her!'

Anxiety warred with happiness in Andrew's face. 'Safer to leave her behind, surely; but even with her there, I should come with the greatest delight if Louise is sure she can be bothered with me.'

'Asked for you specially,' Geoffrey assured him, unable to say that his wife's most desperate need seemed to be for the two of them not to spend their holiday alone.

'Then I shall undertake to keep Madeleine out of your hair,' Andrew promised bravely, '. . . and greater love, I suggest, hath *no* man than that!'

Geoffrey smiled naturally at last. 'I'm not in any danger now

'— Louise assures me that Madeleine is tired of historians! If you don't make yourself too enticing she'll get tired of you as well and we shall all be left in peace.'

He drained his glass and stood up, over-topping his friend by several inches. Andrew watched him for a moment with unselfish appreciation — Geoffrey Carmichael wasn't quite himself at the moment; but he'd become an impressive man in middle age, quietly authoritative, and with the necessary touch of steel about him. Dear old Edward would have been hopeless at the job, and Andrew had had no faith in Justin Harkness, a scientist-turned-businessman.

'It *has* been trying, but perhaps it's all been for the best in the end,' he said suddenly, anxious to reassure his friend.

Geoffrey smiled and ushered him out of the room, using the little commotion of doing so to avoid answering. 'The best' seemed scarcely to describe a situation in which he and Louise performed an agonisingly courteous, formal dance. The only relief came from knowing that there was no chance now of meeting Daniel Goodman. Ruth had seen him leave, and of course come in to tell them so. She'd sounded pleased to see the last of a neighbour who hadn't, she said, quite fitted in. Louise had said nothing at all, and soon afterwards made an excuse to leave the room.

Now when he got home she was just finishing a telephone conversation in French, which meant usually that she was talking to her mother. But she was frowning when she replaced the receiver.

'Not Nadia, as you probably thought — Henri instead, warning us to expect them the day after tomorrow. I said we could call on *them* next week, on our way to Italy, but there seems to be something urgent to discuss. It isn't their health — I asked about that — so what else could it be?'

'Nadia wants to return to her Russian homeland . . . take the veil . . . become a Buddhist! My dear, who knows? We shall have to wait and see.'

She smiled at his suggestions but discovered two days later that at least he'd been right to guess that her mother was at the root of the matter. Like the good Frenchman he was, Henri placidly enjoyed the dinner that was put in front of him, complimented Louise on the perfect hollandaise that accompanied the salmon, and Geoffrey on the white wine. Nadia ate her usual minuscule amount, and sighed when her husband accepted a second helping of summer pudding; but she had obviously been made to promise to let *him* broach the subject that had brought them to Oxford.

'Delicious, my dears,' he said regretfully when the last mouthful had been relished, 'but now to business before my poor Nadia bursts with anxiety!' He touched his wife's hand in a little gesture of affection and then turned to Louise.

'It concerns the Galeries Benoît, and since they're owned equally by you, Pierre, and myself, it means that two of us must agree if changes are to be made.'

Geoffrey saw Nadia about to protest yet again about the infamy of a will that had been wickedly influenced by a woman-hating lawyer, and made haste to intervene. 'There are now changes you'd like to make?'

'In a sense they are forced on us, because Pierre has been offered a brilliant opportunity in New York. I think his future now is there, and I must either replace him – not an easy task when the knowledge required is highly specialised – or we must dispose of the Galeries Benoît to someone else.'

Louise asked the obvious question. 'It's kind of you to consult me, but you scarcely need to if the two of you agree?'

'Alas, we don't agree,' Henri said sadly. 'Nadia and I want more than anything to leave the Rue Jacob and find a pleasant house in Provence. She always feels well and happy there, and I should like it, too. But Pierre is anxious for the Paris connection to remain. He sees it as being very useful, and is strongly against selling.'

'I say it with the greatest reluctance,' Nadia now put in, refusing to be restrained any longer, 'but Pierre is thinking only of himself. He talks much of the name of Benoît and how it must remain part of the Parisian scene, but the last true Benoît – myself! – does not even *own* the galleries, thanks to Maître Clément.'

Anxious to keep them to the matter in hand, never an easy

task when his mother-in-law was concerned, Geoffrey asked a question of his own. 'Supposing that you *could* all agree, is a buyer likely to be found?'

'I have one waiting,' Henri admitted, 'an old adversary of André's, as a matter of fact. That must be made clear, in case you think it a greater betrayal to his memory than selling at all.'

'You would have difficulty finding a buyer who *wasn't* an adversary of my grandfather's,' Louise said bluntly. 'He could be generous, on his own terms, but he certainly didn't die among a circle of sorrowing friends.'

Nadia was temporarily silenced, torn between the pain of having borne so unnatural a daughter and the immediate necessity of not quarrelling with her. Seeing his mother-in-law's dilemma, Geoffrey stepped in again tactfully.

'Louise knows the problem now – perhaps you should give her the night to sleep on it. Meanwhile, I promised Ruth that you'd go up and say hello. She'll be waiting for you.'

Inclined at first to plead tiredness, Nadia remembered that it was always enjoyable to exchange barbed pleasantries with the strange English creature upstairs. Henri concealed a little sigh and followed her, prepared to play the part of umpire as usual.

'Thank you,' Louise said when the door closed behind them. 'I can never guard my tongue when we're discussing my grandfather; but I should, because it distresses Nadia.'

'Is it too soon to ask what you think about the galleries?'

'Oh, I was quite certain about it straightaway. Pierre is arguing for what will suit *him*. The name of Benoît means nothing in itself if there is no longer a family connection to sustain it in the future. Let someone else make what he can of that which André started so brilliantly. I should like to think of Nadia reclining happily in Provençal sunshine, and Henri at last having the leisure to write his great work on ancient Arabic instruments. He's waited quite long enough.'

'You wouldn't feel regretful at . . . at thwarting Pierre?' Geoffrey asked diffidently.

'Not in the least,' she answered after a moment's thought, then smiled as if to say that it concluded the matter.

*

The following morning, waiting for Nadia's complicated toilette to be completed, Louise left Henri talking French politics with her husband at the breakfast table and wandered out as usual into the garden. In the first glorious flush of summer bloom it looked too beautiful to leave, even for Tuscany. But she was aware of how badly both she and Geoffrey needed to escape — he from Oxford, she from memories of Daniel.

She was deadheading Mrs Sinkins pinks when Henri crossed the lawn towards her. There was time to notice that he was a slightly stooped figure now, frailer than she'd realised. It was selfishly unkind of Pierre not to have realised it, too. She scrambled to her feet and smiled at him.

'Come and sniff Madame Hardy — she's just out, and worth all the expensive perfumes in the world.'

He bent to admire the white rose that Louise's hands gently cupped; then he straightened up to examine her face instead. 'This appointment of Geoffrey's is a great honour, I know, but it's a grief for you as well, *n'est-ce-pas*?'

A thorn had drawn a thread of blood across her hand and she licked it away before she answered him.

'I always used to imagine living somewhere else — anywhere except here, in an ugly Victorian house that defies time and all the weather's attempts to improve it! Now that I'm obliged to leave it for most of the year it's suddenly become desirable. Ruth would say I should have known it all along, but she was born here.'

She picked a tiny sprig of lemon balm to sniff as they walked along, and deliberately changed the subject. 'Can you imagine Pierre in New York? I can't, although I see that he might be very successful there.'

'The charm of the exotic!' Henri agreed. 'Yes, he'll be successful, and therefore happy. The only thing my dear son can't tolerate is failure, and I'm afraid he *did* fail with you. But even I can see that it would have been unreasonable to expect anything else. You weren't obliged to abandon your husband and your life here just to keep Pierre happy for us in Paris!'

She smiled at the mixture of perception and dry humour that

was typical of her stepfather, then tackled the subject he'd tactfully left alone.

'Now I'm afraid I'm going to make him still more unhappy. It's time for you to do what suits you and Nadia best. I should like to think of you both settled in some nice old stone house, bowered in shady trees and flowers, with a sunlit terrace for Nadia to recline on, and a peaceful study for you to write in.'

'You really don't mind, Louise?' he asked hesitantly. 'You'd agree to see the Galeries lose the name of Benoît?'

She smiled and kissed his cheek. 'Sell them, and live happily in Provence. I insist on it!'

Contentment bloomed in his face, telling her what the decision meant. She thought Pierre should have realised it too, and remembered with disbelief a time when he had seemed attractive to her. Could vanity have been as blind as that? New York *would* suit him very well if it was what she imagined it to be – exciting no doubt, but a hurrying, selfish sort of place. The thought inevitably brought to mind another man – one who'd been born and bred to its pace and harshness. She remembered with a wave of despair that she didn't know where he would go when he was ready to leave Ann Arbor. How could she imagine him, not knowing? The wave broke over her, receded, left her stranded with the cold certainty that she couldn't allow herself to think about him at all.

She saw the sudden concern in Henri's face and forced herself to smile at him. 'A ghost walked over my grave,' she murmured. 'Now, shall we stay out here a bit longer? Geoffrey can entertain Nadia when she comes downstairs. It will be a little test of character for both of them!' The thought made her smile again, more naturally, and Henri decided that he'd imagined a moment when he'd feared she was about to faint.

CHAPTER TWENTY-FOUR

By the beginning of July the constituents of Oxford's population were changing. Apart from would-be scientists still struggling in the laboratories with practical exams, the Masters and Scholars of the University had mostly disappeared. The streets were filled instead with marauding bands of French and Spanish schoolchildren, marginally under control. Earnest German students tried to decide where Balliol ended and St John's began – a problem that few citizens could help them with – and swarms of Japanese eddied like gnats on summer evenings. The tourist season had begun.

William rather enjoyed the annual influx – he said it kept Oxford from becoming smugly provincial. If a shared language had permitted it, he'd have liked to ask the small Oriental people, especially, what they made of the soaring Gothic splendour of the Divinity School, and the pinnacled skyline of the High.

They were certainly puzzled by the stone heads that glared benignly down from the railings outside the Sheldonian. Stopped for the third time one morning, he sifted again through his stock of explanations. Having already canvassed the claims of the twelve Apostles and all the Greek philosophers, he identified them now as a job lot of Roman emperors. When he reached Norham Grove he explained to Louise that this left his last suggestion in reserve – a dozen of the more austere Victorian Heads of Colleges.

'If you pitch a different story each time it's as well the same people don't stop you twice,' she pointed out.

William waved the objection aside. 'If I can't tell one little Japanese lady from another, why shouldn't she have the same difficulty with me?'

'Because we're a much less homogeneous race. Even

someone from Outer Mongolia would be able to distinguish you from Geoffrey.'

'And you from Ruth,' he felt bound to agree.

She put chilled Vichyssoise in front of him and saw him smile with a child's intent delight as the first spoonful was sampled. 'Perfection! My dear Mrs Maggs does her best, but it has to be admitted that her cuisine lacks finesse.'

'And whatever mine possesses I owe to Marthe – it was she who taught me to cook. I'm so glad she'll leave Paris with Henri and Nadia. She was born in Provence and she'll go back there like a bird to its nest.'

'And Pierre?' William asked. 'Is he resigned now to selling?'

'Not with any good grace. He telephoned, asking me to change my mind, and got very angry when I refused.'

She frowned at the memory of that conversation, and William regretted his question. 'Do you suppose André is turning in his grave,' he suggested instead, 'getting ready to haunt the galleries and fling pictures down from the walls?'

'The new owner is a redoubtable lady, as it happens; well able to cope with even the most troublesome ghost!' Louise looked at her uncle with candid eyes. 'I don't feel guilty about the sale, you know, although Pierre tried to suggest that I should. My grandfather did whatever suited *him* throughout a very long life; now it's time for Henri and Nadia to do what will make *them* happy. Geoffrey will be glad not to have to keep returning to Paris, and I'm not sure I could ever go back again.'

Calmly though she spoke, the strange idea occurred to William that the words had been torn out of her. She looked so desperately tired that he felt bound to try to release her from the burden of entertaining them in Italy.

'My dear, don't think for a moment that I'm not looking forward to our holiday. No eating caviar to the sound of trumpets for me – Tuscany would be *my* idea of Heaven! But are you sure you want to be bothered with us? You and Geoffrey both need a rest.'

'It's what we're planning to have!' she said almost cheerfully. 'We shall offer you generous amounts of food and wine, and otherwise sit under the trees waiting for peaches to drop into our laps. You and Anna will happily entertain each other, and dear Andrew is steeling himself to keep Madeleine amused.'

'It was noble of you to include *her*,' William muttered.

'I don't think so. We haven't hit it off very well in the past, but some sort of understanding has now been reached. Apart from that she's invited for Anna's benefit, so that my dear friend can be convinced no damage has been done to friendship.'

It was an explanation so typical that he thought he might have guessed it for himself. He wanted to say that he loved her very much – wanted *her* to be undamaged by sadness more than he wanted anything else in life; but he was too shy to say so and offered her instead a litany of pleasures in store.

'Think of the Botticellis in the Uffizi, my dear, and – from wherever you happen to look – that incomparable Cathedral dome. Think of Chianti Classico practically on tap, and swallows dancing over a scented garden at twilight. If that isn't earthly bliss at least, I don't know what is.'

'Yes, of course it is,' she agreed readily. 'What a prospect to have in store, knowing that one's worst problem in life at the moment is to decide on what reading matter to take – shall this be the summer to make a determined attack on Proust, or shall I admit here and now that I'd rather stick to Anthony Trollope!'

William saw the sadness behind her smile and knew who it reminded him of – Daniel Goodman, when he'd called in Holywell Street to say goodbye. He was tempted for a moment to put aside the rules by which their lives were played, but reticence was ingrained in all of them now, the fixed habit of a lifetime, and if the rules were suddenly to be discarded what chaos might not follow?

Instead, he touched her hand in a small unspoken gesture of affection. 'Difficult times they've been recently, my dear girl – anxiety over Humphrey's health, the Mastership, those wretchedly disgusting articles . . . but things will get better now. I feel sure of that.'

She nodded, anxious to reassure him. William heard himself say one last thing that he thought he'd meant *not* to say.

'When Daniel left, he gave me his address so that we could be

269

sure to keep in touch. I should have asked for it anyway. He's a friend I wouldn't want to lose.'

Louise still didn't answer, but a small glimmer of joy was illuminating her tired face.

A week later the house party in Tuscany was nearly complete. William and Andrew already felt so comfortably at home that their hostess wondered if they would ever be able to bring themselves to leave again.

Now, with luncheon laid in the shade of the pergola, she and William waited for the return of the others from the railway station in Florence, bringing Anna and Madeleine. William sipped Campari-soda, surveyed the exquisite prospect of near green landscape and distant blue hills, and gave occasional little grunts of satisfaction that made her turn to smile at him.

'A contented man, if ever I saw one!'

'Supremely so, my dear, but not entirely blinded to the well-being of everyone else. I hope I'm right in thinking that this blessed place is working its usual miracle on you and Geoffrey. Sunlight suits you and you *look* better already, but it's the inner woman that counts, not the outer.'

'The inner woman is doing quite well, Uncle Will, and she thanks you kindly for the enquiry!'

He accepted that it was as much as she would say about herself, and about Geoffrey she would say nothing at all. With a tactful change of subject, he speculated next about the carload on its way back from Florence.

'The boot and half the back seat will be piled with luggage – most of it Madeleine's wardrobe, and the rest whatever delicious little comestibles have caught Anna's eye along the way. She and Andrew will be crammed into the rest of the space, and Madeleine will be in front, with a skirt up to her thighs, trying to distract the driver from a particularly tortuous piece of road.' Then he grinned like a regretful cherub. 'Now I *know* I'm getting old – time was when I should have enjoyed the distraction myself!'

But when the car pulled up ten minutes later there was time to see that for once he'd been partially wrong. While Anna was being helped out of the front seat by Geoffrey, Andrew was disentangling himself from Madeleine in the back. Louise ran down the terrace steps to greet them and was wrapped in her friend's embrace. Emerging from it, she smiled as Anna next flung wide her arms, as if to embrace all Tuscany itself.

'You grow accustomed to it by degrees,' she explained, 'but the first glance does rather take your breath away. William's convinced himself that he'd rather live here than in Holywell Street. I tell him that he *is* Holywell Street!'

Luncheon, al fresco, went so happily that Louise felt more confident about her ill-assorted party. Afterwards, when William escorted Anna on a stroll through gardens and vineyard to meet the courtly owner of what he called 'this slice of Paradise', Madeleine announced her own intention – to swim in the pool and sunbathe, at least without the *top* of an abbreviated bikini; she still seemed undecided about the bottom half. Andrew was scandalised but kept his head. Such nudity, he said in the unarguable voice of an Oxford don, would be entirely self-defeating.

'Why, may I ask?' Madeleine enquired dangerously. 'Do I disgust you? Are my breasts too small, my bottom too large . . . ?'

Listening to the dialogue, and certain that he'd never in all his life been called upon to discuss such a subject, Louise thought he managed it with astonishing aplomb.

'I'm sure everything is *exactly* as it should be . . . I mean, *absolutely*, my dear girl; but you're missing the psychology of it all. If what he can see is visible to everyone else as well, the average male loses interest immediately. Why bother to pursue when there's no tantalising mystery, and no private reward?' Then, not waiting for an answer, and chastely shrouded in a robe himself, he bounded down the steps to the pool leaving Madeleine to follow him looking very thoughtful.

On the terrace above Louise stifled a grin, caught her husband's eye, and at last joined helplessly in his shout of laughter. Finally she wiped her eyes and managed to gasp, 'You must warn Andrew. The gauntlet has been thrown down.

Madeleine will subjugate him before a week is out, or drown herself in the pool.'

'I don't think so, my love. He won the first round at the railway station, and we can safely leave her to him now. What's more, I'm damned if he isn't enjoying himself!'

Louise didn't — couldn't — argue. How long since she'd been offered that small, sweet endearment, or anything except a bored 'my dear girl'? Was he even aware of having used it now? She glanced across the table but found him already absorbed in the pages of the Italian newspaper he was disciplining himself to read. The habits of an academic died hard, even in an earthly paradise, but a grain of comfort remained. They had at last laughed together — it was *something*; a little candle of hope for the future ahead of them.

She was still thinking about it when Madeleine reappeared, now more or less decently covered by the towel in which she was draped.

'I've been sent to help,' she announced with an astonishing lack of rancour. 'Andrew says that if I'm *very* good he might consider falling in love with me; otherwise *not*.' Her enchanting gamine smile suddenly appeared. 'It's worth a try I think.'

She stacked glasses on a tray and walked into the house with them followed by her dazed hostess. Louise came back smiling a moment later.

'Still draped in her towel, she's washing dishes and singing "La Vie en Rose" rather out of tune. I'm bound to say she adds something!'

Geoffrey lifted his eyes from the pages of *Corriere* long enough to agree calmly, but there was time as well to register the fact that his wife's thin, brown face was looking less haunted. By the end of the summer, with all the commotion of the move to think about, she'd be herself again — the events of this unfortunate year behind them. They shared a bedroom at the villa; before long, when he'd given her a little more time, they'd become a real married couple again. If he'd asked her to agree she would have done — it was the choice she had made; but for the moment she was deeply thankful for a narrow single bed that would have defeated a husband more ardent than hers had ever been.

The lazy, sunlit days went by amicably and, except perhaps for Geoffrey, too quickly; *his* private undercurrent of delight lay in considering the future. Humphrey had been an outstanding Master, but in times less difficult than College Heads were faced with now. The next few months, especially, bristled with problems, and Geoffrey was aware as well that hidden among the malicious invective of Niall Redmond's articles had been some uncomfortable grains of truth for the College and the University. There was, in short, a huge amount of work to do, and idyllic though this place was, and unexpectedly congenial Louise's assortment of guests, he longed to get started on it.

The end of the holiday was almost in sight when the conversation after dinner turned to the subject of whether or how people were influenced by their surroundings. Anna was definite in her opinion as usual.

'My dears, an antique, civilised landscape, the blessing of sunlight day after day — of course we are changed by these things. Here even *I* become a little bit lovely, instead of the ill-tempered old woman who waits in the rain in Cornmarket for a bus that doesn't arrive!'

Louise shook her head, waiting to be heard amid the laughter round the table. 'As one who has frequently shared the bus queue with you, I can insist that isn't true. But I'll agree with you to this extent — in a place as lovely as this it's surely easier to behave well. Perhaps we should remember that when we allow human beings to live in semi-derelict, inner-city tower blocks and deplore their urge to go out and vandalise whatever they come across.'

'Of course squalid surroundings and squalid lives are linked,' Geoffrey confirmed in his cool voice, 'but the latter aren't inevitably changed by changing the former. Bring a posse of slum children here by all means, but don't expect them to be transformed into della Robbia cherubs overnight, or even at all.'

'We educate them and *then* bring them,' Andrew suggested quickly because he saw the faint tinge of colour in Louise's face.

'And I suppose *we* must go home ourselves clinging resolutely to the loveliness that dear Anna thinks now wraps us round!'

Louise smiled at him, grateful for his tact. Then it was Madeleine's turn to speculate sadly about the future.

'Everything will change now, *n'est-ce-pas*? *Maman* will be alone in our house, because even Gertrud has finally had to go home, as well as Daniel, and I shall be studying in Paris.' Then suddenly she clapped her hands. 'I know . . . Andrew, *you* move in upstairs. *Maman* will take much better care of you than some stupid College servant does, and I shall always know where you are!'

He looked much struck by this idea, but instead of committing himself suggested a last stroll before it was time for bed. William and Anna also accepted the invitation, and the four of them wandered away across the garden into the dusk.

'It isn't such a bad idea,' Louise commented thoughtfully when they'd disappeared. 'Andrew would take care of Anna beautifully for me, I'm sure.'

'My dear, does she need taking care of? Almost more than any woman I know, Anna Ouspenska is capable of managing very well on her own.'

'I was thinking she'd be lonely, that's all,' Louise answered with some shortness, irritated by Geoffrey's offhand tone.

'Spare a thought for Ruth, then – don't you see *her* being lonely without us?'

There was no immediate answer, and the candlelight on the table threw concealing shadows on her face. 'We haven't talked enough about the future,' he said abruptly.

'We haven't talked about it at all,' she pointed out at last. 'It's something that's waiting for us when we leave what Anna calls this antique, civilised landscape.'

Geoffrey frowned and poured more wine for himself, as if a little stiffening of courage was needed for what was to come next.

'I know that you and Ruth haven't always quite . . . quite seen eye to eye, but she's almost the only family we've got, apart from Nadia of course.'

'She'll miss having you in the house, but no doubt you'll find the time to visit her,' Louise said calmly. 'She can even come and visit us when literary endeavours allow.'

'Exactly what I told her.' Geoffrey saw the fence in front of him and took it all standing. 'She was getting very upset, poor girl, but all was well when I said it only meant that we shall all have two homes from now on – in College and Norham Grove.'

'Ruth will look on the Lodging as *her* home too?' Louise enquired after a small pause.

Geoffrey casually tossed off the last of his wine. 'I think she must, don't you? How could we *not* make her welcome? The Lodging is three times as big as we shall need, and we've always been together. It's too late for any change now.'

The evening was warm, but Louise felt the tingle of gooseflesh on her arms. She seemed to be looking down a never-ending vista of things that couldn't change because they wouldn't be allowed to. Prominent among them now was the large, ungainly figure of her sister-in-law, forever beaming at the Master of St Barnabas with delighted approval and pointing out to his wife the continuing error of her ways. She took a deep breath and tried not to shout or shake.

'I would much rather, Geoffrey, that Ruth stayed in her own home. Let her have *all* of it if that would make her feel less upset. We could find somewhere else to escape to from College.'

'That would make her feel *more*, not less alone,' he pointed out in the tones of someone trying to make an irrational child see common sense. Then, as if sensing her despair, he leaned over and grasped her cold hands. 'My dear, *we* have a great deal – Ruth not very much; don't let's be unkind enough to shut her out. She'll probably only want to come at weekends.'

It had been arranged between them, Louise realised, though not mentioned until now. And to object, to flatly refuse, would be the behaviour of an unkind, selfish woman.

'Ruth will be welcome at weekends,' she said at last, 'but she must expect me to be working in the garden at home whenever there is work to be done.'

She withdrew her hands from his and stood up, searching for

something safe to say. 'Speaking of which, I'm full of plans for St Barnabas. Edwina suffered for years the municipal garden displays that Dawkins must have planted out with a tape measure. But we can do much better than that.'

The silence this time was Geoffrey's but at last he answered her.

'He *is* the College gardener, you must remember, with traditions which he follows, like the rest of us.'

'And it would be unkind to shut *him* out as well. Of course – I should have thought of that.' Her calm voice expressed nothing at all, because she felt nothing – only walked away empty of every emotion, having suddenly become the thing that Nature abhorred – a vacuum!

Geoffrey stayed where he was, considering a conversation he'd known would be difficult. On the whole, he thought, it had been easier than he'd expected. It was a pity to have had to warn Louise off interfering in the College gardens, but interference was certainly how it would have been seen – and there were much more important battles for them to fight.

He was reassured when Louise came downstairs the following morning, still the charming, attentive hostess that she'd been all along. When the time came to discuss the journey home he even felt confident enough to tease her about it.

'I was afraid you might be dreading the end of the summer, but the truth is, I think, that you're just as eager as I am to start tackling the work ahead of us!'

She interrupted the packing of clothes into suitcases to agree with him. 'Yes, I'm eager, Geoffrey.' There would be a great deal of work involved in getting the new Master of St Barnabas installed in his College home, but she would do it conscientiously and willingly. Only very occasionally would she allow herself to ask William for news of Daniel.

Michaelmas term – a year since she'd walked into Anna's garden and found a stranger muttering over an inefficient lawn mower. Nervous, new students to be made welcome, half-hostile College Fellows to be won over, the whole cumbersome machinery of the University year to be set in motion again. She watched at closer quarters than before and saw how devotedly and skilfully Geoffrey accomplished it all. Humphrey had been right in knowing who should succeed him.

She played her part well too, she thought, even though the mollifying of Gwyneth Morgan defeated her. Carols in the Cathedral again, snowdrops in the Botanic Gardens, stately dinners in Hall, and scrambled picnics with Anna when time allowed. She helped Nadia and Henri move into their new home on the outskirts of Aix, and came back to Oxford as the willow trees were breaking into bronze-gold leaf.

William, looking suddenly older than she remembered, had what he thought was surprising news – his friend had decided to turn down a professorship at Ann Arbor.

'Can't think why,' he commented, 'the Prof label is what most academics work, scheme and connive for! Daniel's being cagey – doesn't say what he's going to do next, but he isn't the man not to have some plan ready.'

'I think *I* know how it begins,' Louise admitted. 'He's going hunting ... for a millionaire! He told me once that he was going to need one.'

She kissed her astonished uncle goodbye, and walked away, but not back to College, he noticed. Instead, she crossed the High, turned into St Aldate's as Great Tom thundered out the hour of four o'clock, and settled herself at a table in the General Post Office. The message to be cabled to Dr Goodman at the University of Michigan took her a little while to compose, but she was satisfied with it in the end:

Experienced piano teacher waiting for school vacancy. Assures headmaster that music well known to soothe savagest small breast. Hopes to hear, c/o Professior Standish, that he can't manage without her.

She handed in her form, smiled blindingly at the counter clerk who counted up the words, and then walked through the thickening evening crowds back to St Barnabas.